AMANDA PILLAR is an award-winning editor and speculative fiction author who lives in Victoria, Australia, with her partner and two children, Saxon and Lilith (Burmese cats).

Amanda has had numerous short stories published and has co-edited the fiction anthologies *Voices* (2008), *Grants Pass* (2009), *The Phantom Queen Awakes* (2010), *Scenes from the Second Storey* (2010), *Ishtar* (2011) and *Damnation and Dames* (2012).

In her 'free time', she works as an archaeologist.

BLOOD STONES

Also edited by AMANDA PILLAR

Voices (with Mark S. Deniz)
Grants Pass (with Jennifer Brozek)
Scenes from the Second Storey (with Pete Kempshall)
The Phantom Queen Awakes (with Mark S. Deniz)
Ishtar (with K.V. Taylor)
Damnation and Dames (with Liz Grzyb)

BLOOD STONES

EDITED BY
AMANDA
PILLAR

T꙳
p꙳ Ticonderoga
publications

This for my sister, Sarah.
Monsters don't need to be vampires or
werewolves to be awesome.

Bloodstones edited by Amanda Pillar

Published by Ticonderoga Publications

Designed and edited by Russell B. Farr
Typeset in Sabon and Vani

A Cataloging-in-Publications entry for this title is available from The National Library of Australia.

ISBN   978-1-921857-26-3 (hardcover)
       978-1-921857-27-0 (trade paperback)
       978-1-921857-28-7 (ebook)

Ticonderoga Publications
PO Box 29 Greenwood
Western Australia 6924

www.ticonderogapublications.com

10 9 8 7 6 5 4 3 2 1

ACKNOWLEDGEMENTS

Firstly, I want to thank Russell B. Farr. This is my first solo project, and without his support, I'd never have made it this far. Secondly, I want to thank all the authors who contributed to this collection—and of course, those that made it through to final selection. Without your work, I'd have a book filled with empty, soulless pages. Your ideas, thoughts and beautifully written words make this collection what it is.

I would also like to thank the talented Pete Kempshall for his help with proofreading, Seanan McGuire for her wonderful introduction, and Liz Grzyb for her eagle-eyed assistance as well. And of course, I would like to thank my usual support cast of heroes: Tom Bicknell, Judi Jaensch and Boris Dzuris.

CONTENTS

INTRODUCTION

SEANAN MCGUIRE

Everyone knows what a werewolf is. Changing flesh, wolfsbane and silver . . . oh, yes, there's no question that everyone knows what a werewolf is. It doesn't stop there, either, because everyone knows what a vampire is, too. Vampires, werewolves, Frankenstein's monster, ghosts and zombies and the rest, they're familiar monsters. For some of us, they've become almost comforting, the toothy, sharp-clawed equivalent of our favorite childhood blanket. Even when they're given a new twist, they're never really all that different. They're always comfortable, always familiar.

The authors Amanda Pillar has assembled in *Bloodstones* aren't trying to be comfortable. They aren't trying to be familiar. What they are trying to be, above all else, is true. There is an honesty in these stories, unhampered by expectations about the creatures they contain. It's beautiful, and it's terrible, and that makes it very much worth your time.

The idea of building an anthology around "unusual" monsters—monsters who will never have their own breakfast cereal, who will probably never dominate their own horror franchise—could seem a little counterintuitive. After all, we all know that the real money is in vampires right now, that zombies are the hot new thing, that werewolves are getting ready for a comeback. Why bother playing with the little terrors when the big ones are easy to use?

Because there's a special kind of terror in a gorgon's stare, or in the sinuously twisting limbs of the kraken. Because selkies are sweet, but can still be instruments of beautiful revenge. Because even the haunts we think we know can become something new and terrible when viewed from the proper angle, and in the proper light.

Because there's always something new to stay, when you leave the familiar behind.

In *Bloodstones*, Amanda Pillar has assembled seventeen sharp new stories that will defy your expectations, break your understanding of the rules, and turn the accepted standards of horror upside down. They are written with—they are *filled* with—love, and that makes them no less terrifying. If anything, it gives them the power that they need to cut and bite at the reader, drawing you in until there is no way out but to keep on going through.

There was not a story in this anthology that did not surprise and delight me in some way. And that's not just because of the monsters. The writing is crisp, interesting, and best of all, intelligent, piecing things together in innovative new patterns that form a remarkable whole. I picked up *Bloodstones* expecting a few good stories, a few good scares. Instead, what I found was a map to a whole new realm of horror.

One where bones can be everything.

One where the dead can love, and hate, in equal measure.

One where the sea is not sorry, but can still know sorrow.

One that needs no explanations; it needs only to be itself, and to invite you inside.

If this is your first time through this anthology, you're lucky; you're about to walk strange new paths, visit strange new gardens, and eat strange new fruit. If you've been here before, welcome back. I'm not surprised you're making a return trip.

Sometimes it's wonderful to step outside your comfort zone.

SEANAN MCGUIRE
SEPTEMBER 2012

THE BULL IN WINTER

DIRK FLINTHART

The dingy room was spattered with blood and feathers. Bull flared his nostrils and snuffed deeply. The place stank of old sweat, stale piss and black mould. Only the faintest, fading trace of frankincense clung to the tattered corpse nailed to the lath-and-plaster wall.

"They took his wings," Kaia observed, her voice a gutted whisper. "There's nothing left."

"*Someone* took 'em," Bull rumbled. "Didn't gotta be the killers. Plenty of mojo in those wings, for somebody as knows how." He picked his way across the room, through the litter of empty bottles, pizza boxes, and Chinese take-away containers until he stood below the sagging, half-flensed mess. He sniffed again. Up close, the frankincense was strong, cloying. No mistaking it. "Help me get him down. Hold him so's I can get the nails out."

Kaia took a step, then stopped and looked away. "Can't," she said. "I can't touch . . . that."

Bull grunted. "Do it myself, then. Look around. See what you can find. Maybe something to show us what happened." He sidled into position, sliding one powerful arm behind the corpse, under its flabby arse, and hauled it up until it rested messily on his hip. The blood had stopped flowing long since, but it was still moist and sticky. He'd have to throw away his jeans after this. With his free hand, he pinched the head of the big nail that stuck out of one wrist. It was slippery with blood; he had to rub it a bit before he could get a decent grip, but once he got it tight between his finger and thumb, all it took was a good, strong pull. The nail came out of the wood and plaster with an ugly screech, and the arm fell to hang uselessly by the side of the corpse. Bull shifted his grip a little, and gave the second nail the same treatment, then lay the maimed body on the stained brown corduroy couch. As an afterthought, he dragged a dirty sheet over it. "Anything?" he called out.

"Nuh . . . no," said Kaia. She sniffed and wiped her nose on the sleeve of her threadbare sweater. "Doesn't matter, anyway. Nobody can help him now."

"It matters," growled Bull, still looking down at the sad, shapeless lump under the stained cloth. "He was good. He was my friend. He thought I was . . . good. Someone shouldn't oughta done this."

Kaia moved against him then, sliding herself in under his elbow, wrapping her arms around his waist. The blood didn't seem to bother her. "What are we going to do, Bull? He was strong, but they came for him. What can we do?"

Bull shook his head. "I'm stronger'n him. They won't come for us. If they do, I'll smash 'em. They know it." He growled deep in his chest and hugged Kaia close. She felt thin and brittle in the circle of his arms. He wanted to hold her closer still, squeeze her, protect her, but she felt so small he thought she might break.

She coughed, her thin body quaking against his. "I'm cold, Bull," she said. "Can we go? There's nothing we can do here now."

He looked around the squalid little apartment. How long had Angel lived here, among the junkies and the filth, the stink of his own decay? Yet the place was lifeless. Nothing of Angel to be seen anywhere; no photos, no keepsakes. Not even a potted plant. "Like he wasn't never here," Bull said. "Just nobody."

"What are you talking about?" Kaia looked up at him. "There's stuff everywhere. He left a mess."

"Yup," agreed Bull. Gently, he uncoiled her arms from about his waist, and propelled her towards the scarred wooden door that hung slightly askew on rusted hinges. "You get goin'. I can catch you up, eh? Got somethin' still to do."

She hesitated in the doorway, watching him from beneath the straggling green curtain of her hair. "Don't be long?"

He waved her away, and watched until he couldn't hear her footsteps in the hall outside, nor pick up her clean, fresh scent in the general reek of the place. Only then did he turn his attention to the corpse on the sagging, foldaway bed. Clasping his big, scarred hands, he lowered his head, and closed his eyes. "Sorry, buddy," he said. "I weren't there when it mighta helped. Ain't much I can do about it now. I don't even know what kinda words is right. But you'da done right by me, if it was me lyin' there, so I'm gonna do the best I can, okay?"

He opened his eyes and waited, but nothing happened. The corpse didn't move. The stink didn't go away. There were no signs or wonders. Bull hitched his shoulders wearily, and smiled to himself. Signs and wonders. Been a long time since any of that kind of thing had happened. He fumbled in the pockets of his old jacket until he found what he needed, and then he set about doing what ought to be done, near as he knew how.

Tucked into the street-light shadow of a bus stop, Kaia was waiting for him when he came out. Most couldn't have spotted her there, still and small in the dark like that, but Bull knew her ways, and anyhow, he could smell her; all woodland-soft and fresh in the rough, harsh stink of the city. She pulled herself out of the dark as he came close, looking past him to the rotting red-brick building he had left behind.

"You did it, then?" She licked her lips nervously. Kaia never did like fire.

He glanced back over his shoulder at the flames leaping high from the solitary window of Angel's apartment. They'd spread some already, since he came down. The flickery orange-red light showed at the end of the hallway, and as he watched, the window burst, and thick smoke poured out. Somebody shouted, a string of choppy, angry curses echoing round the high walls. In the distance, a siren yowled like a cat somebody had stepped on.

Bull turned away, and dragged at Kaia's coat until she stumbled after him, protesting. "There's people inside," she said. "Someone ought to help."

"They coulda helped Angel," he said. "They didn't." On the sidewalk in front of him, Bull's shadow wavered and twisted as the flames behind rose into the night sky. For an instant, it almost looked like he had horns again. He raised a hand, touched one of the rough spots on his scalp, but no—they hadn't come back. Not yet, anyhow.

They kept walking through the wintry darkness until the city swallowed them up.

*

Kaia woke him in the night with her thrashing. That wasn't so bad, but nights where she did that, she sometimes talked in her sleep, too. Snatches of the Old Tongue. Bull had forgotten most of it by now. Couldn't remember more than a few words, mostly swearing. But the sound of it still gave him sweats and bad dreams; nightmares full of twisting stone passages and the smell of rotting meat. He couldn't sleep, nights when the Old Tongue came to her like that.

By the cold light of the moon through the window, Bull sat up and watched her for a while. He liked to watch her sleep. Her face relaxed, and she turned soft, like she'd been when they met, such a long time back. She was still beautiful, of course. Always would be. It was the nature of her kind. But lately, it was a hard, brittle kind of beauty, like a tree under winter ice.

After a while, he got up and padded naked to the kitchen to get a beer. When he came back, she was awake, looking around in confusion. "Bull," she said, as he approached the bed. "When is it?"

"About three," he said, settling next to her, so that the bed creaked under his weight. "Hours yet 'fore sun-up."

"No, I meant *when*," she said. "What year?"

He studied her, his beer briefly forgotten. Her face was white and lined, her eyes dark, with deep shadows under them. She looked scared. "You really don't remember?"

Kaia shook her head, and pulled the covers close. "I'm cold," she said. "I was dreaming, and it was summer in the old land, and there were olive groves, and my sisters were there, and wine, and dust. And now I'm not sure . . . "

"2012," Bull said. "Christian calendar." His hand felt cold, and he remembered his beer. He popped the top; drained it in two swallows. Thin stuff, but it was hard to find the real thing anymore. Maybe he should figure out how to make his own. People did it. Couldn't be that hard.

Kaia wrapped the raggedy quilt tightly around herself. "Do you ever think about home?"

Bull belched, and crushed the beer can in his fist. "What's home? I can't even remember how long we've been here anymore."

A breeze stirred the leafless pear tree outside the window. Both of them looked out into the night. Kaia coughed, a thin, ugly sound. From the corner of his eye, Bull saw her snake one arm out from under the covers and grab a tissue from the nightstand. She wiped her lips, and crumpled it quickly, but he didn't need to see. The smell was enough.

"Blood," he said, trying to keep his voice even. "How long?"

Kaia looked lost. "Forever, maybe? I don't remember. I've . . . lost things, Bull." Her fingers worked restlessly on the quilt, bunching it up, pinching the nap, rubbing it between her fingertips. "I need to go home. Soon."

Home. Bull tried to think about it, but nothing much came, except the nightmare of stone walls and carrion. How long had it been? Too long. Not long enough. Kaia, though . . . he sneaked another glance at her, cocooned and shivering in her quilt. Her eyes were closed, and her lips moved as though she was praying, but he couldn't make out the words. And shit, anyway, who would she pray to? Been nobody listening for longer than he could remember.

Maybe it was time to talk to someone else.

*

You had to know about the place to get in. Bull knew, all right. He'd just never wanted to get in before. The kind of people who hung out in Sanctuary—stupid name for a nightclub—weren't his crowd. All the black and the velvet, and they wanted you to think they were dangerous, but they acted like a bunch of fags instead.

The door was one of those heavy steel jobs you got in warehouses. There was a little camera over it, and if you looked real close, the word 'Sanctuary' was scratched into the rusted metal door, like how someone might do it with a pen-knife. The door opened if they wanted you. It stayed closed if they didn't.

Bull didn't have a real lot of time for that. He stood there, in the pool of ugly neon light, long enough for the camera to look him over, and maybe a minute or two more just to be polite. But they weren't buying, so he knocked. For real, with his balled-up fist, so as to leave a serious dent in the top half of the door.

That got some attention. Someone yanked the door open, and a guy in a long black coat stepped into the doorway. He pulled out a shotgun. Stupid. Bull took it away from him and snapped it across his knee, all the time with his eyes locked on the guy in the coat. "Lizzy," Bull growled. "I wanna talk to Lizzy."

Coat-guy, though, he wasn't done. "Beast-creature beware!" he cried, and a couple of really sharp-looking knives popped into his hands, like magic. "The Lady is not for you. Only death awaits!"

He was fast. The knives zipped back and forth like swallows, slicing Bull across the arms, cutting up his best leather jacket. Bull stepped into the place, ducking to get under the doorframe, and drove his fist into coat-guy's belly, all the way up to the wrist. "Just wanna talk," he said, patiently as he could, as coat-guy sank to his knees. "Lizzy knows me, okay?"

"Enough, Toro," came a voice like honey and silk and cats. "James will trouble you no further."

Bull glanced down, where the coat-guy was spewing up a bellyful of sour, red wine all over the nice parquet floor. "Don't think he could anyhow," he said. "Sorry, James."

He looked across to see Lizzy, and she was just the same as always. Long dark hair, red lips, pale skin, big eyes, big titties: that was Lizzy's package, and she knew how to use it. This time she wore red velvet, fitted real tight, and black suede boots. She licked her lips. Bull felt the blood pound in his cock, and he laughed. "Don't you start that," he said. "We'll be here all night."

"Not a social call, then?" She took Bull lightly by the arm, and led him past a mess of pale, hostile faces, to a curtained booth by the bar. He didn't miss the way she signalled with her hand, though, and he gave the other two guys in long black coats the same flat, ugly stare they tried to give him. He was better at it. They turned away even before Lizzy pulled the curtain across.

"Nuh," he said then, as they sat. "You're all kinds of trouble." He could say things like that to her. It was part of their history. "But there's less of us around all the time, eh? You heard about Angel, maybe?"

Her face didn't change, but he didn't expect that anyway. That's why he was sitting close, leaning across the table. Not staring at her titties there, but catching her scent, and it told him what he needed to know. He leaned back.

"I was sad to hear about Angel," she said. "You know that, Toro."

Bull watched her for a moment. "Yeah," he said finally. "I know. And it's just Bull, these days. Nothin' fancy." He ducked his head and grinned. "Sorry about your door, there. And that James guy."

"Not your fault. And I'm Lizaveta again," she said. "With the accent. They love it, you know?" She looked more carefully at his head. "The horns?"

"Filed back," he said, though he hadn't had to do it in an awful long time. "Saves trouble. But you've still got the teeth?"

"Assuredly," she said, and flashed him a mouthful of ivory razors. "They are expected of me."

He leaned back against the leather upholstery. Lizzy twitched the curtain, and right away, a skinny, pale girl dressed like one of them French maids showed up. "My friend will have a beer," Lizzy told her. "A heavy stout. Not Guinness. Something sweeter. Some . . . red wine, for me." The French maid did a little curtsey thing, and disappeared. Lizzy leaned back and smiled at Bull again. "So, what brings you here?"

"Kaia," he said. "She's sick. She needs to go home."

"Home," said Lizzy. Her eyes glittered. "Interesting."

"Greece, I think," said Bull. "She dreams about olive groves. Talks in her sleep."

Lizzy folded her hands. "So. My part?"

Bull hunched his shoulders. He hadn't thought too much about the next bit. "Well. You're doing okay. Got your own place. You got people. We don't—we don't got papers, nothin'. Back when we come here, they didn't ask much. We're sort of . . . outside the whole thing, you know? But now, you wanna travel anywhere, there's all sorts of stuff. And money, I guess, but we can get that."

The French maid came back with the drinks. The beer was good: thick, bittersweet, cool but not too cold. Bull put away the whole pint before he thought better of it, and eyed the empty glass sadly. Lizzy smiled, and did the hand-signal trick again. Maybe there would be another.

"I don't think going home will help her," said Lizzy. Her expression didn't change, but somehow her voice sounded sad. "Not everyone adapts, Bull. Look at Angel. Look at the Sphinx."

"Angel was weak," grumbled Bull. "Sphinx was just stupid."

"Michael was the strongest of us once," Lizzy said. "And at one time, even I feared the Sphinx. But they couldn't find new ways to be themselves, and so they died. If you want Kaia to live, you should look to the dragons."

"Dragons," Bull snorted. The French maid returned with a new pint, and he seized it, but made himself wait. "Ain't no dragons no more."

"Powerful creatures," said Lizzy. "Creatures who gather great treasure to themselves, rapaciously destroying entire nations. And the treasure itself takes on the poison of the dragon, so that those who see it are ensorcelled and enslaved, desperate to own it. They will kill even their loved ones to keep it. Are you certain there are no such creatures, Bull?"

An idea came, but it was funny. He laughed a little, blowing foam off his beer. "Sounds like a bunch of investment bankers," he said. "Pricks."

Lizzy's slow smile made his eyes widen.

"Bankers," he said. Could the old drakes really . . . ? "No."

"Why don't you go try to take their treasure? See what happens?" She sipped her drink. It wasn't wine. Bull could smell it. But he hadn't really expected her to drink wine. She almost never did.

"Dragons," he said, his head buzzing. "How'd that happen?"

"They stayed true to their nature," said Lizzy. "They found a niche. As have I."

"Me and Kaia," Bull said. "We're getting kinda squeezed out." Working as a stevedore, a bouncer, anything that took muscle and size. Except machines did most of it better, these days. And Kaia, in the gardens, always with the plants. Nobody much cared about that kind of thing anymore. "And the new ones. Like them as did for Angel. They don't show respect. Hockey masks and chainsaws; shit like that don't scare me none, but Kaia . . . I ain't always home. I can't, you know. Always look after her."

Lizzy looked at him with infinite sadness. "That is the way of it, Bull. The old move on, making room for the new. Unicorns die, and blind, albino sewer alligators are born. If you want to live, you find a way. There is nothing else."

Bull shook his head. "Kaia's right. We get her back to the old land, she'll be okay. It's different there."

"If you say so," said Lizzy. She paused, staring at him like she saw something interesting. "Maybe," she said. "Maybe. You desire my help? There is, perhaps, something you can do for me. Something—" She licked her lips, and her teeth showed, just for an instant. "Something in keeping with your nature."

Again, that rush of blood. He got dizzy for a moment. Felt like the horns were back on his head, heavy and hard and proud. He hadn't felt that way in a long time. He didn't like how it felt *good*. Putting his hands on the table, Bull stood up. "Yeah, no," he said, the words spilling in a rush. "Okay, this was maybe a mistake. But it's good you're still here, Lizzy. I gotta go. Kaia, she needs my help sometimes. I gotta get back."

She didn't move, except to nod her head a little. "All right, Bull," she said. "But if you change your mind . . . "

He was gone before she finished the sentence.

*

"What are you doing?" Kaia looked thin and tired. The quilt was always wrapped around her now. She never used to complain about the cold. Always said winter was part of life.

Bull pushed the untidy pile of papers away from him, across the littered table. His head felt real bad. Reading and writing. He still wasn't much good at it. But Kaia had showed him, an age or two ago, and she'd been right. It was important. So he learned, and he practised. "Stuff I'm tryin' ta figure out," he said. "Papers. So's we can travel. It's not how it used to be. Now they got people checking everything. Wouldn't be good, we got put in one of them places for illegals."

She pushed a chair round the table so she could sit near him. "In the old days, they would help us. For love of me, for fear of you."

"Old times, long gone," said Bull. "Hey, you hear about the dragons? Lizzy told me—" he broke off.

Kaia stared at him. "You went to the Lamia? You did this?"

Caught, Bull nodded.

"Oh, Bull." She slumped. "I'm so sorry. You're worried about me, aren't you?"

He nodded again, his throat too thick for speech, and she sneaked an arm out from under the quilt, sliding it all cool and smooth around him. She rubbed her face against the heavy mat of hair on his chest. "It's not so bad, Bull," she said. "I'll get better in the springtime. I always do, don't I?"

But springtime wasn't what it used to be, was it? Even the birds and the flowers got it wrong, coming and going too early, too late. The air smelled wrong. It always did, lately. "I'm gonna do it," he said, touching her hair, twining it through his fingers. Red streaks in the green, brown in the red. More this year than ever before, maybe. "I'm gonna take you back home. You can see spring there, and summer. And your sisters, yeah."

"My sisters," she murmured, her voice soft, like she was tired. "Don't go to the Lamia, Bull. She helps no-one. There is no giving in her anywhere, only taking. Not love. Just death."

"She knows people," Bull murmured, tilting his head to snuff the rich, leaf-mould scent of her hair. "She's got power. She could get us out."

"Not her," said Kaia, her voice softer still as she nuzzled into his chest. "Never her. There must be others. The great Roc, perhaps? If we ask, it will carry us. Surely."

"Thunderbird," responded Bull. "That's what they called the big ones over here. But they're gone. Long time gone."

She pulled back from him, and looked up. "Gone? The Roc? Did I not see his great shadow only last . . . only last . . . " she faltered, and a look of misery came upon her. "I've forgotten again, haven't I?"

Bull said nothing, but pulled her head back to his chest and held her there, trying to warm her with the fires of his body.

"Not the Lamia," she murmured. "There must be another."

He held her like that until she passed into sleep. Then he carried her back to the bed, and lay her down. She was light in his hands, and stiff, like dry branches. When he pulled the covers around her, he saw her other arm, the one she hadn't put around him. The one she'd kept hidden.

He stared at it. Went to touch it, the rough surface of her forearm, all brown and cracked and dry, like . . . like bark. Pulled his hand away again.

Then he brought the covers up under her chin, and tucked her in, very gently.

*

Sanctuary had a new door. It looked like the old one, rust and all, but it was thicker and heavier. There wasn't no dent in the top half, either. Bull thought about maybe changing that, but this time, the door opened for him.

The new man on the door had that smell. The one they all had, all the Strangers Bull had met in a long, long life. Like a whiff of ozone, and the smell of hot coals. Even Angel used to have it, under the frankincense. Bull looked at the man carefully. He was tall and thin, made out of angles and sharp points, and he wore a lot of black. "Ain't seen you before," said Bull. "You're new."

The red-eyed man doffed his crooked top hat, and offered Bull a bow that wasn't quite a joke. Good thing, too, or Lizzy'd lose her another doorman.

"You're not new," said the man, straightening. "I can feel that. Privileged to meet you, Old One."

"Bull," said Bull. All the titles and the polite stuff made him uneasy. Always had. "My name. You can use it."

"Jack," said the other, and almost, he smiled. But not quite. "The Baroness said you would return."

Bull craned his neck, and peered into the red-lit night-club. "She around? I gotta talk."

"My instructions are to convey you to her at once," said Jack. He did the hand-signal thing, and one of the black-coat boys popped up. "You have the door, William," said Jack. "Don't lose it, eh?" William didn't look like he thought that was funny, so Bull made a point of chuckling. That got him an actual smile out of Jack. It looked like someone had slashed his face with a razor, then filled the wound with teeth.

They went through a door at the back of the bar, into a big space like the inside of a warehouse. It was done up fancy, with lights and plants and carpets and furniture, big video-screens and the rest. There was some kind of party going on, with dancing. Bull smelled marijuana and opium among the sweat and the reek of booze. Lizzy was by herself in a big clawfoot tub in a tiled corner. Her hair was all piled up on her head, and her big titties floated on the milky water, red nipples peeking.

"Bull," she said, and pulled herself out of the tub. "You're just in time!" She didn't have no hair at her crotch, and he could see the fat, pale lips of her quim. It made him tense and uncomfortable.

"It's Kaia," he said. "She's worse. We gotta go. Real soon. I got some money. You can have it all. We need papers, tickets. You got people can get stuff like that."

She towelled herself down, titties wobbling, like she didn't know he was there. Then she shrugged into a little wisp of a black silk robe that barely covered her butt, and she smiled. "Quid pro quo, Bull," she said. "I like you. I will get the things you need, but in exchange, you will do for me a thing for which you are peculiarly suited."

He was ready for this. He'd thought about what to say. "I been with Kaia a long time. She makes things grow. She likes stuff that's alive. She don't hold with killing no-one. I made a promise to her, see? But . . . " Bull took a deep breath. "Like you say. It's my nature. I ain't no good at much else. So—I'll do it. This killing. But then I'm goin' with Kaia to the old land, and I ain't coming back, so you best make sure it's someone you want proper killed."

The look she got on her face, Bull thought he'd gone too far. But then it changed, and he saw she weren't angry or anything. For real, it looked like she was trying not to laugh. "Who spoke of killing, Bull?" she said. "You may yet have murder in you, but in these times, who doesn't? Killing is easy as—" She glanced around, pointed out a man dancing alone, under one of the flashing lights. "Easy as that," she said, and snapped her fingers.

Quick as a snake, that guy Jack crossed the floor through all them dancing, drugged-up people. He grabbed the one she pointed at, and in all of one move, just cut his throat. Slashed it right across with a big old razor, blood everywhere, and all the time him smiling that ugly smile, and Lizzy not even looking his way. Just keeping her eyes on Bull, and licking at her lips.

And nobody cared. Some of 'em looked over at the dying guy, and Jack there, but they looked away again. Right there in the middle of the dancing, that crazy Jack did a murder and nobody did nothing about it.

"That's right, Bull," said Lizzy. "Nobody cares about that sort of thing now. Have you seen their movies? Their television shows? Once upon a time, you were the beast in the labyrinth, the primeval rage kept secret inside every man. Now? The labyrinth is gone, and the beast is loose. Being a killer is nothing special. Everyone's a killer now."

He didn't know what to say to that. He thought of Angel, cut up and nailed to the wall. He thought of Kaia, and then he found words. "Okay. Okay. But you still want something. From me. So what is it?"

Lizzy's eyes glittered in the shifting light, and she slid close to him. The little silk robe gaped, and she pressed her hand against his crotch, sliding it along the thickening length of his cock. "Bull," she said. "They're still afraid of *this*, you know," and she squeezed him, digging in with her nails.

Lamia. Queen of desire.

Bull groaned in real pain, and stepped back. He had to loosen up his clothes. He always wore cargo pants, with plenty of room, but when the rut came on him even they were no good. "Bitch," he cursed, fumbling with the band, breathing hard. He bent at the waist, hunching over as his cock stiffened, and throbbed, and rose. The constriction hurt. With a growl, he bunched his big hands in the tough cloth and ripped.

Long as a child's arm, thick as a fist, his cock sprang free. It quivered to his pulse, all purple and shiny, a single, clear drop hanging from the eye. A murmur went around the big room. People drew in breath, exclaimed like they never did when Jack killed the dancer. They saw his cock, and it shocked them like murder couldn't.

Lizzy laughed, a clear, tinkling note. "You see, Bull? It's your nature. Now, follow me." She turned and sashayed away, her smooth, white butt swinging from side to side. The woman-smell of her was hot in his nostrils, and he panted, his cock aching hard. She led him through a narrow, badly lit passage, out a door that led onto some kind of stage. The lights were bright in his eyes, and there were cameras, but he didn't care. All he could see was her titties, the pink slit of her quim peeking from under that robe.

He lunged at her, but she danced aside, laughing at his clumsy grab. "No, no," she said, and a spotlight came up, showing a girl chained to a big, heavy table. She was naked, splayed wide open. Bull stopped, confused. The heaviness in his cock mixed up with the pain in his head, and the woman-smell, and the stink of the crowd beyond the lights. He hunched his shoulders, and grabbed the base of his cock.

The audience *oohed*.

Bull couldn't see Lizzy no more, but the smell was still there, fizzing in his blood, making his breath hot in his throat. The girl on the table. She saw him. She looked at his cock, and her eyes got real big. She shook her head back and forth fast, so her curly red hair flew. She had gingery curls at her crotch, too. Bull took a step closer.

"That's right, Bull," said Lizzy, somewhere off in the dark. "She's there for you. All for you. A true virgin, like the old days. Take her, Toro, Taurus, Old Bull."

Bull tossed his head. He tried to think. What about Kaia? What would she say? He tried to remember her face, but the scent of Lizzy, the smell of the girl, the sharp tang of her fear, the delicious, pink folds glistening at her crotch—too much. He snorted, and stamped his foot.

"Take her," crooned Lizzy. "Let the Minotaur have his due!"

Bull threw back his head and *roared*.

*

When it was done, when Bull came back to himself, the girl was still there on the table. He couldn't see her proper, with the people crowded round. They were fighting to touch her between the legs. Some were scooping up the blood and jizz with their fingers, smearing it on each other, licking it off. A man even grabbed at Bull's cock, softer now but slick, hanging down his thigh. Bull backhanded him in the head, and he fell away, his eyebrow split and bloody.

Jack came up and took his arm, led him away from the madness into a quiet changing room. "That was well done, Old Bull," he said. "The Baroness is pleased. The footage is already going viral on the 'Net. You're a star. A *legend*."

Bull didn't want to think about that. He saw some pants on a peg. Big, khaki cargo pants. Numb in the head, he put them on, shoving his heavy cock down one leg, like always. The smell of sex clung to it, got on his hand, and he wiped it on a velvet curtain. "The girl," he said. "She okay?"

Jack giggled, high-pitched and crazy. "What do you think?" he said. "Don't worry. She got what she came for." He paused, and looked at Bull, his strange red eyes slitted. He pointed at Bull's head. "Would you like a hat, Old One?"

Bull stopped. He ran a hand over his head. His palm snagged twice, once on each side, above his ears and forward a little. Two hard, sharp projections. His horns, maybe an inch long each.

"Shit," said Bull. "Yeah. Gimme a hat. I gotta go." He frowned at Jack. "When do I get my papers?"

"Within the day, Minotaur."

It was Lizzy, come up from behind. He hadn't noticed her. She still wore the little bathrobe, but now Bull didn't much care. The emptiness and the ache that started in his balls filled up his whole body. He felt flat, bitter like coffee too long in the pot. "Send 'em to me," he said, turning away from her. Jack offered him a beat-up felt hat, shapeless from long use, and he clapped it onto his head, pulling it down hard so it covered the horns. He'd file them back again, later.

Lizzy slid in front of him, smiling. "You can return for the papers tonight, Minotaur," she said, leaning close. "There will be another virgin."

The smell of her, close in the little room, all musky and sweet . . . He got a half-flash, a fragment of a memory: the girl, screaming. The taste of her sweat, where he licked her face. The slickness of her, the tightness as he pounded into her . . .

Bull shuddered. "Not coming back," he said. "You send me the papers." He shouldered past Jack and Lizzy to a door with an 'Exit' sign over it. Looked back over his shoulder. "The Minotaur died a long time gone," he said. "My name is Bull."

*

The little house was empty when he got home. Like it had been when they found it, abandoned. Another mortgage swallowed up by the poison wyrms, the bankers. Nobody'd cared when they moved into it, him and Kaia.

He moved through the place in a daze, going from room to room, calling her name. Sniffing at the air. But there was just the fading green smell of her, no hint of ozone or fire.

Finally he thought to look in the wintry garden of the back yard. Twice he checked, the bitter wind freezing the tears onto his cheeks, but she wasn't there. Except now, there was an apple tree, old and twisted and leafless. He sat in the snow with his back to the gnarled trunk. Turned his head to rest his cheek against the rough bark.

Maybe it would blossom in the spring.

AFTERWORD

What happens to old myths? Where do new myths come from?

This story's crawling with both kinds. The Bull. Lizzy the Lamia, Kaia the dryad, Michael the Archangel and a host of dragons—they're all well known, well worn. But look closer: you'll find blind sewer alligators, Leatherface, and Michael Meyers, and someone who might be Springheel Jack or even The Ripper.

New myth-ideas get born all the time, but only a few are strong enough to make the transition to that indefinable place occupied by the figures of legend. Is Jack the Ripper a myth? He's got to be close, surely. What about Dracula?

Meanwhile, old myths fade. Does anyone really believe in the Minotaur anymore? But . . . what if they could adapt? What would it take for a myth to survive? What new meanings would it acquire—and what would be the price for such survival?

The Old Bull knows.

EURYALE

NICOLE MURPHY

Take ye only the blood from the right side of the gorgon, for it will heal you. The blood of the left will bring you suffering and eternal damnation

As I carried the drinks out to the veranda, Rafael said lazily, "New neighbours."

I looked over the wrought-iron latticework that surrounded the second floor of my sandstone home to the red brick bungalow next door. Two men heaved and panted as they carried a long lounge out of a truck and into the house.

The exertion made the back of their necks flush with blood. I wasn't the only one on the balcony licking their lips at the thought of how easily it could be made to gush forth.

Jon turned and his tongue slipped out between his teeth, tasting the air. "Fresh meat." He grinned as he tapped his stack of poker chips.

Behind the sunglasses I always wear to protect the innocent from my gaze, I rolled my eyes, sure he was just teasing me. "Behave," I said, putting the drinks down and heading back inside. As I passed, Paddy patted my behind and I pursed my lips to pretend it wasn't appropriate, although we both knew I enjoyed the attention.

Leaving my sons and man to their poker game, I went inside. Once I was away from the balcony windows, from possible prying eyes, my first act was to pull the hat from my head. My hair danced and slithered, delighted to be free. It hated being confined.

I sat down at my computer to order the weekly groceries. As the pictures flicked across the screen, my hair played; the hissing sounding very much like laughter as I considered purchases such as fruit and vegetables. In all my centuries, few things had delighted me more than the advent of the Internet. I barely had to leave the house at all—a handy situation for someone trying to hide their identity from the mass of humanity around them.

I thought about the new neighbours. I'd heard the sound of children running inside their house. Children were always the most difficult to avoid—they insisted on looking into the yard, throwing balls over the fence, coming to call to raise funds for their school.

Perhaps it was time to think about moving. When I'd arrived in Australia, this beautiful old sandstone home had been miles away from Sydney, and I'd found a peace that I'd lost as the population of Greece grew.

But now Australia was growing too, and my beautiful home was surrounded by humans. Keeping my agelessness from them was becoming harder and harder.

After ordering the lashings of red meat and alcohol that formed the basis of our diet, I decided to check out the local news before I went out to have some fun. A small notice in a side column drew my attention: VAMPIRE KILLER ON RAMPAGE.

If a vampire had come to town, I'd have to do something about it. Things like this made humans think. Wonder. And they might realise that in all the years they'd known me, I hadn't changed . . .

As I read on, I realised that it wasn't a vampire. Vampires bite into the neck, drain the blood. They don't rip a body apart to suck out the contents of the torso.

A deep tightening of my gut told me this creature was close to me.

What disturbed me most was the date—this story had run nearly a week ago. I should have known about this before now. My boys should have told me.

When I stepped back onto the veranda, once again wearing a hat, I could taste the tension in the air. Rafael and Jon were studiously avoiding looking at each other. Paddy played with a pack of cards, his long slender fingers moving like a blur, shuffling them like they were water.

I sat down and asked, "What is troubling you?"

"I'm sorry," Rafael said. "I went in the house to ask you something and saw what you were looking at. I wanted to tell you from the beginning, but Jon said not to, that you were upset enough over Germaine's latest killing spree and that this didn't really concern you."

"Ain't a snake," Jon muttered. "Snakes don't slash."

I loved my sons as much as any mother, but sometimes their stupidity had me thinking of murder.

I looked at Paddy. The disgust in his clear blue gaze was enough—this was news to him as well. I lightly touched his arm and when he looked at me, I smiled so he would see I wasn't too upset.

Then I turned back to my silly sons. "Do not keep information from me in the future." My voice was so quiet, they had to lean forward to hear me. "We have not been in this land long enough to become complacent about threats."

"Want us to go check it out?" Jon asked eagerly, obviously wanting to make up for his mistake.

"No, he is one of us. I will summon him."

I went into my office and closed the door. I stood before the mirror, took off my hat and shook my head; my hair seethed and spat, understanding that power was afoot. My children had inherited many wonderful things from me—some of the power of my eyes, my longevity, the ability to change forms—but none had inherited my hair. They all looked wholly human and could even walk around with their eyes bare, able to control the impact of their gaze.

Thinking of my children again had me thinking of Germaine— my first, my greatest, my enemy. Leaving Europe to her had been a difficult decision, but she would not move from her determination to destroy humanity and I would not move from mine to leave it be.

After all the centuries, I deserve peace.

Which brought me back to dealing with the creature that was plaguing the surrounding suburbs and threatening, in some part, to reveal me. I threw open my French doors and stood, facing the west. I slipped my sunglasses into the waistband of my shorts, and then I *looked.*

My fabled gaze—the gaze that could turn to stone, that had been feared throughout the world—travelled over the houses, through gardens, around shopping centres and offices. I saw him, the snake, slinking in the darkness, waiting, hunger gnawing at his stomach.

He flinched, then stumbled forward, his feet moving when it seemed his body did not. Satisfied, I blinked and slid my sunglasses back on.

I didn't know who he was, or why he was here, but the snake was about to meet the queen of his kind.

The gorgon.

*

It was after midnight when a moonlit shadow slithered across my lawn; it thickened and distorted until a human shape stood at the base of the stairs to my front door. I sat in my swinging lounge, a gentle tap of the railing occasionally all that was needed for a relaxing rock.

"You may come forward," I said.

It—he—stepped into the square of light thrown by the windows of the lounge room and onto the veranda. He was young—there was still a wildness in his eyes that only time would contain. His body moved jerkily and his limbs were so slender it seemed a wrong step could break them.

I guessed he'd been sick—maybe a druggie, maybe a real disease—when he had been turned. So he not only was dealing with the usual hunger, but with his body's drive to be healthy again.

Who had been foolish enough to make this man a child of theirs?

"What is your name?"

"Paulo." His voice shook.

"Paulo." I sucked some air into my mouth, could taste him on my tongue. He hadn't fed tonight. "Paulo, you are a fool."

His shoulders hauled back and his chin jutted forward. "You can't talk to me like that," he said.

I sighed. "Please tell me you're not so stupid you don't know what I am. I do not wish to kill you. It's messy."

He frowned. He had to know something—had to acknowledge the superior power that had dragged him to my door. That itself should be enough to still his tongue.

"I'm a shape-shifter," he said, thrusting his chin forward and drawing his lips back in a sneer. "Part man, part snake. You can't kill me."

I moved quickly—faster than he would ever be able to. My hand had slammed across his face and I had returned to my seat before his arse hit the wood.

"I will not abide disrespect," I said softly. I lifted my finger to my tongue and sucked the small piece of flesh my nails had scored from his cheek into my mouth. With that, I would always know him.

With that, I knew whose child he was and I sighed. Germaine, my foolish girl. *What are you doing?*

Paulo pressed a hand to his cheek and while he didn't fear me, his eyes were wary and that satisfied me.

"You have awakened the humans," I said. "Your inability to control your hunger, your actions; they have put me at risk and that is something I cannot accept. You will leave this city, and you will find another place to settle; you will control yourself and feed only in a manner that does not arouse suspicion. If not, I will come for you. I will make you suffer so that you will wish you had never lived."

He stood slowly. I shook my head, loving him as I always did my family, even though I despaired of his creation. "You are Germaine's get. That daughter of mine is too impetuous for her own good."

His body quivered with the need to defend his maker. "You will not speak ill of her," he growled.

"I will speak in the manner I deem fit," I said. "You, little boy, are the one who must control his tongue." I rose, my limbs unfurling, uncoiling.

He needed to learn, needed to understand, so I reached up and pulled the hat from my head, satisfied it was late enough and dark enough that my neighbours couldn't see. My hair crawled, slithered, danced around my ears and shoulders.

He fell to his knees, staring up at me in horror. His mouth opened and closed, as if he wanted to say something, but terror had rendered him mute. Germaine looked so human—he hadn't expected the truth of what I am.

I bent down and some of my hair reached out to him. He shuddered as tiny forked tongues caressed his skin.

"You do not want to test me, little boy," I said. "You are one of mine. I wish to let you live, learn; become great as you can be. But if you do wrong, I will punish you. Like any good mother."

"Yes," he whispered.

"Have you fed tonight?" He shook his head. "There is blood in the fridge. Microwave it for thirty-seven seconds. Then you will sleep—take the room at the top of the stairs. Tomorrow night, you will leave."

He ran into the house. Desperation and fear lingered in the air.

I smoothed my hair back into a dark shell, calming my lovelies. Then I sat back on my swing and with a gentle push of my toes, set myself to rocking again.

"Will he do as you asked?"

I looked at Paddy, who leant against the doorframe and stared at me. His skin and hair shone so brilliantly that even behind my sunglasses it hurt my eyes. My beautiful Irish love.

"He will," I said. "Or he will die. It is a simple choice."

Paddy grunted. "The young rarely make the simple choice."

"Then it's a good thing I am a mother that follows through on her threats."

Paddy nodded. "Good night, lovely one." He kissed my forehead and drew his hand lightly over my hair. The tiny snakes shivered, entranced and I pushed his hand away.

"Set your spells on those that need them," I said.

Paddy laughed and went inside. I looked out over the dark suburb and enjoyed the peace and sanctity, watching until dawn came.

*

As evening crept in the next day, Paulo sauntered from his room. I was waiting for him and ushered him into my office.

He sat at the edge of his chair, staring at my hair. I regarded him closely, noting the pink in his cheeks and the softness of his hair after it had been washed.

"I wanted to talk to you about how best to live the life you have been given," I said. "You can be great and glorious, if you learn to be smart."

He nodded and I smiled at the seriousness of his expression. "Stick to feeding from beasts—native animals are best, because they are rarely missed. From time to time, you will wish for a larger meal; then you can look to one of the herd animals the humans keep. Take care to rip out the throat, and make other wounds on the animal, so the humans will believe wild dogs have attacked."

His eyes widened. He nodded again and I thought I could sense the information sinking into him.

"Resist humans, as much as you can," I said. "Covering their deaths, finding explanations for them, is very difficult. I will know if you fail. If it seems that you are putting us at risk, I will kill you."

"I will resist," he said.

"Now, go to the kitchen, feed. There is a satchel by the door. It contains more blood and meat and will keep you satisfied for the next few days. That will give you time to find a home, work out your routine and ensure that you remain a secret."

"Thank you." Paulo stood, bowed and left.

I hoped that Paulo would do well, out there and alone. Next time I spoke to Germaine, I would counsel her to keep her children close.

Except that would start the argument over why I left her.

My daughter. My beloved. Shaking my head, I went out to enjoy the night.

*

Two nights later, my boys suggested a game of baccarat. As the men trash-talked each other and Paddy dealt, I took a moment to connect with my newest family member. What I felt in his mind made some of my blood chill and the rest heat.

Hunger. Desire. Despair. Need.

Crushing, aching need.

I'd been wrong to let him go—he wasn't ready to be out on his own. My foolishness—no, I would be honest, my laziness, my unwillingness to stir myself from the comfortable situation I had found for myself—was going to cost human lives.

"I must go." I pushed my seat back and stood. I shook my head and some of my hair slithered down from under the hat, hissing, writhing, feeling my upset.

Paddy laughed. "Don't be too long, lovely."

If there was one thing to love about leprechauns, it was that snakes didn't bother them. They didn't realise they should.

"Eat, drink, be merry," I said. "I hope to return before midnight."

Then I was gone, flashing across the dark lawns, avoiding the pools of brightness from the streetlights, focusing on the sensation of the one I'd let go.

As the centuries had passed, somehow my ability to move had sped up. If Homer had thought me terrible three thousand plus years ago, imagine what he'd think of me now.

Paulo had fetched up for the night in the tiny town of Wilcannia, in the west of New South Wales. There were less than a thousand residents, so not the best choice for a child of a gorgon to live, but it always had lots of fresh blood, being surrounded by dairy farms.

I followed my senses to a hotel on the edge of town. He was staying in the room furthest from the lobby—I had to give him that much. Standing by the door, I could hear whimpering and deep breathing, and the suck of liquid through pursed lips.

I took off my sunglasses, hung them on a belt loop, and pulled the hat down to ensure it covered my agitated hair, which was desperate to be free. I was risking revealing myself to humans as it was.

Using both hands, I forced open the door.

It flew open with a loud bang. Paulo looked at me and barely had time to register shock before his body stiffened like stone.

I kicked the door shut so we would not be seen and put my sunglasses back on. Then I bent over his victim. A giant slash laid open her rounded stomach and within, something wriggled.

So, my arrival had been fortuitous. I looked at the woman's face. Ordinary—none of the beauty of my children.

It did not bother me, seeing adults die. I had killed enough myself before I'd sought peace. They'd had their time and had usually wasted it. And human blood was very sweet.

But I didn't hold with killing babies. Innocents, squirming potential.

That Paulo hadn't yet eaten the infant meant this woman was going to get a second chance.

I lifted my right hand and with a slash of my fangs over a wrist, drew blood. I dripped it over the wound, over the dying foetus, then opened the woman's mouth and trickled it on her tongue.

Then, while she was healing, I dealt with Paulo. I hated what I had to do, but I had told him the consequences. Hold punishment from one child, and I could lose others.

I picked him up and laid him on the bed. I gave him some blood from my right wrist, but just as he was starting to soften and waken, I slashed my left wrist and dripped some of that blood onto his tongue.

Take ye only the blood from the right side of the gorgon, for it will heal you. The blood of the left will bring you suffering and eternal damnation.

Or turn you into a gorgon, if you weren't already one.

I turned my back on Paulo's convulsing body and picked up the girl. I sniffed, and was able to follow her scent to the room she had been using before my child had lured her away. She was still some time from awakening—her injuries had been bad, although the wound on her stomach was knitting—so I was able to clean her up and put her to bed without detection.

When she woke, she'd remember the most horrifying dream of her life, but hopefully would think it no more than that.

I went back and cleaned the other room. Then I collected Paulo and bore him away. Let them think he went for a walk in the middle of the night and got lost in the bush. I did not care.

The burden of his body slowed me down and so it was near daybreak when I returned home. Paddy was waiting for me, standing by a deep dark hole near the back steps.

"The things I do for you," he said.

Ah, my sweet Irish love. He knew me too well. I put Paulo's body in there and we covered it up. Then I kissed my shining leprechaun.

"You are a good, blessed man," I said.

"Germaine will not be happy."

"I know," I said. "But she will find that I am angrier still."

He patted my hand, offering me what consolation he could.

*

It was a month before Germaine arrived. She must have been caught up in Europe, for it to take so long.

She slunk into my study, long limbs and sinuous torso, clad appallingly in black leather with her golden hair trailing down her back.

"You killed my boy." Germaine glared at me. Her eyes were remarkable—golden, like her hair, and glistening with rage and destruction. Millions would cower, die, under that gaze.

Not I.

"If you had taught him how to be, I would not have had to. Why was he here, Germaine? Why not in Europe, with you?"

She smiled, mouth wide, pointed teeth glistening in the sun. "I thought he'd like to meet his grandmother."

So he'd been sent here precisely to do as he had done—disturb my life, make it impossible for me to remain here. Draw me back to Europe.

Back to Germaine, and her push to destroy humanity.

"He did meet his grandmother. It is a shame he did not listen, or he would still be alive."

Germaine hissed. "It is not your place to punish my children."

"If I could have waited for you, I would have. But the humans—"

"Fuck the humans. We can defeat them. Let us do so."

I shook my head. "No. They live, as we do, thus they are deserving, as we are."

"You didn't think my child was."

"I gave him the chance. He proved unworthy. Next time, choose a more able subject."

"Perhaps I should choose you." Germaine flew at me.

I could have avoided her, but I felt guilt for letting her boy go and not keeping him safe with me. I let her hit me. Once.

My hair lashed about my head, hissing, spitting. Some must have hit, because Germaine lurched away, clutching her eye.

"Fucking snakes," she said.

"Germaine." My heart clenched. My child was in pain. How could I resist her? I lifted my right arm. "Here."

She looked at me through her uninjured eye, balefully, regretfully. Then she grabbed my arm and sunk her teeth into the tender skin of my wrist.

She tore a piece of flesh away and swallowed it. Then she lapped at the blood that poured from the wound. I stroked her golden hair.

"Hush," I said. "I was wrong to kill your get. You were wrong to not train him better. We have both learned. Let us live in peace."

She stepped away, releasing my arm slowly, reluctantly. I glanced at my injury then dismissed it from my mind—it would heal.

I looked at Germaine's face—the blisters caused by the poison my hair had spat were already disappearing and her eyes were both golden and clear; once again ready to steal someone's soul.

"My son should not have died for a human," she said. "Humans should die for us."

"I will not join with you," I said. "And without me, you will fail."

"You're pathetic," she sneered. "Euryale, second of the sisters, griever of Medusa. An immortal, feared, reviled and look at you—hiding in the backwater of the world."

"Your flattery will not change my mind," I said.

Germaine swore, spun on her heel and slammed the door behind her. I stood and listened to the squeal of tires as she sped away from the house.

The door opened. "So, when do we return to Europe?"

I smiled at Paddy. "We do not," I said. "I like it here. It's so lovely and hot, and the nights are so clear. You can see the stars. It's so hard to see the stars in Europe."

"You believe Germaine will not succeed?"

I nodded, although deep in my heart, I wondered.

AFTERWORD

When I first wrote this story, it was a vampire story. I love reading vampires, but I don't want to write them unless it's completely new. So I started thinking—I've got this woman, kinda snaky, who can do some really bad arse stuff and BAM! Medusa. But Medusa is dead. Generic gorgon, I thought. Then I did a bit of research and found Medusa's sisters—Stheno and Euryale. I played with the mythology a bit—there's mixed reports over whether they had snakes for hair and could turn people to stone with their gaze like their sister, but I decided to go with it.

Making my protagonist a gorgon added a whole layer of interest and beauty to the story for me, particularly in the opportunity to have her hair become its own character. After all, the snakes are alive, part of her, so there's got to be a relationship there.

Then I surrounded her with men. The gorgon myth is one of the ultimate in scare stories about women. The power of a gorgon cannot be refused.

A SMALL BAD THING

PENELOPE LOVE

The Toyol was small and sly and meant no harm. He was not one of the *hantu raya*, the great ghosts. He was a petty thief who liked to steal coins and sweets. He could be scared away by mirrors, for he hated his own reflection. He could be distracted by a shiny scattering of dry beans.

He spied on the couple when they visited his apartment that night. He ran through the wall cavity, looking out through cracks in the plaster as they moved from the front door through the kitchen to the living room and then the bedroom. There he clung to the apartment's timber frame, inside the plaster, beside the long crack in the bedroom wall.

They were not like the folk he knew. They were big and pale. Their hair was wispy. They wore shoes indoors. They clattered on the tiled floors. They filled the space with the sound of unknown words.

The man was wide and tall. When he was excited he expanded to take up room. His shoulders broadened and he flailed his arms. He even breathed himself bigger, throwing out his chest.

The woman was thin, freckled, bony and intense.

"This place is not as old as I thought. It's the weather that makes it shabby," the woman said to the peeling paint and sagging plaster. "This horrible humidity." She stood with her back to the air-conditioning, her arms clamped to her sides.

"I like it," the man said. "These rooms are the largest we've seen. It's got character and it's cheap."

"Why is it cheap?" the woman asked. "The air-con cuts out at night? The elevator breaks?"

"I'm sure it only needs a lick of paint," the man said

"I don't like it," the woman said to the geckos crawling along the window frame.

The man drew a breath so deep that his head heaved up and down between his shoulders. He let out a long, slow hiss. "We must have looked at twenty places. You didn't like the last one because it was soulless and modern." His voice rose with every sentence. "This is old for Kuala Lumpur. Now you say you don't like this one either. I don't have time. I have to work. What do you want?"

"I don't know." The woman shrugged, not meeting his eye. She grimaced with distaste at the long crack in the bedroom wall. The Toyol quickly ducked out of sight.

"Will you just make up your mind!" the man shouted.

Shouting? The Toyol was so interested that he peeped through the crack again. He watched as the man stomped out before the woman could answer.

"I didn't want to come here," the woman said, low and sullen to the man's broad back. Her eyes sparked. She followed him slowly, with one last backwards look of disgust.

After they left, the Toyol mouthed their unknown words. "What do you want," he said, experimentally. "I didn't want," he replied. The words were not Malay or Hindi or Hokkein. They sat strangely between his sharp teeth.

The Toyol was small and grey. A *bomoh* had made him from a stillborn baby. His master had given him a cup of milk, morning and night, and an urn to live in. In return, the Toyol had stolen money for him. He was born of old, dark jungle gods of blood and vengeance.

When his master died old and alone in this apartment, no one came to claim the Toyol by giving him a cup of milk or to speak the words that released him. The Toyol was glad to be forgotten. Worse than anything he feared being trapped in his urn and thrown into the ocean, where slowly, slowly the waves would wash him away. The Toyol hated the sea worse than his own reflection. He shuddered at the thought of seeping into nothing.

Night after night and day after day he crouched on one of the mould-furred windows of the tenantless rooms. He gazed at the lights of the city with red, wondering eyes and twitched his pointed ears at street noises, cars, motorbikes, music and hawkers' cries. The Petronas twin towers of metal and glass gleamed in the distance. He misunderstood their size. He thought they were baubles he could steal if he could only get outside. He watched and waited and dreamed of all the sweets and coins and shiny things he could not reach.

He had seen people come and go from these rooms before, but nothing ever came of these visits. Soon, he forgot that the pale people had come.

The Toyol was curled up in the wall cavity late one rainy day when the apartment door burst open and men hauled furniture into the kitchen. Men piled boxes and filled the rooms with scrapes and shouts. The Toyol peered out through the cracks. Sound and movement and shiny things, so many shiny things. He was beside himself with excitement.

"I thought you said the place would be replastered and repainted before we moved," the woman muttered as she walked in. Rain rattled against the windows.

"Yes but you know KL. Things get done in their own time," the man said.

The woman glared at the crack in the bedroom wall. "Don't think that I'm going to sleep with a dirty great draught at my back," she said.

"Hello sir, hello madam," there was a clap of hands at the door. A plump, middle-aged man stepped in. "Allow me to introduce myself. I am Mr Durajaya, your neighbour from downstairs. Welcome sir, welcome madam, to our happy home."

The men heartily shook hands. "I'm Andy. This is Meg."

"It is so wonderful to get new neighbours," Mr Durajaya beamed. "This place has been empty for too long."

"Why is that?" Meg spoke too sharply. The frail scaffolding of male camaraderie shuddered uneasily.

Andy scowled at her. Mr Durajaya hunched backwards with a

nervous laugh, raising his hands. "No reason, no reason," he said. "What is the trouble?"

"There is a crack in the bedroom wall," Meg said with deep resentment.

"Let me have a look," Mr Durajaya bustled inside. He took in the problem at a glance. "A little plaster and paint and all will go well," he assured her.

"Let me do a quick fix for now," Andy shoved the headboard of the bed sideways with one big hand. "Ta-da," he said as the headboard covered almost the entire crack.

"Very good, very good sir, ha, ha, ha," Mr Durajaya applauded.

Aggrieved that his view was blocked just as it finally got interesting, the Toyol climbed out to peer over the headboard. His eyes met Meg's. She screeched. "What's that?"

The Toyol ran for cover, back into the crack and between the concrete wall and the plaster frame.

"I didn't see anything," Andy said.

"It was big as a rat," Meg said.

"Perhaps it was a rat," Andy suggested.

"Ugh. I should have known there would be rats in this horrible place." Meg whirled to confront their neighbour. "Mr Durajaya—" she stopped, disconcerted.

Mr Durajaya was in full retreat. He had taken out his wallet and was clutching it tight.

"I thought you said you liked this apartment," Andy said to Meg, with a quick gesture at Mr Durajaya and their audience of removalists.

Meg didn't take the hint. "I said I might like it if it was cleaned up a bit," she snapped back.

"You have to expect rats in KL," Andy said. "So much street food."

"So much *ghee* you mean. God I hate the stuff. It smells like popcorn gone off."

"Not one rat have I seen in this apartment building the whole time I have lived here," Mr Durajaya assured them both, and fled.

"Did he think we were going to mug him?" Meg asked.

"Perhaps he really doesn't like rats," Andy suggested.

Once safely downstairs, Mr Durajaya felt a twinge of remorse. "I can't tell them. They won't believe me," he told his wife, who was as plump as himself. His two glittering, bewildering, teenage daughters laughed over their phones on their way out.

Meg spent the evening cleaning. She scoured and mopped and dried with savage, compressed force. A horrible musty smell lay all over the place that she was determined to scrub out. Why had she said she hated *ghee*, she asked herself. Was it just to offend Mr Durajaya? She liked it, really. *Ghee* filled the food courts of the malls with the happy movie scent of hot butter. Once, she could be kind when she chose. Now, every time she opened her mouth something unpleasant spewed out.

It hadn't been like this before. Singapore had been fun. Brussels was great. She liked the expat lifestyle. She did. She had. There had been a long wearing down on her reserves until all at once, she could not cope. She said stupid things and alienated Andy's friends. Andy tried, he really tried, but he didn't understand.

She and KL had somehow not hit it off. The city felt too big, in a way which had nothing to do with its actual size. She could never orientate herself within it. She felt lost in a maze of glaring, intense heat, and humidity so high it made her eyeballs sweat, even when the rain pounded the pavement with brute, tropic fists. The city wouldn't slow down and it played by its rules, not hers, yet she felt she could be happy here if she could only seize the chance. She loved shopping, for a start. She loved the vibrancy, the colour, the chaotic traffic, the hordes of motor scooters, the dense crowds strolling, eating and chatting in the streets. She felt as if somewhere within this labyrinth of sweating concrete a warm heart beat, but she kept missing it.

She closed her eyes and drew a deep breath. She should treat this apartment as a fresh start. Things would be different, if she wasn't so angry. But it was no use to think on that. She got it from her mum; her mother was an angry woman. Always had been. Anything bad that had happened to her mum had been Meg's fault; she'd been locked in her room for hours without end. Now, her mind moved in circles when she was left alone. Only anger cleared her head.

She filled the crack behind the headboard with several tubes of builder's putty. The putty dried and shrank swiftly, leaving a large gap.

*

That night, the Toyol had no trouble wriggling through his crack as soon as the couple were asleep. He stole beneath their bed, listening to the reassuring sound of deep breathing. He climbed up the handles on the dresser drawers, one at a time, head cocked and ears straining for any disruption to the steady rhythm of their dreams. At the top of the dresser he found coins, ten, twenty and fifty sens, carelessly lying in a glittering heap. He carried them off to his stash behind the wall, then returned for more.

Andy's trousers lay discarded on the back of a chair. The Toyol rummaged in the pockets and found a wonderful shiny thing. It was red with a silver streak, as long as a man's thumb. There was a plastic clicker on the top and when he pressed with all his might, a spark shot out. Clutching his prize, he retreated behind the walls again.

The next morning Andy searched his pockets, checked the dresser, even stooped and peered under the bed. "Honey, have you seen my lighter?" he asked Meg.

She lay coiled beneath the sheets, reluctant to face the day. There was no reason for her to get up. "I thought you'd given up smoking," she said.

"Yeah, but you know sometimes when I go out with the boys," Andy said vaguely and retreated to the kitchen. "I've lost my change, too. Can I borrow some for the train?"

"You'd lose your head if it wasn't screwed on." Bitterly, vindictively, Meg rolled out of bed. She didn't need to get up. Andy knew where her purse was. She willed herself upright to make him feel bad. A simmer of rage bubbled. It was better to feel anger than emptiness. She found her handbag in the kitchen, got her purse, and slammed coins into his outstretched hand.

"There's no need for that," Andy said.

"I thought you'd given up smoking," she snapped.

"Look, I don't know what's eating you. Why don't you get out to a mall?"

"It's too hot."

"The malls are air-conditioned."

"Don't tell me where to go, all right?" The spark hit the tinder and ignited.

"No need to get snarky. I'm trying to help."

"How exactly are you trying to help? By telling me where to go; is that it? You want some trophy career wife?"

"You know that's not what I meant." Andy spoke quietly, but his frame swelled.

Meg stood before him, fists clenched, and dared him. "I saw you flirting with Stella and Imogen at that KLIA cocktail party. You thought I didn't? It made me sick. You know they were laughing at you behind your back?"

The rising tension fell flat. "Don't be ridiculous. You should get out more," Andy said. He turned and left, very quietly closing the front door.

Meg stood in the empty apartment. Her anger subsided into a dull throb of defeat. "I want to go back to Melbourne," she said aloud. No, she didn't. And yet . . . once upon a time, Andy would respond to her goad. He'd shout back. They'd have a fight and make-up sex. Now, she was a failure even at that. She couldn't make him mad anymore.

She had made a fool of herself at the KLIA party. One minute she was cool and collected, the next she was horribly aware that she was wearing the wrong dress. There she'd been, clutching a drink with shaking hands and blurting all to Stella and Imogen. Stella was Andy's manager, Imogen the vice-president's wife. And what had she been talking about? Her baby, born too early to survive. Miscarriage. What a stupid word. As if he hadn't truly been born in blood and pain, as though he hadn't lived when he was within her, and she'd wanted so desperately to give him everything good in all the world.

He would be a year old now and she would have had an instant circle of friends; mothers for coffee, shopping, movies and book club, all the little things about expat life that she really liked. Instead, she had blurted out an incomprehensible hurt in the wrong place and the wrong time, then cried in the toilets until Andy, with barely concealed annoyance, took her away in a cab.

"You should get counselling," he had said.

"I'm depressed, I know that," she had replied. "I can deal with this myself."

Her mother had tried counselling. It hadn't helped.

"I'm sorry," he had said. "I'm so sorry. I really am, but you have to move on."

She knew he was right. She had to get a grip on herself. She couldn't remain prey to this emotion. Was it truly grief? Grief was painful and sharp and stabbed when she least expected it, but it didn't speak. What burnt so long and loud? Could it be anger at that little, lost soul who hadn't tried hard enough to live?

Now she faced the empty apartment. The thought of going outside hurt, the sheer futile effort of braving the crowds, the glare, the instant soaking sweat. She felt tired and defeated. She had better have a shower, she decided.

Brace up and face the day.

Be a trooper.

You'll be okay.

As she walked to the bathroom she heard behind her the patter of tiny, phantom feet.

Her back prickled with a cold shock. She rushed into the bathroom, slammed the door and shot the bolt. She looked around for a weapon then unscrewed the metal rod from the towel rack. She raised the rail threateningly, and sniffed incredulously as a horrible, musty smell flooded the room. Drains, she thought, before she remembered she was nine floors up.

She faced the door a long time, listening. The footsteps had stopped. An echo of her own, perhaps. Stupid, pathetic woman. Useless. Worse than useless. Couldn't even have children. She put the towel rail back with shaking hands and turned on the shower. She stood a long time before she realised she had forgotten the hot water. She was freezing cold and shivering.

*

Things continued to go missing. They couldn't understand it. Never anything large, never enough to call the police or lay a charge; never anything they could complain about to anyone except themselves; loose change, lone earrings, rings and keys. They spent their mornings searching through pockets, peering under the bed and lifting the sofa cushions. Andy kept running late as he rummaged for his train fare.

"This is getting old," he complained.

Bad feeling began to grow. It was small at first, but it swelled into a pall of ill will. It thickened in increments, with each lost coin and missing lighter, and every mismatched earring. It flooded the rooms, but they kept thinking they could live with it until it got too deep, suddenly, and spilled over their heads.

"All right, all right, I get it," a tired Andy said one morning to Meg, who was curled up in bed. "I shouldn't smoke. I'll give it up, but not right now, okay. You've made your point, but I need them. Just give them back."

"Give what back?" Meg asked without interest.

"My cigarette lighters. You must have a right stash," Andy said.

"I haven't got them," Meg rolled over to the other side of the bed.

"I don't see anyone else here," Andy said.

"Are you calling me a liar?" Meg scrambled out of bed.

"I'm calling you a thief," Andy said. "A klepto. A smoking vigilante. I don't know."

Meg strode right up to him, fearless. She glared at him. "I— didn't—take—anything." She punctuated each of her words with a strong shove to Andy's chest.

She drove him against the dresser. A musty smell choked him. His eyes watered and stung. "Jeez, what the hell is that?"

For an answer, Meg shoved him again.

He put his hand on the dresser to keep his balance. He looked down at the exact spot where he had left the change for his train fare. No coins were there. Frustration and rage stabbed home. "Quit shoving me," he shouted.

"I'm not a thief," Meg yelled, and shoved him harder.

"Stop it!" Andy hit her, hard and flat.

Meg reeled back, stunned and clutching her cheek.

"What, wait, I'm sorry," Andy cried. He half-lifted a hand to touch her cheek, then snatched it back.

Meg's eyes filled with tears. "You beast." Her cheek was a hot, ugly, appalling red. She ran to the bathroom and slammed the door.

"Meg, love, I'm sorry. I don't know what came over me." As Andy tried the handle, he heard her slam the bolt. "Don't shut me out!" he shouted. He raised both fists and hammered the door.

"Get out! Get out!" Meg cried, muffled.

"I didn't start this." Andy ran his hands through his hair. Then he slammed his fist into the wall by the door. The plaster broke. He cracked his knuckle on the stud beneath. "Christ!" He hunched over his hand as blood flowed.

Meg opened the bathroom door and came out clutching the towel rail. "Take that, you pig!" She hit him across the shoulders so hard that the rail bent. The musty stench flooded over everything, infuriating them more.

Andy grabbed her wrist and bent it, forcing her to drop the rail. Blood dripped onto the floor from his injured hand. "Meg, get hold of yourself," he shouted. Her eyes were glazed, her eyelids red, and her face streaked with tears and snot. "Stop it! Just stop it!"

Her eyes snapped back to the present. She dropped to the bed, crying hard.

He stood with his hand held out to her, uselessly, for he dared not touch. Then he went into the bathroom. He washed and bound his torn and throbbing knuckles. He moved very deliberately and carefully. When he came out, he spoke softly, "I've got to go to work. You should have a shower. Wash your face. Let's deal with this when I get back."

He realised in the elevator, with a surge of pure frustration, that he still didn't have any change. "Bugger it," he said, and waved down a cab.

Mr Durajaya and his wife and daughters heard the sound of the fight overhead.

"This cannot keep happening. It is getting worse. You have to tell them," Mrs Durajaya said.

"I can't." Mr Durajaya feared ridicule more than ghosts.

The girls texted their friends about it on their way out.

That evening, Mr Durajaya met Meg in the elevator on the way up. She had a bruised and puffy cheek, badly concealed beneath thick foundation.

"Dear me, that looks painful," said Mr Durajaya innocently.

"I ran into a wall." Meg stood in unhappy, fraught silence as the elevator rose.

It was her silence that tipped Mr Durajaya over into speaking. He felt so sorry for her and the strong, stern wave of pity washed away his fear of looking a fool. He clutched his briefcase tightly before him in self defence. "There is a Toyol in your apartment," he blurted out.

Meg just stared at him.

"Everyone knows. A Toyol is a thief," he said, then regretted ever opening his mouth. He was trapped in the elevator and the floor obstinately refused to swallow him. The silence drew on, scathing, disbelieving. He looked at his sweating reflection in the elevator mirrors. The door opened on his floor with a triumphant ring. He rushed out, happy to escape.

The doors hissed shut behind him then opened again. Meg had thrust her hand out. "A thief," she repeated.

"A little thief. It steals small things only. Keep it away with mirrors," he said.

"Thank you for letting me know," Meg said. Her strained face lit into a grateful smile. Then the elevator doors shut again. This time she did not stop them.

"There. I told her. You know, I actually think she believed me," Mr Durajaya told his wife that evening as they watched television. Relief made him feel light headed, and he went to bed content.

*

Meg went out that night and bought a large mirror. She set it on the dresser and put her small change and rings and earrings and keys before it.

Andy sent a text to say he was working late. He had not returned by the time she went to bed.

In the morning, Meg's little pile of treasure was still there, gazing placidly at its own reflection. "Andy, look!" she cried joyfully, turning to share.

But Andy wasn't there.

His side of the bed was cold and empty. There was no sign he had ever been in. She got up and dangled the earrings and rings with shaking hands. She jingled the keys, then poured the coins through her fingers, ten, twenty, fifty sens.

Andy texted later that day. He was staying at a friend's place for a bit.

Meg had breakfast at the hawker stall downstairs. She talked to the man making pancakes. He laughed off the Toyol. "It is an old story. It doesn't belong to modern Malaysia," he said.

She talked to the men playing chess in the street, the scooter riders, the taxi drivers, the girl at the durian stall, and the stall-holders at the market. She heard the old tale of the village miser who fed the Toyol with a cup of milk, morning and night, and how the Toyol stole from his neighbours until they chased the miser away. Story by story, she learned how to make a Toyol and dismiss it, and of the salt water that would slowly, slowly, wash a Toyol away.

Andy dropped by to collect some clothes. He had a white bandage wrapped around his knuckles. He could not even raise his eyes to hers.

"I'm better now," she said.

He didn't stay to listen.

That night, she poured milk into a cup and left it by her bed.

In the morning, the milk was gone.

Her coins and jewellery sat innocently by the mirror. Her keys stayed in place. She had not realised until now how much the constant petty pilfering had bothered her. She was filled with exquisite relief.

A plasterer and a painter finally arrived. They cut away the torn plaster next to the bathroom door to patch up the hole in the wall. She was in the kitchen when she heard them laughing. She returned to see them scooping glittering handfuls from the wall cavity. Coins were packed in a thick pile below. Afloat in the sea of small change was a flotsam of earrings, rings, keys and cigarette lighters.

"You must have a Toyol," the plasterers joked.

"Ha ha ha," she said.

The men patched and painted the hole. They promised to come back tomorrow to fix the crack by the bedstead.

That afternoon, she sat before her mirror and combed her hair. She regarded herself steadily over the heaped pile of loose change. The swelling had subsided and the bruise faded. The pain was gone.

She visited the Indian supermarket downstairs and bought a large glass jar with a screw-top lid, the kind used for pickling mangoes. She lugged it to her apartment and set it down on the bedroom floor.

She sat on the cool tiles as, outside, the sun set in a blaze of orange and blood red. Below the traffic blared and muttered. The evening darkened to night, until the street lights cast a pale glow against the walls. In the distance, the Petronas Towers wept great streams of glittering pearls.

"I know you're here," she said to the Toyol. "Come out."

Nothing stirred in the apartment.

She poured milk into a cup and set it before her. "You've drunk my milk. I am your master. Come out now," she ordered.

A shadow slipped from the crack behind the bedstead and stole beneath the bed. Its large head bobbed beneath the mattress. It peered at her with red eyes and reached with tiny fingers like the beloved dead. She breathed in the musty stench of jungles and blood.

The shadow stopped at the end of the bed.

"Drink the milk," she said.

It lifted the cup with both hands, drank, then licked its lips. It spoke to her, guttural and soft. She could not understand it.

"Get in the jar," Meg said.

The grey creature climbed inside. It was a large jar, but it was too small for the creature. The Toyol could only fit by squatting with its arms around its shins and resting its head on its knees.

Meg screwed the lid shut. She lifted the jar and shook it, so the thing inside flinched. Its red eyes blinked. "This is all your fault," she said.

She thrust the jar into the crack between the concrete and the plaster, as far and deep as she could reach.

The next morning, the painter and plasterer filled the crack and painted it over, then put the bedstead back. Meg sent a text to Andy. "I'll get counselling," it said.

He called later that day.

"I am so sorry about everything," she said.

"We'll go to counselling together," Andy promised her.

Meg told Andy that she didn't want to stay in that old apartment. They moved to a bright, modern tower surrounded by fellow expats. She found her lost rhythm. She made friends. Her days were filled with coffee, walks, lunches and shopping. She knew she had done a small, bad thing. But she did not dwell on it long. It was the choice she'd had to make to be happy again.

The Toyol crouched in darkness with his chin resting on his knees and his arms wrapped around his shins. He was not one of the *hantu raya*, the great ghosts. He could not free himself. There he sat, night after night and day after day, and the kind waves of the sea never came to wash him away.

AFTERWORD

I was delighted when I heard about the *Bloodstones* collection last year, as I was travelling to Malaysia for a wedding in early 2012. I figured this would be great chance to write a story based on my firsthand experience of a foreign city. Kuala Lumpur is such an amazing place that it was a natural location for my story. Several of my friends lived the expat lifestyle and I also wanted to make use of that experience—especially when one partner is working and the other is not. I already knew of a couple of suitably gruesome Malay monsters: the *Penanggal* (a floating woman's head that trails entrails), and the *Pontianak* (a female vampire who lurks in banana groves), so even before I left Australia I was toying with the idea of a story about female anger. However, when I sat down to write the story on my return, the *Toyol* showed up. By the time I had finished, I had realised the story was still about female anger, and that the *Toyol* wasn't really the monster.

A MOVEABLE FEAST

JENNY BLACKFORD

"Benji isn't really a baby, you know, Aunty Jessie," Angela said. Fluoro-bright ice cream was smeared orange and green around her wide mouth; more dripped from her fingers onto the floor. "He's a durga-monster."

Jessica nodded, and looked back at the notebook's screen. Angela's world was full of monsters that no one else knew about: moon-leopards hunted through her nights, and stranger things stalked her by day.

Jessica kept staring at the screen, but she could still feel Angela looking at her with those huge brown eyes—as if she didn't have enough problems already. On cue, the idiot, incessant voice inside her head said, *He doesn't love me anymore. I wish I was dead.*

She gritted her teeth and copied some financial data from the company's website into her report, trying not to hear the drip drip drip of melted ice cream puddling on her sister Sophie's floor. She would mop it up off the slate later; poor Sophie had enough to worry about—but Eric needed this report fast, and she was determined to finish it.

Jessica managed to grind out one more painful paragraph, her eyes stinging with suppressed tears, then she saved and closed the file. Eric had torn her heart into small bloody pieces and stamped on them, but that wasn't Angela's fault.

She smiled as convincingly as she could manage, and said, "Okay, chicken, what's a durga-monster?"

Angela beamed a fluoro-bright smile. "A durga-monster looks like a baby most of the time. It's *very* cute. It makes people love it and cuddle it, but it turns into something else when no one's watching."

That sounded nasty; silly, but nasty. The figments of Angela's imagination were seldom cute, or even comfortable. "Oh. Is that why you were screaming last night, possum? Because Benji turned into something?" Jessica still remembered night after night of her own evil dreams, when she was Angie's age.

Angela shook her head so violently that Jessica could almost hear her brains rattle. "No, silly. Benji was in Mummy's bed all last night. He can't turn into something else when he's in bed with Mummy."

"What made you scream last night, then?"

Angela stuck her ice cream-dripping fingers in her mouth and mumbled something incomprehensible.

Jessica said, "Take your fingers out of your mouth, Angel, and tell me what happened in the dream."

Angela looked furtively around the family room. "Don't want to."

Jessica frowned, remembering that feeling. The poor kid was still terrified. "If you don't want to tell me about it, that's okay. Just put the ice cream stick in the kitchen tidy and wash your hands. I've got to finish this report for my boss." (*Even though he doesn't love me anymore.*)

The girl turned her head away and mumbled again.

"Angela," Jessica said, warningly. She remembered her mother saying "Jessica" in just the same tone, each syllable perfectly distinct, and winced. It was strange how all the tiny, niggling pains could still hurt, even when one's whole being was flooded with misery.

Angela stared at her feet. "The lady from the stars was looking at me." Her voice was soft and fast.

"What lady from the stars? An alien? An astronaut?"

Sophie boasted about her daughter's imagination—unlike their mother, who'd labelled Jessica *over-imaginative* as if it were a notifiable disease, and forced her to study accounting instead of Medieval English and the Norse poets.

Angela stamped her foot. "Not from the *stars*, from the *stairs*! Don't you know anything? The lady from the stairs! The scary lady!"

"What scary lady? And what do you mean, she was looking at you?"

Angela almost shouted, "The lady wants me to go to the party!"

"What party?" But by the time the words were out of Jessica's mouth, Angela was gone, stomping down the long corridor towards the front of the terrace house, then up the stairs to the bedroom where Sophie was trying to get Benji to sleep. Jessica put her head in her hands. Another failed conversation, in a lifetime of failed conversations. But crying would be too great a luxury. Eric wanted this report on his desk by morning. She had to get it finished, and it had to be perfect, absolutely perfect, even if he didn't love her anymore. Especially because he didn't love her anymore.

*

Jessica woke, thirsty, around 3 am, in the spare room at the back of the old house, behind the upstairs bathroom. The bedroom was tiny, but she was grateful to Sophie for letting her sleep there until she found somewhere of her own. She padded barefoot down the two flights of stairs to the kitchen, and gulped down a giant glass of water. On the way back, her stomach now uncomfortably distended with liquid, she saw a door she'd never noticed before. It was bright apple-green, and it led off the half-landing just down from the bathroom door.

Jessica hardly saw the door at the time; she was still immersed in the dream she'd been having before thirst woke her. She'd been floating through the void between the stars with a dozen ancient god-beasts, horned and tentacled—or was she fleeing them? While she was at college, her mother had donated all Jessica's tatty paperbacks to charity, and she'd been too busy for fiction since— but the heavy-duty sleeping pills that the doctor had prescribed gave her strangely vivid dreams. At least they stopped the suicidal ideation, as the doctors called it, most of the time.

Afterwards, she lay back in bed despairing, remembering Eric's hair, as soft and pale as corn silk, and his blue eyes, cold as the south wind. But she was puzzled about that green door. She'd thought that she knew all the rooms in Sophie's old inner-Sydney terrace house. What room could possibly lie behind that door?

*

While Jessica was setting up her laptop in the family room after work the next evening, she saw the dried-up puddle of fluoro ice cream on the slate. She'd forgotten to mop it up for Sophie after all—too absorbed in the report for Eric, damn him. (*Why doesn't he love me anymore? Am I so old, so ugly, so fat?*) With a shock, she remembered Angela's lady on the stairs, and that green door she'd seen in the night. In her frenzy to get to work in the morning, Jessica had forgotten to check exactly where that door led.

It was time to get to the bottom of this door thing, Jessica decided, so that she could concentrate on editing Eric's new presentation. She left the clever silver machine to run a virus scan and walked up and down the stairs three times, looking for the door.

It wasn't there. The bathroom door was right next to the spare room door, on the back landing. The stairs went down from it to a half-landing, then up to the front landing, with Sophie's big bedroom next to Angela's smaller one. But there wasn't a door anywhere near the half-landing, let alone a bright green one. There was nothing but old bricks, stripped bare of their plaster back in the clueless 1970s. No green door, no nothing . . .

Jessica shrugged, and went downstairs to Eric's presentation. He had chewed up her heart and swallowed it, then decided he didn't want it anymore. It was a mangled mess now, and her life would never be the same, but he still *needed* her. She was the *best*. One day, he would realise what a fool he'd been.

She crossed her fingers, hoping that the day would come before despair sent her over the edge.

*

That night, music woke Jessica from her drugged sleep. Giant tripods straight out of *The War of the Worlds* had been hunting her through twisting lanes, their death rays coming closer and closer to her head. It was almost a relief to be awake—but what was Sophie doing, playing music in the middle of the night? Sophie was still miserable about James leaving her and the kids, and she wasn't exactly rational; but if the music woke Angie and Benji now, nobody would get back to sleep. She staggered to her door to investigate.

On the back landing outside her room, her eyes more than half-closed, Jessica listened for the source of the music.

The bathroom? Sophie was playing music in the *bathroom?* Jessica swung the door wide open. There was the slightly grimy claw-footed bath crowded with plastic toys, the almost-clean sink with the grey slick of slime around the plug-hole, Sophie's thick paperback of short stories by H.G. Wells sitting dog-eared on the cane stool next to the toilet—but no Sophie, and no music.

The music had to be coming from *somewhere.*

Jessica stumbled sleepily off the back landing and down a few stairs to the half-landing. The music was louder now. She opened her eyes wide, and saw that door again. It was apple-green against the bricks of the wall, and it sounded as if there was a party going on behind it: music and loud voices, and the sharp, bright tinkle of ice in glasses.

What? Sophie wouldn't have a party without inviting her, would she? Her only sister?

Jessica grabbed the big brass handle at the centre of the door and tried to turn it, but the handle wouldn't move, no matter how hard Jessica tugged. Surely Sophie hadn't locked her out of a party. *Surely not.*

After pushing and pulling at the handle for ten minutes with no result, Jessica went back to bed, furious and baffled. She thought she'd never sleep, but all too soon the alarm clock dragged her out of the control room of a space-ship that was falling infinitely slowly towards the event horizon of a black hole.

As she woke up, she remembered the night. How could Sophie have held a party and not asked her? Not even *told* her? It was unimaginable.

But as she was stomping down the stairs, tears in her eyes yet again, she saw that the green door was gone. She put both hands out, touched the space where the door had been in the night. All that she could feel was gritty old hand-made bricks.

She shook her head to clear it, but it only made it hurt more.

"It must have been a dream," she said aloud. "Just a dream."

Angela's door at the top of the stairs creaked open, and the kid stepped out onto the front landing, in her blue-green dragon-scale pyjamas.

"Did you see the lady last night, Aunty Jessie?" Angela asked.

"What lady, chicken?" Jessica said warily.

"The lady on the stairs. She was playing music. She wanted me to go to her party."

Jessica just shook her head. This couldn't be happening. It was too much to deal with before she'd even had the first coffee of the day. Especially after the music in the night. But if there wasn't a door in the wall, how could there have been a party behind it, or music?

Too much thought too early. Jessica changed the subject to something more interesting. "Hey, Angie-pie, what does a durga-monster look like when it's not pretending to be a baby?"

Angela looked doubtful. "Well, it's got a lot of legs," she said slowly. "*Long* legs, like a spider. And long black wings. *Furry* wings, like a moth."

Over her muesli, in the family room, Jessica watched Sophie spoon pale sludge into Benji's mouth. Now and then, Jessica felt Sophie glance at her green snakeskin stilettos (too high) and the neckline of the black dress (too low), her sister's face creased with worry. Jessica couldn't possibly ask Sophie about what had happened during the night.

Jessie tried to imagine dropping it into the conversation casually: "Hey, sis, did you know that your house has a door that appears in the wall in the middle of the night? And that there was a party behind it last night? Loud music, and everything?"

No way. Sophie already thought Jessica was insane for moving in with Eric last year. Jessica couldn't possibly tell her sister that she'd seen a door that wasn't there.

Still, she had to say something. "Sleep well?" she asked, oh so casually.

"Like the dead," Sophie said, with a huge smile. Her eyes were clear and bright, without a trace of the dark circles that late nights always gave her.

"You didn't hear any noises in the night? Music?"

Sophie raised her eyebrows. "I keep telling you, you've been working too hard. You have to slow down, sweetie. Read a book. Fiction, not finance."

"I'm okay, don't worry about me. It must have been just another bad dream. I've been dreaming a lot lately." Too much, obviously.

Benji waved his anemone-like fist.

The baby, Jessica thought. Now, that was a thought to hold onto amongst the misery. He was *such* a sweet little nephew. And it was so sweet of Angela, too, making up the story about Benji being a durga-monster, whatever that was.

Jessica tried to smile, despite the night she'd had, and despite the day she was expecting in the office. There was Sophie, her adorable younger sister, being such a good mother, putting yet another spoonful of sludge into Benji's warm, wet, open maw.

The baby gazed at his aunt with dark, ageless eyes. He put a hand up in the air, and waved his fingers like an octopus's tentacles. Then he winked, very slowly. Jessica shuddered.

*

"Well, did you see the lady last night?" Angela demanded at half past six, kicking repeatedly at the leg of the table Jessica was trying to work on. "You didn't tell me. You have to tell me if you saw the lady."

"What lady, Angel-pie?" Jessica said. But she was only pretending. This thing with the door in the wall, and the lady, was starting to seem more important than the endless stream of urgent reports and presentations that Eric apparently needed her to work on until midnight every night. Perhaps he was just trying to drive her out of the firm with over-work, now that he didn't love her anymore.

Angela said, "The lady in the green dress, silly. The one who wants me to go to the party."

"Where does this lady live, chicken?"

"The second star to the right, and straight on till morning. That was what she said, one time."

"In the stars? Is she an alien, Angie-poo?"

Angela shrugged. "Maybe. I don't know. Do you want to go to her party with me tonight?"

None of this could possibly be real, but she might as well go along with Angela's fantasy—make her happy. The kid wasn't having an easy time any more than Jessica or Sophie was: her beloved father was off in Europe with his new wife, Sophie's younger and thinner replacement, and he hadn't seen Angela for months. No one mentioned his name, or even that he existed, anymore.

"Sure, why not?" she said. "I'll go to the party with you."

Angela nodded. "Good. She'll like that. She said she wants to meet you."

I can't imagine why, Jessica thought. *No one else wants to know me these days.* She said as breezily as she could, trying to be a good aunt, "Has your brother turned into a durga-monster lately?"

Angela picked up her favourite fluffy toy, an orange and gold dragon the size of a toddler, and held it over her head. "He's a durga-monster all the time, silly. He looks like a cute baby most of the time, to make people love him, but he's *always* a durga-monster."

Jessica tried again. "Um, has he changed into the thing that he looks like when he doesn't look like a baby, then?"

Angela threw the dragon into the corner. "He looks like a baby *now*. Mummy's in the front room with him. But he looked like the other thing *before*, while he was taking his nap and Mummy was watching Sesame Street with me. He looked like the bad thing, then."

"Oh, darling, I'm sure your baby brother never turns into a bad thing, really." *Even if grown men could turn out to be such bastards.* "Why don't we find a DVD for you to watch, just while I finish this presentation I've got to write?"

*

That night, Jessica woke gasping from a dream of sinister blood-sucking moths flying at her eyes and mouth. Angela was patting at her face and throat with small, sticky fingers.

"I want to go to the party, Aunty Jessie. The lady won't let me in unless you come with me. Wake up!"

What? Jessica blinked several times. But she might as well humour the kid, now she was awake. "Okay, Angel." It had to be better than dreaming about evil moths, or despairing over Eric.

Jessica got out of bed, feeling hazy, and walked behind Angela down to the half-landing. Eyes half-closed, she held Angela's hand while the kid knocked at that impossible green door in the wall, and saw a tall woman open it. Jessica blinked, and rubbed at her eyes.

The woman in the doorway wore silk the colour of green apples, with strings of pearls dripping from her neck and shining emeralds laced through her blonde hair. Behind her was a ballroom full of revellers. (That wasn't possible, of course. Jessica knew there wasn't any space behind the green door for a *ballroom*.)

This had to be another dream. One of the people behind the woman in the green dress had a curly pink tail poking through her blue velvet dress, and another's sleek body shone bright gold all over. On the floor near them there were two huge panthers, gloriously spotted, playing with a golden ball; and the man to the left, serving drinks, had long furry ears, and grey whiskers on his donkey muzzle.

"Come join the party, Angela, Jessica," the lady said, and smiled at them both. "The endless party."

Jessica was suspicious, even if this was just a dream. "Endless, like endless night, or endless sea?"

"Exactly. But this is an endless *party*."

Jessica didn't like the sound of that, any more than she liked the look of the green-silk woman. There was something not quite right about her.

Angela let go of Jessica's hand and rushed into the room. Jessica suddenly panicked. What if this *wasn't* a dream? Jessica could see her niece racing towards the corner of the room, where small people in silver space-suits were dancing around a table loaded with fairy-bread. Within seconds, a piece of fairy bread was in Angela's mouth, and another was on the way.

The woman in green smiled widely, and Jessica shivered. Her teeth looked very white, and very sharp. "You won't see your niece again, my dear," she said, "not unless you join us, but don't worry. She'll be happy with us. And everyone in your world will simply forget her. Even you will forget her, in time. In a week and a day, you won't even remember what colour her eyes were."

The door closed. Jessica just stood and looked at it, for a moment. "What? Let me in, you bitch! You've got my *niece* in there! Give her back to me!"

Jessica beat against the door, when the handle refused to turn, until her hands started to bleed. The door had gone, and there was nothing left but old handmade bricks.

"Shit," she muttered. "What am I going to do? I have to get Sophie. She's the kid's mother. That strange woman *has* to let Sophie in to the party, if Angela's there."

But no matter how long Jessica stood over Sophie's sleeping body, shaking her shoulder, Sophie just slept on, with Benji snuggled smugly against her side, his red mouth lolling open.

By dawn, Jessica was a snivelling mess. She was still sitting at the side of Sophie's bed, working her way through a large box of tissues, when Sophie finally stirred.

Jessica screamed at her drowsing sister, "Angela's gone. The woman on the stairs took her. The one who lives behind the green door."

Sophie grabbed Jessica's hand and stroked it. "No, darling. That wasn't real. You're just having a nightmare. Everything's all right." Beside her, Benji seemed to nod agreement.

"Angela's been kidnapped, I tell you—"

Sophie's voice had tears in it. "No, sweetie. I know you miss Angie. But she's still in Paris with her bastard of a father. It's just another nightmare, like when you were little. Go back to bed. I'll call your work, and tell that stupid bastard Eric that you're sick."

"Paris? But she was here last night!"

Sophie said, slowly, "You're still in your nightmare. It used happen to you when we were kids, remember? And it happens to Angela all the time. Just go back to bed, sweetie. Please."

"But Angela's—"

Sophie sighed. "Oh, darling, don't you remember the postcard I showed you yesterday? Go to the dressing table and have a look. Then you'll remember."

Too distraught to disobey, Jessica walked the three steps to the dressing table. Right in the middle was a postcard of the Eiffel Tower; on the reverse, Angela's wobbly writing and a French stamp. It was dated eight days earlier.

"Oh," Jessica said. "Angela's in Paris. You were right. I must have been dreaming. But . . . "

"Go back to bed, sweetie," Sophie said, and Benji gurgled happily beside her.

But when Jessica went downstairs for lunch, after a long, uncomfortable time of tossing and turning in the narrow spare bed, wondering whether she was having a nervous breakdown, the golden dragon was lying on its side in the corner where Angela had thrown it, and the dried-out fluoro ice cream was still puddled on the slate floor. She almost pointed them out to Sophie, but Benji looked at her with those deep, dark eyes, and she knew there was no point. What she had to do was to get in through that door and rescue Angela, no matter what.

*

For three days, Jessica let Sophie answer the phone whenever Eric rang to see when she was going to be well enough to finish the presentation for him. He didn't love her anymore, and probably he never had, and maybe she would never be truly happy again—but her misery about him was just a backdrop to her guilt and rage about Angela. Her only niece was *gone*, kidnapped and taken somewhere unimaginably strange in time and space. Jessica wanted to scream and cry, to rail against her fate, but that would do no good.

Instead, she babied herself by day: took afternoon naps, ate chicken soup and chocolate, read magazines in bed. But for those three nights, as soon as Sophie's bedroom light went out, Jessica sat on the landing and watched the wall.

Nothing happened: no door, no music, no party.

The fourth night Jessica slept, but woke in a panic. What colour were Angie's eyes? Brown? Green? She ran downstairs for Sophie's photo albums, and dragged them back to her bed. There were hundreds of photos of Benji, and even some of his father, but none of Angela. Jessica shook too hard after that to get back to sleep.

The next day, Jessica stayed in bed until Sophie went to the supermarket with Benji, then she rang Angela's school. They must have photos, records of her classes . . .

"Sorry," the school secretary said, "a girl of that name was enrolled with us last year, but she's never attended the school. Her father took her to Europe, I believe."

*

A week and a day after Angela had disappeared, when Jessica had almost given up, had almost decided that it was she who was deluded, not everyone else, she woke from a dream of matt-black spaceships hovering over the house's corrugated iron roof. Her mouth was dry as the vacuum of outer space. She started to walk downstairs for a glass of water—and there was that damned door again, bright apple green, the brass handle shining, and party music filtering out. The endless party.

Her heart pounding, Jessica knocked.

The woman in the green dress opened the door and smiled. Jessica looked past her, scanning for Angela. The room seemed to go on forever—where was the kid? Over to the left were five or six things with too many long legs, and furry dark wings trailing to the floor. *Durga-monsters.* They were dancing in a ring around Angela, who was singing at the top of her voice, and spinning around. She was still wearing her dragon pyjamas. Jessica squinted: did the monsters have claws at the end of those furry wings? Did they look hostile? She hadn't decided when one of them waved to her and winked, just like Benji had. *Shudder.*

"Give her back to me," Jessica said. "She's my niece."

"But she's happy here," the woman said. "You'd be happy here, too."

"Where is *here*? Where exactly *is* this party? It can't be inside the house. The room's too big—I can't see any walls—so where is it?"

"You should know that. You'd have known when you were twelve. You've spent too long reading the wrong books, Jessica."

What was she reading when she was twelve? Paperbacks with pictures of unicorns on the cover, or monsters—or aliens. "Angela said that you live in the stars."

The woman laughed. "Sometimes we do. Sometimes we live on an island of glass, or under the burial mound of a warrior-king. Our kingdom is a moveable feast. You stay here, and I'll find your niece and bring her to talk to you. Meanwhile, why don't you have a drink? What harm could it possibly do?"

The long-eared waiter came up to the doorway. On his tray was a bunch of white grapes and a single crystal glass full to the brim of wine the palest of yellow-greens. He held it out to Jessica. Automatically, she took the glass and lifted it to her nose. It smelled of spring. The shadow of a memory niggled at the back of her mind—but what harm could it possibly do to take a single sip?

*

Sophie answered the phone, Benji on her right hip.

"I've already told you, Eric," she snapped. "Jessica's in London. I have no idea what this presentation is that you're carrying on about. She's been there for weeks. And I don't care why you want to know, I'm *not* telling you what colour her eyes are. If you didn't bother to find out before you dumped her, you're a fool."

Sophie slammed the phone down. Jessica's eyes were brown, of course; dark chocolate brown.

Or were they apple green?

AFTERWORD

Unlike Jessica, the readers of *Bloodstones* should have little difficulty in recognising the elegant blonde in the green dress as the alluring Queen of Faerie, and the green door as one of the occasional gates to her marvellous, dangerous realm. Some of them might even remember the green door in the old brick wall from H. G. Wells' wonderful story "The Door in the Wall", which has haunted me since childhood. That door was in a street, not a house, but it led to an enchanted space that held "beautiful strange people" (including a tall, fair girl in a green dress and two spotted panthers playing with a ball)—and, all too possibly, death, or something like it.

The immediate thrust of inspiration for the story came from my niece Alexandra, who informed her mother that her little brother (whose name is not Ben) was a cute, but dangerous, durga-monster. She drew a moon-leopard for me, once.

DEAD INSIDE

PETE KEMPSHALL

Ian can see the silence. Emanating from the corner of the room, it's heaviest at its source, those closest to it stooping under its weight. It steals the purpose from the knot of blue-clad men and women, robs them of their accustomed urgency so they appear to move in slow motion, their work over before it even had the chance to begin. Donna's screams are muted now, too. Her wails have faltered, collapsed into defeated little bursts of sound, and Ian knows he's expected to go to her. Instead he stares at the corner, at the absence that sucks the life from the place.

He feels nothing.

Finally, one of the women remembers he's there. Standing in the room, yet so very much outside of it, Ian finds he's aware of even the smallest details of her appearance, as if his brain is compensating for the silence by drinking in other stimuli.

She's a perfect fit for her job: a head shorter than him, and a little too round for her height, she's . . . matronly, Ian decides. Her face is the colour of porridge, stark against hair dyed a fiery red. Ian supposes she wanted to look special, a bit different, to stand out. All it's done is make her look grotesque.

Her sky-blue tunic is rumpled, darker in spots where it had been stained not five minutes earlier. As his eyes track across her ample, yet unappealing bosom, they latch onto a badge she's pinned there. A nameplate. She's adapted it, small felt-tip pictures of multi-coloured balloons festooning the letters: 'Alana'.

Her eyes are small and dark, and they lock with his, widen with an emotion Ian can't place. She holds the look for what must be forever, then stiffly reaches down to pick up a small bundle from the table. Three waddling steps are all it takes to cross the room and stand beside him.

"You should see him," she says. Her voice sounds flat, lacking in sympathy.

She places the bundle in his arms. Ian looks down at it.

There should be noise. But the silence swallows everything.

*

The sun caught the brass plaque, flaring on the warm metal and causing Ian to squint. A moment later, the small box was deep enough into the hole for the light to no longer reach it, and the inscription resolved.

STEPHEN ALISTAIR CONNELL 2012

Ian watched the coffin until it nudged onto the soil at the bottom of the grave, as much to avoid looking at Donna as anything else. There was nothing left of the woman he had fallen in love with. The moment the ultrasound had failed to detect a heartbeat, she'd started to collapse in on herself. But it was when she had realised what would have to happen next, that it was too late in the pregnancy and the baby too big for her body to simply expel it . . . that's what had finished her off.

Donna had been staying with Roger and Maureen since the hospital released her. Now, at the graveside, her parents insisted she stand with them, not him. It was the first time they had shown any interest in their daughter since she'd told them she was moving in with Ian. Back then they'd cut her off without a cent; now they were volunteering to pay for the funeral.

Leaning heavily on her father for support, Donna shuffled forward and dropped a single flower into the grave. It landed gently on the coffin, bright against the dark wood. Suddenly weak at the knees, Donna staggered at the edge of the hole, and Ian heard a collective intake of breath from the mourners as she teetered on the brink. But Daddy was there, latching a firm grip on her shoulders. Ramrod straight, he turned her away from the grave and escorted her to her seat, a signal for the press of black-clad friends and relatives to come forward and cast in individual handfuls of dirt.

Again, Ian hung back. It was a good turn out from the neighbourhood—piss-broke they may be, but they all pulled together when it counted, and he didn't want to get in their way. Let them pay their respects. He had nothing more to add.

He felt a hand clap him on the shoulder, another grip his arm, silent gestures of support. If anyone noticed his lack of emotion, no one said anything. Compared to the display of grief from Donna and her family, anyone would look cold. Dead inside.

As the procession of mourners passed, he let his eyes wander. In the middle distance, a lonely figure picked his way through the headstones. Layered in filthy clothing, arms laden with ragged plastic bags, the man stumbled along, looking as hunched and defeated as the other living occupants of the cemetery. It wasn't unusual to spot homeless people in this neck of the woods—God knew enough of the locals were one missed benefit payment away from swelling the numbers—but something about seeing one here seemed wrong to Ian. Repellent.

He continued to watch the vagrant, only dimly aware of the messages of condolence being offered by those around him, finally losing sight of the man in a bank of stone crypts.

And then the ceremony was over.

The mourners drifted towards the cemetery gates, and Ian found himself trailing the pack. On the road outside, a dark-windowed car waited, hired by Roger to transport the immediate family. The older man tucked his wife and daughter into the vehicle then slipped in after them. Ian didn't even warrant a backward glance.

The car pulled away smartly, and Ian watched it vanish up the road.

Message received.

*

Rob's grip on the trio of pint glasses was slipping by the time he got them back to the table, and he half-placed, half-dropped them onto the sticky wooden surface. Dark beer slopped out to add to the table's filthy patina—created from years of being wiped down with a dirty cloth, if at all. The Jacaranda Hotel was nothing if not classy.

"Careful, dickhead," growled Mitch. He shuffled his seat away from the table a little, to avoid booze dripping onto his trousers. Like everyone else, he was still wearing his funeral suit, and like everyone else, wanted to avoid having it cleaned if possible.

"Sorry," Rob muttered and slid one of the diminished pints across to Ian. Without a word, Ian snagged the drink and raised it to his lips. He took a third off the top in one hit. Across the table, both his friends watched him with expressions like slapped puppies.

Annoyance flared within him—he let it smoulder and die. No point getting stroppy with them: truth was, people just didn't know how to act around him anymore.

They'd been like that when he first moved into the neighbourhood, the shittiest little suburb in the west. All those fuckers in the city, crapping on about the Mining Boom, they had no idea places like this even existed. Ian certainly hadn't.

He'd had to watch himself back then, watch the people, see the little things that bound them together and mirror them. In the early days, he didn't give away that he was well-educated, from a different social stratum. But drugs and unemployment are great levellers, and when they saw he was just as hard up as the rest of them, brought just as low, the locals had soon warmed to him. When he'd helped out with Gemma that time, he'd become a favourite son.

It was a tight-knit community. That much poverty, you stuck together. Now though, ever since word had got out about the baby, people had backed off. What the fuck did you say to someone whose unborn son had just died?

Nothing, apparently. You just take them out and buy them drinks and avoid eye contact all night.

Ian swallowed another mouthful of beer, set his glass down and stared at Rob and Mitch. He could practically feel them squirm.

"I'm fine, all right? Fine."

Rob shuffled his arse on his seat. "We're just worried, mate, you know?" His gaze was downturned, as if the puddle of beer on the surface in front of him was the most interesting thing he'd ever seen. "You're so quiet, we thought—"

"—I'd be locking myself in my room and crying like a girl? You feel better if I did that, would you?"

"No, but you're not—"

"I'm. Fine. I'm dealing with it. You want to help? Really want to help?"

Both men nodded like novelty bobble heads.

"Stop acting like I'm made of glass." He drained what remained of his beer. "Only glass you need to be worried about is this one, and who's filling it up next."

Mitch shook his head, half a smile on his face, and reached across for the empty. He was getting to his feet when the door on the far side of the bar crashed open, letting in frigid winds and warm laughter.

Bill McCoy tumbled in through the door, followed by a younger, slighter man Ian didn't recognise. Bill was a pillar of the community, or a rampant pain in the arse, depending on who you asked. Ian had no opinion one way or the other; he caught Bill's eye, nodded a greeting. Bill looked away, embarrassed.

Christ, not another one.

"Sorry, mate," Rob muttered, barely audible over the bar noise, then looked back at Ian. "I didn't think . . . "

"About what?"

"Fuckin' dickhead," Mitch muttered.

"What is going on?" Ian enunciated the words like an adult to a particularly stupid child.

Mitch sighed. "Bill got a call last week, some bloke from the city. Turns out he'd had a one-nighter with a bird up north twenty-odd years back; ended up with a boy he didn't even know about."

Ian regarded him blankly—usually he'd have heard about this straight away, grapevine being what it was. But people had been avoiding him . . .

"Kid grew up with no idea who his real dad was," Mitch continued, "gets old enough to start sniffing around and tracks him down, doesn't he? Long story short, Bill's over the bloody moon and—"

"—Bill likes to come here for a drink."

Mitch looked as if he wanted the ground to open and swallow him up.

"You're all right," Ian sighed. "No harm done." He thought for a moment, glanced over again at Bill and his long-lost son. Happy families.

He downed the remains of his drink. "Come on, Maguire's is open late. You're buying."

Rob exhaled loudly, as if he'd just been given permission to breathe. "You sure, mate? I mean—"

Ian scraped back his seat and stood up, feeling as if every punter in the room was looking at him. The dark emotion that had gnawed at him ever since he'd walked into the pub intensified.

"Let's just go, eh?"

*

By the time Ian staggered through the front door of the tiny house he shared with Donna, he'd already stopped to puke three times on the lawn. The prickly odour of regurgitated alcohol burst in through the door with him and followed him through to the kitchen, where he spent another couple of minutes retching into the sink. When he was done, his mind connected the lack of verbal abuse with the fact that Donna wasn't there, and his surge of gratitude coincided with the next surge from his stomach.

Pushing himself upright and away from the sink, he went over and pulled open the fridge, plucked out a can of cheap beer and took it to the living room. There, slumped in his favourite knackered old chair, he fought a short battle with the ring pull, took two swigs from the drink, and was asleep.

*

He woke late, the sun already slanting through the ill-fitting blinds in the bedroom. At some point he'd relocated there, flat on his back and comatose under the covers, like someone had come along and tucked him in. He had no recollection of the journey. He stared up at the immobile ceiling fan and tried to remember.

After what felt like hours, he half-climbed, half-rolled out from under the doona, and struggled into his tatty robe. He only wore it when he anticipated a day spent not going anywhere. He wore it a whole lot more often than not.

Rob had got him an answering machine about a year ago, direct from the spot where it had fallen off the back of a lorry, and Ian mooched over to check the display. A blocky zero proclaimed that Donna hadn't felt the need to ring, tell him that she wouldn't be home. Probably off her tits on Maureen's Valium the moment they got her home. *Fucking hypocrites.* Ian grunted and wandered towards the front door.

Unlocking the deadbolts, he stepped out onto the veranda. Without the blinds to filter it, the sun was several orders stronger, and he was obliged to squint until the pain in his eyes faded. Slowly he shuffled down the path that bisected the straggly patches of grass, nodding absently at Gemma in the house next door. He was as used to seeing her peering through the kitchen window as she was used to seeing him bimble around in his robe. While Ian could simply find no motive to go out, Gemma was properly scared to: she'd never really recovered from the attack. The police had been bloody useless, as always, so the locals—Ian among them—had ended up sorting it out for her.

He smiled at the memory. There was no life for her, stuck in her poky little shack, but he liked to think that even if Gemma never came out anymore, she at least felt a little safer.

At the foot of the path, he stopped at the mailbox and flipped open the small door in the back. A thin stack of envelopes sat inside. He fished them out and riffled through. Junk. Junk. Bill.

Crap.

He was disappointed, but not completely surprised. It'd been a slim hope, so early on . . . He trudged back to the house, where he tossed the unread communications on the floor, shrugged off his robe and went back to bed.

*

The hammering on the door syncopated with the hammering in his head. Two more nights of solitary drinking had swollen Ian's brain to a point beyond which his skull could contain it, the constant pulsing of its attempts to free itself nailing him to the bed from which he was already loathe to move.

Neglecting even to grope around on the floor for the robe, he staggered to the front door. The pounding continued, inside and out, as he willed his numb fingers to disengage the locks . . . and then the door was open and he was staring into the hard face of a policeman.

An icy flush purged his system.

"Mr Connell?"

A brisk "Who's asking?" was halfway to Ian's lips before he caught it. *They know already . . .*

"Yes."

The officer, half a head taller than Ian and as clean cut as Ian was debilitated, cleared his throat. "My name's Senior Constable Warwick, this is Constable McGann." He indicated a second, smaller cop standing off to one side of the door, where Ian had thus far failed to notice her. Ian's thoughts slipped around, tried to gain purchase. All he could focus on was that he was wearing nothing but boxer shorts.

"Sir?"

Ian snapped back into the moment. "What?"

"May we come in?"

"Yeah. Right."

"After you, sir," offered the Senior Constable, his body blocking the front door.

Ian nodded and led them into the living room, shifting a beer can from his best chair before plopping himself into it. He gestured for the cops to do the same—the senior constable declined politely, choosing instead to remove his hat and tuck it under his arm. His partner stood solicitously by his side.

"How can I help you, officers?"

"I'm afraid we have some bad news, sir."

Ian's thoughts raced ahead of him. "I don't—"

"I'm sorry to say that there's been an incident at the cemetery." Ian's speeding neurons crashed down several gears as he saw the policeman's face redden. *What was that? Shame?*

What the fuck's happened?

Warwick cleared his throat, refusing to make eye contact, just like everyone down the pub . . . "We had a report of vandalism to one of the graves. I'm sorry to say the grave in question was your son's."

"Vandalism?"

"A . . . theft." The cop's face fell still further. In a flash of insight, Ian knew why he'd brought a policewoman. "Someone's stolen . . . Someone's stolen your . . . "

But all Ian heard was silence.

*

The papers got hold of it straight away. Grave robbing? They were all over it like blondes on a footballer. And of course that meant that the police couldn't be seen to let it go.

Thing was, the cops had no chance. Around here, no one talked to the law, no matter what. Around here, justice was more immediate. Ian stared into his mug of cooling tea and thought about Gemma next door, the man who'd attacked her. No police there, they'd taken care of that bastard personally. Rob reckoned Bill still had the bits, buried in a jar somewhere.

But this sick bastard . . . If the lads caught up with him, made him disappear, the cops'd just keep on looking. Had to, or the journos'd eat them alive. There'd be coppers all over Ian and his business, twenty-four-seven.

And he couldn't have that.

He got to his feet, crossed to the sink and emptied his tea down it. He'd have to find the fucker himself. Point the coppers in the right direction. Best thing was, he knew exactly where to look.

Pulling the front door shut softly behind him, he set off down the path. On the way past, he checked his mailbox again, but found it empty.

*

He half expected to be creeped out by the cemetery after dark, but as Ian scaled the back wall of the graveyard and dropped quietly to the grass on the other side, the tingle he felt was of expectation, not fear.

He'd watched the cop car out by the front gate for more than an hour, until he was satisfied that the police presence was for show alone. Sure, if they heard someone digging holes, they'd be on the case quickly enough, but it was a chill night and neither of the officers were going to go out of their way to patrol a crime scene that had long since turned colder than the weather.

Everything pointed to the vagrant. No way that dodgy bastard didn't have something to do with all this, hanging around the graveyard like that. Ian wasn't sure the man actually lived here, beyond an itch of intuition, but he had to start looking somewhere.

When he spotted the faint, flickering light from a mausoleum at the far corner of the grounds, he knew he was on the money.

Ian padded softly across the grass, staying well clear of the gravelled footpath; on a night as clear as this, the sound of crunching footsteps would carry even as far as the dozing lawmen in their patrol car. Closer to the crypt, he could see that light was leaking out from under a stout wooden door.

He wondered if anyone had even noticed there was someone living here. The cops clearly hadn't. Those useless pricks were supposed to have searched the whole cemetery.

The padlock and hasp on the crypt door were both more or less intact—Ian could see how the hinge had been prised away to allow access to the tomb within, but the new, living tenant had done it in such a way as to minimise the noticeable effect. Anyone standing at the top of the path and looking down on the entry way would be hard pressed to spot the interference unless they were specifically looking for it. Maybe the cops weren't so crap after all—if no one had tipped them off that there was more than the dead inside the crypts, they'd never know to look. And around here, no one tipped the police off about anything.

He grasped the door handle and gave it a gentle tug. The door opened a fraction, and the trickle of light from within became a flood. There was just enough room to slip inside without needing to tear away the carefully arranged lock, so Ian turned himself side-on and did just that.

The stone room beyond was cramped, but its small size gave it a pathetic cosiness. Certainly Ian noticed the difference in temperature as he surveyed the hidey-hole; the warmth generated by inhabitation was several degrees more comfortable than the chill air outside. A pair of milk crates took up most of the floor space, ersatz seating, and a small electric lantern provided the mellow glow by which to see. Four shelves were set into the wall, two each side. Three held coffins, their wood lacklustre in the dim light. The fourth, too, was occupied.

The vagrant lay curled up beneath a grimy blanket—closer up, Ian could smell the booze from where the man had drunk himself unconscious. Half a dozen beer cans were scattered around the makeshift bed, the same brand Ian had in his fridge at home.

He crossed the short distance to the sleeping man, and without pause, gripped him around the throat. The vagrant's eyes bulged open, a choke escaping as Ian squeezed his windpipe.

"Where's my son?" Ian snapped, tiny droplets of saliva speckling the man's face.

The homeless man gurgled, a stench like rotten vegetables and sour milk leaking from his mouth. Ian recoiled, easing up on the pressure.

"Don't," the vagrant gasped. "Wasn't me!"

"Bullshit!"

"Wasn't me!" The man's eyes were pleading, terrified.

"Who?" Ian snarled.

"Woman. Saw her," the man gabbled, desperate to please. "Late at night, woke me up."

"What did she look like?" Ian's conviction wavered, his grip with it.

"Dunno, was dark wunnit? Short. Fat. Walked funny."

"Bullshit!"

"No, for real."

Ian snarled, tightened his hold again. Words spilled from the vagrant's mouth. "Red hair! She had red hair."

The fuck? Ian's mind raced. The nurse at the maternity ward . . . Shit, what was her name . . . ?

Alana.

He let go of the gasping itinerant, and wiped his hands on his trousers. "Better not be lying," he said, "or I'll be back."

"Not lying. God's honest truth, it were a woman."

Ian made for the door. Behind him, the vagrant grunted. "Chance of a couple of bucks?"

"You've got to be kidding."

*

It would've been the easiest thing in the world to just throw the bitch to the wolves. Fuck, he was so tempted to do it . . . Trampling home through the slowly lightening, frosty streets, the thought of the deviant cow getting carted off by the police kept him warm deep inside. It wasn't the way they did things in the neighbourhood, but who was going to blame him for shopping her to the law, given what she'd done?

Yeah, the cops'd have to have her. But that didn't mean he couldn't have a little chat with her before . . .

*

He headed home first, arriving just in time to run into the postman. It was a new guy, Ian noticed, nervous-looking, probably shat himself when he found out he'd be making deliveries here. Anyone who lived around this way knew it was safe enough—the local version of the neighbourhood watch kept it that way—but from the outside looking in, this was only a couple of steps up from Beirut.

"Anything for seven?" Ian asked, and the postie forked over a single envelope, hand shaking, no thought about asking for ID. "Cheers, mate," Ian said, and wandered up to his front door without a backward glance. All his attention was on the envelope and the return address in the top corner. With a thin smile, he stuffed it into his pocket and let himself into the house.

*

He had boosted a knackered old Ford from the cinema car park in the city, heading straight to a supermarket and switching the plates with another vehicle. Couple of years hanging around with Rob and Mitch, you pick up some tricks. It wasn't foolproof, the car would show up as nicked eventually, but he only needed a few hours. No point following the nurse out of the hospital and watching her drive off while he was stuck on foot.

Bernice at the Jacaranda had phoned the maternity ward for him—for twenty bucks—and asked for Alana, and Ian now knew the nurse wouldn't start until later in the day. His strategy was simple enough. Hang around outside the ward, then follow her home when she quit for the night. Unshaven and rumpled from his night at the cemetery, he had enough camouflage to pass for a stressed new father. So long as he kept his head down, there was a good chance she wouldn't spot him.

She came on duty just after lunch—Ian almost missed her, his attention temporarily focused on getting something sugary from the vending machine. The brief impression of red out of the corner of his eye was enough, however, and he watched the short woman with her ludicrously dyed hair amble across the foyer and through the swing doors to Maternity. As far as Ian could tell, she didn't have the faintest idea she was being watched. The vending machine was tucked off to the side of the entrance and didn't warrant even a sideways glance from the evil little bitch.

He looked at his watch. After 36 hours without sleep, he'd be struggling by the time the nurse finished up for the night. He prayed the vending machines did better coffee than their snacks.

*

It was close to midnight before she emerged. Ian tracked her over the top of a newspaper he'd found folded up on another seat in the waiting room, staying in his seat until he was comfortable that she had just enough of a lead, then slipping out after her.

Outside, the temperature had dropped dramatically and the brisk air achieved what all those cups of instant coffee had struggled to do. Immediately awakened, preternaturally alert, he shadowed the rotund figure across the hospital forecourt. He felt the adrenalin ramping up in his arms and legs, and forced himself to breathe deeply and heavily to offset the effects. Clouds of warm air billowed in the frosty night as he exhaled the tension.

He'd been expecting the nurse to head straight to the car park or straight out the front gate—instead, she cut to the left, and down a covered walkway. Ian's neck hairs prickled. The semi-tunnel was a little too enclosed for his tastes; it'd be too easy for her to spot him tailing her. But he couldn't back off now. Letting the distance between them stretch a shade further, he kept after her.

Another left off the walkway and she was briefly out of sight, Ian needing to hustle to make sure he didn't lose her. It turned out there was only one place she could have gone—the passage ended at a pair of green double doors, marked with an institutional plastic nameplate.

HOSPITAL SERVICES.

He'd had enough shit jobs to read between the lines. This was where the porters hung out. The scut workers.

He eased the doors open and peered inside. At that time of night, the corridor beyond was quiet, deserted, but while the sensation of absolute isolation caused Ian's bowels to clench involuntarily, the silence did make his prey easier to track. From down the corridor came the noise of a swing door closing.

Ian hurried in the direction of the sound, sacrificing some stealth for haste. Every second she was out of sight was a second the woman could get away. He passed a series of doors, all identical except for more small plaques announcing the function of the rooms behind: storage, waste disposal, electrical. Arriving at a corner, he was in time to glimpse a flash of red hair as the nurse pushed the release bar on an emergency exit, and vanished through it. Again, he picked up the pace and bundled through the door after her.

She was already halfway up the street, again bypassing the car park. Ian swore quietly—he needn't have bothered jacking that car after all.

As he walked, he noticed the woman's arms were wrapped around herself against the cold. There was something awkward about the pose, however, something that didn't quite . . .

She was carrying something. She'd wrapped her coat around it, hugged it to her chest so it couldn't be seen by anyone she met on the street, but she was definitely carrying something.

She hadn't been, before she stopped by Hospital Services.

Down the hill past the office buildings that lined the approach to the hospital, then a turn towards the old high street, Ian kept just enough distance between them to avoid detection. She had a decent turn of speed for someone her size, and it was only twenty minutes before she arrived at her destination. By then, Ian's face was red and tingling from the cold and exertion.

The covered markets had been one of the first things to close when the recession hit. Skyrocketing rents and falling spending had driven the stallholders out of business so quickly that the decision was made to shut down the art deco terraces almost before anyone noticed. While promises to sell and redevelop the site were made and broken, the corner block had slipped into disrepair. Sheets of plywood had been nailed over all the access points and flyposted to such a thickness that they could deflect bullets.

The nurse made straight for it. Sidling around the back of the block, away from careless observation, she'd disappeared entirely by the time Ian caught up. Not that it was difficult to find out where she'd gone—at one of the old entrance points, one side of the plywood barrier had been pulled free of its nails to allow access.

Ian gave her a minute or so, then pulled back the plywood sheet as far as it could go without cracking and ducked inside.

The gloom in the market hall was close to absolute, and he had to stand for a moment to allow his eyes to adjust. Dark shapes resolved themselves into empty stalls, abandoned without ceremony by their tenants. At first, the interior appeared lifeless, then he became aware of more dark shapes that flitted at the edge of his vision, startled by his intrusion and hurrying to safety.

He strained to listen, hoping to locate his quarry. Inside the market hall, the space seemed vast, so much larger than it did from the street outside. She could be anywhere.

In the end, it was easy. The nurse's footsteps had created a path through the accumulated grime coating the market floor. All Ian had to do was wait for his eyes to focus, and follow it.

She'd stopped at the back of the market, at an old stall over which a small section of the roof had collapsed, leaking a modicum of light from the street. The bilious glow illuminated faded signs in and around the small alcove that offered fresh bread, pastries, hot pies.

The glass-fronted cases in the bakery stall held nothing now but shadows, and through them Ian could see the bulky figure of the nurse busying herself with . . . what? A cardboard box sat on the countertop, but the woman's focus was elsewhere, on a plastic sack, like a bin bag but lighter in shade. As she rooted around inside the bag with her hands, Ian caught a glimpse of the warning on its side.

CLINICAL WASTE. SPECIALIST DISPOSAL ONLY.

When the nurse extracted her hands from the sack, they were dark and dripping. She kept them cupped, bearing their contents down to the bakery benchtop with exaggerated care.

The object was small, only about 10 centimetres in length, he guessed—it was curled in on itself, making it hard to judge. About a third of it was a bulbous protrusion, giving it the appearance of something close to a tadpole. It was another few seconds before he recognised arms.

His stomach contracted, a violent spasm that travelled up his throat, where he caught it before it could burst from his mouth. It was enough for the nurse to notice his presence, and she raised her eyes from her work. Her gaze pinned Ian like a butterfly to a display card, and in that moment he found he was completely incapable of movement. Vomit spilled from between his insensate lips, rivulets tracking down his chin and onto his chest, malodourous.

The nurse watched him with the vaguest of curiosity, and began removing her clothes.

Stripped down to her pasty skin, heavy breasts folding down over a thickened waist, her body started to change. Unblinking, Ian watched as her hands bent back upon themselves, curling against the natural angle of the wrist. Feathers—or scales?—no, feathers seemed to sprout from her flesh, to be there and yet not be there, mocking his ability to trust his vision. And her eyes . . . From the dark brown of her human aspect, the orbs became as red as her cheaply dyed hair, then redder still. Empowered. Demonic.

Ian's bladder joined the list of muscles to fail him, although he smelled the change more than felt it. For everything that was happening in front of him, he remained physically numb.

The transformation shimmered and blurred around the nurse, shifting her from human to birdlike and back again. Ian could only stare as she lifted up the small curl of tissue she'd rescued from incineration.

It whimpered.

The nurse raised the mewling lump of flesh to her breast. Ian felt a charge building in the air and the woman's eyes rolled back into her head, a halo of energy crackling around her.

Once—oh God, it seemed like so long ago—Ian had watched a TV show about the natural world, and had seen a film someone had made of a flower. They'd shot it from the moment the seed sprouted through to the point where the flower died, petals curling and falling from the stem. Sped up, the whole thing had taken less than a minute. He saw the same thing now, the pitiful twist of skin and bones growing before his eyes as it leeched life from the creature that had chosen to mother it. Six months passed in half a minute, the foetus becoming larger, stronger, firmer. Raising its fully formed hands, it clutched at the nurse's swollen teat, as if to drag it all into its mouth, sate the insatiable.

When it was done, the nurse removed it gently and reached into the cardboard box for a blanket. She wrapped the baby and placed it in the box, where it cooed for a little, and fell asleep.

Exhaustion etched deep lines in the nurse-thing's face, and once again Ian saw it change, features melting back into those of Alana, labour ward assistant. Without bothering to dress, she approached him, looked him up and down, a cold, clinical assessment.

"You come to do me harm," she said, a bald statement of fact rather than a question. "I see it in you as clearly as I saw into you the first time we met."

Ian tried to speak, to curse her out, but his tongue still refused to obey orders and all that emerged was a small grunt.

"I am sorry," Alana said. "Permit me."

Ian felt control return to his vocal cords. "What are you?"

The nurse turned and walked back towards the box on the counter. She peered inside. "A spirit. Some of my people came here for a fresh start. I followed."

"You took—"

"Your child is safe. Safe and well."

"He's—"

"Alive. Yes." She reached into the box with a finger extended and Ian shuddered to see a small hand clasp it tightly. The nurse smiled, making small clucking noises.

"It's so much easier here, you see. In my homeland, I was obliged to work with less. Moon's blood, those born too small, too soon to live. Here . . . you people have so much intercourse, yet so few of you are prepared to live with its result." She gestured to the crumpled plastic refuse sack. "So much raw material."

Alana approached, standing close enough now for him to smell her, a contrary aroma of cinnamon and excrement. He barely felt her touch as she dipped a hand into his pocket and pulled out the envelope he'd stuffed into it that morning. "It finally arrived, I see."

"How did you—?"

She held the crumpled paper up in front of his face where he couldn't help but look at it. "I told you. I can see into you quite clearly."

And he felt her in his mind, sorting through memories like anyone else would sort laundry.

Meeting Donna, that first night at the party, the edges taken off her face and his nerves by six pints of IPA and a couple of tabs, she as drunk as he was and as lonely and needy and ready . . .

Fucking her in the disabled toilets, because he happened to be walking by her office and he was horny and she was there. Making it a regular thing, her text message summoning him, his text alerting her to his desires, coming together to stick two fingers up to the rest of the world because they wanted each other and the rules didn't matter . . .

Her turning up at his house, bags in hand, thrown out by her parents when they found drugs in her room again and when she'd promised she was clean, she'd promised . . .

Losing his job, seeing his friends lose theirs, their homes soon after. Being forced to move to the crappy new house, whole days spent inside it, waiting for Donna to get home so he could screw her, go out with her, spend her pay cheque at the pub with her, strangle the dead thing inside him that consumed him one dream at a time . . .

The arguments, Donna laying into him about when he's going to get back out there, get a job, help her out. Going to the pub without her to waste money she'd earned, dreading the idea of returning home and being there with her, watching him, looking at him like this was all his fault . . .

Wanting to leave her, wanting to be free again so badly, but there's no money, he can't survive without her, he needs her and it's killing him . . .

She tells him she's pregnant and he sees the hope in her eyes, sees that this is what he needs to reclaim responsibility, what he needs to pick himself up again, and it feels like a trap closing on him, sealing him in, cutting off the light, cutting off the light . . .

Sitting at home, daytime TV numbing his last nerve, the talk about baby bonuses, the big wedges of cash you get just for having a baby, and thinking how useful that would be, all that money, and watching some more and seeing that you get it anyway if the baby dies before it's born, you get it all the same, compassionate payment . . .

Ian choked on the memories, the flood of emotion, unleashed in an instant and driving the breath from his lungs, almost ending him.

The nurse held the letter from the welfare office in her hands, eyed it with wonder. "All those weeks of slowly poisoning your wife so you could take the money and run. And here it is, notification of payment. You must be so pleased." She placed a hand on the side of his face, and he felt it burning coldly at his skin. "Do you know why I do this? Why I bring them back?"

"No."

"I do it because everything on earth deserves to be loved." From out of the corner of his eye he saw her raise herself up on tiptoes, place her lips by his ear.

"Almost everything."

*

Ian had no idea why the creature let him live. But coming to his senses in an alley outside the markets, his body frozen and aching and his face flat against the cold, wet pavement, the 'why' didn't matter. Whatever that thing was, it had missed its chance to finish him. He wasn't going to give it another one.

Sometime in the last few hours, his watch had stopped, but the faded indigo of the sky told Ian it was nearly dawn. He had to move quickly. Three streets over, where it still attracted a decent amount of foot traffic, there was an ATM where he could empty the bank account. He'd take every cent of the baby bonus, head to the main road, hail a cab . . . within an hour he could be on a flight to Sydney.

It wasn't until he was standing outside the bank, punching his PIN into the keypad, that he felt it, worming its way up through his chest to freedom . . .

The laugh burst into the still morning air, dozens of siblings rushing after it. He'd done it. Fuck Donna, fuck her parents, fuck that . . . that thing. Fuck the lot of them. He had his way out now; he'd got away with it.

New city, new home, new life. Free and clear.

*

The light from the bulb stained the room yellow and stale like old piss. Ian's hand hovered by the bedside lamp, but as he stared at the low-yield bulb with hot, gritty eyes, he knew he wouldn't switch it off.

Couldn't switch it off.

In the dark, he would feel every fibre of the sheets, prickling the bare skin of his back and legs like sackcloth. In the dark, the noises would be louder, every punter who walked the corridor outside this cheapest of motel rooms grating at his raw, attenuated nerves.

In the dark, he'd be back at the market again, looking into the creature's eyes as it prised clear his secrets, sifted his memories, and stopped at an image of Bill McCoy.

And grinned.

Every time he closed his eyes now, that's what Ian saw. Bill McCoy in the bar of the Jacaranda Hotel, laughing and joking and happier than he'd ever been, reunited with the son he'd never known he had. And every time Ian closed his eyes, he knew.

That's why the creature had spared him.

One night just like this, lying in bed too fearful to sleep, he would hear footsteps outside that didn't pass by. One night, Ian would watch, with those his inflamed, insomniac eyes as the handle turned and the door opened onto the night, and he'd see the man, unexpected but awaited, unknown but familiar. Wanting answers. Wanting revenge.

Wanting his daddy.

AFTERWORD

Back in 2007, I spotted a story in the news about people who were taking advantage of a legal technicality to make a fast buck. All they had to do was kill their babies. At that time, if her child died late in the pregnancy, an expectant mother was still eligible for the Australian Government's baby bonus. A number of women cottoned onto this compassionate gesture, and a trend emerged for terminating babies and taking the cash. Some mothers admitted to having done it more than once.

Jump to 2012, and my search for a creature for *Bloodstones*. When I read about an entity from the Philippines called the *Alan*, something reminded me of that old news story. You see, the monster's party trick was to create people from reproductive waste, and . . . well, you'll know by now where I went with that.

I've used a little poetic licence in the story, for which I hold up my hands right now. First, I've set the story in the present day, and the loophole that would have once prompted Ian's cold-blooded crime has long since closed. Secondly, it was never completely clear to me *why* the *Alan* gives life to the unborn. The reason I've given seemed reasonable in this context and, of course, serves to highlight the real monster of"Dead Inside".

SMOKE GETS IN YOUR EYES

MLD CURELAS

"Fran! We're going to be late!" Bennie's thin fingers squeezed my hand as she skipped ahead of me, my arm the tether that kept her close. She glanced over her shoulder, wisps of pale hair floating around her temples like a cloud of dandelion fluff. Her dark eyes sparkled. "Slow poke."

I smiled in spite of myself. Bennie's usual lethargy had vanished, granting me a glimpse of the woman she'd been before she'd fallen ill. At least, I assumed this was how Bennie had been in years past: we'd only been on a handful of dates, quiet evenings at cafés that had sprouted up in Seattle like mushrooms in a bog. Sipping fancy coffee over tight games of Scrabble had been the most strenuous activities we'd shared, so the prancing, singing woman before me filled me with delight. I was a little surprised that she hadn't suggested a date like this earlier, since she enjoyed music so much.

After a clumsy pirouette, Bennie came to a halt, panting. The feverish sparkle in her eyes worried me; she tired so easily. Concerned, I tugged on her hand, reeling her to my side. She laughed, tilting her head, and I honoured the invitation, kissing her. A warm tingle zinged up my spine, and my pulse quickened. I halted, twining my other hand in Bennie's flaxen hair.

Laughter bubbled against my mouth. She pulled away. "Frannie, we can't be late."

"Not even a little?" I teased, tracing a finger down her cheek.

Bennie shook her head, the spark of amusement fading from her eyes. "Not even a little." Still holding my hand, she resumed walking, and my heart sank at the abrupt change of mood.

The Ballyhoo Pub's green neon signs blazed in the creeping darkness of twilight, the twinkle lights in the windows giving the building a jaunty air. At this time of day, the shabbiness of the brick building was concealed, the chipped paint of the window panes and doors not as obvious.

Bennie giggled. "Fairy lights!" She spun in a circle, hair fanning out in a pale gold halo.

"If you say so," I said, rolling my eyes.

Bennie paused, one hand resting on the door handle, and looked back at me. "What's wrong with fairies?"

"Other than that they're for kids? Nothing." Her eyes clouded with sadness and my gut twisted with anxiety. An unhappy Bennie signalled a quarrel on the horizon. I stretched out a hand, brushing her shoulder. "Hey, let's not fight, okay? Not about twinkle lights."

"My little sceptic." She smiled, although her eyes remained shadowed, and turned back to the pub. My anxiety faded. Bennie scuffed her boots along the welcome mat and pulled open the door. A blast of light and warmth hit me, and another smile quivered on my lips. The pub was cramped, patrons rubbing elbows with people from other tables. At the far end of the pub was a tiny square stage, with an even tinier square dance floor. Bennie found a table by the corner of the stage. We forced the chairs against the wall, so that we could both see the stage, and squeezed into the seats.

I plucked a menu from a wire condiment and napkin holder and gave the contents a quick scan. I frowned. "What's good here, Bennie?"

She peered over my shoulder. "It's pretty standard Irish fare, Frannie me girl."

"Oh." I blushed.

Bennie hooted. "Frannie, don't say that you haven't had Irish pub food? *You*, Frances *O'Brien*?"

"I might be of Irish descent, Bennie, but that doesn't mean much in Seattle. It's not like I live in Boston." I shrugged. "Anyway, the Irish blood is pretty thin."

"Oh, *aye*," she mocked softly, tweaking one of my red braids. "Thin indeed."

When the waitress came over, Bennie peeked at me over the menu. "Want to split?"

I shook my head, careful to keep my gaze on her face. If she caught me examining her sharp clavicles and shoulder bones, it'd spark another fight. "I didn't have lunch. I'm starving."

Bennie nodded and ordered for both of us, asking for Irish stew, soda bread, and pints of Guinness. Bennie gave me a quick kiss and excused herself.

The waitress returned, placing two glasses on the table. I inspected the dark beverage in front of me with the thick head of foam, looked up at the waitress and asked for a diet Pepsi. She chuckled and left again.

As members of the band wound through the tables, I pushed the Guinness off to one side. The band members stepped onto the stage, carrying various stringed instruments. One stopped by my table. "I see that your pint is going to waste. May I?"

"Sure." I pushed the glass over to him. He carried a strange guitar that had a fat, round body.

I must have been staring, because he grinned. "It's a mandolin. My name's Mike." He offered a hand, and I took it.

"I'm Fran."

Mike grinned again, sweeping the pint off the table. "Pleasure's all mine, Fran." He saluted me with the pint glass, and joined his bandmates on stage.

Bennie came back from the washroom, sliding into her chair. As if they had been waiting for her, the band started up. Although unfamiliar with the music, my toes were tapping the rungs of my chair within seconds. My hand crept under the table and cupped Bennie's knee. She didn't draw away.

Her fingers drummed the table in time with the music, and then her lips parted and she started singing. Not loudly, but the keen edge of her voice cut through the hubbub of the patrons. The mandolin player, Mike, looked up from his instrument. His gaze flicked between me and Bennie, widened, and settled on her.

Bennie seemed to enjoy his attention. She continued singing, her swinging foot kicking my shin in time to the music. Her dark eyes focused on him, like she was drinking him in. Mike ducked his head. I didn't hear anything wrong, but a few of the other musicians shot him quick stares.

A bowl of stew appeared in front of me and Bennie. I ate, watching Bennie watch the band. She took a few swallows of her Guinness without taking her eyes from Mike. With her mouth open just enough to release her wordless song, revealing the pointed tips of her eyeteeth, Bennie looked . . . wild. Feral. I pushed away my unfinished stew. I was beginning to realise how little I knew about her.

The band's singer tucked a strand of hair behind an ear. "Folks, we're going to take a short break. Danny back there— wave a hand, Danny—has CDs and other merch that you should check out."

Instruments were laid reverently in cases, and the band trickled off the stage, heading straight to the bar, or to the kitchen as they fumbled in their pockets for cigarettes and lighters. Since smoking indoors had been banned years ago, I figured they were using an employee door in the kitchen. The mandolin player was the last to leave. He stopped by our table.

"Hey, Fran," he said, "since I stole your pint, maybe I can get you something else? The bar'll serve me first since I'm with the band."

"Oh, I don't know . . . " I'd been hoping to talk with Bennie during the quiet of the break.

"Go ahead," Bennie whispered in my ear. "I think it's important."

I cocked an eyebrow at her, disconcerted by the pleased smile on her face. She didn't want to spend the few moments of relative quiet with me? Pasting on a fake smile to hide my hurt, I pushed back from the table. Spending time with the mandolin player was suddenly more appealing. "Sure, Mike, thanks."

While the bartender poured our drinks, Mike bent his head close to me. "Do you know what she is?"

I glanced at Bennie. She watched us through half-closed eyes. "What do you mean, 'what' she is?" I glared at him. "A lesbian? I know that, she's my girlfriend."

Mike shook his head. "Bah. Like I care about that." He grabbed our drinks and handed one to me. He knocked back his shot of whiskey and plonked the glass onto the bar. "She's not human."

I laughed. "Wow, are you drunk already?"

"Look at her!" he whispered. "Take a good look."

Even though he was full of crap, I found myself turning my head. Bennie smirked like a cat who'd got the cream. A light flush stained her porcelain cheeks, her lips were plumper, and the shadows under her eyes had faded.

"It's just the alcohol," I said. I barrelled my way through the mass of people surrounding the bar, letting out a sigh of relief when I got back to the table.

"Thank you for your concern, friend," Bennie said, leaning forward, looking past me. Her shoulders seemed less bony. "It's done me a world of good."

I pivoted, scowling. Mike had followed me.

"Sorry, Fran, but I hadn't quite finished." Avoiding Bennie's gaze, he clasped my hands. "You get out of here," he told me. "You're in danger."

I jerked my hands away. "You're creeping me out."

Mike's eyes flicked to Bennie. He crossed himself. "She's no good, I'm telling you. But if you won't listen . . . " He backed away from the table, fishing a pack of smokes out of his pants, and bee-lined for the kitchen.

"Bennie," I said slowly, picking my way through thoughts and words. "What was that about? And why do you look . . . different?"

"Belief is a wonderful thing, Fran."

"Belief in what, exactly?" My dinner churned in my stomach.

Bennie's eyes flickered. "Well, Fran," she sighed. "I hadn't wanted to tell you this way, but he's right. I'm not human."

I forced a chuckle out of my mouth. First Mike, now Bennie. That Guinness stuff must really be something. Bennie's sudden glow of health was nothing more than a combination of the dim lighting in the pub and the effects of the alcohol in her system. "Sure, Bennie." I reached down and patted her hands. "You're not human."

"You're so thick-headed. I don't know why I—" Bennie shook her head. "Let's get down to brass tacks, Frannie. I'm a bean-sídhe. Do you know what that is?"

I started to shake my head, then hesitated. Bennie's strident singing voice rang in my memory, and I shivered. "A banshee? Don't they sing or something?"

Bennie sighed again. "Yes, we 'sing or something'. We're harbingers of death."

"That sounds like fun," I said, cramming every inch of sarcasm that I could into the words. The band was returning, bringing with them the odour of rain and cigarette smoke. "Bennie, I need to pee before the band starts back up."

Bennie grabbed my wrist, yanking me down until our faces were scant inches apart. This close, it was hard to deny the changes that had come over her. Her face was less gaunt. She had put on weight since we'd entered the pub, which wasn't a side effect of drinking that I'd ever heard of before. My arms broke out in goose pimples.

"Listen, Fran," Bennie hissed. "I've suffered a lot over the years in this miserable piss-hole of a country. My beauty, my *power* has diminished as belief in my kind—in *me*—has waned." She released my wrist, but I couldn't move, ensnared by her angry gaze.

"I have a duty to fulfil, but if nobody can hear me, then I just lose more power. I . . . fade." Bennie's mouth softened. "I'm sorry, Fran, I like you, I really do, but I need you to believe in me."

"Why?" I asked, rubbing my wrist.

"Because I need you to be able to hear me when you die tonight."

I gaped at her.

"You're an O'Brien. It's only right that you get the warning."

I stumbled away from her. People milled between the tables and chairs behind me, blocking the exit. I could feel tears brimming in my eyes. I hated crying in front of strangers. I swivelled on my heels and fled to the washroom, which was tucked down a short hallway across from the kitchen. Behind me, the band started playing.

There was only one stall, and it was empty. Tears streaked my face, blurring my vision, and I struggled with the lock for a few seconds before realising that it was broken. I screamed, a low, throaty sound that rasped my throat, and kicked the door. It swung out with a *thunk*, then drifted shut.

"That'll show you," I muttered. Bennie's face floated in front of me. My foot flew at the door again, but I miscalculated. My heel smashed through the cheap plywood partition of the stall, and I crashed to the cold tile floor.

For a few terrifying seconds I couldn't pull air into my lungs, and I gawped like a fish. Then air rushed in, and I gasped and choked until my breathing evened out. My ankle throbbed. Glassy pain lanced up my leg, and I lifted my head off the floor. My foot was still wedged in the partition; my leg twisted down at an odd angle from my ankle. I scooted around on the floor until some pressure was taken off my leg and it looked less like a pretzel. "Hey, anybody out there?" I called.

Nobody answered, which didn't surprise me. Enthusiastic stomping from the restaurant rang in my ears. Who would hear me? I wiggled my foot, ignoring the twinge of my ankle.

A shrill buzz drowned out the music and the stomping. The fire alarm! Screams and shouts, muffled by the alarm, drifted to my ears. I tensed my abs and curled into a half-sitting position and yanked on the boot. "I am *not* dying with my foot stuck in the bathroom door," I growled.

The possibility that Bennie wasn't crazy or drunk, that she actually was a banshee, flitted through my thoughts. She'd said I would die tonight, and here I was—alone, trapped—in a burning building. Either it was one helluva coincidence, or my girlfriend really was a banshee. A ball of anger blossomed within me. "She knew, she fucking *knew*, and she dragged me here instead of keeping me safe! Lousy *bitch*." My breath hitched and something like a sob escaped me and my vision blurred again.

This made me even angrier and I swore a blue streak as I twisted and pulled on my foot. The sounds of people had faded. Tendrils of smoke snaked underneath the washroom door. With a panicked shout, I pressed my free foot against the trapped boot, wrapped my hands around my calf and pulled. My foot slipped out.

I crawled out of the washroom, vague memories of fire safety classes prompting me to stay low to the ground where the air would be fresher. Thick, grey smoke filled the pub, so I didn't see Bennie until I bumped into her knees.

"There you are," she said. "Right on time."

My anger returned in a rush, boiling up inside me, begging to be released. She *knew* and she hadn't warned me! Clenching my jaw, I grabbed her ankles and jerked her to the floor. I scrabbled to her side, drew back a fist and punched her in the face, a savage grin twisting my mouth as I felt skin and cartilage shift beneath my knuckles. I hit her again. Bennie squealed, her hands flying to her cheek.

Then her hands drifted down, revealing a blackening eye and a split lip. Her cheek had started to bruise. Bennie laughed, the sound tapering into a sob. "It's too late. I'm sorry, but it's too late. *You believe.*"

Even with the smoke curling around us, I could see the truth of her words. The trickle of blood oozing from her lip sparkled like rubies, her dark eyes were velvet, her skin the finest marble. She was so otherworldly that my eyes hurt just looking at her. My belief had revitalised her.

Fire crackled, orange flames spiking through the thick clouds of smoke. My chest ached, and I coughed. I sagged to the floor. Bennie caught my arms and eased me down, the bruises I had given her already fading. A fit of coughing rattled my chest.

"I *am* sorry," Bennie whispered into my ear. Tears flowed down her face, mixing with the drying blood; diamonds and garnets to my bedazzled gaze. She threw back her head and screamed, a shriek of such grief and longing that my heart clenched. It was my death knell she wailed. It reverberated through my soul.

Weariness bogged my body, and my eyes drifted shut. "Bennie . . . " My lips moved for a few seconds before I could push out the words. "You bitch." I was so tired. Bennie's wails of grief swept me into darkness.

*

Snatches of words. Sirens. Shouts.

I opened my eyes and stared at the chaos around me: the emergency vehicles, the firefighters and police, the curious onlookers crowding against barriers.

"Thank the Mother. Fran, look at me."

I blinked and turned my head, gravel digging into my scalp. Bennie's familiar features filled my gaze. She knelt on the ground beside me. "You're dead, too?"

She pursed her lips. "Nobody's dead."

I laughed, then coughed. "You were wrong then? The mighty banshee?"

"You *did* die. I resuscitated you." Bennie smoothed a strand of hair from my face. "It took so long for you to come back, I worried that I'd miscalculated the timing, didn't do the CPR soon enough."

Miscalculated the timing? "I'm glad that I was dead long enough to give you your fix."

"Now, Frannie," she said, patting my cheek.

I pushed her hand away with shaking fingers, remembering her needy look when she'd fed off Mike's belief. "Don't. Just . . . don't touch me." Bennie's eyes clouded with confusion and pain. A few hours ago I would have done anything to wipe that look off her face. Right now a dark satisfaction filled me at the sight of her distress.

"You can't mean that, Fran." Bennie bent over me, her ruby red lips brushing the corner of my mouth, tendrils of her golden-blonde hair skimming my face and arms. I shivered. It was an exquisite taste of how *good* things could be with a powerful, rejuvenated Bennie. It would, I had no doubt, be the best I'd ever had and *would* ever have.

My breath caught in my throat again, and I wheezed for several seconds before my lungs filled themselves with sweet air. *Miscalculated the timing.* Had she really been worried about me, or about the loss of her personal food source? My anger bubbled to the surface again. "I do mean it, Bennie. Get lost. I don't want to see you again."

"Very well." Bennie's gaze grew sharp, and I squirmed under her intense regard, feeling as if my soul was laid bare. After several seconds, she smiled wistfully. "Even after all these years, I sometimes forget how clever you mortals can be." Bennie held out a hand. "I'm fond of you, Frannie, in my own way, and it pained me to watch you die. Shall we part as friends?"

I stared at her hand for a few seconds. It wouldn't be wise to insult an immortal creature—I'm sure she had a long memory—but the thought of touching her goosed my heart rate into a frantic pace. Fortunately my brain kicked in, overrode my fear, and I reached out and squeezed her hand.

Bennie's fingers curled around my hand and she pulled me up into a sitting position. Our faces were close enough to kiss. Her red, red lips parted, revealing delicately pointed teeth. "I *will* see you again one day, Frances O'Brien."

"Hopefully not for a long time. Goodbye, Bennie." I forced the words through numb lips. Her smile became more knowing, cruel, and I knew she could hear my frantic heart beat.

I watched her leave. The kernel of belief that had taken root in my chest swelled, sending icy tendrils of fear throughout my body. I don't know which frightened me more: that such creatures as Bennie existed, or that I had won. For now.

AFTERWORD

The idea of writing a story about a bean-sídhe, or banshee, trying to survive in modern times has been kicking around my head for a few years. It occurred to me that a banshee's purpose (reporting a death within a human family by shrill keening) relies a lot on having humans believe in her existence, and that she would suffer more than other Faeries from a decline in the belief of Faeries. The banshee idea made it onto paper at one point—as a flash fiction piece of less than 1,000 words—which really didn't work. It was terrible. And so it languished, until Amanda Pillar's *Bloodstones* prompt inspired me to haul the banshee story fragment out of mothballs. Only I couldn't find it. I had to start over (for the best, I'm certain), answering these two questions: If a banshee screams, but nobody believes in her, is she heard? What if that banshee befriends a mortal and reveals her existence for the purpose of creating a new believer? Thank you, Amanda, for spurring me to revisit the story and write it properly. Thanks also to Jason for reading this story in both forms.

SANAA'S ARMY

JOANNE ANDERTON

Sanaa was lying face down against the threadbare carpet when the doorbell rang. She drew one final, deep breath, savouring the many-layered scent of death rising from the basement, and gradually sat up. From their smell, she could predict, to the nearest inch, the thickness of flesh or fur on the carcasses beneath her. Not enough clean bones. Not yet, anyway.

Her kneecaps took advantage of the movement to flee, hiding somewhere in her hips. Her femurs rallied in response, stretching and bulging to fill the gap. It made standing difficult.

Cat Box, At Christmas dragged itself toward her. One of her earliest works: a cat's skull with a wire neck, a shoebox body filled with flickering Christmas lights, rib-cage legs and a battery pack tail. It was a good pet, always tried to help even though it wasn't much use. As long as she remembered to change the battery.

Sanaa struggled to her bare, misshapen feet and shuffled down the hallway, clinging to the walls for support. She pulled up the hood of her dark jumper, shook her long fringe loose and tightened the drawstrings to hide as much of her face as possible.

She opened the door to three dirty children, carrying a large cardboard box between them.

Oh, how they smelled of death. The not-too-fresh odour of whatever offering they carried, and the lingering touch of their own, slow decay. The inevitable shortening of hard little lives.

"We found something for you, miss," the middle one said. A girl, maybe twelve.

Sanaa smiled as best she could. She liked it when they called her miss. "Alice, isn't it?" she asked. The girl nodded. "Don't know these two." Sanaa leaned forward and sniffed at them.

Alice swallowed visibly. "This one here's Matt." Another boy, about the same age, gaunt and empty as a shell. "The little guy's Pete."

Sanaa stepped back to let the children in. Their smell wrapped around her, stronger than usual. There was something odd about it, a depth that did not belong to their living flesh, even flesh as starved and abused as theirs.

Artworks reached out from their canvasses on the wall as the children walked down the hallway. Lonely fishbone fingers stretched; thick layers of oil paints undulated; seashell castles with insect kings rattled. Sanaa chided them silently—they were bored, locked away in her dark townhouse, but it wasn't polite to scare the children. Alice knew to keep her head down, not to encourage them. The little one gawked, open-mouthed, at every single moving bone. The older boy hardly seemed aware of anything, and Sanaa focused her breathing there. The smell definitely came from him.

"Put it down," Sanaa said, patting the tabletop with her crooked hand, as they entered the kitchen. She didn't have much food, didn't eat much. But the kids weren't fussy. She found them milk still within its expiration date, clumpy chocolate powder, frozen bread and Vegemite.

"Move to the other end of the table," she instructed. "Don't eat near dead things. It isn't healthy."

She left them to their reward, and lifted the lid on the box they had brought. Several pieces of dead animals, each at a different stage of decay. An electrocuted fruit bat, a couple of rats, severed wings complete with feathers. A possum—by far their best find. It had been dead a while, the tail was gone, some of the vertebrae too, but skull and claws and hind legs all remained intact.

"It's good, right, miss?" the girl—Alice—asked. "We did good this time, didn't we? Better than usual, even?"

Sanaa glanced down the table. Was the child actually attempting to engage her in conversation? The street kids who brought her dead animals in exchange for food were usually too grateful and terrified to talk. Alice wasn't eating, which was odd. Instead, she was trying to push a half-frozen sandwich into the older boy's unresponsive mouth. Odder still.

Unsure how to react, Sanaa collected a knife from the table and pried loose some of the possum's hard skin. It came away clean, revealing pale bone beneath. She quivered, her entire skeleton rattling. "Yes," she said. "Good."

"Then, miss, I had wondered—" Alice hesitated "—if you would, if you could—" She had one hand wrapped around the older boy's chin and was making his jaw move, forcing him to chew.

Sanaa shuffled closer. "What's wrong with him?" she asked, even as the currents of that rotten scent wrapped warm and heady around her. He smelled wrong, so wrong. Not like a living thing at all.

"It's been calling him, miss," Alice answered. "Breaking him, slowly, until he don't eat, don't speak. Soon, when he don't bother to breathe, it'll call him one last time and never give him back."

Sanaa leaned closer. He was thin, yes, but they were all thin. Dirty, but they were all dirty. He looked just like the rest of them. Her small street army of carrion gatherers. "What has been calling him?"

"Dunno," the little boy piped up, mouth full, eyes wide and fearful. Alice pinched him until he added a squeaking, "miss! I seen it, but dunno what. Got eyes, got teeth. Stays in the darkness. Gotta keep the lights on all night, miss. Once it touches you, you're good as dead."

"I thought," Alice whispered. "I hoped, if we brought you good animals, lots of animals, a whole possum even, that you could, that you might—"

"—help us," the boy finished for her, and drained his glass of milk.

Sanaa staggered back, clutching the table to keep herself upright. Her kneecaps had still not returned. "Help you?"

"No one else believes us, miss," Alice pleaded. "Thought you might."

That made a hard kind of sense. Why wouldn't Sanaa believe in a monster hunting them from the shadows? After all, she was a monster herself. But what did they expect her to do? "Shouldn't you go to the police? Or community services?" Sanaa had been well known to the department as a child. They'd thought all her broken, dislocated, freakishly altered bones were proof of parental abuse. Wouldn't listen to her explanations. Wouldn't believe. Tried to give her to foster families who refused to let her play with the dead things she found—

She closed her eyes against the memories.

Alice didn't answer. Didn't need to. Sanaa understood the street kids. Maybe they knew that. Maybe that's why they trusted her.

Why they asked for her help.

"I don't know what I can do," Sanaa whispered. She glanced over her shoulder. Her neck twisted too easily, too far. Several vertebrae slipped away to pester her elbows, and her spine stretched out to compensate, her muscles seized up and the nerves down her arms screamed.

The front door behind her loomed large, its peephole a sinister bright eye. Sanaa hadn't gone into the too-bright, too-revealing outside world in so long. The kids brought her the bones she needed, her agent sold her artworks (the ones that had exhausted the strength of their second life and were finally ready to move on), and the Internet delivered the rest. How could the kids know what they were really asking?

"Please," the young boy whispered. "We got no one else to ask."

Damn him for looking up at her, so small and lost. Damn them all for putting her in this position. And damn her, for softening. For starting to care.

Sanaa drew herself up as straight as her skeleton would allow. If she was going to do this, she would do it properly.

"You—" she struggled to remember the little boy's name "—Pete, finish the food and watch your friend." She tried to sound like she was used to organising children. "Alice, pick up the box and follow me."

She led Alice to the basement.

Cat Box emerged and followed eagerly, winding its awkward way around her ankles, and sniffing derisively at Alice's bare feet.

The girl once again proved her worth by neither screaming nor running at the sight. That pleased Sanaa, though she couldn't have explained why.

"Here we are." She switched on dim lighting.

Her collection of bodies rested on layers of slatted, metal shelves. The top row was cleanest: mostly bones and dry skin. The lowest wiggled with insects. The floor beneath them was thick with newspaper, which she changed once a month.

Alice did as she was directed, slotting the rats and the bat toward the bottom, and carrying the possum through to Sanaa's studio. She helped find an appropriately sized piece of corrugated iron to use as a canvas.

"What're we doing, miss?" Alice asked. She hung back against a cold brick wall while Sanaa suspended her canvas from the ceiling, and collected her blowtorch, drill, and small hand-held saw. "Going to be dark soon. Going back is dangerous in the dark, and the others are waiting."

"Be patient." Sanaa stripped the possum of its desiccated skin. It was laborious; her uncooperative fingers itched to escape and dot the landscape of her back. "I can't go like this. Not yet."

Despite Alice's anxiety, Sanaa took her time over the possum. Carefully, gradually, she gave it a new life, a clean form, woven through the iron's waves. Art, for her, could never be meaningless. Every inch and moment of its creation was tied to her own body in ways she'd never understood. For with each piece of bone she glued and wired into shape, her disobedient skeleton settled down. Claw-tipped paws tore through rust like the dead rising—and her fingers calmed. Skull, inverted, jaw hinged loosely with copper wire—and her back realigned. Final touches with ink and the roar of the blowtorch—and her kneecaps returned.

Cat Box watched her work. It coiled and glowed, empty sockets following as she threaded the possum's spine.

"*Possum On A Hot Tin Roof*?" she asked it.

Cat Box's lights died instantly, and one of the possum's legs jerked.

"No?" Sanaa didn't like leaving her artworks without a name, but maybe it didn't matter this time. She was already feeling stronger.

Nothing like fresh bones.

She turned to Alice, unafraid for once to show the girl her face. "And now we can go."

While Alice and Pete extracted Matt from the kitchen, Sanaa prepared as best she could. She changed into fresh tracksuit pants, plaited her hair back tightly, wrapped a scarf around her head and did up the zipper on a high-necked, knitted jumper. All in black. She took *Possum* up from the basement and hung him in a storage room, where he'd have plenty of new friends to talk to. "Think about what you'd like to be called," she said, and ran a finger across his skull. So many bones rattled around her, all tense with concern. They could sense her apprehension, feel her fear. They were, after all, a part of her, each joined to her strange body through the life she had given them and the relief they gave in return. *King Rat Trap* tried to follow her, so she placed him in *RooStone's* arms.

"You're always with me," she whispered. "Don't fret, I'm never alone." But it was hard. As she learned against the wall, just outside the door, listening to *King Rat Trap* struggle and *Possum* kick, *Cat Box* rubbed against her shins. She scooped it up before she could have second thoughts, wrapped it in a towel and shoved it into an old, dusty backpack. "Not alone—" she whispered, as it struggled "—never ever." She gave it two replacement AA batteries to keep it quiet.

Almost as an afterthought, she included her most portable tools. The saw. The pliers. A small roll of copper wire. She was setting out to face a monster. What other weapons did she own?

Then Sanaa made her slow, reluctant way down the hallway, patting each of the artworks there. "It will be all right," she tried to reassure them as they clutched and snapped after her. "I'll be back soon."

It was evening by the time Sanaa stepped out into the world. The sky was quiet, muted by clouds. A cold breeze touched her face and she found the unfamiliar, fresh air pleasant. Alice and Pete, holding Matt's hands, waited for her in the street. Sanaa steadied shoulders that for once complied, and followed them.

There were too many lights on. They beamed out of shop windows and restaurants, sparkled and wound through treetops. The last time Sanaa had walked down this street it'd looked nothing like this. All boarded up windows, empty shops, and homeless old men. Just the kind of place where no one would notice the smell of rotting animals, or care about the strange woman who lived above them. *Cat Box*, responding to her distress, kicked tiny holes in the side of her backpack, the movement drawing looks from a group of well-dressed women walking past. Sanaa drew her scarf down, almost covering her eyes.

The children took her to the train station. This was a shock—didn't they live just a few minutes down the road, squatting in the old community housing? She stopped, turned, peered down the street. The fibros were completely gone, replaced with sleek white apartments. "Jesus. When did this happen?"

Her guides paused reluctantly. "Miss?"

Sanaa shook her head. How could the inner city have changed so much around her? How could she not have noticed?

"We need to hurry, miss."

One last look. The park on the corner, where no one dared to tread after dark—now full of people and bright market stalls. Music playing. Women laughing. Sanaa caught a glimpse of something small scurrying in the darkness of the gutter and took comfort in the idea that at least the rats and stray cats remained. Just like her, they were last remnants of an older, dirtier time.

The train station had been developed, too. It was neat, clean, and well-lit. It made Sanaa's skin crawl just to look at. "N-No way I'm going in there," she stammered. Too many people, too close together. Ticket machines, turnstiles, guards all watching, watching. Her teeth chattered, involuntarily. "You'll just have to look after yourselves. I can't, I won't—"

But Alice, brave Alice, took her hand. Her fingers were dirty, but still pale against Sanaa's dark skin. Alice drew her not into the station itself, but through a gap in the wire fence and onto the tracks. "Good spot here," Alice was saying. She talked smoothly, constantly. "Always find a bird or two, and usually a bat. I think it's the wires—" Sanaa glanced up at the snaking cables above, so thick and full they hummed with hidden power "—they land on them and get fried." The children wound a complicated pattern along the tracks, avoiding the trains that rattled fiercely past. "But you gotta be careful not to get hit—"

In the end, and to Sanaa's intense relief, they didn't catch any trains. The children led her away from the station, down one of the lines, past abandoned carriages rusting away and an old unused platform, to another break in the fence. They pushed through untidy bushes, shopping trolleys, and onto backstreets where decrepit townhouses, empty warehouses, and vacant lots were ringed by colourfully spray-painted walls.

Now this was more like the city Sanaa knew. Most of the streetlights here were broken. It was so dark in places that she couldn't even see the vermin that followed them; the critters scratching cement and splashing in an overflowing drain.

They arrived at a bizarre little camp, in the corner of one warehouse. Two more children sat with their backs to the wall, surrounded by countless lights all rigged up to a single power point.

"I brought her!" Alice and Pete broke into a run, dragging Sanaa and Matt along with them. "See, didn't I tell you? I brought her!"

Sanaa quailed and pulled her hand free. Lights. Too many lights.

"Quick, miss," Pete called. "It'll come now. It must have seen us, must have heard. It knows we're here!"

Cat Box was squirming against her, kicking and tearing through the backpack.

"Miss?" Alice tried to push Matt into the light, but he held his ground. "Please, miss. Help me."

Sanaa's throat clenched as three teeth cracked loose from her jawbone to shimmy into her neck. Too much exertion. All that walking and talking and worry were eating quickly through the strength the possum had given her. Would have been better just staying at home. Would have lasted longer.

Then Matt turned, all of his own volition, and stared intently into the darkness behind her. "Coming," he said, and stepped forward. Alice, white with fear, allowed Pete to draw her into the circle of light.

Sanaa froze as Matt walked past her. He walked awkwardly, chest thrust forward as though a hand had hooked into his ribcage and pulled him.

With a great clatter of bones and a tearing of fabric, *Cat Box* finally freed itself. It pressed its dented shoebox against Sanaa's shins and arched as best it could. Sanaa turned. She blinked, squinted— something moved. Faintly pale, a bulging face, teeth and eyes. Sanaa clutched Matt's wrist and dragged him against her. His smell wrapped around her—unnatural decay and too-clean bones.

"Don't," Matt gasped, but he didn't fight her. "Let me go." There was no conviction in his words. "I have to go."

Sanaa swallowed hard against her loose teeth, and lifted her head. "Who's there?" she called. Even as she spoke, her right shin shattered; shards migrated to wedge themselves between her ribs. She didn't so much as flinch.

When nothing answered she glanced down at *Cat Box*, with its bright Christmas lights. How she hated to ask it to do anything more than she had already forced it to. "Will you show me?" she asked. *Cat Box* tensed, dimmed. "Shine your lights? Show me the monster that has been hurting these children." It didn't move. "They brought you to me, do you remember that? Found you when you were nothing but a dead cat on the side of the road, gave you to me so I could make you live again. They helped you. They help me. Now it's our turn." A battery-tail twitch. "For me?"

The steady lights of *Cat Box's* bulbs revealed a man. A strange, small, twisted man. He was bent on one horribly dislocated knee, all his fingers were on backwards, one foot stuck out at the wrong angle, his neck bent, one shoulder missing, face a mess of mountains and valleys—

Though his skin was white and he was a man and she'd never, ever seen him before, she knew that body immediately. Intimately.

"You—" Sanaa gasped. "You're—" She couldn't speak. "Not possible."

The man looked up. His eyes were sunken and dry. "Possible. 'Nother one," he said, his words so distorted she could barely understand them. "Not met one for long time. Never one looks as good as you." He stood with a groan and a million painful pops. He nodded to *Cat Box*. "What this?"

"*Cat Box, At Christmas*," Sanaa answered, as though in a daze. "It's my pet." She clicked her fingers and *Cat Box* returned to her. The man followed, keeping within its light.

Matt flinched and tried to pull free. Sanaa held him, while she still could.

"Wanna use?" the man asked. He scanned the children. "Doesn't bother. Plenty more." He held out his hand. Oh, but he must be in such constant pain. His elbow was long gone, his shoulder had worked its way around to his chest. "Already got started on that one. You take others. He's mine."

"Have to," Matt hissed, trying to pull away. "Hurts. Let me go. Have to."

"I—" Sanaa swallowed hard. "I don't understand. Are you an artist, too?"

He laughed at that, and it was horrible: mouth too slack and throat shaking, all his bones bouncing beneath his skin. "Artist? Me?" He waved at Matt. "Show."

Sanaa released him as Matt pulled off his thin, torn shirt. She sucked in a horrified breath at the body underneath. Broken, so broken. His upper arms were all terrible indents and lumps from bones shattered, then poorly healed. His ribs were a mess, all wrong angles, some in visible pieces. When he started to tug his pants down she caught the knobbed edges of misaligned hips—

"Stop," Sanaa gasped. "Don't. That's enough."

The pale man grinned, mouth too wide and teeth misaligned. "Break the bones, move the bones, turn them into something new." He nodded slowly. "See now, like artwork. But more. Belongs to me, part of me. Feels what I feel. Comes to me when I call. Needs to. Only way to ease the pain."

Matt stepped forward. "Please." He glanced at Sanaa. "I have to. He's hurting now, hurting so much. And I can feel it all. So let me go with him. It's the only way to stop—"

"Quiet!" the pale man snapped. "No more talking. Come now. Hurting *now*!"

"But," Sanaa whispered. "He isn't dead. You know what it feels like—the pain, the body that won't do as it is told. How could you possibly inflict that on anyone else?"

The man tipped his head like he just didn't understand her. "Look you, stand all tall. You must, too."

"No, no I don't. Not like this. And I won't let you keep doing it. I can't!"

He chuckled, a low sound that reverberated in her chest and left hairline fractures in its wake. "Stop me?"

Matt, poor alive innocent Matt, stood between them. "I'm sorry." His lips hardly moved. "If you don't go away, he'll make me hurt you. I'm sorry, I can't stop it."

Sanaa, torn, unsure what she could possibly do, held her breath. "Please," Pete whispered behind her, where he huddled in the light. She met Matt's terrified gaze, eyes wide and cheek twitching, but the rest of him still and hard as stone.

Then the smallest, strangest noises echoed through the warehouse. Scratching, like dozens of rats' claws against cement, then the screech of metal on stone. It grew faster, closer, louder, until even the pale man turned to peer into the darkness behind him.

Possum On A Hot Tin Roof led the way, kicking and clawing into the light. Then the others emerged, all of them. *King Rat Trap* in a chaos of steel and tiny limbs, helped *RooStone* drag its heavy granite body. Her favourites from the hallway walls, the pile she'd thought too powerless to move anymore and therefore ready to sell, half-made sketches in feather and bone, massive pieces from her larger installations. Their canvases were muddy, their paint scratched. Most had parts missing. One had definitely been run over by a train.

"You followed me," she whispered. "How did you know I would need you?" *Possum's* empty eyes peered up at her. *Cat Box* rubbed against her shins. They were a part of her, bound to her, bones to bones, death and life. How could they not have known?

The pale man had Matt. Sanaa had an army.

She didn't even need to tell them what to do, at least not out loud. Her artworks swarmed over the man, covering him in bones and wire and steel mesh, bearing him down to the ground, pinning him. When Matt turned to fight for him they smothered him too, but gentler, immobilising but never hurting. Careful with one of their own.

It looked to Sanaa like a work of art, each piece a part of a powerful whole, with the cement floor as its canvas. Watching, avid, she slipped the broken backpack from her shoulders. "Alice," she called. "Get my tools out."

Saw in hand, she crouched, inspected. Measured with her eyes, and imagined. "*Pale Man?*" she whispered, and glanced at *Cat Box*. "What do you think about that for a name?"

*

Sanaa bought the old warehouse for a fraction of the cost of her house and moved in straight away. Boxes of dead animals would have been a challenge for any removalists, but her army of carrion gathers made it easy. No questions to answer, either.

She bought beds for the kids, and let them sleep with the lights on. She set up an enormous studio and was more productive than ever. She even went outside, on occasion. Rare occasion.

All thanks to *Pale Man*, and his unending strength.

Every morning, before she helped Alice prepare breakfast, before coffee—which she was developing a taste for—Sanaa visited *Pale Man* in his room, secure behind a heavy metal door and *Cat Box*, ever guarding.

His bones, wiped clean, were pale indeed, and shone far whiter than his skin had. He'd made the most beautiful installation piece, and the strength he gave her never faded. She wasn't cruel, not even to him. She'd made him far more perfect than he would ever have otherwise been.

She'd made him human.

All the right bones in all the right order, tied together with copper, silver, and dotted with flecks of gold. His wrists were bound to the ceiling and his feet to the floor, and he floated in between, suspend on a spider web of wire. Fairy lights surrounded him, like those she'd seen in the trees on her street. She'd installed a fake window, with a lamp and a fan behind it, so he could feel the warmth of a pretend sun, and the brush of a cooling breeze.

She fed him tiny, nameless artworks, made from bird wings, or mice. Just enough to make sure he never tired and, she hoped, alleviate his pain. This wasn't punishment or revenge. This was art.

He might have been a monster, but, after all, so was she.

AFTERWORD

"Sanaa's Army" was inspired by a strange combination of myth and real life. It started with a friend and co-worker of mine who, like Sanaa, collects bones and creates artworks with them. I've seen her carry away the corpse of a possum trapped in the roof at work, and she regularly asks for any mice caught in the kitchen traps. The act of creating something new and beautiful out of the discarded parts of a dead body felt just like magic to me. So I looked to shamanism, in particular the world of the Indonesian dukun. Children, and their bones, feature prominently in their magic. Children's bones are so powerful that their graves are robbed, even today. Dukun are also known to summon a servant-spirit called a *Toyol* from the bodies of dead children. It's all about trapping them in a new body, you see, and in some traditions these new bodies are carved from the child's own bones.

Sanaa and the *Pale Man* are shamans and artists, in their own way. They are also servants to their magic, and bound to their artworks. Shaman and spirit both.

A MOTHER'S LOVE

RICHARD HARLAND

It's the normality of normal things I love. When I came back to Lyell Street, our lawn was an almost luminous green after the rain, and the brick of our front wall was a soft, ochre red. In our driveway stood Mum's old silver-grey Fairlane; beside the path were the yellow zinnias I planted myself five years ago. I grew up in the Sydney suburbs, first Werrington, then Bossley Park, and I'm sure there's no better place in the world.

I checked the letterbox before remembering it was Saturday. At the front door, I shifted my carry bag to my other hand and fished for my keys. Mum usually keeps the house locked up when she's alone. She called out before I even opened the door; "Is that you, Sean?"

I went through into the lounge before answering. "Now who else would it be, Mum?"

She was sitting in her leather recliner in front of the TV, but the set wasn't on. White hair in a bun, hollowed-out features, rimless glasses, blue house-jacket . . . all exactly as normal. All except for the tension that radiated from her like beams from a fire.

"Where have you been?" she demanded.

"For a walk."

"Let me look at you."

I put my carry bag down on a chair. I was feeling on top of the world, and I wasn't going to lose my good mood. I stood still and let her study me.

"You were shaky and trembling when you went out before," she said accusingly. "I saw you. Now you're as calm as calm."

I smiled at her upside-down logic. "Isn't that good? You should worry if I was still shaky."

"What have you been doing to get so calm?"

"I told you when I went out. A long walk, all the way round Wylde Park and Flora Park. Shall I draw a map?"

"Don't take that tone with me, Sean. I care about you."

"I know. But you spend too much time sitting and brooding over every little thing I do. You need to be more active. Normal exercise, like me."

"I can't help brooding when—"

"Why not do something now? Get up and make us a nice cup of tea. Don't you think that would be good for you? While I go and have a shower."

"You're brushing me off, Sean."

"No, Mum, but you blow everything up out of proportion. Okay, my walk took longer than you expected. It's not a major event."

She moved out of her angry phase, into her self-pitying phase. "You'll never love me the way I love you. You don't have it in you."

I could have reminded her that I was twenty-seven, and no normal mother expects to know everything a twenty-seven-year-old son does. *I can work out my own problems,* I might have said. And I had worked them out. The kind of all-enveloping love my mother wanted to give me was no longer appropriate. Heavens, she was fifty-five herself! *It's over the top,* I might have said. But I didn't want to start old arguments again.

"Stop fussing," I told her. "You won't change anything by getting into a state. How about that cup of tea? Should be just right by the time I'm out of the shower."

I was halfway to the door when she stopped me with a "Wait, Sean."

"What?"

"Bring me Chango."

She was referring to one of the dolls on top of the glass-fronted cabinet. There were five of them, and they all had individual names: Chango, Osun, Ellegua, Obatala and Yemaya. They weren't normal dolls, but wooden sticks with scratched-on faces, dressed in exotic, multi-coloured costumes. I didn't like them, and they were completely out of place in our house. In fact, they were the only remaining souvenirs from Mum's globetrotting days when my father was still alive. Over the years, I'd managed to get rid of the rest, but she had a special attachment to these dolls, which seemed to comfort her in some way. Perhaps Chango would comfort her now.

I picked up the doll—even its costume felt odd and wrong, as if made out of coarse twine—and passed it across. My cup of tea had been relegated to the back of her mind, I could see. I turned on the TV, selected a channel for her and handed her the remote. Then I went off to have my shower.

In these moments, I love a long shower with the water turned up hot. Everything clean and pure, everything under control. I hadn't lost my serene mood. Eventually I would get rid of those outlandish dolls—but all in good time, all in good time.

I put on my bathrobe, came back to the lounge and found Mum crying. She had got up out of her recliner, dropping both doll and remote on the floor. Now she stood against the wall and stared at my carry bag, which she had lifted up onto the table. Obviously she had been looking through it.

"What are you?" She turned her eyes on me. "What did I bring back?"

Her eyes seemed strangely dark and deep behind the tears. The look she gave me didn't belong to my mother.

"Are you even human?" Her voice was no more than a whisper. "You've done it before, haven't you?"

"Sit down."

"I ought to kill you. I ought to have killed you long ago."

"Now you're being silly." I spoke slowly and calmly, trying to bring some normality back into the situation. "*Sit.*"

"I nearly did once. Do you believe me? One night a year after we came back from Cuba, when I *knew* there was something wrong. I took a knife out of the kitchen drawer. I might've done it then."

"But you didn't." I gripped her by the arm and propelled her to her chair. "And now you can't."

She didn't want to sit, but I pressed down on her shoulders. She put her head in her hands and let out a wail. "It's my fault. I made the choice. I did a terrible, bad thing."

I gave her a smile, still standing over her. "Not you. Not my Mum. You're too good to do bad things."

"What would you know about good and bad?" She looked up at me with a sharp, fierce glare. Then her mood switched again. "I did it for you."

"Thank you."

"You don't know what it was."

I didn't know and didn't care. I only wanted to calm her down. "Don't over-excite yourself. Everything's all right."

"No, it isn't. You need to know what it was. You remember your father died in Cuba?"

I didn't understand the jump to that last sentence. "You told me. I was too young to remember."

"Five years old. You were there when it happened."

I shrugged. I had no memories of my father or his death. I'd been told he was a university lecturer in sociology, and was always going off to do research in faraway parts of the world. Communist Cuba had been just one of his crazes. Mum was forced to accompany him, and after I was born, that meant me, too. I was glad I didn't remember my father, because I'm sure I wouldn't have liked him.

"It was 1989," she went on, "just after Australia established diplomatic relations with the Castro government. Of course, your father had to be one of the first to visit."

"You should've stayed home in Australia."

"I *loved* him, Sean. People do things out of love. He wanted to observe the effects of Cuban-style socialism on an agrarian society. So we went out beyond Havana to talk to people on farms, in small communities. And that one day he forgot his Ventolin inhaler. In the main street of Antón Diaz, near Santa Clara . . . it was horrible. He started wheezing, then he couldn't even wheeze. His skin and fingernails turned blue from lack of oxygen. It was the asthma that killed him, though the doctor who did the autopsy said it was heart-failure at the end. I couldn't do a thing to save him."

She was gasping for breath herself, crying tears of a different kind now. I grimaced, and pictured a hot, dusty street in a foreign country where a man lay doubled up on the ground with strangers all around. I don't normally have a vivid imagination, but this was an exception. I couldn't help thinking my father had brought it on himself.

"I didn't need to hear that," I said.

Mum pulled herself together. "You haven't heard anything yet. What happened with you was three days later."

"Then I don't want to hear. Not now."

"Yes, now." She directed a meaningful glance towards my carry bag. "It's who you are. It's *why* you are."

I could've left the room or turned the TV up to maximum volume. But she was determined to tell her story whatever I did.

"Three days later," she said in a loud voice. "I couldn't wait to get us back to Australia. After all the arrangements had been made for the body . . . thanks to that doctor, he was wonderful help. I hired a taxi in Santa Clara to take us all the way to Havana airport. I had to hold you in my lap in the front seat with our luggage piled up behind. No seat belts, of course."

"Third world country. Of course."

"Oh, Cuba's not simply third world. The public medical service is first world standard. But backward in other ways. A mix of modern socialism with Catholicism and Santería—"

"What's Santería?"

She shook her head. "I have to tell you about the crash first."

For some reason, I had been expecting there would be a crash. She paused and re-gathered her thoughts.

"It was a tyre blow out. We weren't going all that fast. The taxi swerved across to the other side of the road and smashed into an old American limousine, a 50s Pontiac, built like a tank. Our Lada didn't stand a chance. I thought I had a firm hold on you, but a suitcase hit the back of my neck, and I must've let go. You went flying forward through the windscreen. You bounced on the bonnet and fell down out of sight."

She was talking about me, but it didn't feel like me. That five year old sounded like someone else's child. Cuba was just a name, not a place *I'd* ever experienced.

"Don't blame yourself," I said.

"What?"

"Don't blame yourself for not holding on to me. You couldn't help it. And I survived."

"Did you?" She looked at me with an unreadable expression, compressing her lips and screwing up her eyes. There were no tears there now. "I re-live that day every moment of my life. Every time I look at you."

I waited. She seemed to be going into herself, into her memories. She dropped her gaze and studied her hands in her lap. Her fingers clenched and loosened, clenched and loosened, as she told the story. It was like a story she'd rehearsed a thousand times before in her head. Perhaps she'd been rehearsing it for this very occasion of telling it to me.

"I hit my head hard on the dashboard. By the time I got out of the taxi, four people had got out of the limousine. There was the chauffeur, wearing an official-looking peaked cap, and two female passengers—rather beautiful women with jet black hair and dusky skin. The fourth was a big man in a fawn suit, gold jewellery and sunglasses. He'd picked you up from the ground and held you cradled in one arm. I think he must've been some local boss or high-ranking party member.

"My taxi driver recognised him, and couldn't apologise enough. 'I'm sorry, Mr Padrón, it was the tyre. I couldn't do anything. The steering went out of control.'

"You were a dreadful mess, Sean, covered in blood. Mr Padrón was getting blood all over his expensive suit, but it didn't seem to bother him. I stepped forward to claim you, and he inspected me through his sunglasses.

"'I'm his mother.' I understood Spanish better than I spoke it, but I spoke it well enough to communicate.

"Mr Padrón passed you across. For such a heavily built man, he was surprisingly gentle. He shook his head in a way that filled me with sudden terror.

"'What?' I cried. 'He'll be all right, won't he?'

"I don't know why I expected Mr Padrón to be an authority— he just had that air about him.

"'No, señora.' Another shake of the head. 'Shock, blood loss, head trauma. He is not long for this world.'

"I couldn't, I *wouldn't* accept it. You had no obvious wounds, Sean, even though you were covered in blood. As I rocked you in my arms, your leg kept kicking and moving.

"'Look at that! He's fine!'

"'Yes, the leg moves, señora, but not the head or the heart. The life-spirit is leaking out of him.'

"*Life-spirit*—that was Santería thinking. I wasn't interested in superstition, only in modern medical intervention. 'We have to get him to a hospital,' I said.

"My taxi driver spoke up. 'The nearest hospitals are in Havana, señora, over an hour away.' He turned to Mr Padrón. 'Is it possible?'

"'I could take him there, yes. Unfortunately, he will not live that long.'

"My driver looked desperate. He didn't want to be responsible for the death of a child. 'But you can save him, Mr Padrón. Use your *elekes*.'

"There was a horrified gasp from the two women. Mr Padrón's own chauffeur faced the other way and seemed to be making the sign of the cross.

"The big man frowned. 'It is too late.'

"'I'm begging you.' My driver turned to me. 'You beg him, señora. He can do it.'

"'I don't understand.'

"'Mr Padrón is an *olorisha*.'

"I knew the word *olorisha*. It meant a priest in the local voodoo religion. Vodoun in Haiti, Pukkumina in Jamaica, Santería in Cuba. It still exists, even under Communist rule. Castro was always less worried about local Santería than organised Catholicism.

"'He can bring him back,' my driver insisted. 'As long as any part of his life-spirit remains.'

"'She has no idea of the consequences,' Mr Padrón said sternly. 'You should know better than to encourage her.'

"'Her plane flies out this evening, then they'll be gone. She'll take him away to her own country. You'll never come back to Cuba, will you, señora?'

"'Never.' I was very sure about that.

"Mr Padrón leaned forward, and touched and tapped you with his index finger, Sean. Your legs, chest, head, like a doctor conducting an overall examination. You didn't cry out or recoil— only your left arm and leg moved in response.

"'You see?' he said. 'So little life-spirit. He has gone too far.'

"Oh Sean, that was when I truly believed you were dying. I couldn't bear it. Three days after watching your father die—it was the same again. Worse. I felt like my insides were being ripped out. If I lost you too, I'd have lost everything I loved. I *couldn't* let you go, Sean. You understand that, don't you?"

As she spoke, Mum's hands moved from her lap to the arms of her chair. Her fingers were like claws, she gripped so fiercely onto the padded leather. I didn't like it when she talked about love, and I had never really understood her love for me. Right now, though, it was all in my favour that she couldn't let me go.

She looked up at me, but I don't think she found what she was looking for. She dropped her gaze and went on with her story.

"I pleaded with Mr Padrón to save you. I didn't know how he could do it, but I was desperate enough to believe in anything. I promised him money—all that I had and more than I had. But he didn't want to use his powers.

"'It is too much against nature,' he said. 'The child will never be complete again.'

"I didn't care. The two women couldn't change my mind either, though they kept saying how wrong and horrible it was.

"'You don't know what will come back,' said one.

"'Let him go in peace,' said the other. 'Accept your loss. Give his body a dignified burial, let his soul fly free.'

"I don't remember their words so much as the expression on their beautiful faces—a kind of terror and a kind of pity. The pity would've persuaded me, if anything could. But I blocked out their warnings and turned to Mr Padrón. 'I'll die if my son dies,' I told him. 'If you don't save him, you'll kill me.'

"Finally he agreed. He wasn't interested in payment—I think he was moved by my utter despair. One of the women let out a small shriek of horror. The other began to shout at him until he halted her with an upraised hand. The two of them went off and sat in the limousine with the chauffeur, not wanting to watch.

"I could hardly watch myself. I seemed to see it all from a distance, through a blur. Mr Padrón unbuttoned his shirt collar and drew out a string of coloured beads that were hanging around his neck. He let it dangle over you as he performed the ritual. He began chanting words in a strange language that wasn't Spanish—probably a dialect from West Africa, where all those voodoo beliefs come from. The names of the Santería gods were in it: Ellegua, Obatala, Yemaya, Chango, Osun. And all the time he kept stroking your body, Sean, like a massage that started from the fingers of your left hand and the toes of your left foot, pushing up through your arm and leg towards your heart. That's how it looked, as if he were squeezing the life-spirit you had left back into the rest of your body, spreading it back into your heart and head. He wasn't pressing hard on you, yet a sweat broke out on his face and he was panting for breath. It lasted . . . I don't know how long. Minutes or hours. It was like a dream."

A dream . . . and I'd had the same dream myself. I've never stopped having it, once or twice a month. It's always begun the same way; in the dark and gliding along as if borne on some stream in an underground tunnel. Then I hear a chant in a foreign language, and a sudden jolt wrenches me to a stop. I look up and see a great glittering web — like a necklace stretched across the dark, blocking my way. The wrenching continues and drags me back against the current—I can't explain how horrible it is. Then, very gradually, the dark gives way to daylight, and there above me are two heads silhouetted against the brightness. One is very close, with enormous black pits of shadow for eyes.

That's how I'd always thought of it—enormous black pits of shadows for eyes. But perhaps what I was seeing were sunglasses, Mr Padrón's sunglasses . . .

"So, I was brought back to life by black magic?" I asked incredulously.

Mum shook her head. "No, you never died, not completely. You mustn't believe that. Some of your life-spirit remained, or Mr Padrón couldn't have done what he did. He regenerated you from the part that was still alive."

Other images had started to drift through my head: dusty streets, bright sun, strange architecture, people gabbling in a foreign language. They were like something I'd read in a book or watched on a screen—very vivid, but not *my* memories. They seemed to belong to someone else.

My head swam. I took a backwards step, and my foot came down on the doll that was still lying where Mum had dropped it. Chango! I lost my balance and went down painfully on one knee.

The fall cleared my mind and brought me back to myself. I stared at that bizarre stick of wood in its multi-coloured costume. Chango . . . Santería . . . *olorishas* . . . witchcraft. No, Chango was no god of mine. I picked the doll up by its feet and snapped it clean in two. Mum let out a quavering moan.

I rose and held the halves in front of her face. "That's what I think of Santería," I said. "Enough of this junk. I'm going to throw the lot out."

I carried the remains of Chango through to the kitchen and dropped them into the bin. Then I came back, scooped up the other dolls from the cabinet and disposed of them the same way.

"All gone," I told Mum. "We don't need *them* cluttering up our house."

Mum didn't look at me. She seemed smaller, collapsed in on herself. She muttered something about "decision" and "consequences", but I wasn't listening.

"Shush," I said. "Calm down. Isn't it nearly time for your game show?" I picked up the remote and changed the channel for her. "There. Now I'm going to make us a nice cup of tea."

*

I'd lost my good mood, but not so much as to become shaky. It would be weeks before *that* started up again. And later I recovered my good mood, anyway.

I deliberately didn't move my carry bag from where Mum had left it on the table. We had dinner in front of the TV and watched the news. Then I got up, collected the bag and a roll of paper towels from the kitchen.

I went to my bedroom and unlocked the special cupboard. There was my collection, exactly as it should be. I took the kit out of my carry bag and stowed each item in its proper position on the bottom shelf. Chloroform bottle, pad, mask, garrotte, surgical saw—I cleaned the saw with a paper towel before putting it away. The disposable plastic apron I rolled up into a neat, tight bundle.

Next I brought out my little souvenir in its resealable plastic bag. As I'd expected, the girl's thumb had leaked a lot of blood. I took it into the bathroom, washed it under the tap and patted it carefully dry on another paper towel.

Back in the bedroom, I prepared a glass jar for it. Formaldehyde is expensive, so I poured in the minimum amount necessary. I dropped the thumb in, watched it settle to the bottom, then placed the jar in the cupboard alongside the rest of my collection.

I wouldn't let myself relax, though, not yet. First I had to get rid of the bloodstained apron, plastic bag and paper towels. I took them through to the kitchen and mixed them in with the garbage in the bin, including Chango and the other dolls. Mum still sat in her recliner in front of the TV, and never once turned her head as I went past.

Finally I could relax. I closed and locked the bedroom door, then opened the cupboard again. My collection now took up nearly two shelves: nine jars containing three fingers, two thumbs and four toes. One more souvenir, and I would need to start a whole new shelf! And when that shelf was full, I would need to buy a whole new cupboard!

I stood there admiring my collection, feeling a kind of love for every single one of those digits. That was when my good mood came back to me.

AFTERWORD

This is a story with several starting-points! The first was when Aileen and I travelled to Cuba five years ago, and saw a Santería shrine in the town of Trinidad. Unbelievable! In the middle of a supposedly secular, rational-minded, communist state was this continuing practice of the original religion brought to the Caribbean by slaves from West Africa—the religion usually known as voodoo and associated with Haiti. I don't remember many details of the shrine except that it was in an ordinary domestic household, it made use of blue cloths and mirrors, and it incorporated a few token Catholic symbols.

That bit of real life stayed in my mind until a second starting-point arrived in the form of a favourite fairytale motif, namely, the idea of a magic that gives you your heart's desire, but exacts a higher price than anything you could ever have imagined. I love to reinvigorate the huge emotional power of old ideas like that. I soon focused on the most absolute desire of all—a mother's determination to save the life of her dying child.

The last starting-point was completely out of left field. Not my own idea, but Amanda's idea for this anthology as horror in a suburban context. I don't know why I jumped across to the idea of Santería in Cuba or a magic that exacts a terrible price for bringing a child back to life—what could ever be further away from suburbia? Yet that play of normality versus the exotic is the thing I'm most pleased about in "A Mother's Love"—once I started working it into the main character's mental state, the story just wrote itself.

Last (and probably least) was another snippet from real life—a rather well-known obsessional habit of serial killers!

FERREAU'S CURSE

CHRISTINE MORGAN

Eleven Years Ago . . .

"She's been in the same spot for over an hour . . . "

" . . . think she's all right? Maybe we should . . . "

The voices were pitched low, almost lost in the general background murmur, but they got through Renee's fog of distraction. Footsteps approached. "Miss?" Addressing her in the professional tones of a museum employee, the woman sounded a step removed from a librarian.

Renee flicked a glance up at the woman. Her appearance was a step removed from a librarian, too. Sensible shoes. Pants suit. Minimal makeup. Renee looked at the small gold pin on her lapel, which read STAFF.

This was a public museum. Admission was free, but she'd left a donation in the box at the door, anyway. Like she did every time. Didn't that mean she could sit here as long as she wanted?

Why did they have to bother *her*?

It wasn't fair. Boys made crude jokes and jerk-off gestures in front of the display of African fertility masks, while gangs of little kids stampeded around the dinosaur exhibits. There was even a wino slumped on the bench by the elevator.

But they singled *her* out, the girl in the St. Theresa's uniform, alone and quiet in the Arts and Antiquities wing, bothering nobody. The woman's librarian voice spoke again; "Is everything all right, miss?"

"Yes," Renee said. She looked at the woman, and the museum volunteer lurking behind her. "I'm just sitting here."

"Yeah, all afternoon," the volunteer said. "And almost every day last week."

"I come here after school sometimes. What's wrong with that?"

"Nothing's wrong with that," the museum lady said with a phony smile. "Does your . . . family know you're here?"

Renee nodded slowly, not missing the significant pause. Did her grandfather pay them to keep an eye on her or something?

The museum employee ramped her phony smile up a few notches. "I can tell you're interested in Egyptian artefacts. Could I answer any questions for you?"

And get me out of here? Renee thought. *Keep me out, keep me away from him? You'd like that, I bet.*

Aloud, she said, "No, thanks."

She waited to see if they'd push it, but they decided to let it go. They knew who she was; and they'd made sure that *she'd* known that they knew. They probably didn't really want to deal with her family unless they had to.

As soon as they'd gone, she swivelled back around and resumed gazing through the thick pane of glass. She knew the exhibit's details by heart, but memory never seemed to be enough. Stone walls covered with hieroglyphics . . . fake torchlight gleaming on gold . . . a fabulous full-size statue of Isis with her rainbow-plumaged wings outstretched . . . an entire mummified bull with gilded horns . . . sealed jars of grain, honey, seeds, spices . . . and the sarcophagus.

Renee picked up a set of headphones and donned them, then pushed the orange button set into the wall. She knew the presentation by heart, too, but she let it drone comfortingly into her ears as she scanned the colourful frescoes. Her gaze lingered on one particular figure. Tall. Straight. Regal. Eyes outlined in dark khol. Handsome. Perfect.

"Here we see the tomb as it appeared when it was discovered in 1958 by Professors Thurbridge and Carstairs. Prince Atensef, one of the many younger sons of Pharaoh Rameses the Third . . . "

PRESENT DAY

The side-view mirror exploded. Renee Ferreau ducked, swore, and twisted the keys before her conscious mind fully registered the gunshot and cascade of fragments.

The second shot skidded along the side of the truck, screeching, showering sparks. Pulses of red and blue light splashed across the museum complex's many-angled reflective façades. What looked like a dozen cop cars veered into view.

"Shit!" Eddie scrambled up into the cab, grabbing for his seatbelt. "Go, go, go!"

"What about—?"

"Screw 'em! Go!"

Renee jammed her foot down on the gas pedal. The engine roared. Rubber-stinking black smoke whirled up from the shrieking tires. Spin . . . spin . . . traction! The truck lunged forward, taking out a parking meter.

Her arms felt wrenched halfway out of their sockets. Power steering? Dream on. She yanked and hauled, throwing her weight into it.

Heavy things slid and shifted as they took another hard corner. Renee winced, braced for the sound of breakage, but lucked out. This time.

If anything happened to . . .

No. She wasn't going to let herself think about that.

Two wheels bump-ka-thumped over the kerb. "Hang on!" she said. Better late than never.

"Where'd you learn to drive, sweetheart? The bumper-cars at Devil's Beach?"

She ignored Eddie, blasting through an amber. A cab, creeping forward, anticipating the green, skidded to a stop. The driver gave her a horn blare, a one-fingered salute, and a shouted remark about her mother.

"There!" Eddie pointed to a narrow side-street.

Renee took the turn, wincing again. Everything slid back the other way, making the truck rock on its suspension. Odds and ends made a jingling slot-machine noise as they spilled across the corrugated metal floor.

Side street? Little more than an alley. The jolting wedge of headlights revealed graffiti, garbage, Dumpsters and cardboard boxes. Cats, rats and bums scattered ahead of the truck.

Eddie cranked down his window, stuck his head out, and peered backward. "Looks clear."

She brought them to a stop, slumping in her seat with her head back and her eyes closed. "What about Marco and Tank?"

"They're big boys. They can take care of themselves. We got what we came for, right?"

"Right." She hoped. What if they'd missed something? Forgotten something? There wouldn't be a second chance.

"Don't be so glum, sweetheart." He clapped her on the shoulder. "Even if they rat on us, what's the worst that could happen?"

Renee twitched away from his meaty, sweaty, too-chummy hand. "My grandfather could kill us."

Eddie paused. A worried frown creased his big face. "Uh . . . I meant, besides that?"

Five Days Ago

"A thief? *My* granddaughter, a common *thief*?"

Renee bowed her head, cheeks flaming. Through the hanging veil of her hair, she could see the police report on his desk. He rapped it, his bunched knuckles knocking through to glossy wood.

"A thief," Vincent Ferreau said again. "When I think what you could have made of yourself. You're breaking your grandmother's heart, not to mention disgracing your father's reputation. A young lady with your intelligence and education and talents, and *this* is what you do with your life?"

"I didn't—"

"Don't interrupt!"

The venom in his voice made her flinch. She risked a glance, saw him glaring at her from the depths of his big leather chair. Behind him, on the wall, various Ferreau ancestors cast their own disapproving scowls.

"I read over this, and it makes me want to vomit," he said, giving the papers a contemptuous flick. "What next? Purse snatching? Shoplifting? Where is your good sense?"

"I'm sorry, Grandfather."

"Look at your brothers, the biggest gun runners and arms dealers in this part of the country. Your aunt oversees an empire that brings in girls from all over the world. My father, he never got arrested *once* in forty years. But you? You, Renee? Robbing jewellery stores? Have you no ambition?"

She wanted to protest, wanted to mention some of the other less-successful relations. Like the uncle doing twenty-to-life, or the cousin who'd changed her name and become a squeaky-clean district attorney in another state.

But doing that would only *really* bring on the old man's wrath. He didn't care for any reminders that went against his vision of their criminal empire; a familial dynasty spanning generations. The fact that his son had married the daughter of a 'stuffy academic' was already bad enough.

"I stole the Heart of Isis!" Renee said instead.

"Pfft." He waved a hand. "Worthless."

"It's one of the rarest and most valuable—"

"Which means it can never be sold. Too distinctive. Too recognisable. All you did was acquire a pretty paperweight that your mother used to tell stories about. If you want to impress me, you'll have to do better than that."

"Well," Renee said, "there is this one job I've been thinking of pulling. A big one."

His expression didn't change, but she could tell that she'd managed to pique his interest. "What kind of a job?" he asked.

"A museum heist."

"Renee, Renee, Renee." He pinched the bridge of his nose, the underworld king in despair.

"This one is a done deal, Grandfather. I've got it all planned out, a buyer lined up, everything. All I need is a team and some equipment. Come on, please? One last chance to make good?"

*

Now here she was, parked in an alley with Eddie, while Marco and Tank were probably either already arrested or gunned down.

"Why the hell did they go back in?" She unbuckled her seatbelt, agitated. "We would have been out of here clean if they hadn't gone back in!"

"They're idiots," Eddie said. He shrugged. "Gold does that to some guys. This one time, me and your dad . . . " He launched into some rambling story that Renee tuned out as she clambered into the rear of the truck to check on its contents.

"Please be okay," she whispered, her guts in a knot. "All in one piece, come on, what do you say? Give me that much, at least."

She righted the small square crate and pried up the lid. Four bubble-wrapped objects nestled down inside contoured hollows in custom-cut foam padding. The curators had done a diligent packing job. The artefacts looked undamaged, felt undamaged. So far, so good.

Had word of the bungled heist gotten back to her grandfather yet?

Who was she kidding?

Of course word had gotten back to her grandfather.

The old man had all the contacts he needed on either side of the law. He'd already know that the job had gone bad. He had given her this one shot to prove herself, and she'd blown it.

Well, it might still be worth it. If she could get to the old man . . . if he really could do what he *said* he could do . . .

Even if it meant she'd have to kill him afterward.

She'd never killed anyone before, not on purpose anyway — *getting* someone killed wasn't the same, that didn't count. But there was a first time for everything, and this was important. Since obtaining the Heart of Isis, she found she worried a lot less about the little things.

She went to the longer, rectangular crate. It had shifted and slid, but likewise looked undamaged. She opened it and clicked on a penlight. She smiled.

"Gorgeous," she said.

An explosive sneeze right behind her made Renee stifle a yelp.

"Sorry," Eddie said. He leaned over her and looked inside. "Huh. Gorgeous? Dunno about that, sweetheart. How much is it worth?"

"Priceless."

"A little dusty, dontcha think?" He sneezed again. "What's that funny smell, anyway?"

"Oils, spices, linen, natron crystals." Renee let the penlight's beam rove slowly over shining gold adorned with bands of polished lapis lazuli and red carnelian. Screw Eddie; this was spectacular. The moment she'd been waiting for.

"Who-what crystals?"

"Natron. A sodium compound. They used it to dry out the body for mummification."

"Like salt, you mean?"

"Yeah, Eddie. Like salt."

Everything seemed to be okay, nothing crunched or broken off. Renee let out a long, relieved exhalation.

"Hey, check it out!" Eddie reached past her. "It's one of those Egyptian bug-things."

She smacked his hand. "Leave it!"

"Ow! What's the deal? You want one? Look, there's a bunch of them, all tucked into the cloth."

"I said leave it!"

"Okay, okay. Don't get your panties in a twist over a couple of stone bugs."

"For one thing, they're called scarabs," she said. "For another, there could be as many as a hundred protective amulets—"

"So nobody'll miss one or two."

"We can't disturb the wrappings."

"Why not?" He barked a laugh. "This isn't where you tell me there's some kind of mummy curse, right?"

Renee groaned. "The buyer won't want to pay up if the merchandise has been pawed over and looted, that's all. He's an archaeologist, not a treasure-hunter."

"That why we had to cart off the whole stiff? Because it would have been a lot easier to dump King Tut's musty butt out of this damn stone coffin and just take the mask and necklace."

"That's why," she said. "Also, he's *not* King Tut, and it's a sarcophagus, and a pectoral . . . oh, never mind. Here, help me with the tie-downs, in case we have to make any more sudden stops."

The truck came equipped with canvas straps, but Marco hadn't bothered to secure the cargo before he and Tank had decided to go back and help themselves to a few more trinkets from the Hall of Kings' exhibits.

Her orders had been so much wasted breath. Yeah, she might be Vincent Ferreau's granddaughter, but she was only a chick, and a novice as far as they were concerned.

She kind of understood their point of view. All that gold: statues of spearmen and dancing girls and animal-headed gods; ankhs and sceptres; that jewel-studded miniature chariot complete with a pair of golden horses; they were supposed to leave all that behind? For what? A dried-out ancient dead guy and some jars?

As they got back into their seats and she started up the engine, Eddie said, "I didn't know you were so into all this history stuff. Like what's-her-name, that video game babe with the big—"

"Lara Croft? Not hardly," Renee said. "I just used to go to the museum all the time when I was a kid."

*

The garage door rattle-rolled up, revealing a cavernous warehouse dimly lit by hanging bulbs. A maze of stacked crates and boxes stretched off into the darkness.

"You sure this is the place?" Eddie asked dubiously.

A thin, prissy old man in a brown suit hurried into view. He gesticulated, urging them to hurry-hurry-hurry. His movements made Renee think of a nervous little dog that needed to piddle every thirty seconds. As soon as the truck was inside, he hit a remote and the door trundled down again.

"Okay," Renee said. "Here we are."

"That the guy?" Eddie frowned. "Fussy-looking fella."

She nodded, cut the engine and climbed down, looking at the old man. "Professor Thurbridge."

"You did it? You actually did it? You have the prince?"

"In the back."

"Let me see him. I want to see him. And the jars? You have the canopic jars? All four?"

"I have the jars." She went around to the rear of the truck.

Professor Nigel Thurbridge fidgeted alongside her every step of the way. She was amazed his blood pressure could take the excitement. The last thing she needed was for him to pop a vessel and croak on her before they had concluded their business.

Eddie got out. "So what's the deal with the dead dude, Prof? You go to school with him or something?"

"Not now, Eddie." Renee opened the doors.

Thurbridge was past her in a flash, scrambling up, amazingly spry for a man his age. His gnarled hands caressed the lid of the sarcophagus. "Oh, my . . . my goodness! Prince Atensef! At last! I only had to outlive that bastard Carstairs, and now you're mine . . . all mine . . . I will be proved right! After all these years!"

Eddie sidled over to Renee, eyebrows raised in a query. To keep him from shooting off his mouth some more, she explained. "The professor was on the expedition that discovered Prince Atensef's tomb. With another Egyptologist, Albert Carstairs. There was a . . . well, a difference of opinion over what to do with the mummy and the treasures. Carstairs wanted to donate everything to a museum."

"And ol' Prof here didn't, huh?"

"Basically."

"I will be vindicated!" Thurbridge crowed. Only then did he take a quick, perplexed look around the interior of the truck. "Didn't you have more men with you? I said you'd need at least four to safely move the sarcophagus."

"There was a problem," Renee said.

"You weren't caught, were you?"

"Not all of us," Eddie said. "The cops showed up, and—"

"The police!" The professor clutched at his chest. "You said you knew what you were doing! You said you had it all arranged! And you still bungled the job?"

"We got him here." Renee nodded at the lid. It was sculpted into an image of Atensef in repose, arms crossed, one hand gripping an ankh, the other a sceptre in the shape of a hooded cobra. "The cops didn't follow us. You can do what you've been waiting all these years to do. It's time."

"Hang on," Eddie said. "What's he wanna do? I don't know if I like the sound of that. Is it kinky? Is it gross?"

"Eddie, shut up." Renee leaned conspiratorially close to the old professor. "If you're right, this is going to make you more famous than anyone since Howard Carter. Think of what you'll be able to discover. Better yet, think of what you'll be able to *prove*! You'll have answers and knowledge no other archaeologist has ever dared to dream of having!"

"Renee—"

"Shut *up*, Eddie, or so help me, I'll shoot you in the leg."

His mouth snapped closed, but his eyes bugged with astonishment.

"I wanted to try it forty years ago," Thurbridge said, his tone at once wistful and sullen. "When I first found the papyrus and the Osiris Scarab. But that pompous fool Carstairs wouldn't agree to it."

"You don't need his permission anymore," Renee said. "He squeezed you out. He cheated you. Took all the glory. Now's your chance. Do it."

She realised her mistake too late. She'd let the eagerness show, and it had penetrated Thurbridge's own. His narrow, suspicious gaze fixed on her.

"You haven't asked for your money yet," he said.

Eddie stirred. "Yeah, hey, what about our money? We've delivered the goods. Let's get paid and get gone."

Now she *wanted* to shoot him in the leg. Or staple his big mouth shut.

"In fact, come to think of it," Thurbridge said slowly, "*you* sought *me* out. You'd read that paper I wrote, you knew about my research on Queen Nefertegi's papyrus. You even brought me the Heart of Isis to ensure I'd take you seriously. This was all *your* idea!"

"I wanted to see if your theory was right," she said, trying to make light of it. "I'm curious, that's all."

"Hey now, hang on, hold the phone, I want to know what's going on here," Eddie said, all truculence and belligerent jaw-jut.

Renee kept her attention steady on the professor even as she spoke. "Rameses the Third had several wives," she said. "One of his favourites was the sorceress Nefertegi, who worried that her son, Atensef, would be in danger of getting murdered by his half-brothers to remove him from the line of succession. She was right. Atensef was murdered. So she put a spell on his body, with the idea that she'd be able to sneak into his tomb after he was mummified and buried, and bring him back to life."

Eddie snorted. "That's nuts."

"It most certainly is not!" Thurbridge bristled. "She wrote it all down, and left detailed instructions with one of her daughters, in the event that she herself was unable to complete the ritual. I have that very papyrus!"

"She was caught trying to break in," Renee said. "Caught and executed by order of another of Rameses' sons."

The professor nodded, eyes bright, always ready to leap at the chance to lecture on his pet subject. "The daughter, however, failed to keep her promise. She hid the papyrus away, along with the Osiris Scarab."

"The what? Those bug-things?"

"Not an ordinary scarab," Thurbridge said. "The Osiris Scarab was carved of purest onyx, a sacred token of the god of death and rebirth."

He brought a small box from his pocket and opened it. Inside, nestled in folds of cloth, were two shaped and polished chunks of precious stone, each the size of a plum. One was sleek and midnight-black, a scarab beetle with gold hieroglyphs inlaid on its glossy carapace. The other was a rounded half-globe of deep red diamond. Upon it, inlaid in silver, was the image of a kneeling goddess with feathered wings sprouting from the undersides of her outstretched arms.

"According to the papyrus," Renee said. "When the organs from the canopic jars are returned to his body, the Osiris Scarab is set upon his brow and the Heart of Isis on his chest, Atensef will be restored to life."

"And you guys *believe* that crap? I mean, you're talking magic spells here. Give me a break!"

"The world of the ancient Egyptians was quite different from this stark, clinical modern age," Thurbridge said. "Do not sneer at their ways simply because they are beyond your feeble understanding!"

"Oh, sure." Eddie sneered. "Go on, then, Prof. Bring the mummy back to life. Let's see you do it. I bet you a thousand bucks that you can't. A thousand bucks cash. Right here and now."

Huffing, Thurbridge drew himself up to his full spindly height. "I refuse to be mocked and bullied by the likes of you. I've half a mind not to go through with this at all, if this is the kind of attitude—"

"Do it," Renee said.

"You think I'm going to fail? Is that it? You want to discredit me, and then see me thrown in prison? Why, it wouldn't surprise me if you've been working for Carstairs' people all along! I should have known!"

She drew her gun. As she did, the old man choked and sputtered, and Eddie took a step back with his hands half-raised.

"Hey, now, sweetheart . . . "

"Do it," she said. "Or I will."

TEN WEEKS AGO

The attendant at the information desk just about jumped out of his skin when Renee rushed up and slapped her palms on the marble surface.

"Where is he? Where are they taking him?" she demanded.

"Huh . . . wha . . . pardon me? Where's who?"

"Prince Atensef!"

"Ma'am, I don't know what you're—"

"From the Hall of Kings," she said, resisting the urge to reach across and throttle some sense into him. "The tomb of Prince Atensef. Where is he? What's happened? The sign says the exhibit is being moved!"

"Oh!" He chuckled, relaxing. "It's going on tour. The curators are crating everything up. Mummy and all. In a couple of months, it'll be on display in Vegas. A special showing at the Luxor."

"When will he — it — be back?"

"Ma'am, are you okay?"

"Answer me!"

"After Vegas, it's headed for the Royal Museum in Cairo," he said, eyeing her as if his hidden hand was straying near the emergency button. "It isn't coming back."

*

"What the hell? You seriously think you can bring this thing back to life?" Eddie spluttered at her, but his eyes stayed on the gun.

"They were going to take him away," Renee said. "I couldn't let that happen. Not when I'd already obtained the Heart of Isis. And the professor here was so keen to try out the spell — so keen to prove himself."

They both stared at her like she'd read one too many paranormal romances.

"You're crazy," Eddie said. "You're in love with a guy who's been dead for a hundred years?"

"You don't—" she began, but the professor's outburst at Eddie interrupted her.

"Good heavens! Did you never go to school? A hundred years, indeed! For your information—"

"Save it." Renee raised the gun again. "Let's do this. Now or never."

Thurbridge hesitated, even with the black bore of the gun staring him in the face. "My dear girl . . . you do understand . . . the chances of this . . . "

"Don't start doubting your own theory now."

"All right," Nigel Thurbridge said. "All right. Unpack the jars."

*

The golden deathmask, depicting the face of a prince, noble, handsome and serene, had been lifted away and set aside. The pectoral as well, with its weight of precious stones.

Strips of brittle, brownish linen, a hundred and fifty yards of it, made a loose heap on the warehouse floor. Protective amulets, engraved with scarabs and ankhs and other symbols, were collected one by one during the ritualised unwrapping.

The alabaster canopic jars each had a different lid: a jackal, a man, a falcon and a baboon. These were gold, done in exquisite detail, decorated with malachite and onyx. Their dried, shrivelled contents — stomach, liver, intestines, lungs — had been carefully replaced into the mummy's body cavities, once packed with bags of spices and sawdust.

And there he was. Prince Atensef.

"He's beautiful," Renee said. "Perfect."

Eddie kept his mouth shut. He'd made one smartass remark about beef jerky early on, but the threat of a bullet in the foot had taught him the value of silence.

"Go on," she said. "Finish it."

Thurbridge's old hands shook so badly that he dropped the Osiris Scarab. It fell, twinkling in the gloom like a black star.

She had a brief and terrible vision of it cracking to pieces, then caught it herself, mid-air.

With an accusing glare — if she'd thought he had done it on purpose, she would have killed him there and then — Renee put the onyx scarab on Atensef's brow.

"Now the Heart of Isis," she said. "Though if you don't mind, I'll do it myself. Just in case you're still feeling clumsy."

The rich red jewel was as cool and satiny-smooth to the touch as it had been when she'd first lifted it from its display case. She settled it gently onto the prominent bony ridges of Atensef's chest. Her hand lingered on his coarse, dry skin.

Several seconds passed.

A minute.

Papyrus rustled as Thurbridge anxiously re-read the ritual. "I . . . I don't . . . "

"Jeez," Eddie said, with an embarrassed laugh. "You two kooks had me halfway convinced it was really going to—"

There was a faint rasping sound, like an arid desert wind stirring across dry palm fronds. A whiff of incense and spices drifted on the air.

The Osiris Scarab and the Heart of Isis sank into the cadaverous husk. The mummy's dessicated flesh closed over them, so that they were subsumed, like stones slowly swallowed up by a shifting sand dune.

Long-unused tendons creaked as Prince Atensef turned his head.

His eyelids were leathery flaps half-stretched across empty sockets, but his hollow gaze fixed somehow upon Renee. Wizened lips drew back from crooked yellow teeth. Stiff, sticklike fingers grasped her wrist.

Eddie took a couple of tottering steps. "No way. No effin' way."

Professor Thurbridge stood where he was, swaying, muttering in an amazed whisper.

"Return," Renee said, in a language even older than the mummy and artefacts. She'd memorised each word with care. "Rise and return, son of Rameses."

More tendons creaked and cartilage crackled as he sat up. Dusty flecks of skin sifted from his moving joints to powder the bottom of the sarcophagus with fine brown grit.

She touched his brow, where the Osiris Scarab had merged into his skull. "*Sheut* . . . the death-shadow . . . is yours again."

"The hell's she doing?" she heard Eddie ask.

"And *Ib*, the blood of the mother-heart." She set her hand on his ribcage. Beneath her palm, the jewel embedded there gave a sudden throb, a kick.

"This is not part of the ritual familiar to me," Thurbridge said, eyes wide. "Miss Ferreau, what is that incantation, and where did you get it?"

"Let the *Ren*, your name, be restored to you now," Renee said, ignoring him. "Atensef."

"That Egyptian she's speaking, or what?"

The professor, as if relieved to be on more solid scholarly ground in the face of the inexplicable, started in as if by rote about dialects, geography, and periods in history.

Eddie looked sorry he asked. His bored expression changed to surprise in a hurry when Renee finished speaking, turned from the sarcophagus, and shot him in the side of the head.

Blood, hair, bone fragments and brain matter burst out in a chunky spray. Eddie crashed into the crate that had held the canopic jars, tripped over it, and dropped hard. He sprawled face-up on the warehouse's concrete floor. A dark red lake pooled and spread around his ruined skull.

Thurbridge made some squeak of protest or disbelief. Renee ignored him. She stared at Eddie's corpse, watching, waiting.

The dead man's throat worked, the bulge of larynx moving, as if he was trying to speak. A glottal choking gurgle issued from his slack mouth. The bulge moved again. Eddie's jaws parted, forced wider from the inside. Something emerged, struggling to pull itself free.

It was pinkish and wet, this thing birthed from death. On its bald round knob of a doll's-head, the malformed face resembled a half-melted, infantile version of Eddie's. The body was that of a plucked or newly hatched chicken, wings pasted to its sides by viscous fluids. A sodden mess of stringy feathers coated its wrinkled skin. Weak claws dug into Eddie's lips as it tried to balance upright and unstick its wings from the gluey mess of mucus and slime.

"*Ba*," Renee said, seizing it. "Corporeal strength, power of physical life." It squalled, thrashing, slick and disgusting in her grasp.

She gave it to Atensef. The mummy wrung its neck in a single violent twist. Wrenching his own jaws wide with another creak of tendon and another sifting of dusty flakes, he devoured it whole.

The professor had backed up until he was pressed to the side of the truck. His chin quivered. Tears trickled unnoticed down his sallow cheeks. A soft whimpering was the only noise he made.

Renee almost felt sorry for him. All his intelligence, all his scholarly learning and education, an entire career dedicated to this very subject . . . and none of it had prepared him to believe.

Atensef, after consuming the *Ba*, bent double. He shuddered. His withered flesh began to fill out, tissues restoring themselves.

Patches of skin peeled off in dry, papery curls and fell away to reveal smooth, unmarked tissue beneath. New nails sprouted at the ends of his fingers and toes. He slowly raised his head, then stood tall and straight.

Beautiful. Perfect. As she'd always dreamed, and known, he would be.

His shaved scalp and hawklike features gave him the regal profile of countless busts and murals. His eyes were also hawklike, dark and intense, even without benefit of kohl. His slim but muscular torso could have been a sculpture brought to life.

"And now," said Renee, still in that language as rich as the Nile valley when the pyramids were new. "That which is spirit and life, vitality. *Ka.*"

Nigel Thurbridge did not try to run or resist as the reinvigorated Prince Atensef approached with the lithe grace of one of Bast's hunting cats. Ancient but young and supple hands settled upon stooped old shoulders. The hawklike head tilted as if to better examine a choice piece of prey. Their gazes locked.

"Albert Carstairs never told you," Renee said, speaking English again. "That he could trace his ancestry back to Queen Nefertegi and her surviving daughter, did he? That's why he hid away the last piece of the puzzle, the final incantation. He didn't believe the stories, but he was afraid to risk finding out if they were true. He passed the incantation on to his own daughter for safe-keeping. Then she passed it on to hers." She gave him a razor-thin smile.

Thurbridge gasped a tremulous breath, but as he was about to exhale in another whimper, Atensef inhaled sharply.

Renee saw it happen, the stream of smoky tendrils and flickering embers that rushed out of the old man's mouth and nostrils to be drawn into Atensef's. The prince's back and neck arched. He released Thurbridge's shoulders and the professor collapsed in a loose, lifeless heap.

"Atensef," she said.

He turned toward her. His dark eyes, formerly opaque and empty, glittered with awareness. He touched her face, his fingertips gliding smoother than fine sand over her cheek, sending a delicious shiver through her body.

"It seems almost that I should know you," he said, and his voice was as she'd always dreamed and known it would be. Rich, honeyed, with a hint of exotic spices. "What is this place? How long has it been?"

"Ages have passed," Renee said. "The world you knew is gone, and Egypt is far away."

"Then what am I to do?"

"Your mother promised you a kingdom. An empire, a dynasty. She promised you wealth, fortune, power, immortality and revenge."

Atensef nodded.

"All of those will finally be yours," Renee said, then smiled. "Ours."

*

"Well, there you are," Vincent Ferreau said as the door to his private study opened. His lips pursed into a scowl. "Finally come to explain yourself, have you? It's far too late. I've already heard from Marco and from Captain—"

He glanced up and the scowl faltered into a puzzled frown as Renee strolled in with a stranger at her side.

The frown became alarm when Vincent saw that past them, his usual bodyguards were crumpled on the hall carpet. There'd been no gunfire, no sounds of a struggle, no signs of violence or bloodshed. But the guards were unquestionably dead, mouths gaping, eyes bulging.

Old though he was, there was nothing wrong with Vincent's instincts or his reflexes. He grabbed a gun secured to the underside of his desk and had it levelled at them before they'd crossed half the room.

"Hello, Grandfather," Renee said. Dark amusement danced in her tone.

Where was the bumbling but earnest family screwup he'd always known? In that moment, she looked uncannily like her mother, that Carstairs woman. Intense, focused—full of confidence and purpose.

"Not another step," he told them.

The young man with her — tall, slim, bald, foreign, aristocratic, well-dressed, but wearing ridiculous eyeliner and far too much ostentatious jewellery — took another step.

Vincent fired.

The bullet punched a hole in the man's very nice suit and rocked him back on his heels, but there was no other discernible effect.

The wound didn't even bleed. Unperturbed, the stranger continued his advance.

"This is Atensef," his granddaughter said as elegant scarab-ringed hands closed on Vincent's shoulders. "I don't know if you have much more life left in you than the professor and your goons did, but he's still hungry."

AFTERWORD

My introduction to mythology goes back to a book of Greek myths I got when I was in grade school. Since then, that initial interest has grown and diversified alongside a love of history in general into a fascination with ancient cultures.

And, when it comes to ancient cultures, few are as fascinating, impressive, and just plain COOL as the Egyptians. The style, the art, the architecture, the beast-headed gods, pharaohs and pyramids, mummification . . . they win for sheer style.

I'm also a fan of heist and action movies, and "misfit/bumbler gets revenge" stories, so I thought it might be fun to throw all that together and see what I got. This was the result.

SURVIVING FILM

THORAIYA DYER

It's the wedding dress of a dead woman.

It was saved from a flood in an attic. Meanwhile, the rest of the town, including the bride and groom, were washed away.

Katie is drunk, but not drunk enough to let me try it on.

"I never said you could take things that are currently on display," she admonishes in a whisper. I don't know why she's whispering. There's nobody to hear or see us. The high, open galleries and glass ceilings of the mid-renovation museum hold only dust motes, starlight and the bronze starfish of the sprinkler system. "What's wrong with you, anyway, wanting to try on a dead woman's dress?"

I can't tell Katie what's wrong with me. Not after what happened with Nick. She's my best friend and I need companionship.

She restores antiques and Michael needs access to the museum. She's my flatmate and I need a place to live.

"This," Michael says reverently, tracing the back of a shabby Bath chair made of leather and wood. "This is perfect, can we borrow this?"

Watching him glide about the chair, pale where Nick was dark, all moonlight and shadow like a Rembrandt come to life, I want to blurt at him: *I could love you like you've never been loved before.*

If only I could be sure.

If only I knew that you wouldn't be afraid of me.

"Better than a shopping trolley," Katie giggles; a shopping trolley is what we wheeled her home in, the last time. She wobbles a bit and her smile grows uncertain. "I have to go to the bathroom."

She leaves me alone with Michael.

Michael's our prop master. I'm the digital imaging technician. It's taken him three whole projects to notice me. We're working together on a Louis Le Prince thriller that's to start filming in three days.

It's a bit incestuous, really. Film-makers making a film about the first film-maker. Like when journalists report on celebrities asking to be left alone by journalists. Only, Le Prince supposedly got murdered by his competition before he could publicise his first moving picture, and that's never happened to the Channel 9 news anchor.

Le Prince's wife, Lizzie, blamed Thomas Edison. The director's being careful not to get sued, so Edison isn't actually shown stabbing Le Prince and chucking the body off the infamous Paris-bound train, except in the disturbed dreams of the wheelchair-bound widow.

"It's kind of moth-eaten," I say. "Makeshift. Lizzie's sons wouldn't have hammered a few old bits of wood together for her. We're talking after the First World War. She'd have had a proper chair with a metal frame."

Because I love him, I try to make him hate me. Why? I don't know. If the wry compression of his lips and the fall of his black fringe were raw images from the day's rushes, I'd advise the Director of Photography to change the lighting; I'd allow detail to be lost from the image in compression and I'd leave notes to increase the contrast in post-production, to make a monochrome God of this man, this mover and maker of things, whose essence is white hands and raven eyes.

"Most of it will be covered by the costume," he says. "Besides, authenticity is in the eye of the beholder."

I turn away from him and there's a camera, sitting with other, more modern cameras on a hardwood work table.

"A camera," I say, but Michael shakes his head.

"We've got cameras. That was the very first thing we had made. Replicas of Le Prince's cameras. They were twice the size of that one. We've got cameras coming out our ears."

He reaches out and tucks a strand of hair behind my ear.

All the stages of love thrill through me, like the stages of grief.

Denial. *He's getting a spider out of my hair, surely.* Anger. *You never gave me a clue that you liked me, too, you bastard.* Bargaining. *If I'm going to have a short life, let me at least have love.* Depression. *There is no point in any of this, he'll hate me as soon as he knows.*

Acceptance. *He's interested in me. That's all. See where it leads.*

I keep gazing at him until Katie comes trotting back into the room and we both turn towards her.

"Find anything else you want?" she asks.

Michael flicks his eyes back to me for just a fraction of a second, but it's long enough for me to go through the five stages all over again.

"No," he says.

At the same time, I say, "Yes," and pick up the too-small camera to busy my hands. It rattles softly, like there's something inside.

"Then let's get out of here," Katie says.

*

At home, days later, I slouch on the couch, oblivious to the muted television, reliving the hair-tucking moment.

Already, I forget the exquisite detail of it. If only a film could have been made of it through the lenses of my eyes. But film couldn't have captured the unexpectedness of it, the sensation in the roots of my hair, the surge of feeling and colour. Film is not life. It's a voyeur's window to the dead.

The camera from the museum is hidden behind the blender. Katie won't find it there. She never uses the blender; not since I forced her to clean it five days after she made a banana smoothie and then left it all gunked up in the sink for me to clean.

If she sees the camera, she'll demand to know why I took it when it's obviously not being used as a prop, and I can't bear to admit I was so stricken with adoration that I simply forgot to let go of it after I'd picked it up. I only had eyes—brainpower, breath— for Michael.

"I've still got my wedding dress, you know," Katie says. She's curled in the snail chair, watching episodes of *Antiques Roadshow* on her iPad. If I answer her, she won't be able to hear me, because she's got earbuds in and the volume turned up.

So I just listen, with my eyebrows quirked to show that I'm paying attention. Even if I'm not; not really, because I've heard the story before. Her voice is loud and awkward like a deaf person's.

"The drunk bastard spilled champagne down my back while we did the wedding waltz. I can't believe all those people just watched. They knew he was sleeping with her and they just watched. Like I was a soap star and my wedding was an entertaining prelude to the final, fun-filled episode."

I wasn't at Katie's wedding. As I recall, I was at home in the pit of despair. My boyfriend had dumped me in a rage, accusing me of being the one responsible. But I couldn't have been the one responsible. He was the first person I'd ever slept with. I hid in my house for four weeks, pretending to have the flu.

It felt like the flu. Coughing. Vomiting. Sleep-deprived delirium. Katie emailed me the wedding snaps and I knew that I would never get married. Nobody would ever want me, now that I was HIV-positive.

I had wanted her marriage to fail.

That is, I thought I had wanted it to fail, until she turned up on my doorstep crying and saying something about happiness being like a Gonsalves painting.

When Katie's sleeping, I creep into the kitchen and slide the camera out of the cupboard.

Inside, there's a reel, but it isn't like any film I've ever seen. More like a roll of lace. When I look closer, it's definitely sequential images, woven of something that could be spider silk. The detail is too fine for me to see.

Under a magnifying glass, I search the first image for something familiar. There's a face. It's tiny.

Fascinated, I lay the roll flat under my scanner. Length by length, with the hour growing later and later, I digitally capture the tiny frames and set my computer to compile them.

What is the stuff? Who made it? I've never heard of it, and I studied the history of film.

When it's ready, I hook it up to the projector and pull down the blind in the living room. Tinsel left over from Christmas glitters on the curtain rod holders that Katie and I can't reach, and books are stacked into skyscraper cities on the cockroach-strewn floor.

I turn off the lights. My bum hits the couch. My finger hits the preview button.

For a moment, in the white square of light, there's only the hourglass symbol of the computer thinking.

Then, a man sprawled in a ditch under a night sky. He's colourless, like an etching in glass, covered in mud and wearing a top hat.

He throws up his hands as if to shield his eyes from the light of the projector. The coincidence makes me feel queasy. The film crew must have turned a spotlight on the man. My throat tightens with the beginnings of a nervous laugh.

Then the man scrambles out of the frame, landing silently on his stomach on my cockroach-strewn floor.

My legs try to shrink up into my body like a cartoon elephant avoiding a mouse. The tightness in my throat turns to a choke. I'm freaked, but I've never been a screamer. If I'm to die of unexpected supernatural phenomena, it will be in silence.

Silence surrounds the ghost as it rises shakily to its knees.

"*Je suis où?*" the man asks, taking off his hat and holding it to his heart.

His words are soft. They are the only sound he makes as he clambers to his feet, an apparition sans-sound-effects, like an unfinished film. He puts no weight on his left leg.

"Who are you?" I ask in reply, though I know who it is. I recognise the tall, straight figure, the ardent eyes, the angular cheeks above steel wool mutton chops.

"I am Louis Aimé Augustin Le Prince."

Immediately, my sanity falls under suspicion. If I'm to have waking nightmares about someone, who more likely than the man whose story has been uppermost in my mind for months? The man whose story made me cry in a particularly poignant pre-menstrual moment?

"I'm Chrissy Wick," I say. "And you've been dead for almost a hundred and twenty-five years."

"Dead? Is this death? Perhaps it is. If so, why do I not rest?"

"What happened to you?" I ask.

"They came into my compartment to kill me," Le Prince says. "When I leaped in desperation from the train, I landed on my valise, splitting it. It was late afternoon in the French countryside.

When I was sure no bones were broken, I thrust the design papers into muddy puddles, so that the ink bled off the paper, and then I shredded them with my fingers. I left my valise behind and ran in the direction of Dijon."

"Couldn't you have gone into another train carriage? Somewhere with witnesses? Stayed in the company of strangers until you reached Paris?"

"I'm afraid I could only have endangered their lives as well as mine. The men chasing me were professionals. Lean as lawyers. Poised on their toes. They were on my trail mere moments after I abandoned my valise. They called out, keeping in range of one another, coordinating their hunt. I could smell their tobacco. I could hear them, rustling like snakes. They circled, forcing me away from the town. When night fell, I found myself in ill-tended farmland with not so much as a full moon to keep me from breaking my leg in a bog-hole."

"Who sent them?"

"I cannot know. Exhausted, in agony, I fell into a ditch, shivering in the dark, clutching the camera. All I could think of was Lizzie and how I would never see her again. Then *they* started rising from the ditch. First I thought they were shapes in the fog."

"They?"

Le Prince laughs.

"The ghosts of starved Parisians. Louis Napoleon led the Second Empire into a disastrous war against Prussia in 1870. The Prussians captured him. They besieged Paris. I was a volunteer for the National Guard, but my bayonet rusted while I buried the victims of malnutrition, exposure and smallpox. And some of those ghosts remembered me."

This isn't a story I could have invented. I don't know where Prussia is. Perhaps I've fallen asleep with a documentary playing on the telly.

I feel calm, though. I feel awake. My heart beat is slow and steady.

"Did the ghosts hide you from the men that were hunting you?"

"They were insubstantial. They could not conceal me like cloaks. Indeed, they said that the men could not perceive them. Only the ones who cared for them in life could see them in death, they said, and I had tended their wounds and taken the gnawed corpses of rats from their frostbitten hands. They entered into the camera, which was a mock-up, a mostly empty box, and they whispered to me to turn the lens on myself."

"And the lens captured you. I mean, really captured you."

"I had dreamed of a camera that could truly capture life. It was great joke to play on me. They told me the words of the spell I must utter: *There is no 'I'/ but the eye / of the loving beholder.*"

"The men never found the camera."

"Nor did the police, evidently. But now, you say, my Lizzie is dead. All who cared for me are gone, and I shall be visible to no-one but the holder of the camera."

"I'm sorry. I think you still have family who care for you. We had to get their permission to work on a film about you."

The ghost turns his back to me. I can still see his face, sort of inside-out. I swallow hard and look away from it.

"My heart is breaking," he says hoarsely. "But it seems I am no longer able to perish of such an affliction. I must find the place where her bones lie. Perhaps my devotion can raise her again."

He limps away in silence, a tall man in a ruined three-piece suit, bog-water leaking from his leather shoes.

"I hope you find her," I call.

He passes through the wall into Katie's room. She's sleeping. According to Le Prince, she can't see him, anyway.

I wonder if she'll stir. I wonder if she'll dream of him. Perhaps she is, already. Perhaps I am.

The Le Prince film starts shooting in the morning.

*

An afternoon thunderstorm rumbles.

The day has been a blur of call times and insertions, wet, whirring golf buggies and sprinting gofers shielding their heads from the preliminary drizzle with their jacket sleeves. A woman in a red coat exercises three muzzled greyhounds in the wind tunnels between sound stages. Traffic rumbles on the other side of a sound barrier.

I have ten minutes to spare.

Like a programmed machine, I navigate towards the espresso van, caffeine priority one. I half-expect to see the ghost of Le Prince. Perhaps the lead actor, an approximation of the real thing. I'm so jumpy about the prospect of seeing either of them that I forget to be jumpy about the prospect of seeing Michael.

He's there.

"Hey, Chrissy," he says, sipping, his sharp nose dividing the rising steam of a flat white with 'no sugar' checked on the side.

He likes me. Everything about him is warm, despite the greyness of the day. I pay for my short black and move away from the queue. Michael moves with me.

"Monsieur," I say, bunging on an accent. "How do you find your beverage?"

"Hot," he says, and kisses me behind a concrete pylon.

I want to cling to him, but my arms are spread wide to keep from knocking him senseless with my laptop bag or scalding him with coffee. He's teetering the same way. We press together, mirrored in a strange, crucified pose.

His lips are soft. My skin tingles. There's pleasure and paralysing fear.

He's kissed me. I have to tell him. I can't let him kiss me without knowing.

But my memory plays me a best-of reel. Nick, smiling for the cameras, holding up some golden statuette while I hang back in the shadows. His ex-wife turning up at the award ceremony for the Deadlies, brushing crumbs off the kids, turning cold when the little tykes recognise me; run to me.

I don't want my children around her, she tells him. *She could infect them. It's not safe. I won't have them visiting you if she's living in your house. It's her or them. You choose.*

And there's no choice. Not really. My Nick, so careful, so loving, so determined that my being positive wouldn't make any difference, closes the door on me for the last time, even though he thinks we're soul mates.

Soon. I will tell Michael soon.

I lean back against the pylon with my eyes closed, sick with my own cowardice. There's sudden lightness and coolness. I open my eyes.

Michael is gone.

I check the time. Four minutes to get to the train station set. I pull out my laptop and quickly load the new call sheet.

No changes.

Yet everything is changed.

*

I play the scene again, but Le Prince isn't in it.

Only fog and the long grass, mysteriously lit.

It isn't possible. I load the original scans of the spider web film. Even they are somehow altered. I start scanning it again, and Le Prince just isn't there.

"What's up?" Katie asks, yawning. "Go to bed. It's late. You've done enough staring at a computer today."

She's not usually allowed to hang around the set, but today she wanted to see her Bath chair in action, so Michael scored her an invite and she turned up around lunchtime. The chair gave a stunning performance. All three visible inches of it.

I think Katie was disappointed all over again by how boring and technical she thinks my job is. She doesn't understand, though she should. When the cameras are rolling, history is running through me.

She likes to keep history at a distance. She prefers picking bones out of the soil to picking them out of her own self.

"Gone," I mutter. "Like it was never there."

"What's gone? Don't tell me you've stuffed up on the first day."

She makes no sense to me. I can't think straight. My hands want to stay busy. If they don't, they'll pick up the phone and call Michael.

Then it will be over and I'll be on the other side of the camera. I'll be like Le Prince, a wandering ghost that nobody can love because I'm not really amongst the living.

"G'night," Katie sighs, seizing my head in both hands and kissing the crown of it.

I should tell her.

I can't tell her.

At least when Michael is gone, Katie will still be here with me. I should just get it over and done with.

Alone, I pick up my phone with clammy hands. I've never called him, though I've had his number since the emergency contact memo went around.

"Yeah?" he says sleepily, and I curse myself for forgetting the time.

"Michael, it's Chrissy," I say in a small voice.

"Who? I can't hear you."

I'm not sure I can bear to make myself louder. What if Katie hears me? It was a stupid idea to tell him over the phone, but it's too late to hang up.

"It's Chrissy," I half-shout.

There are rustling sounds, like he's sitting up in bed.

"Chrissy," he says, yawning. "How are you?"

"Nervous," I say.

"How come?"

"I have to tell you something."

"Yeah?"

"Michael, I really like you."

"Ditto. Don't be nervous about that."

"I have HIV."

Silence. Like LePrince's limping ghost. Like the silence in outer space between two cracked and crater-pocked planets that kissed once and then flew away in opposite directions forever.

"I just thought you should know," I say, and my voice has gone all barely audible again, but somehow he hears me.

"Um. Okay. Thanks."

I read a thousand things into those four syllables. They're flat. Deep. Dark. Disappointed. He's drawing away.

"See you tomorrow?" I ask, wildly and irrationally hopeful. He just needs time to come to terms with it. To think it over. To see me skipping about the set without a care in the world; to realise it's not a death sentence these days, just a chronic illness to be managed. Nick took a few days to accept it, didn't he? I squash the urge to babble about how I'm not a junkie or a whore.

"Yeah. See you," he says.

He'll be fine with it. Tomorrow. We'll talk again tomorrow.

*

In the afternoon break, he isn't at the coffee van.

He isn't anywhere that I can see. I feel hollow, like a log eaten from the inside. The little viruses within are laughing diabolically.

I order a short black and a flat white with no sugar. Michael must already be at the carriageworks. The focus puller and the clapper zoom past in a buggy and I flag them down to beg for a ride.

They tease me mercilessly. I've never brought a coffee to any of them. But they take me straight to Michael. He's showing an actor how to operate the crank of a prop that's all gears and blue light through falling glass positives.

"Your coffee," I say to Michael, holding it out to him.

His face goes blank. His fingers curl away behind his back, as though they're slugs that I've poured salt on.

"No," he says. "I mean, no, thank you."

I stare at him. The actor turns, surprise on his face, the very image of the young Le Prince, but I can't peel my eyes away from Michael. It seems like we face each other for an eternity.

"Take it," I say, trying to pretend that he's joking, holding it out to him.

He steps back. My grip loosens on the cup; I'm in disbelief. He has to take it.

It falls to the ground. The actor gasps. An assistant zeroes in on the mess, ready to clean it up.

"You shouldn't touch that," Michael says quickly to the assistant.

When I meet his eyes again, there's anger in his. As though my tainted blood is a malevolent creature, possessing me, eager to use me to strike him down, that I've somehow failed to protect him.

I want to be angry at Michael but I am too hurt. I can't breathe.

I can't go home, either. That would be weakness. I am strong.

First, I envision my immune system, fighting even though it is corrupted. It's fighting. It's fighting. I am fighting.

"I'll clean it up," I say, and do.

Then, I focus on my next task; adjusting the variables in six high-definition Viper Filmstream cameras that are being positioned in the carriageworks for the exploding dynamo scene. The cinematographer knows what he wants but the camera operator doesn't know how to get it; not since they took her 35 mm cameras away from her. We are soldiers in a trench together. I am needed.

I am needed. I am needed.

Glimpses of Michael are like knives in the back. He avoids looking at me. I avoid looking at him. It will break my concentration. I have to focus on the cameras. The footage. How the sensors are reacting. How close we are to capturing the perfect shot.

Capturing life.

Somehow, I keep it together until I am home.

Katie's had a long, interesting day at work sorting boxes of tinsmithing tools, and she wants to tell me all about them.

This time, she notices that I'm not listening.

"Did something happen with Michael?" she asks. "Did he turn out to be an arsehole? Want me to go and take the Bath chair back?"

"No." I manage a sort-of-laugh. "Actually, he's finished with the little camera that we borrowed. I wonder if I could borrow your keys and code and take it back to the museum tonight."

"Tonight? What for? Give it to me. I'll take it to work in the morning."

My brain won't come up with a reasonable excuse, so I spew out the truth.

"Please, Katie. Tonight. I want to look at the wedding dress again."

She bites her lip.

"I'll come with you. Even if you won't tell me what's really going on."

On the pedestrian bridge that leads to the museum, her quick little footsteps in expensive heels make a patter like my heartbeat. Inside, the renovations are nearing completion. Some of the walls are painted. Some of the signage is re-hung.

The wedding dress falls from the shoulders of the mannequin like blossoms from apple trees.

"Please, Katie," I whisper. "Let me try it on."

"Why don't we go home and you can try on mine? You can keep it."

I touch the glass of the display case with the fingertips of my left hand.

"You know what I love best about movies?"

"No. What?"

"Being able to rewind it back to the beginning."

If only I could undo what had been done. But that can't happen, any more than a young and virginal bride can undo the wrath of a river breaking its banks.

"Let me take the camera," Katie suggests. "I'll put it back."

But I hold it out of her reach.

"Katie, please let me try on the dress. Just long enough for you to take a picture. With this camera."

"With that camera? It doesn't work, Chrissy."

"Will you just try? Will you promise me you'll try, and if it works you'll take the film out and scan it with my computer and project it onto the wall?"

"That sounds hard. I'm scared of your computer. If it works, you can do that part."

There's resignation in her voice. I hug her, squeezing as hard as I can.

"Thank you," I say. "I love you."

She sighs and unlocks the display case.

"Yeah. Love you, too."

As a ghost, I will be harmless.

Yet, according to Le Prince, I will be visible to those who truly care about me. Katie loves me. I will still live with her, after she's resurrected me from the spiderweb inside the box.

Nick loves me. We're soul mates, he said. He would have stayed with me, if he wasn't afraid for his children. He still loves me. I might marry him, once I'm safe. He'll be able to see me. How beautiful my ghost will be, in the doomed wedding dress in the moonlight. Film is not life, but I can still find love on the other side of the camera.

The dress fits me as though it was made for me.

"I'm ready," I say. "That is, there is no 'I' but the eye of the loving beholder."

And I smile.

AFTERWORD

I was trying to explore an Australian myth that is also persistent across many cultures—Hindi, Swahili, Native American—the myth that a photograph can steal away all or part of the soul.

I couldn't resist mixing that up with the legend, or, more accurately, the suspicion, that Louis Le Prince—inventor of the motion picture—was murdered by agents of Thomas Edison.

And ghosts are nice and mythological, too. I really enjoyed myself with this one, though my inexperience with the film industry possibly still shows. Much gratitude to Claire Corbett for her assistance. Any errors, of course, remain mine.

AND THE DEAD SHALL BE RAISED INCORRUPTIBLE

KAT OTIS

Ann Amelia was skimming through a copy of the *Evening Standard*, waiting to start her last tour of the day, when she noticed the article. She read it through twice, hoping she'd misunderstood it the first time, then left the porter's lodge to find David. The balding human porter was just on the other side of the cemetery's wrought iron gates, handing out release forms to the waiting tourists.

She couldn't go out to him—even just approaching the cemetery gates made gravelings relive their deaths—so Ann Amelia studied the tourists while she impatiently waited for David to come back inside. One of them had to be investigative reporter Eric Taylor. The idiot who'd written the article, declaring his intention to sneak away from his tour and spend the night in Highgate's East Cemetery. The idiot who was going to get himself killed if she didn't stop him.

Her bet was on the sandy-haired man chatting to the other tourists and writing their responses down in a notebook.

As soon as David came back through the gates, Ann Amelia hurried to his side. "That one—Eric Taylor—he can't come in."

"Why not?" David asked, turning to look back at the man.

"Didn't you see his article?"

David shrugged. "He signed the release, the same as everyone else."

"I don't care. Cite health and safety, or whatever you have to say to get rid of him."

"If he's really a reporter, he'll throw a fit. He's over eighteen; we have no legal grounds to refuse him entrance—"

"David!" Ann Amelia snapped. "I'd rather him throw a fit over being denied access than the world throw a fit when he ends up dead." David was old enough to remember the public outcry over the series of deaths four decades earlier that had nearly seen the cemetery closed. There had even been talk of disinterring the bodies and razing the cemetery to the ground.

David sighed. "All right, I'll try to talk him out of it. But if I can't, you're just going to have to keep an eye on him."

Ann Amelia watched, eyes narrowed, as David went out to talk to the reporter. *Just.* As if keeping an eye on *any* of them was that easy. There was a reason she took the last tour every day, and it wasn't only because she, alone of all the gravelings, actually enjoyed interacting with humans. No, she didn't trust the others to keep track of all their tourists. During the earlier hours, there was always time for her to gather up anyone who'd gone astray, but sunset came too close for comfort to the last tour. She had enough trouble keeping her tourists safe on a regular evening, without adding a suicidal reporter to the mix.

"So, that's the fresh meat," a voice behind her said.

Ann Amelia didn't bother to turn around. "Not if I can help it, Liam."

The other graveling took up a position on her right, studying the reporter. "You're such a bleeding heart."

"Does everyone else know, already?" Ann Amelia asked, ignoring the familiar insult.

"Of course. Katherine saw the paper before you did."

And Katherine was the biggest gossip in the entire cemetery. Ann Amelia shook her head. "How are the ghosts?"

"Riled up," Liam answered. "The underslabbers, too."

The underslabbers had too much respect for her to openly attack a tour under her protection. The ghosts were another matter—the underslabbers only hated the living, but the ghosts hungered for flesh. "Riled up enough to manifest before dusk?"

Liam shrugged. "In the shadows, maybe. But most of them are too busy fighting over the Privilege to waste their strength manifesting."

The Privilege. That wasn't what Ann Amelia called it, but it had been decades since the ghosts had listened to anything she had to say. They saw her vigilance in protecting the humans as selfishness, and a betrayal. Maybe it was, maybe it wasn't. Ann Amelia only knew that she couldn't stand aside and do nothing while the ghosts cut more lives tragically short.

David opened the gates and began ushering the tourists through. Eric Taylor didn't so much as pause before stepping inside, his gaze fixed on Ann Amelia and Liam. The others milled through more slowly, not quite certain where they should be going, drifting along in Eric's wake.

"Well, enjoy," Liam said, touching the brim of an imaginary hat before turning and heading down the wide, paved avenue that led deeper into the cemetery.

"Can he just *do* that?" asked a grey-haired woman who looked like she'd be more at home surrounded by grandchildren than tramping through an overgrown cemetery.

"He's a graveling, ma'am," Ann Amelia said. "We live here—Highgate holds no secrets from us."

"A graveling?" The grandmotherly woman shook her head. "You both look human to me."

The tourists began gathering around Ann Amelia, murmuring amongst themselves and gawking at the handful of proud mausoleums that crowded the cemetery's entrance. The reporter was still scribbling away in his notebook. Ann Amelia craned her neck, trying to read the upside-down writing, then realized he was quoting her. *Highgate holds no secrets from us.* She grimaced, then remembered the rest of the tourists and hastily smoothed her expression.

"Welcome to Highgate East. My name is Ann Amelia and I'll be your guide today. I ask you all to remember that, while every effort has been made to provide a safe environment for this tour, the cemetery *is* a dangerous place. Please remain with the tour at *all* times." She gave Eric a pointed look; he affected not to notice.

"I'd also like to remind you that photography is strictly prohibited during the tour, with the exception of Marx's monument."

"Why's that?" drawled a man in an unfamiliar accent—she might have spent the entire tour trying to analyse it, if it weren't for the reporter.

Ann Amelia gave him her best chagrined smile. "Most of the cemetery's residents lived and died before photography was widespread. We find the experience of being photographed rather disturbing. But Marx doesn't mind, so we make an exception for him." Complete rubbish, of course. Karl Marx had never risen—though none of them knew why—so there was no ghost to mind.

"So, if you're a graveling, where exactly do you, ah . . . " the strangely accented man hesitated, obviously searching for the right words. "Live?"

"My grave is at the corner of Kirkaldy and the Opened Casket," Ann Amelia said, watching Eric's pen fly across the pages of his notebook.

"Opened casket?" That came from a younger woman, who looked delightedly scandalised as she clung to the arm of a bored young man.

Ann Amelia fell back on the safety of routine, projecting her voice so the whole group could hear. "There are many opened caskets and graves in Highgate East. The fence path by the north wall is full of them, but we won't be going that way—there are too many underslabbers. They mostly stay underground during the day, but they'll come out if they hear travellers on their paths." As she spoke, she started walking backwards, guiding her tourists past a line of dirty stone angels and crosses, liberally covered with wildflowers.

"You mean there are paths where the underslabbers live?"

"The underslabbers do have physical bodies, so they create paths to and from the graves where they live. As do the gravelings," Ann Amelia said, gesturing at some of the dirt paths that branched off the main avenue and disappeared into the shadows.

Her group looked around sceptically, and Ann Amelia didn't blame them. The forest had grown wild in the six decades since the groundskeepers had left. The area around the gates was largely still intact, but the rest of the cemetery was in ruins. Trees grew through graves and pushed down headstones, ivy cracked the statues and choked the slabs that once covered crypts, and high grasses swallowed entire ranks of headstones. It was a wilderness of life and death intertwined.

"Is it true that underslabbers and gravelings are related?" Eric asked.

"There are some apparent similarities between us," Ann Amelia side-stepped the dangerous question with the ease of long practice.

"*Apparent* but not actual?" Eric persisted.

"We're both corporeal, as opposed to the ghosts of the dead buried here," Ann Amelia said, then changed the subject before he could get in another follow-up question. "Speaking of which, if everyone will look to your right, we're just approaching the monument to Karl Marx. If anyone would like to take photos, now's your chance."

Ann Amelia moved to the side of the group, so she wouldn't be caught in their photos by accident. She kept watch as the tourists photographed the tall, boxy monument, decorated with an image of Marx's head and his final exhortation: WORKERS OF ALL LANDS UNITE. Some of the tourists took turns posing by the monument, while others began stealthily photographing nearby graves. Ann Amelia let them—she was more concerned about the reporter than a few illicit photos.

Eric sidled up beside her. "So how well do you know Marx?"

Ann Amelia gave him a sharp look. "What do you mean?"

He smiled, innocently. "Gravelings can talk to ghosts, can't they?"

"How well do you know all the staff who work for your newspaper?"

"I'll answer your questions if you answer mine," Eric offered.

"No, thank you."

"Just think about it."

"I really have no interest in knowing anything about you," Ann Amelia lied. She would have loved to know what Eric thought he'd accomplish by sneaking away from the tour—and why he was doing it. She'd half-hoped he would make his move at Marx's monument, when there was still time to get the others to safety and search the cemetery for him, but he obviously had no intention of obliging her.

Eric shrugged and started to move away.

"Ten minutes," Ann Amelia said, impulsively. "I'll give you ten minutes to interview me if you leave when the gates close tonight."

He was quiet for a moment, considering her offer. "You'll answer any question I ask?"

Ann Amelia hesitated.

"I won't be difficult," he said. "Easy questions only."

"I'm not sure you and I agree on the definition of *easy*," she said. The questions he'd already asked were dangerous enough to give lie to his reassurance.

"How about an example? Rumour has it that despite your youthful appearance, you're actually the oldest of the gravelings. Can you confirm or deny?"

Confirm or deny? She could do neither and both. She was the oldest of the surviving gravelings, but she wasn't the first. Ann Amelia had only to close her eyes to see Jonathan again. He'd taken flesh only moments before her and they'd spent a whole glorious summer together, learning the rules of their new existence.

Then he'd tried to step through the cemetery gates and she'd watched in horror as his body began to warp and decay around him. If he'd pulled back and given up, he would have at least survived as an underslabber—his body ruined even though his spirit still clung to it—but he was too stubborn for that. He'd pushed onward through the gates and left her behind. Alone.

"Everyone knows that no graveling's record goes back as far as mine," she said. The newspapers occasionally ran specials on Highgate at Halloween; they would put old photos of gravelings side-by-side with new, showing them unaging through the decades, and speculate on what they did or didn't know about the cemetery's undead residents.

"That's not a real answer."

"It's the best I can give you." She didn't talk about Jonathon with anyone, especially not a human who could use the knowledge of how to kill a graveling against the rest of them.

"The best you're *willing* to give me, maybe. No deal."

Ann Amelia sighed, and Eric moved away to take his own photos. She gave her tourists a minute longer, until the bored young man turned and brazenly took a photo of her. For a second she couldn't breathe and her mind reeled with panic, just as it had done in the last moments of her life. Then the feeling passed and she glared at the offending tourist. "If you're all *quite* finished?"

At least his girlfriend had the grace to blush and snatch the camera out of his hands. The rest of the tourists didn't seem to notice the exchange as they gathered around her again. Ann Amelia gave the young man one last Look, then started walking backwards again.

"Is there any chance we'll see a ghost?" That came from a man near the rear of the group, who kept looking hopefully over his shoulder.

I pray to God not. Ann Amelia forced a smile to her face. "The ghosts only come out at night, if they come out at all. Some of them sulk in their graves and won't speak to you no matter how often you visit."

"Ghosts *sulk*?" A few of the tourists laughed.

"The newly dead tend to sulk for weeks, if not months, before they finally admit they've risen." Ann Amelia waved a hand at some of the newer graves on her right. "The older ghosts—the ones whose headstones have sunk beneath the earth or whose inscriptions have worn away—those are the ones that sulk the most."

It really was ridiculous. But some ghosts were content just to stay in their graves until they faded away into nothingness. The very thought sent shivers down Ann Amelia's spine. That was *true* death.

"What about pre-World War Two, before the first ghost sightings here? Were all the ghosts sulking then?" Eric asked.

Ann Amelia chewed on her lower lip for a moment, trying to decide how to answer that. "No. Not sulking." Would the truth help her or would it only encourage him? Any answer was treading a dangerous line; she risked giving out information that might be used against the cemetery. But the reporter was as stubborn as Jonathan had been; continuing to stone-wall him would not convince him to leave. "Pre-World War Two, there were still full-time groundskeepers here. Ghosts apparently don't rise in well-tended cemeteries."

The reporter's pen began flying across his page. "Why?"

Ann Amelia shrugged. "God only knows."

"And after the ghosts? Then came the gravelings and the underslabbers?"

"That's how it happened here," she allowed, glancing over her shoulder. They were nearing the old eastern gates, which gave her the perfect excuse to change the subject again before the reporter could pressure her for more. "Let's stop here for a moment. I want to draw your attention to the inscription on this grave slab here. *Resting where no shadows fall.* Well, most of Highgate is wooded and lays in shadow year-round, which makes it easier for the ghosts to manifest. Exceptions to this are the areas around the gates—here, obviously, being one of them—and the field of flowers, which you'll see as we make our way to Fireman's Court."

The tourists obediently peered around, looking at the inscriptions on the grave, a few wandering closer to the gates to inspect them. Ann Amelia let them for a minute, then said, "From here on out, the footing will get a little uneven, so please, everyone watch your step."

She turned so that she was actually walking forward, though it made her shoulders itch to have her back to the tourists. This would be the perfect opportunity for Eric to slip away. But he fell in at her side and listened attentively, taking notes as she pointed out various landmarks to the group. She'd almost begun to relax when he jumped into one of her pauses, pointing at a side-path. "What's down that way?"

"That's not part of the regular tour," she said, shortly. "If you want to investigate other parts of the cemetery, you can pay to have a tour specially designed for you."

"Hmm, I haven't had much luck arranging for a designer tour," Eric said, his eyes crinkling in amusement.

Of course he hadn't. Ann Amelia could just imagine the porters' reactions when he had begun listing the places he wished to visit. She was certain that list included all the most dangerous spots in the cemetery—perpetually shady areas, where the underslabbers lurked and it was dark enough for the most strong-willed ghosts to manifest by day as well as night.

"Maybe I could help with that," Ann Amelia said, slowly. Was this her way out? A private tour of wherever he wanted to go, but at least it would be in daylight? She could keep the underslabbers from him, so long as it was light out, but she wasn't so certain about the ghosts, especially now that they'd gotten their hopes up.

The light was beginning to fade, twilight stealing over the

cemetery. She looked over her shoulder to count her tourists. All there. But behind them, in the shadows, she could sense movement. None of the ghosts had manifested—yet—but they were all watching and eager for the chance to seize any unwary human who wandered too far away from her.

Eric still hadn't responded to her offer. When she turned back to him, he was studying her with a thoughtful expression on his face. He was interested, but not convinced. Not yet.

"Look, what good is finding out the truth if you end up dead?" Ann Amelia asked.

"Death isn't the end of everything—this cemetery is proof of that." Eric shrugged, casually, but there was pain in his voice as he added, "Besides, I'm already dying. Pancreatic cancer. I've got three to six months, tops."

Ann Amelia bit her lip. That would be a horrible death—fully as bad as her own had been, slowly suffocating as polio paralysed her. But letting the ghosts take him would be far worse. "Not all deaths are the same."

The gleam returned to his eyes. "Yes, and this way I'll die on my own terms."

She'd lost him. Furious with herself, she lengthened her stride to put some space between her and the reporter, and raised her voice. "Now, to your left you'll see we're approaching Firemen's Court. There's not a lot of space in the court itself, so please wait at the benches and allow just a few people to go in at a time."

Eric would have been one of the first to go out onto the paved square of the Firemen's Court, but she caught hold of his arm.

"Yes?" He raised his eyebrows at her.

"If you sneak away now, you won't be the only one to die."

"If that's supposed to scare me—"

"No. It's the honest-to-God truth." She let go of him and struggled to keep her voice down so she didn't frighten the other tourists. "Stay with the tour." It was hard to admit defeat, but she forced the words out. "Stay and I won't let them throw you out when the gates close."

He grinned. "Your word on it?"

"My *word*," she spat.

"All right, then." He turned towards Firemen's Court. "That wasn't so hard now, was it?"

Ann Amelia dug her fingernails into her palms. "I'm trying to save you."

"I don't need to be saved."

"Then I'm going to save as many as I can," she said, stepping away from him before she could lose control of her temper and say—or do—something she shouldn't.

The shadows lengthened as her tourists took their turns investigating Firemen's Court, lingering by the marble slab that commemorated London's Fire Brigade and bending over to read the bronze plaques on the foot-high stone that bordered the court. Ann Amelia wanted to shout at them to hurry, but she held her tongue and instead kept a wary eye out for manifesting ghosts. She could *feel* them all around her, hungering to have flesh once more.

Finally, after what seemed like forever, the last of her group took their turn. She gathered them all up, hoping she didn't look as anxious as she felt. "That was the last stop on our tour. If everyone would please follow me in an orderly fashion, we'll head back to Swain's Lane."

"I thought tours were longer," complained the man who'd hoped to see a ghost.

"During the summer we sometimes close later, but you can see the light's failing," Ann Amelia said. "It is absolutely critical that all humans be out of the cemetery before dark."

"It wasn't always forbidden," Eric said loudly enough that the whole group could hear.

"True, before the Friends of Highgate Cemetery acquired the freehold, all sorts of people were in and out at night." Ann Amelia shrugged with a casualness she didn't feel. "More came in than ever made it back out. Hence we no longer admit anyone except on guided tours."

"Well, *I* felt safe the entire time," the grandmotherly old woman declared.

"Why thank you, ma'am," Ann Amelia said, dredging up a smile. "I'm glad that you felt like you were in good hands with me. Please tell your friends. Or even better, make a donation to the Friends of Highgate Cemetery on your way out."

Though she was alert to the possibility of trouble, none of the ghosts manifested before she got her group back to the gates. David was waiting in the porter's lodge and relief crossed his face when he came out to see the reporter was still with her. The tourists all filed out, except Eric, who stayed planted by her side. David frowned and opened his mouth to say something.

Ann Amelia shook her head.

David's frown deepened. "I'll just lock up for the night, shall I?"

"Unless you've changed your mind?" Ann Amelia asked Eric.

"Not unless you've changed yours? I want the truth—I don't care how I get it."

She wished she could. She wished she *dared*. But to give Eric the answers he sought would be as dangerous as letting him disappear—more so, maybe. "Close the gates, David." When he looked like he might protest, she added, "Hurry, please. The ghosts are restless tonight."

David hesitated a little longer, then bowed his head and locked the gate behind him. He looked back several times as he left.

"So, what's next?" Eric asked, for all the world as if she was still playing the part of his tour guide.

Ann Amelia glanced around at the ghosts, shimmering on the edge of manifestation. "This is a complete and utter waste."

"What are you talking about?" Eric demanded.

"Your death." Liam said as he emerged from behind the porter's lodge, the other gravelings trailing in his wake.

"Not just his," Ann Amelia said, regarding the group warily. Most of them shared Liam's amusement at her squeamishness, as they called it. They deferred to her because she was the eldest, but there were so many things they disagreed on that the gulf between them was unbridgeable. She and Jonathan had taken flesh accidentally, drawn to a pair of teenagers exploring one another's bodies under the light of the moon, but the other gravelings had all taken flesh with the full knowledge that they were committing murder. "Who won?"

"Christopher," Liam said.

Christopher. He wasn't strong-willed enough to oust Eric from his flesh. "We'll lose them both."

Liam shrugged. "I know. But the ghosts don't care—they won't let an opportunity like this slip away."

Eric yelped, grabbing for her arm. Ann Amelia spun, heart pounding, then relaxed when she realised that none of the ghosts had manifested.

No, he had been frightened by the appearance of the underslabbers.

They were terrible to look at—a hideous mockery of human form, features twitching and sliding across their faces, never quite settling on one visage. Flesh dripped from their limbs, mostly hidden by the rags of their clothing. Few if any were capable of human speech anymore. The older they got, the more they disintegrated, until they fell to living pieces—eternally caught between life and death.

"What happened to them?" Eric whispered.

Ann Amelia sighed. There was no reason to lie to him—it was far too late for him to escape. "Ghosts aren't always able to properly possess a human body; sometimes the original inhabitants are just too strong to completely subdue. So now their bodies decay by daylight, when their hold is the weakest. We call them underslabbers because hiding underground helps, but it's not enough to save them."

"Possess?" Eric looked her up and down. "You're a ghost, possessing someone's body?"

She nodded. "When spirit is stronger than flesh, we can reshape the bodies to look as we did during our lives."

Ann Amelia waited, expectantly, for Eric's nerve to break. Everyone tried to run once they realised what was about to happen. The ghosts were expecting it, too—they began closing in around the gravelings in a tight circle. A few even manifested, translucent images shimmering into existence in a pale mockery of the forms they had worn during life.

Eric took a step backwards, then planted his feet in the grass and flipped to a new page in his notebook. "So it began with the ghosts rising?" His voice shook a little, but strengthened as he continued. "Then possessing human bodies, with varying degrees of success?"

Ann Amelia stared at him, unable to understand why he wasn't trying to save himself. "Yes. And tonight one of those ghosts is going to possess *your* body."

"Good luck with that, by the way," Eric said. "So, were you the one who figured out how to possess people? Since no graveling's record goes back as far as yours?"

"You know no one is going to ever see your notebook, don't you?" Ann Amelia asked, looking around to see the other gravelings had pressed in closer to the reporter, curious now. The ghosts maintained their distance, apparently willing to wait for the night to deepen—so long as their prey showed no sign of trying to escape. Possessions done during twilight hours had less chance of succeeding than those done after full dark.

"So why not answer my questions?"

"She was the second," Liam said, and Eric's gaze snapped to him. "Jonathon was the first, but he's long gone—he tried to leave the cemetery and neither flesh nor spirit survived."

The other gravelings murmured their disgust and Ann Amelia found herself defending Jonathon, as she always did. "Don't you judge him! All of you made a choice to take flesh again, but we just wanted to *feel* again—to try something we weren't old enough to do in life—we didn't know we were killing them!"

"Bleeding heart," Liam said, smirking.

"So you possessed someone by accident?" Eric asked. "And afterwards found yourself trapped?"

"Jonathon found a way to undo it, at least in part," Ann Amelia whispered, mesmerised by the movement of Eric's pen. "But it didn't save the boy, like we hoped it would. His spirit was already gone; there was nothing left to reclaim the flesh. And then they were both gone." Leaving her alone for fifty long years. Yes, other ghosts had followed her example and taken flesh, but for all that they had defied death, none of them were interested in *living*. It was as if, having already lived full lives, they were now contemptuous of all things human.

"A waste," Liam said, shaking his head. "Jonathon was given immortality and he just threw it away."

"There's more than one kind of immortality," Eric said as he closed his notebook and tucked his pen into its spiral binding. Then, to Ann Amelia's surprise, he turned to her and held out his notebook. "I want you to have this."

"Why me?" Ann Amelia demanded, taking the notebook.

"Because you tried to save me—you wanted to make a difference." Eric turned towards the ghosts and pulled his camera out of the pocket of his pea coat. "Whenever you're ready."

Ghosts began manifesting by the dozens as Eric lifted up his camera. The flash went off and Ann Amelia flinched backwards, dropping the notebook as she raised her arms to protect her eyes.

When there were no more flashes, she cautiously lowered her arms and blinked away the afterimages. The ghosts had scattered, but Eric's reprieve only lasted a few moments. They manifested again and Christopher surged forward into Eric's body.

Eric fell to the ground, thrashing about and trying to scream, but no sound emerged from his tortured throat. Ann Amelia approached him carefully and used her foot to nudge him over onto his back, so she could watch the battle as it raged across his face. Her stomach lurched as his features fought—and failed—to rearrange themselves into Christopher's form.

"It's not too late," she told them. "One of you must yield, so the other can survive. One of you. *Either* of you. Don't be stubborn— don't let yourself be stuck in-between like this forever."

"They won't listen to you," Liam said. "They never do."

"This time is *different*." Ann Amelia clenched her hands into fists again and struggled against the urge to kick the body writhing on the ground before her. She wasn't sure who she was angrier with—Christopher, who didn't care what happened to the rest of them so long as he got flesh, or Eric, who wouldn't let her save him. "He's famous, people will notice." She turned to the manifested ghosts. "You're going to destroy us all!"

"*You all*," the ghosts said, their voices the whisper of the wind. "*It matters not to us.*"

"There will be no more bodies for you," Ann Amelia snapped. "No more possessions, no more chances, no more *Privileges*!"

"*There will always be fools*," the ghosts said. One by one, they began to fade away, flitting back to their graves now that the entertainment was over.

The underslabber that had been Eric, that had been Christopher, groaned in pain.

"Damn you," Ann Amelia whispered. "Damn you all."

"Ann Amelia—" Liam began, putting a hand on her arm.

"Leave me alone," she said, throwing him off.

The other gravelings and underslabbers scattered. Two of the latter paused only long enough to drag their newest companion away with them.

Eric's camera and notebook still lay on the ground. Ann Amelia picked them up, retreated to the nearest wooden bench, and opened the notebook.

Highgate holds no secrets from us. The words were scrawled across the first page. Above it were two questions, circled repeatedly: *Why no cameras? What are they hiding?*

She should have saved him. All she'd had to do was answer his questions with the truth. Maybe he was right—maybe she wanted to make a difference—but, unlike him, she'd been too afraid to. It would have doomed her and the other gravelings. But in a way, they'd already doomed themselves by taking flesh that wasn't theirs. She and Jonathan might have done it by accident, but the others had known exactly what they were doing when they'd seized the bodies they now held.

Life and death, entwined forever, unchanging, incorruptible . . . and unnatural.

To distract herself, Ann Amelia set the notebook down in her lap and picked up the camera. It seemed okay, turning on when she hit the power button. Curious, she switched modes and began to scroll through his photos. He hadn't cleared the memory card in a while—there were dozens of old photos of a smiling woman who she assumed must be his wife. Then she found a few of the cemetery gates, David, and the other tourists. He'd only taken one of Marx's monument before moving on to the surrounding area. Then there was his last photo—most of the ghosts had shimmered away in the split second between the flash and the photo, but a half dozen of them hadn't been quick enough.

She started to turn the camera off, then hesitated and looked at the last photo again. Six ghosts. Had she spotted any of them afterwards? She closed her eyes, trying to remember what she'd seen as she argued with the ghosts. No, they hadn't been among the ghosts who'd come back after Eric took his photo.

Was it because they *couldn't* come back?

Her breath caught in her throat and her hands shook as she hit the power button. It made perfect sense. But it didn't matter. Even if she was right, no humans would ever know enough about Eric's death to come to the same conclusion.

Unless she told them.

Ann Amelia hugged the camera to her chest, horrified with herself for even considering the notion. But then she looked back down at the notebook in her lap and Eric's questions seemed to leap off the page at her. She could still answer those questions. It might be too late to save Eric, but how many others could she save with her answers?

Slowly, Ann Amelia pulled out Eric's pen and began to write.

*

Afterwards, Ann Amelia sat on the bench until dawn began to colour the horizon and she heard the motor of an approaching car. The other gravelings must still have been trying to give her space, because none of them were close enough to notice when she rose and walked over to the cemetery gates.

It wasn't long before the woman from the photos appeared on the other side of the iron bars.

"Mrs Taylor?" Ann Amelia asked.

The woman nodded, her eyes fixed on the camera and notebook in Ann Amelia's hands.

"I am sorry for your loss," Ann Amelia said, stepping closer to the gate. Her heart began hammering her in her chest, her lungs struggling to inflate, black sparks dancing in front of her eyes. She fought down the memory of her death. There was nothing wrong with her—not yet. She could still run back to her grave and pretend nothing had changed.

Or she could die again—on her own terms this time—and maybe make a difference.

Holding the notebook by its edge, Ann Amelia slipped it through the bars. Mrs Taylor's eyes watered, but she remained silent as she took it. The camera went through next, and then it was done. Done past all undoing.

They stood there, staring at each other, as the sun rose. It wasn't quite fully light when David arrived, keys in hand. He froze when he saw the two of them and all colour drained out of his face.

"Ann Amelia?"

"Open the gates, David," she said. "Please?"

"He's dead, then?" David asked, his Adam's apple bobbing as he swallowed. Mrs Taylor made a soft sobbing sound and finally turned away.

"Everything you need to know to stop the ghosts is in the notebook." Ann Amelia nodded her head in Mrs Taylor's direction. "His story—the one he died for—it's in there. Please, open the gates before I lose my nerve."

"Why?" David asked, but he fumbled out the keys.

"Mrs Taylor," Ann Amelia added. "If his camera has a video mode, you need to film this."

"What are you doing?" David hesitated, one hand on the gate, but he'd already turned the key in the lock.

Ann Amelia gave the gate a gentle push and it swung open. "Something I should have done a long time ago. Something Jonathan had the courage to do, but I did not."

"Jonathan?"

She closed her eyes and drew in a deep breath. "It's time for me to make a difference."

Then Ann Amelia opened her eyes and stepped forward out of darkness, into the light.

AFTERWORD

The Highgate website warned me to come early, but apparently half an hour wasn't early enough; the 2 o'clock tour of the famous West Cemetery was already full. No problem, I thought, I could check out the East Cemetery for a bit then catch the next tour. A few hours later, the sun was setting, the gates were closing, and I had the first draft of this story written. I never did make it to the West Cemetery.

Death is an inescapable consequence of life. Visiting cemeteries, those liminal spaces between the living and the dead, is one of the ways we try to come to terms with that truth. Speculating about undeath—ghouls and zombies, ghosts and revenants—is another. And then there are those of us who sit in a quiet corner of an historic cemetery and scare ourselves silly by writing about the murderous undead. The first story I ever submitted for professional publication was written in a cemetery. I doubt this one will be my last.

EMBRACING THE INVISIBLE

KAREN MARIC

While her master watched without interest, Chen Ying undressed. Fear made her brash. She tossed her jeans onto the bed's unused feather pillows, twirled her bra around her index finger before flinging it away, sent her panties flying over Mr Li's head.

Naked, she flopped into the armchair beside the wide bed. She was achingly aware of her boniness: her spine pressing against the stiff leather back, her elbows against the wooden armrests. She felt gawky, unlovely. Ashamed.

Mr Li sat opposite her in a matching armchair, clad in his usual charcoal suit. The only light came from a small bedside lamp. It left shadows lurking around his black eyes and deep hollows beneath his formidable cheekbones.

Mr Li ran a thoughtful finger along the tight line of his lips.

"Did you bring my other requirement, Miss Chen?" he asked.

The bedroom was overheated. Though outside snow lay in crisp dirty piles on the streets, Ying could feel sweat trickling down the back of her neck and gluing her long hair to her skin. She tilted her head at her handbag. "Help yourself."

He did not chastise her for her rudeness. He never did. Instead, he rose and began rummaging through the handbag she'd dropped on the dresser.

Ying fought to hold onto her brashness, to hide her unease and disgust.

He drew out the plastic bag. It rustled in his hand. Lamplight gleamed off his wedding ring. Her roommates and fellow student-mistresses Liu Ling and Huang Luodan claimed their masters removed their rings during their trysts. But Mr Li was nothing like their masters.

The faintest hint of stale menstrual blood wafted from the plastic. Mr Li shoved the bag into his trouser pocket and returned to his chair.

For a time, there was silence. Mr Li watched her, finger stroking his lips, while Ying breathed slowly to hold back the fear that made her want to leap up and run. She could smell the bedroom's sickly floral air freshener, and beneath it, the faint sourness of her sweat. From outside came the sounds of car horns and traffic. Inside was only their breathing.

Every Friday night was the same. He'd order her to undress. And then he'd watch her. Yet his opaque black gaze never registered any arousal, and he'd never touched her or himself.

Mr Li took his hand away from his mouth. "You look at me as if you hate me," he said, his voice flat. "Would you rather I was fucking you?"

Ying crossed her bare legs and managed a strange, unsteady sort of laugh. "At least then I'd understand you."

"It is not necessary for you to understand me, Miss Chen. It is only necessary that you do whatever I pay you to do."

Her head jerked backwards as if he'd slapped her. A hot tide of blood rushed up her throat to her cheeks. "I need a drink." Without waiting for his permission, she dragged on a dressing gown and stalked out the door.

In the hallway, his hand caught her shoulder. "It's cold," he said, almost gently. "I'll make it. Go back into the room."

She stared at his back for a moment before retreating.

Sitting alone in the bedroom, arms folded beneath her breasts, her unease, as always, intensified. It tightened her nipples, shrank her too-brown skin into gooseflesh, made her breath come shallow and fast. This whole situation smelled exactly like one of those urban legends that did the rounds of China's microblogs. Another lurid warning why impoverished university students should never become student-mistresses. The only thing missing was the tale's conclusion, in which he'd lunge at her, black eyes finally coming alive with blood lust, and tie her up and—

He'd left his suit jacket draped neatly over the back of his chair, Ying noted.

Despite her initial attempts to draw him out, he'd volunteered no information about himself. All she knew about Li Bai was that he was a businessman involved in exports, just like tens of millions of other Chinese businessmen.

Ying glanced at the bedroom door. Distant clinks sounded as he stirred a drink in the kitchenette. Heart racing, Ying rose and patted his jacket down. The wool was luxuriantly soft against her palms. Her touch stirred up the smell of his aftershave, musky and expensively masculine.

She found his wallet in the inner breast pocket and tugged it out.

A wad of crisp, red hundred-yuan notes fattened it. A flick through told her there was at least five thousand yuan there—more than ten times her parents' monthly income from their tiny farm in the mountains of south-western China. Enough to keep her at university for a year. Ying stared at it, shaking with the desire to slip a few notes out and into her jeans pocket. But if Mr Li discovered any missing . . .

Forcing that urge aside, Ying checked the wallet's other pockets. She found his Chinese identity card listing his address as here, in Wuyishan, and some yellowing business cards giving an address in Shenzhen. Behind the cards, her scrabbling fingertips touched a stash of tiny, folded paper squares. She dug one out and unfolded it.

Handwritten characters, small and neat, covered the top half of the sheet:

> *If I should fade until I am like a candle flame at noon, know that my love for you will always burn as brightly as the sun.*

Ying frowned as she read the note's signature. *Ni de qixi, Yao Ziyan.* Your wife, Ziyan Yao.

Beneath that, in larger hand, was a reply:

I would throw everything in this world on your flame to keep it burning, for without your light, the sun's light means nothing. Your husband forever, Li Bai.

The tiny papers all seemed to hold florid, ardent love letters. Ten? Twenty? Maybe more. All written by Mr Li and his wife.

Footsteps sounded in the hallway. Ying replaced the notes before shoving his wallet into his jacket pocket and speeding back to her chair.

Pulse roaring, sweat slicking her armpits, she fought for calmness as Mr Li re-entered the bedroom. He placed a cup of hot rice wine on the dresser beside her before sinking back into his chair. Ying stared at the floor rather than meet his passionless gaze.

So you can *feel,* she screamed at him silently. Or at least he pretended to, when he and his wife were fashioning themselves as heirs to Mr Li's namesake, the great Tang Dynasty poet Li Bai. Yet if he loved his wife more than the sunlight, what was he doing here with her?

Nothing much, really. Just watching her, and collecting her menstrual blood.

Fear swirled in Ying's veins, searing her like acid, like poison, driving her to her feet.

She snatched her underwear off the floor. Hopping around as she dragged it on, she said, "I-I have to go."

Li Bai leapt upright, eyes bulging. "No!"

Ying stopped hopping and stared at him. *This is it,* she thought, bowels knotting and cramping with terror. Because he looked desperate. Mad.

"You will stay for two hours," he ground out. "That is our agreement."

Ying slithered into her jeans.

"I'll pay you double, Miss Chen. Triple!"

She pulled on her sweater and coat and slung her scarf around her neck. "Mr Li, you can't pay me enough."

She ran outside into the winter night, her heaving breaths flying long white banners behind her.

*

Her roommate Wang Yue hammered at the bathroom door. "Finished in there, Ying?"

"Almost." Standing before the mirror, Ying twisted her waist-length black hair into a ponytail at the nape of her neck. "Done."

After the steamy heat of the bathroom, the dormitory's cold was like a punch in the face. Six of her seven roommates sat eating breakfast, arrayed on the bottom levels of the four bunk beds. Shudders wracked them: even with eight young women packed into the tiny room, the cold that emanated from the tiled floor and concrete walls was staggering. And unlike the more expensive four and six-bed dorms, here there was no space for desks. They ate, studied and socialised on the bottom bunks.

"He sent you another gift, Ying." Ai Wei tilted her head at the parcel near the door.

"You can have it," Ying said. "I'm not interested."

She took a steamed pork bun and a plastic bag of soybean milk from Liu Ling, who was on breakfast-buying duty that week. As Ying shoved a straw into the top of the plastic bag, she could feel her roommates' gazes on her.

"He's sent you gifts and flowers every day since you last saw him," Wei said. "What happened? Did he finally sleep with you?"

Ying put her untouched soy milk down. "No."

Huang Luodan, a student-mistress like Ying, shrugged. "Then I'd be counting my blessings. He helps pay your way through university *and* you're still a virgin." A single pallid beam of wintry sunlight entered the dormitory's narrow window, highlighting the bitter twist of Luodan's lips. "At least *you* won't need to fake being opened on your wedding night."

Ying looked down at her hands, which were twisting in her lap. "I ran out on him on Friday night. That's what the gifts are about. He's trying to coax me back."

Her roommates gaped at her.

"Ran out? Why?" Wei demanded.

Ying said nothing. How could she explain? *Because he pays me to bring him my used sanitary napkins. Because he's utterly oblivious to my nakedness, yet writes steaming love letters to his wife.*

Her phone rang. Ying answered it eagerly, grateful for the distraction.

"Yes?"

"It's Mama."

Ying's hand tightened on the phone. She forced some lightness into her voice. "Mama!" She slipped outside the dorm room, onto the balcony. Beyond the balcony's concrete parapet, leafless branches creaked and sagged on the garden's plum and cherry trees, weighed down by layers of snow. "Mama, what is it?"

"Ying, I-I put five hundred yuan into your bank account yesterday. I hope . . . I'm hoping it will be enough to last you until you get home for the Spring Festival."

Ying pictured her mother holding her breath, awaiting her daughter's reply, while she stood by the pay phone outside the general store in Ying's home village in Yunnan Province, two thousand kilometres away, and for a moment, she could not reply. Her chest tightened; she felt overburdened, suffocated by the scope of her parents' hopes and expectations. They were poor farmers, she their clever only child and their sole hope for a reasonably comfortable old age. *If* she could finish university and land a job which paid enough to support them all.

"It's plenty, Mama," she lied, ignoring the dread that came worming through her bowels. "And if I run low, I'll just take some more part-time work." Yet the local supermarkets and teashops paid students three yuan an hour. Fine for those students whose parents could spare more than five hundred yuan, but for Ying . . . She'd have to work so many hours to make enough to live on she'd have no time left to study for her exams.

Whereas Mr Li paid one hundred yuan. For sitting naked for two hours in a heated bedroom. You could hardly even call that work.

And after all the sacrifices her parents had made to get her to university, filial piety demanded she do whatever it took to get her degree. *Whatever* it took.

She called Mr Li as soon as her last class ended.

"I'm sorry, Mr Li," she said, voice quaking. "But I've discovered I can be bought after all."

He spoke with an impatient, breathless kind of relief. "Well, whatever your price is, I'll pay it."

She recalled the thickness of the notes in his wallet. "I want five thousand yuan. Half next time we meet and the rest next year, when my tuition fees are due. And I'll work for you every week until I graduate."

He didn't hesitate. "Done. Now, I'll need you to come to the opening of my new teashop on Friday night."

Ying's belly clenched. He wanted to parade her in public? But she said, "All right."

"And I'll give you an extra two thousand at the end of the winter vacation, but only if you spend the break here in Wuyishan. I'll have need of you. Understood?"

Ying winced at the thought of her parents celebrating Spring Festival alone. They'd clean their small, mud-walled farmhouse and hang a red lantern over the door. Then they'd slip what tiny amounts of spare cash they could scrape together into a red envelope she wouldn't be there to collect. But she did understand: seven thousand yuan would ensure she finished her degree with the highest grades possible.

On Friday night, she smoothed down the front of her new, fur-trimmed winter *cheongsam* and walked to the entrance of Mr Li's teashop. Beneath the honks and snarls of the traffic, she could hear the hissing of the air compressor that inflated the gigantic red dragon gate which arched over the shop's façade. Bouquets of red and yellow carnations, pink roses and palm leaves stood on plinths in twin rows beneath the gate, attracting luck and wealth to Mr Li's latest enterprise.

Inside the shop, occasional downlights illuminated tables that were draped with white linen and covered with champagne glasses, bottles of wine, and free sample boxes of tea. Slick-haired men in shiny suits and women in silks and furs hovered near the drinks.

Mr Li met her at the door. A white suit had replaced his usual blacks and greys. He looked handsome, but his darting eyes betrayed an uncharacteristic nervousness that immediately made Ying tense.

"Miss Chen." He slipped a fat envelope into her hand. Ying peeked inside it, saw the red hundred-yuan notes, and then glanced up to make sure no one else had seen. She quickly shoved the money into her handbag.

She let Mr Li draw her inside.

And froze when she noticed the woman.

Clad in scarlet, the beautiful woman stood alone beneath one of the downlights, a solitary splash of splendour amongst the dim and glittering crowd. Glossy ebony hair rippled down her back to her thighs. Her huge eyes gleamed like black jewels within her flawless white face, and her lips looked as blood-red and slick as the silk of her *cheongsam*.

Standing beside Ying, Li Bai stared at the glorious woman with a yearning so naked and raw it sent cold nausea coiling through Ying's belly. There was something perilously close to madness in the intensity of his gaze.

The woman returned his stare without blinking, with a look of infinite sorrow. It was the look, Ying thought, of someone whose soul had been profoundly and terribly wounded. By Li Bai, she wondered?

Before Ying could voice any of the questions that burned inside her, Mr Li thrust a champagne flute into her hand and gestured at a sallow-faced, suit-clad man who'd just joined them.

"Miss Chen, meet Weng Qiabo, my associate. Mr Weng, my new assistant, Chen Ying." Without a word to excuse himself, Mr Li slipped away, leaving her alone with Weng Qiabo.

Ying tried to attend to Weng Qiabo's chatter, but her gaze kept sliding between the woman and Mr Li. Mr Li padded around the room, nodding at and greeting various guests and supporters, all the while circling ever closer to the woman, a hunter creeping up on his prey.

The beautiful woman stood alone and silent, seemingly as paralysed by her sorrow as a rabbit by a car's headlights.

Then her head rolled from her shoulders—

And vanished.

Ying shrieked. Her glass fell from numb hands, yet she scarcely noticed the champagne splashing her ankles or the crystal shattering on the floor.

Impossibly, the woman remained upright, a slender, headless body encased in blood-red silk.

"Miss Chen? Miss Chen!"

Ying glanced up and saw Weng Qiabo staring at her in bewilderment. She glanced back at the woman. Her lovely head was right where it was supposed to be, attached to her slender neck.

An intense, pounding dizziness swept through Ying. She knew what she'd seen. Knew she hadn't imagined it. And yet . . .

Like a long white worm, the woman's left arm fell from her torso and disappeared before it struck the floor. Ying blinked, moaning—and the arm reappeared in its usual place.

Weng Qiabo was following her gaze. Ying could tell from his non-reaction that he hadn't shared her vision. Fear tightened around her lungs. Was she going mad?

"I-I'm sorry," she managed to say to Weng, though her voice shook violently. "I thought I saw—"

The beautiful woman abruptly turned and strode away between the aisles of tea. With every step she took, her right leg quavered like a mirage, sliding in and out of visibility.

"She's mesmerising, isn't she?" Weng Qiabo said.

Ying drew in a slow, steadying breath. "Do you know her, Mr Weng?"

Weng Qiabo looked askance at her. "Of course I do, Miss Chen. Her name is Zhang Mei. She's your boss's wife."

Ying gaped at him.

Weng Qiabo's lips parted in a thin smile. "You know, you look uncannily like her, Miss Chen, although your skin is considerably darker. Perhaps that's why Li Bai chose you to be his 'assistant'."

The clamour of Ying's thoughts almost drowned out his words.

Mr Li had brought his wife *here*? To the same event to which he'd summoned his student-mistress? Did he *enjoy* humiliating Zhang Mei?

And what of the love letter in his wallet? The one signed, *Your wife, Yao Ziyan*?

"So Zhang Mei is his second wife?" Ying asked as casually as she could manage. She had to know.

"I don't know about that," Weng Qiabo said. "But I do know that there's something very strange about Zhang Mei."

"No, really?" Ying said, poker-faced.

Behind them, laughter broke out amongst a group of revellers.

Weng Qiabo lowered his voice. "Zhang Mei never touches any food or drink at these public events. It's as if she has some morbid fear of food poisoning. Or—" He winced. "I'll leave you to talk to them, shall I?"

He hurried away, revealing Mr Li and Zhang Mei heading straight for her. Mr Li was gripping his wife's smooth white arm with force enough to bruise while hissing orders in a fierce whisper.

A clearly reluctant Mei was shaking her head and pleading with him, her black eyes swimming with that unbearable, unrelenting sadness.

Ying's lips peeled back from her teeth. If Li Bai thought she'd stay here and wait to speak to his wife, then he was badly mistaken.

She backed away, towards the door.

Pain sliced into the ball of her foot. Ying yelped and stopped.

She'd trodden on a sliver of the glass she'd dropped when Zhang Mei's head had disappeared. Whimpering, she lifted her foot and plucked out the shard that had penetrated the thin sole of her slipper.

When she lowered her foot, blood squelched between her toes.

"Miss Chen."

Ying glanced up. Mr Li and his wife stood before her. Zhang Mei's form rippled like a reflection on a windswept lake. But Li Bai, and indeed everyone else in the room, carried on as if oblivious.

"Miss Chen," Mr Li repeated tightly. "I'd like you to meet my wife, Zhang Mei. Mei, this is Chen Ying, the girl I—"

The pain in her foot and the sheer weirdness of the visions boiled up in Ying, and she exploded. "You *bastard*. You prick. How could you do this to her? To me?"

People were staring at them, but Ying didn't care. She tugged off her ruined, bloody slipper and flung it at Mr Li's pale face. Then she spun on her heel and stormed out.

Passing the dragon gate, she stabbed it with the sliver of glass she still held and smiled savagely when she heard the flatulent sounds of air escaping. Within moments, the inflatable red arch began to sag. Mr Li stood beneath it, clutching her bloody slipper in both hands, his face white and hard with fury.

Ying wondered if he'd sniff and gloat over her slipper, too, or if only menstrual blood did it for him. But it didn't matter. He wouldn't get any more of her blood. And he could keep his two and a half thousand yuan. She'd take a job in the supermarket and work thirty hours a week, and learn to live on four hours sleep a night.

She waved down a three-wheeled taxi and ducked inside.

"Xing Xing University," she said. "Dorm building B."

Back in her dorm room, she ignored Ling and Yue's sleepy questions and said to Wei, "I need your laptop. Please." A laptop was a luxury the daughter of peasant farmers could not afford.

Wei blinked. "Now?"

"Now. Please." Because now that she'd made it back here, Ying was desperate to learn all she could about Mr Li and his beautiful wife. She had to know if Zhang Mei's partial invisibilities were a symptom of her own madness, or whether they might be something even darker. Because what if the horrible visions were premonitions? What if Li Bai planned to dismember Zhang Mei?

What if he planned to do the same to her?

And what about Yao Ziyan, the woman to whom he'd written those ardent love letters signed *Your husband forever, Li Bai*?

Ying climbed onto her bunk and set Ai Wei's laptop on her lap. At least the computer helped warm her against the room's vicious chill.

She typed 'Li Bai and Zhang Mei' into the Baidu search engine. Zhang Mei's name yielded nothing. Li Bai's name brought up millions of results, but a quick glance showed Ying that the foremost sites were all for Li Bai the poet. She'd have to refine the search.

She remembered the old business cards she'd found in Mr Li's wallet. They'd listed an address in Shenzhen. Quickly, Ying typed 'Li Bai and Zhang Mei, Shenzhen'.

Success. The results listed numerous articles from the *Shenzhen Daily*'s online archives, many from the business section. Ying clicked on the newspaper's homepage and ran another, internal search, setting the filter to sort the stories from the oldest to the most recent so she'd be able to read them in chronological order. There were stories about his burgeoning business empire; his wedding to renowned beauty Yao Ziyan in 2002; their attendance at movie premieres, fashionable restaurants, local festivals and community events.

Then she came to a blurry photograph of Yao Ziyan and Li Bai arm-in-arm outside a theatre in 2005 and her heart skipped several beats.

Yao Ziyan and Zhang Mei were the same woman. Or were they?

The more Ying stared, the more she noted minor differences. Yao Ziyan's face was not as preternaturally pale and flawless as Zhang Mei's. Her eyes, though beautiful, lacked the unbearable sorrow of the woman Ying had seen tonight.

Biting her lip, Ying clicked on the next article. It was dated April 5th, 2009.

WIFE OF PROMINENT SHENZHEN BUSINESSMAN GOES MISSING.

Ying's fingers jerked off the computer's mouse.

Police say they hold grave fears for the wife of prominent Shenzhen businessman Li Bai, 35. Mr Li's wife, Yao Ziyan, disappeared during a shopping trip to the Dafencun art markets last Friday.

Police urge anyone who saw Yao Ziyan at Dafencun to contact them. Mr Li is offering a substantial reward for information leading to the return of his wife.

Ying tasted blood. She'd bitten her lip too hard. Pulse pounding, she navigated to the next article.

POLICE QUESTION LI BAI OVER WIFE'S DISAPPEARANCE

Amidst rumours of marital difficulties and domestic disputes, police have taken businessman Li Bai in for questioning over his wife's disappearance.

"Initially we suspected kidnapping," Detective Cai Song said on Thursday. "But no kidnappers have come forward to confirm our suspicions. Therefore, we need to investigate all avenues."

Detective Cai would make no comment about whether police have found any evidence linking Mr Li to his wife's disappearance.

The next few articles continued the terrible story. Two weeks after her disappearance, Yao Ziyan was discovered, mutilated and scarcely alive, on the floor of an abandoned factory on the outskirts of Shenzhen. She had died before her ambulance had even reached the hospital. Li Bai was subsequently charged with masterminding his wife's kidnapping and murder, but the charges were dropped due to a "lack of evidence". And Ying knew that "lack of evidence" did not necessarily mean that Mr Li had had no involvement in his wife's death. "Lack of evidence" could simply mean that Mr Li had enough *guanxi*, enough connections within the police force, to have the charges against him quashed.

And then, soon after Yao Ziyan's funeral, Mr Li had moved sixteen hours by rail north of the metropolis of Shenzhen, to the isolated Wuyi Mountains. Where he now lived with a woman who looked remarkably like Yao Ziyan. A woman of whom there was no trace on the Internet.

That night, as Ying lay sleepless, she tore open a seam in her tattered Xi Yang Yang toy, a relic from her adolescence, and shoved the rolled-up hundred yuan notes inside the little goat's fat belly. Afterwards she stitched the seam up again.

Morning came, and the dawn sky looked grey and curdled, hinting at more snow. When Ying stepped from the dorm to buy *baozi* and soy milk for breakfast, she found two policemen standing on the ice-slicked balcony. Waiting. Both wore grim expressions. The older one had thinning black hair combed sideways across his scalp, the younger the long, lanky body and pale skin of a northerner.

"Chen Ying?" the older policeman said.

Ying nodded mutely.

The lanky one took her elbow in a painfully tight grip. "You're coming with us."

Ying arched her back and sucked in a breath to scream.

A pricking sensation in her neck . . . She glimpsed the older policeman's hand falling, thick fingers curled around a hypodermic needle . . . Her vision blurred. Doubled.

She felt as if she was flying above the cold concrete as the men dragged her towards Mr Li's black Audi, nonchalantly parked beneath the No Parking sign outside Dormitory B. Then blackness swamped her vision, and she slept.

*

Ying woke to a powder-dry mouth and a terrible pounding in her skull.

Skyscrapers streaked past the car windows, neon lights brilliant against the burnt orange sky of a city at night. She shoved herself up in the seat. Beside her, Mr Li stared straight ahead, his face tight with fury.

"Where . . . where are we?" she croaked.

Silent, he stabbed his index finger past his driver's shoulder, indicating a green road sign up ahead.

Huifeng Street. Central Shenzhen.

Ying moaned. Shenzhen—or the Overnight City as it was called, having appeared almost that quickly—was also the country's kidnapping capital. Entrepreneurs made and then lost fortunes here; millions of desperate migrant workers from western provinces like Xinjiang and Gansu flocked here seeking jobs. For some of those people, kidnapping and ransoming Shenzhen's *nouveau riche* was the quickest route to riches of their own.

Ying wondered if Li Bai had driven Yao Ziyan down this same road on the day she met her death.

And then she saw her handbag, lying on the seat beside her. Mr Li's friendly policemen hadn't confiscated it. Surreptitiously, she worked her hand into the bag and felt around for the pen she always kept inside. Closing her fingers around it, she drew it out and into her right sleeve, keeping its sharp point against her palm.

The Audi lurched over a pothole. Ying's head smacked against the window.

Unconsciousness claimed her again.

*

When she came to again, she found herself slumped on a brocade couch in an enormous sitting room. In Li Bai's mansion in Shenzhen?

On the walls, antique scrolls swam before her unsteady gaze. Images of Huang Shan's mist-swathed peaks and sprigs of cherry blossoms flickered in and out of view.

Two table lamps made lonely spheres of golden light kept apart by the room's many shadows. Zhang Mei sat stiff and silent on a couch beside the farthest lamp, cloaked in sadness and a lavender dressing gown. Her wet eyes met Ying's once before sliding away, eyelids fluttering with distress.

A metallic clink sounded behind Ying. Startled, she leapt off the couch. The movement brought star-speckled darkness rushing towards her. Through it, she saw a scowling Mr Li lifting a pair of handcuffs from a desk drawer.

Ying curled her fingers. Felt the pen, still caught in her cuff.

Without hesitation, she slid the pen into her palm and drove the point into her neck. Hot, sticky blood spurted over her fist. She shrieked, swayed, staggered, but remained upright.

Mr Li stared at her, aghast. He reached out a hand. "Don't—"

"If you come near me," Ying slurred, "I'll stab myself again. In the jugular." She could feel the sickening, excruciating sensation of the pen bobbing in her neck as she spoke. "I know what you did. I'm not going to let you cut me up like you did Yao Ziyan."

To her astonishment, Mr Li gave a bark of bitter, humourless laughter. "You think *I* killed my wife? Well I did not, Miss Chen. Certainly it was my fault she died, but I am also the reason she lives again now."

"What . . . ?" Reeling, Ying backed further away from him, staggering past the dim form of a tea table made from the upturned, sanded and lacquered base of a laurel tree. Blood soaked the collar of her shirt and jacket, making the warm, wet fabric stick to her cold skin.

Ying struggled to move past her dizziness. To *think*.

What had Weng Qiabo said? *She never touches any food or drink . . .*

The pale skin . . . the disappearing limbs . . . the awful sadness in Zhang Mei's black eyes . . .

"Zhang Mei *is* Yao Ziyan," Ying whispered with difficulty. "You-you resurrected her."

Mr Li nodded. "I did."

"But . . . how?"

Mr Li lowered the handcuffs and stepped nearer, his expression pleading, his voice soft. "We had a . . . a difficult marriage. As a husband I was neither attentive nor kind, though I loved my wife more than I could say. Yet until she was kidnapped, I, like so many people in this brash new China of ours, believed that money was everything. It is not, of course. Love is everything.

"It was a business rival of mine, a man whose livelihood I'd destroyed, who kidnapped my wife. He ordered me to tell my friends in the police force nothing. Said he'd let her go if I gave him what he wanted. But in the end he murdered her anyway. After my beloved Ziyan's death, I searched from Song Shan to Emei Shan for a *waidan* master capable of bringing her back to me. And eventually I found one: my money, at least, allowed me to carry out such a search and buy the necessary ingredients."

"*Waidan*," Ying murmured. It was a combination of alchemy and necromancy. Its practitioners sought to bring the dead back to life, to even grant immortality. All by stuffing the newly dead with gemstones and the rarest, most potent of herbal concoctions, by preparing sacred salves and potions in accordance with arcane recipes.

Ying could feel the blood ebbing and pulsing down her neck. Had she nicked her jugular after all? If she pulled the pen out, the blood loss would accelerate . . .

"But I-I don't understand," she said dizzily. "I saw Yao Ziyan disintegrating . . . I thought I was seeing premonitions of what you'd do to her . . . And why-why do you need me to pose for you? Why do you need my blood?"

"Because the resurrection did not work as it should have. My wife's body was mutilated, her body weeks old by the time I found Master Wu. I wanted him to make her into a *xiannu*, an immortal woman. But the damage done to her was far too great. And mere months after her resurrection, after we'd left Shenzhen and everyone who knew of Yao Ziyan's death far behind, my wife began dying again. Literally fading and falling apart before my eyes, as your premonitions showed you. I took her back to Master Wu. But he said there was little hope. All I could do was search for a woman who resembled my wife. If I added that woman's moon-blood to a sacred tea, if I forced my wife to meditate upon the woman's unclad form and thus absorb her *ch'i*, perhaps I might share a few more years with Ziyan."

Ying wondered where Yao Ziyan had been hiding as she sat naked in that overheated bedroom in Wuyishan. In the next room, perhaps, staring at Ying through a spyhole? Or huddled in the built-in wardrobe, too ashamed and appalled to join her husband and tell Ying why she was there?

Mr Li went on, anguish cracking his voice. "I sat outside the university gates for three weeks, despairing, before I spotted you, Miss Chen. And I had planned, at the teashop opening, to tell you about my wife in the hope that you'd agree to stay with us and help her. I see now that that was unrealistic. And I'm not letting you run from me again. From now on, you'll stay here." Grief pulled the lines of his face down. "And keep Yao Ziyan alive as long as possible."

Ying's legs gave way. She dropped onto the tea table. She heard the pen fall from her neck, felt the fresh spurt of blood through the fingers she clapped to the wound.

Zhang Mei—*no*, Ying reminded herself, *Yao Ziyan*—gasped.

That was the only sound she'd made since Ying had found herself in this room, and Ying realised then that although Yao Ziyan was only one generation removed from hers, the distance that separated them was impossibly vast. Li Bai's wife came from a time when a Chinese woman's most important duty was to obey her husband; Ying was the product of the One Child era, singularly responsible for her entire family. And she could not let Mr Li steal her from the mother and father whose future relied on her.

"I bet you've never asked your wife what she thinks of all this, have you?" Ying said. She'd wanted to sound tough, taunting, but the frailness of her voice frightened her.

Li Bai stared at her, eyes burning.

"Before you lock me up here as your prisoner, why don't ask her what she wants?"

Li Bai shot a wild glance at his wife. "I—"

Yao Ziyan suddenly rose from the couch, her black eyes like orbs of night sky floating in her moon-pale face.

"I love you, husband," she said softly. "I always have . . . "

Li Bai slid to the floor. On his knees, he looked up at his wife, his face ashen. "Don't—"

Yao Ziyan lifted a hand, silencing him. "But every day, I spend my every waking moment trying to hold myself together while every cell in my body screams with the memories of my murderer torturing me. I didn't ask to be brought back to life. Like this—" She raised her flickering hand higher; it shed and regrew fingers in a terrible, ceaseless dance "—like this, I am nothing more than an earthbound ghost, ever fading, unable to eat or drink anything except that awful blood-tea. Unable to ever give you a child."

Li Bai pressed his face to the floor and began weeping softly, in sobs that shook his entire body.

Slowly, Yao Ziyan came gliding towards Ying. She pressed a thick envelope into Ying's hand. Her form writhed like smoke in a gale and Ying realised it had been more than two weeks since Yao Ziyan had last absorbed her *ch'i*.

Yao Ziyan said, "This is the money my husband promised you. Take it. You'll need some for the doctor and the train back to Wuyishan."

Ying took it.

"Now go," Yao Ziyan said.

Ying was so dizzy from blood loss she wasn't sure she could make it to the door. Yet she did, weaving an erratic red path across the tiles.

In the doorway, she paused and glanced back.

Li Bai and Yao Ziyan were kneeling, embracing each other. Ying could see the tea table through Ziyan's nebulous form. She blinked, and Yao Ziyan was gone, but still Mr Li knelt, arms extended as if embracing her, delaying the moment he'd have to let his arms fall and admit that this time, she was really gone.

Ying was halfway down the circular drive when she heard a gunshot ring out inside the house. She turned. Floodlights set in a winter-brown lawn made the mansion glare whitely against the dark orange sky. Ying waited a moment, panting and whimpering, yet she heard nothing more. Only her own muted cries and the rustling of leaves in the chill night breeze.

Clutching the envelope of cash in her bloody hand, she stumbled on towards the street.

She hoped that in whatever afterlife awaited Li Bai and Yao Ziyan, they would soon be embracing again, in a gentler place than this.

AFTERWORD

For the past two years, I've been lucky enough to live and work in China, and the initial idea for "Embracing the Invisible" came to me courtesy of one of my Chinese colleagues. One night, over the course of a discussion about student life in China, he introduced me to the concept of "student-mistresses", modern-day concubines who become the mistresses of wealthy businessmen in return for the financial help necessary to get their all-important university degrees. I was fascinated. I decided then and there that I wanted to write a tale in which the protagonist is a student-mistress, and so the character of Chen Ying was born. I am also constantly fascinated by the relationship between old and new here. The frenetic rush towards modernisation, the Middle Kingdom's 5,000 year old history—both seem to mix, mingle and clash at every turn, just as in my story modern social dilemmas like the One Child Policy merge with beings from myth like the *xiannu*.

THE BONE PLATE

DAN RABARTS

The only god I ever knew is dead.

He fell, like all his demons, carved open under the pale sky. I watched his blood run black, air bubbling through torn lungs like dark rain chuckling over broken glass.

He was the god of lies, the only true god.

I held the knife as I stripped away his immortality, leaving nothing but agony and the same cold dusk that falls over mortal hearts. I came to pull those immortal bones from inside him and make them my own.

I was his dark angel.

*

Back in the black old days, we called it the Bone Plate. Wasn't worth your life to touch the Bone Plate. It made men kings, back in the black old days. Mine was a trashcan lid, piled high with gnawed, soot-stained remains, the bones of rats and cats and stray dogs and pigeons. Only the bones of that which you had killed and stripped clean with your own biting, smiling teeth were allowed on your Plate, and whoever had the biggest Plate ruled the windswept world of trash and frost that sprawled beneath the overpasses. I remember jamming more and more bones on top of each other, wrapping them up with wire and twine and whatever else I could find amongst the trash, until mine towered taller than anyone else's under the 'pass. It had made me king, and Hania my queen.

Hania and I, we liked to huddle close together and watch things die. It was romantic, knowing that something had to give its life up for us to live. We pulled our ragged layers of clothing tighter and fed the fire, the flames' warmth holding back winter's hunger, while dozens of hollow eye-sockets stared out blindly over our domain from the heights of my Bone Plate.

Far as I could remember back there under the 'pass, there wasn't anything magical about the Plate, but I knew there was *something*, something that mattered, something powerful, but not magic the way people think of magic. Lot of folk thought it was, though. Fools. Sucking brain from a hot rat skull didn't make me some sort of shaman or give me psychedelic insights. But damn, it scared the locals, and frightened people will do just about anything you tell them. Plus, the eyeballs gave me something to chew on during those long dark nights, when I'd stare at the slivers of sky peeking between the curves of the overpass high overhead, and wonder what had come before the black old days. Wonder where I'd ever learned about it all; the Bone Plate, the rituals, the rules. Those nights when I'd wonder what the hell I was, what I had been before the world had chewed me up, stolen my memories, and spat me out down here amongst the trash and the frost and the wasted souls, where all I had was my pile of bones, and Hania.

Then one night the spooks came for me. I remember the dry scuttle of my bones scattering under someone's boots, the obligatory cloth wrapped around my face, and the black as it swallowed me whole.

*

The spooks told me I'd been a soldier once.

Said I had known how to kill a man with my bare hands, or cold steel, or from a half-mile away with the right sort of gun.

Said I'd had some sort of psychotic break.

Said it got ugly.

It made for bad press, that sort of thing, and they couldn't just lock up a Black Ops crackpot in any old prison. No, once someone'd snapped, that was it. They couldn't even drop me in a hostile situation and put me at the wrong end of a burst of friendly fire, because with men like me, that's a way to invite all the wrong sorts of accidents.

So they'd strapped me down in a lab and bleached my brain, locked away all that nasty killing shit where I couldn't get to it. Spat me out as just another homeless vet with a chip on my shoulder and a mean streak a mile wide, but otherwise harmless. It was their way of being merciful, they said. It explained why I hadn't been able to remember anything before the black old days under the 'pass; they'd left a gaping hole in my head where my memories should've been.

Now they said that they needed me back the way I was.

I guess I just looked at them.

They told me that there was a man I had to kill. This man, they said, was very bad.

This man needed to die.

They said that they'd turn me back into the soldier I once was so that I could do it. When the job was done, they promised, there'd be a nice hospital where they could fix me properly this time, and a pension so that I'd never need to work again.

I shrugged. *What have I got to lose?*

Yes, they agreed, *what indeed?*

*

I woke in an alley, head thumping, everything hurting. Apart from that, I didn't feel much different. I wasn't dressed for war, no guns, no knives, nothing. Just a hunk of small bills wadded in my pocket and a business card that was blank except for a scrawled address, someplace in a city a bus ride away.

Took me three days to find Hania. Turns out I'd been gone awhile longer than I thought, and she'd had to scarper; she'd shacked up with the sisters down in the Barrens. Greasy Pete was running things under the 'pass now, she told me, threw out my Bone Plate and everything. I told her not to worry; we didn't need no Bone Plate no more. Told her we had a place to go, and we caught that bus. We had cash, real cash, so I sprung for food and coffee at a truckstop somewhere in a high cold place where we could smell the snow coming down off the mountains.

We ate fried chicken. I didn't keep the bones. No honour in collecting another hunter's leavings; even worse, a farmer's. There's no challenge in breeding chickens for slaughter, not like there is in trapping rats. That's survival, that is.

The bus took us down to the city, where the streets crawled with vermin, most of them the two-legged kind. We beat feet to the address on the card in my pocket.

"You haven't told me what happened, Terrance," Hania said as we walked. "When you disappeared."

I shrugged. "I don't remember rightly." It had always been a good enough answer in the past. Guess it was good enough this time around, too, because she didn't ask me where we were going. As long as it was warm, and there was food, and now and then we could roast dead things over hot coals, she'd stick with me.

Place was a church, or so said the sign outside: *Church of the Divine Flesh.* More like a halfway house that dished up salty soup for its visitors alongside some flavour of god, but it was no god I'd ever heard of. This god didn't even have a name, at least not one that any of its followers dared to speak. A god of hope, they said, which meant it was a god of desperation. Hania and me, we took to desperation like rats to a sewer.

It was all going well enough, desolate god-botherers and salty broth and all, until some fool brother had the bad sense to make a move on Hania. There was no blood, just the crack of snapping vertebrae and the brother being far less alive when I finished moving than he had been when I'd started. My hands remembered things that my mind didn't. That could be useful, dangerous.

After, I scanned the congregation and tried to look mean. I expected someone to call the cops, who would haul me away and lock me up darker and deeper than ever before. If it happened, I could try calling in a favour with the spooks, but they'd no doubt brand me a nutjob and deny all knowledge. But I needn't have worried. Instead, a couple of the brothers efficiently scooped up the body and took it away, leaving us alone. The rest of the congregation got themselves as far from us as they could manage.

That night, the brothers put us on a plane south, a long way from the smog and snow of the world I used to rule with a bone fist. Drove us from the airport through the wee small hours in a mini-van, the back section framed off, something heavy sliding around in there while we tried to doze until the sun came up. When we could see, we found ourselves driving through a sprawling vastness of rolling hills, tussock grass and roaming cattle.

"Injun country," I said, looking out the window.

The brothers had brought us to an honest-to-god ranch. Not just a country home, but a *ranch*. Me, I'm a hunter. Way I see it, *rancher*'s just a fancy word for farmer. No respect in farming, not from a man who survives by killing and eating his prey.

A horned skull gaped over the villa's front door. Reminded me of my own little skulls, staring back at me. Seemed like a kind of blasphemy.

But we were a long way from the Bone Plate here, or so I thought.

Soon as we'd dropped our things in the room where they told us we'd be staying, sun barely up over the hilltops, a house servant arrived to deliver our invitation to lunch later in the day with Victor Metzger.

Victor Metzger. High Priest of the Flesh Cult himself.

Same man that the spooks wanted me to kill.

I never did much believe in luck. Never believed in gods before that day either, or angels, or demons. But I'd never stopped believing in the Bone Plate.

*

First thing I noticed was the plate. It was set right in the middle of the table, beside the basket that held bottles of Tabasco sauce, salt, pepper, ketchup, butter, pretty little napkins and toothpicks; just like some homely south-west diner, except the table was long, polished oak, like the sort you might get the whole family around for Thanksgiving dinner. But it was just Hania and I sitting across from each other, looking over the plate.

They brought us chilled water and warm little bread rolls and a dish of oil and vinegar, like we were the regular swank. The first I knew about there being anything truly divine in that place was when the smell hit me. My mouth watered like it never had, the aroma of roast meat and hot gravy almost overwhelming. Then Metzger came in and sat down.

I don't know what I was expecting, but Metzger wasn't it. Prophets and messiahs should have something about them, a look, a walk, a style, something that defies the ages and transcends our mortal failings. Metzger was just a dude in an expensive suit with a bad haircut. He gave us each a quick nod, not meeting our eyes, and sat at the head of the table. By the time he was seated, waiters were dishing up.

Alongside steaming greens and crisp potatoes, the staff placed a plate of ribs in front of both Hania and I, smothered in thick gravy and glistening with glaze.

Metzger gave us the slightest of nods. His plate boasted a slab of steak, slowly bleeding into his potato. I guessed the rebuke for killing one of his clergy was to wait until after we'd eaten. Wolf-hungry, I feasted.

The meat slid effortlessly off the bone. If it was beef, it had the most delicate flavour of any cow I'd ever tasted, but what was I, some sort of fucking beef gourmet? Maybe it was veal, or maybe this was just what ranch beef tasted like, on account of all that fresh air and sunshine. Might've even been pork, for that matter, though I couldn't remember the last time I'd tasted anything so decadent as pork. But good goddamn, whatever they were, they were the best ribs I'd ever eaten.

I sucked the first bone clean and tossed it, out of habit, onto the plate in the centre. Felt good to have a Bone Plate again, even if it wasn't strictly within the rules. I'd stripped three ribs and tossed the remains before Hania had chewed through one.

Her hand flicked, and the bone clattered onto the plate.

Metzger paused, his eyes locked on her bone lying amidst my three. His gaze was fiercer than words, more damning than blame.

That was when it came to me. Metzger understood the Bone Plate. The thought, and everything that came with it, almost turned my stomach.

Hania's chair clattered to the floor as she fled the room, her hands clutched to her mouth. She understood the Bone Plate, too.

I looked from Metzger to the offending bone and gingerly flicked it back onto Hania's plate. "Not her kill?" I asked.

Metzger just went back to chewing on his—boneless—steak. I surveyed the ribs on my plate, split clean through, their true shape and size disguised by the artistry of knife and condiment.

But damn, ribs had never tasted so good.

As Metzger dabbed at his mouth with a napkin, he nodded at my Bone Plate. "It was a good kill," he said. "Or so I hear."

I nodded.

"Do you remember, Terrance, where we met? The first time?" He forked bloody steak between his teeth.

"I don't remember much," I said. Never really been one for small talk, me.

"I heard you had a breakdown." Pale pink juices spilled over his lips. "That you were living under a bridge."

I tried to laugh, ignoring the worms that twisted in my guts. "Seems you know a lot about me. Seems a lot of people do."

"You never forgot how to kill. You never forgot the Bone Plate." The cut of the knife, the stab of the fork, the scrape of steel on china.

I shrugged. No harm pretending he was right. "Some things you don't forget."

"I taught you its power, before they took you away. I'm glad you're back."

"I've been here before?"

Metzger chuckled, a sound like water bubbling over open graves. "Not here, no. Where we met was a darker place, a darker time. It took me many years to build this. Many, many years. To ensure that what we have continues to grow I need disciples, like you, who know the power of the Bone Plate. I see the bones still call to you. Do you hear them?"

I nodded. I couldn't resist the call of the bones.

"Good. There is more you need to remember."

"More?"

"It will come in time. You think you are awake now, but you are not. The bones will wake you. Consecrate them to your purpose. They will make you strong."

I nodded, staring at my Bone Plate. No longer the gaping eye-sockets of rats and pigeons, just a cross-hatching of sauce-streaked white which once had sheltered lungs, heart.

"Welcome back, Captain. Fill your plate."

I wasn't hungry anymore, but the bones called to me. "They can truly bring back my memories?"

"All that the evil men have taken away, the bones will bring back, in time."

I resumed eating, piling my Bone Plate high.

"In the coming days you will eat your kill until it is gone. Then you will begin your service to me." Metzger pushed away his dishes and stood. I eyed Hania's serving, and as Metzger left I reached for the bones, for the past.

*

Eat only that which you kill. Consecrate the bones to your purpose.

In the weeks the followed, I heard the story of how Metzger had killed the steer whose skull graced the stoop, like Theseus had slain the Minotaur, strangling the beast with his bare hands. That was the power of the Bone Plate. Such a man could truly change the world.

Metzger's god of gluttony, which measured individual value by how much one could destroy and consume, was the most honest and human thing I had ever seen in any religion. There was no room for mercy, tolerance, or pity. The Church of the Divine Flesh was founded on the fundamentals that had underscored the rise of every great empire, and eschewed the weaknesses that had seen them all fail.

Beneath Metzger an army of devoted followers waited on his beck and call, ready to pile their own Bone Plates high in his honour. They got me cleaned up, bought me new clothes and nice shoes, ceramic blades and silenced handguns, a dozen identities. I served the Church of the Divine Flesh and its High Priest, doing their work near and far. My ascendance was swift. Across the country and beyond, the enemies of the Flesh Cult fell to my hand; I stripped the bones from my kills and left their bodies flayed open to the sky, flaccid and broken, like some unsigned missive from beyond the gates of hell. The brothers shipped the bones back to the ranch, where Hania cared for them. She cleaned them, dried them, wrapped them and layered them. At first my Bone Plate was a chiller inside the ranch, then an underground ossuary buried in the rolling hills beyond.

Yet somehow I knew that my growing collection was as nothing compared to Metzger's Bone Plate. It seemed like the ranch itself creaked with the grind of bones more ancient and crumbling than the man himself, brittle with ages past, broken with horrors lost to memory. Metzger had mastered the power of the bones and consecrated that power to the unholy beauty of the Flesh Cult, to his own worship. He had turned his Bone Plate into a Bone Empire. Where, I wondered, did Metzger draw the line between priest and god? How deep ran the power of the bones? As deep as the power of the Man? Surely not. A system that cast out a war hero to scrape and hunger under a windswept bridge amongst the detritus of society could not compare to the ultimate glory offered by the bones. Thus it was that I forswore the spooks, abandoned the false mission they had sent me here to carry out, and donned the mantle of darkness. Thus it was that I became Metzger's angel of death, his true disciple.

*

The Man sent spooks after me, but they underestimated what they had created. After enough of their assassins had found their way onto my Bone Plate, they gave up.

Or so I thought.

*

While the police pored over the filleted corpses of my victims, hunting for clues, the media speculated on who I was, and on what happened to the missing bones. Was I working alone? Of course not, they said. My work was spread out across the country, sometimes across continents. *I* became *we*. Were *we* a militant wing of some extremist sect? Did *we* hail from the Far East, or darkest Africa? Terror lay like a bloated corpse in the sea of questions that surrounded *our* motives. The false prophets of the world prayed for *our* souls on international television.

With every kill, the power of the Flesh Cult grew.

With every kill, every bone torn from hot sinew, I clawed back more fragmented memories.

*

A darker place.

Hot jungle, biting insects, screams in the dark. Bamboo slivered razor sharp, blood pooling around pierced flesh. Fingers digging into muscle still hot and flexing, pulling flesh back from the bone.

A darker time.

Make it yours, by your hand. Consecrate it to your purpose.

Initiation. Sacrifice.

The living cling so tight to their precious ivory. Make it yours.

Bones, exposed beneath stubborn flesh pulsing blood.

Master the art by hand, by jaw, by the bones of your own body, only then may you take up the knife.

No knives. Fingers, and then teeth.

Hot blood in my mouth, screams in my ears, cries that could never drown out the song of the bones, the wordless voice that calls, fills, lifts, completes.

Metzger, obscured by smoke and shadow, somewhere in the back of my head.

Good, Terrance. Put it on your plate with the others.

The Plate. Ceramic, this one, its colour lost beneath the swill of blood. Every hard-won trophy striking it like the ring of a celestial gong, soaking up the cries of the sacrifice.

You always remember your first.

*

Hania turned the spit and thin grease hissed into the coals. She had caught the rabbit herself, gutted it, skinned it. "Did you know this place used to be a burial site, hundreds of years ago? The ruins of a Meclan temple are still up there in the hills."

"Hmm?" I stared into the glowering embers, wandering through memories I had thought lost forever — memories that bubbled up out of my mind's murky depths with every bloody bone I cut from the unworthy.

"They buried the dead in the valley. Down under the ranch." While I was away she roamed the hills, hunting, but also learning the place's secrets, its history. Getting a feel for the bones of the land.

Hania pulled the smouldering delicacy from the fire, tore away a limb and handed it to me. "Who are they? The ones you kill?"

The question was unexpected. I bit into the meat and looked over the high rolling hilltops, chewing. The entrance to my ossuary was concealed nearby, and I could feel the pulsing warmth of all those bones stacked up together, crosshatched, creaking. "Politicians, military people, church people. Metzger's enemies."

She stirred the coals, didn't look at me. "You never told me how you learned about all this. Do you remember anything more about the night you disappeared?"

I remembered the spooks. I remembered the needles and the bright lights and the sinking dark. I remembered waking up, no longer a king but a puppet. I remembered the taste of salt and copper and treachery in my mouth. "I don't remember," I said.

"What happens when they catch you? What happens to me?"

"They won't catch me."

"They will. I don't like it here. I don't like any of this."

"We can't leave yet."

"*I* can."

"Then who will care for my bones?"

She gripped my hand in hers, the odd familiar shape of her pinky resting at a strange angle on my palm, the bone disjointed long ago and never quite healed right, comforting at a time when I hadn't thought I might want comfort. "We don't have to go back to the 'pass, but we can't stay here. It feels wrong. I feel it . . . in my bones."

I chewed, swallowed. Decided. "I never told you why I came here."

"You said you didn't remember."

"I remember," I said.

She gave me a sharp look. "Well?"

"I came here to kill someone."

*

All the devices of gods and angels and demons can be undone by the failings of men. Like Judas and his love of silver, the mighty will fall for the false pleasures of the unworthy. So it would be for the Flesh Cult.

I had to leave for a few days, take care of some business down on the coast. I promised Hania that when I came back we'd finish what we came here to start, and that would be the end of it. She didn't have to know that it was the Man that wanted me to do this thing, to kill Metzger, and I doubted that they would back me up now, not after I'd had to dismember all the agents they'd sent to kill me. In the end, though, I was still playing their game. I'd earned the mark's trust, just like they wanted, but I wasn't doing it for the Man. I was doing it for Hania.

Of course, at the time, I still hadn't put all the pieces together, still hadn't figured what Metzger really was. If I had, I would've taken Hania, turned tail and run, even though I would've known that I could never run far enough to escape. The last time I ran from him, my only escape was into madness.

I wanted to call Hania on the drive back, but she might've been at the ranch, and I didn't want anything we might say to be overheard. The only safe place we had to talk was in the high lands, or the ossuary, and it was late. She didn't like being in the ossuary after dark. Place made her skin itch, she said, like she could hear the bones whispering to her, words she didn't want to hear. So I didn't call her. Instead, I checked my guns again, checked the knives with their ceramic blades and bone handles. Metzger would be surrounded by his security men, I knew; they hovered around his shoulders and in the shadows and beyond each door like vigilant gargoyles, waiting to strike. I knew them all, knew their strengths and weaknesses. They were strong, sharp-edged demons, but I was the dark angel. They would fall, like everyone fell. Like Metzger would fall.

Metzger was eating when I found him. His lips moved over a bone, dripping juices onto his plate. He didn't stop eating, simply gestured to the wait staff to set a place and dish for me. A cold knot of doubt twisted in my stomach. Without Metzger, I would still be scratching out a pointless existence among the trash and fumes beneath an underpass far away, chewing on rats' eyes for kicks. I would still be a ghost, living out my hours in the fog of the black old days. Now I was going to kill him, bring down everything he had created, add the power of his bones to my Bone Plate, because Hania had asked me to.

They brought me a plate, but even the magic his chefs could work would not distract me from my purpose.

"Are you pleased with the progress?" I asked, taking up knife and fork.

Metzger nodded. "Most pleased."

I carved a slice of meat, forked it, chewed slowly as I scanned the room, noting where each bodyguard stood, arms crossed, hips bulging with cold metal, judging how quickly I could put a bullet in each of them or drag a knife-edge across their throats. Collecting the bones would have to wait.

"Where do we go from here?" Metzger asked suddenly. "The government will eventually destroy us. There is little profit in all of this, only death, however glorious."

The meat in my mouth tasted sour, to hear him speaking such words of doubt. I was right to stay my course, then. "Death is profit," I said. "The bones are their own reward."

Metzger chuckled. "Spoken like a true disciple. Words that sound profound, yet mean nothing. Think, Terrance. What is the point? We punish the weak for their weakness, the corrupt for their corruption, yet the unworthy remain in power, their own Bone Plates empty." Metzger dabbed away blood and gravy with a napkin. "How can we move forward, when the very poisons we seek to cleanse from the world run through our own veins?"

I dropped my eyes to the food on my plate. Fingers, crisped and curled gently towards the ceiling, basted and grilled in their own juices. A delicate, thin wrist. Neither the hand of a cowboy, nor a soldier.

Metzger tossed a bone to clatter on the plate before him.

For the first time, I saw the spread of his meal; a plate with delicate strips of crispy meat on the bone, resting in a herbed garlic sauce. It was upon these that he was dining, the severed and slivered metacarpals of whomever had offended him most recently, each fried and grilled into an appetizer worthy of the finest gourmet.

Another strip of bone clattered onto the plate, gnawed clean.

The monster was devouring his kill.

"Do you remember now, Terrance? Do you remember who you were when I found you? Do you remember the places where the bones sing? Do you remember their taste?"

I stared at the plate. The bones I had collected in my months serving Metzger had brought me many memories, memories from before the black old days, the days when I had been a killer for the dark powers who ruled from their ivory towers in distant cities. Memories of dark places, months of jungle heat and bitter cold. Brief moments of unspeakable violence, tracer fire slicing through the darkness, the hollow thump of silenced weapons, the whisper of steel in the black, singing to the aria of falling blood, the chorus of the bones.

Memories of childhood, of the dark places where I had learned to hide. Of the voices that had spoken to me in those places.

"I remember many things," I said, forking meat into my mouth so that I didn't have to speak further. The food sat like lead in my stomach.

"Do you remember Corporal Johansen?"

My mouth stopped moving. My vision narrowed to a tunnel, scarlet mist blurring around the edges.

You always remember your first.

Yet until that moment, I had not remembered her. Not remembered, at least, that it had *been* her. Not remembered that she had been the one who had opened my eyes, and my mind, and my soul, to the glory of the Bone Plate. She had fed my madness, given it life.

Whether she had wanted to or not.

"They are always so very succulent, the ones we love."

Metzger seemed to swell on the edges of my vision, something vast and ghastly in the rushing black that poured from the depths of my mind. But all I could see were the bones, scattered on the plate before me.

"The way you cut her open, with nothing but sharpened bamboo slivers and your own fingers, it was almost tender," Metzger went on, speaking through a mouthful of gore which suddenly seemed rank, offal spilling from between his lips like dead worms. "Had I not known how much she meant to you, I would never have believed that she was your lover. But her bones, they sang the sweetest song, didn't they? Like a chorus of angels, calling you in, drawing you down, into something so much deeper, so much more meaningful. Hmm?"

I couldn't speak. I wanted to reach for my guns, unleash them into his chest, and to hell with the security goons who would cut me down before I could turn on them. All I could see was Johansen, her sweet fine lips, her ice chip eyes. All I could hear was her voice, her laugh, her screams for mercy.

I remembered all too well.

I turned to look at Metzger. The vision that had swelled in my periphery did not fade like some rage-induced nightmare. The man was no man, but a demonic apparition of bone, tooth, and claw. Organs pulsed inside its ribs, glowing with a sickly purple and green light. Rotten meat fell from between its fangs to wriggle, seething, on the table. The fiend's maw moved in a gross parody of speech while its words lanced into my brain. "Sometimes, we must break a heart to touch the wholeness of what lies beyond. Tell me Terrance, are you ready to pass out of your dying shell and join me in the promised glory? Are you ready to take the next step?"

A waiter entered the room, bearing a silver platter. He set it on the table and whisked off the lid. Despite the horror of the creature before me, my eyes were drawn down to the platter, to the steaming hunk of meat that lay upon it.

I had cut open enough chests to know what I was looking at. Aorta, atrium, ventricle, sliced delicately down the centre, cooked long and slow to make it more tender. Hearts can be tough, yet fragile things. This heart was small. Not the heart of a warrior.

I looked from that small, delicate heart, to the hand on my plate, the small, delicate fingers, the gentle arching of the joints, the way the pinky was offset slightly. A familiar hand. One I had held on many a cold dark night, back in the black old days.

And the heart to go with it.

My guts clenched. My gorge rose.

I felt the power of the bones, centuries of them, layer piled upon layer locked in the earth of this hallowed ground. Hundreds, maybe more, had been laid to rest here to appease the hunger of the Meclan's ancient god, a god of dark places and desperation. A malign spirit which had not died with its people, but which had burrowed down into the soft, rotten earth and hidden amongst the bones laid there for it as a refuge, a fortress.

As if the thatchwork of bones that creaked beneath the manse were reaching out to fill my head with memories that were not mine, I remembered hundreds of years of hunger, of lurking in the shadows, of whispering to the unwary, of the hollow sweet song of wind passing through empty skulls and luring in those rare few who could hear the promise of immortality. But bones are not the key to eternal life. Bones are the warrior's strength, courage, resolve. Bones bear up the living, and remember the dead. Immortality is a darker, more elusive beast. To live forever takes heart, and the breaking of such, for nothing can be won without loss.

For centuries, the bloodthirsty god of the vanished Meclan people had languished, slowly gathering its power, seducing followers, growing its army. Waiting for its dark angel to arise and take his place at its side. Back in those days, before the black old days, it had found its champion. It had found me, bent me to its will, broken me. I had escaped once, into the haven of madness, but there would be no escape this time.

"Taste it, Terrance. Take it, all that remains of her love for you, like you took Johansen, like you fed on her screams. Eat of her heart, and join me in eternity."

The fork shook in my hand. Metzger was not just a guy in an expensive suit with a bad haircut. No man, not even an assassin, could end this being's existence with anything so banal as hot lead and razored ceramic.

"Eat. My chefs have done something with this morsel which I'm sure you will find quite . . . divine."

Everyone knows that mortals cannot kill gods. Centuries of myth and legend have ingrained this into our psyches so firmly that even if it wasn't true, I would have no choice but to believe it. It is what makes gods gods, and leaves us mortals to bend and scrape and decay at their feet. Only other gods, or demigods, or maybe the immortal, can pierce the armour of the eternal. If I wanted to destroy Metzger, if I wanted to make this creature pay for Johansen, for Hania, for what it had done to me . . .

I lifted the fork to my lips. Dark red meat quivered in anticipation of my bite. It seemed to cry out to me gently, achingly, like a string orchestra sawing one long, sonorous chord that echoed through my ribs and swelled inside my skull.

Hania had never tasted so bitter, nor so sweet.

I chewed, swallowed, took another mouthful, and another. The power surged, trapped, desperate to be unleashed. For a moment, I thought my skeleton was trying to burst free of muscle and tendon and throw itself apart. I realised that my limbs burned with pain, though I could barely feel it over the crescendo of unearthly music that filled my joints and half-blinded me.

"Welcome to my world, Terrance."

I chewed the last bite, savouring the final taste I would ever have of Hania's sweet flesh, and stood. Metzger smiled, like he didn't know what was coming. Or maybe, I thought later, like he *did*. Like he had *always* known.

"You killed her."

Metzger nodded. "She was misguided. But now you see the truth. Now you can bleed forever. If not for her, if not for me, you would still be a frail thing of finite days. Now you are . . . so much more."

"Yes," I said, my hands drifting to the guns resting across my chest. "I am."

For a time, all I knew was rage. The urge to destroy was both fluid and total.

The pistols barked hot and fierce, drilling holes through Metzger's security men. I was fast, so very fast, faster than I had ever been. In seconds they lay dead and I was launching myself at Metzger, smoking guns tossed to the floor, a bone-handled blade in each hand. I heard the knives scream with me.

Only later did I realise that I had been deceived. By then it was far too late, both for Metzger, and for me. But that didn't matter, because it was already too late for Hania, just as it had been for Johansen. All far, far too late.

The god let me come, let its men die. It didn't scream as the knives carved through its ribs and raked across its skull, stabbed through its eyes. It didn't scream, not even in death, this doubting god who had lived too long in the dark and that had seen, at last, that nothing ever changes. A god swelled to bloating with the ages of sacrifice, and yet who still suffered endless, devouring hunger. A god that has finally seen that the world it preys upon is a thing of rot and poison and decay. A god whose taste for innocent flesh could never be sated, for there is no innocence left in the world. A god who needed to create a weapon powerful enough to complete one final, sacred task, and did so the only way it knew how: with lies and murder.

A god who wanted to die, forever.

Before I had time to break a sweat, it was over.

The god I had known, the god of lies, the only true god, was dead. I knelt in its blood, black and chuckling as it gushed from punctured lungs. I began my work. The blades rose and fell, severing skin and shearing flesh. I cut the bones free, laying them in a pile, one by one.

Ulna, radius, humerus.

I had no Bone Plate to lay them in, to catch their precious juices, but these were no ordinary bones. These were the bones of a god, taken in dark vengeance by its most deadly of angels.

Fibula, tibia, femur.

Metzger's power, the power of the bone empire, the power of all the ancient deaths which had made it what it was, flowed into me as I tore bone after bone from the corpse. A pile of offal steamed on the floor beside us, so much waste in the architecture of mortality.

Clavicle, scapula, rib.

Through the haze of blood I thought to wonder at it all; at the words of doubt falling from the lips of a god; at its silence as I took its life, as though it was pleased to die. Only later would I understand these truths, that it had sacrificed my only love for the sake of its hubris, and that I was still, even in this, nothing more than a puppet in the schemes of greater, more wicked creatures than I.

Vertebrae, mandible, skull.

I was gone by the time the spooks arrived. Later, sitting in a truckstop stirring coffee which somehow no longer smelled as strong or as aromatic as it once had, I watched footage of the raid on the late news show. From on high, a helicopter relayed shaky images of the manse swarming with black-kevlared operatives. What would they think, I wondered, when they found my Bone Plate? What about when they began to dig down into those layers and layers of ancient dead?

I didn't know if the spooks had waited for me to do my work and had let me get away before they descended on the ranch, or if they had just arrived too late to catch me. Either way, I'd done their dirty work, like they had known I would. There would be no special hospital or miracle drugs at the end of this mission, however. I had walked too far into the shadow, too far beyond the brink of redemption, for them to ever take me back.

But I had a new Bone Plate now. It was an iron chariot, a holy icon all of its own, a wheeled arc of the darkest and most bloody covenant, which could make fifteen miles to the gallon on the open road. In the trunk were the artefacts of power torn from this ordeal — all that remained of a treacherous god. What was I then to do with this, the makings of a new bone empire? What to do now that I was no longer a creature of finite days? Now that I might bleed forever?

I dropped a handful of cash on the counter and stepped out into the night, crossing the carpark as an eighteen-wheeler rumbled by on the freeway. The V8 coughed to life, its bass growl a fitting counterpoint to the dissonant echoes of the bones and the ringing of the eternal strings in my head. I put the truck in gear and pulled out, knowing that somewhere down this black highway, somewhere down the long stretch of days that lay before me, I would find others like Metzger. The Meclans were not the only people to feed the dark spirits with hot blood and the screams of the living, and not all those gods had grown tired of their hunger.

Somewhere, someone else had a Hania, or a Johansen, or a Christa, or a love by any other name, and somewhere there was another Metzger waiting to devour their screams and feed their hearts to the unwary.

This dark angel rides the highway, and my hunger is fresh and raw. Nothing will sate me now but the blood of gods.

And I am so very hungry.

AFTERWORD

The inspiration for "The Bone Plate" came from many sources, both historical and mythical. Perhaps the strongest of these draws on the significance to my Maori ancestors of the bones of the dead, and how these represent the strength, wisdom, and *mana* gathered by a person over the years of their life—how the bones store the memories of the past. There are places on our land in the Coromandel which are *tapu*, or sacred; places where we do not go, caves we do not enter, for they protect such sacred remains. To disturb the bones is to dishonour the *wairua* of the dead and, at worst, raise their *kehua*.

I also drew upon the various legends of human sacrifice that litter the ancient cultures of Central and South America, for the purpose of appeasing their hungry gods.

But the story itself had its origins in a far humbler manner, with the inspiration for the title. Staring down a steaming dish full of succulent barbeque chicken drumsticks, we decided that we each needed a bone plate, and my four-year old son and I had a competition to see who could pile up the most bones during the meal. I would've won, too, except the little scamp grabbed all my bones when I wasn't looking and put them on his own plate. Cheated.

CEPHALOPODA OBSESSIA

ALAN BAXTER

I don't really know where to begin, but it all started with a drink and a bet, as is so often the case. Usually things never work out quite as the drinkers and gamblers would expect or hope, though I doubt anyone could have foreseen this. I'm sure my employer never did.

Working for Lord Selwyn Gascoigne started as a dream job. "I don't want a bloody staff, Rebecca, I want a Man Friday who knows everything and you're just the woman for the job!" Of course, he had a staff too. But the dream job quickly degenerated into a labour of grinding teeth and forced smiles.

I'd thought the employ of a real Lord, a member of the British aristocracy, would be all international parties with fascinating people and access to the secrets of power. It turned out to be a lot of juvenile, ignorant bigots celebrating each other, with open contempt for 'the common man'. But it paid well. My skills were often tested beyond the merely challenging and I maintained hope that I would gain exposure to things that might help my own path, be it life, career, financial or a combination thereof. So I stuck it out, managing my Lord's affairs like the first class PA he told everyone I was.

Gascoigne's problems started at a dinner party during the Football World Cup. His house was packed with frocked-up nobility — their teeth preceding them into every conversation — who talked about things that made no difference to real people. A blueblood by the name of Jeremy Hancock hollered for quiet during the brandy-soaked after-dinner conversation, turning up the television as he did so.

"Look at this!" he cried.

Numerous wealthy eyes turned. The screen showed an octopus in a tank. In the water with it were two plastic tubs, lids concealing a tasty mussel. On the front of the tubs were flags, one the Spanish national standard, the other that of the Netherlands; finalists in football's biggest competition.

"This damned thing has been predicting all of Germany's games successfully," said Hancock. "Now it's going to pick the winner for the final."

Someone else scoffed. "Predicting what exactly?"

Hancock didn't take his eyes from the screen. "They say he's psychic. Whichever food he chooses first is his prediction. He's had a hundred per cent accuracy so far this World Cup."

Gascoigne shouldered his corpulent way through the people, brandy swilling in his glass. "Bloody nonsense," he said, voice blustering like a stormy day. "How can a bloody octopus be psychic?"

"It's picked Spain!" Hancock shouted, ignoring the host.

"A hundred per cent, you say?" Gascoigne asked, eyes narrowed.

Hancock flicked the volume down. "If he's right this time, it'll be eight from eight. I'm placing a big bet on Spain right now."

Gascoigne barked laughter. "Bloody rubbish! You're betting on Spain? I'll bet *you* a thousand pounds they lose."

Hancock laughed. "Excellent! I'll take that bet." He pulled his phone from the inside pocket of his tailored jacket and headed out to the veranda, chatting animatedly.

Gascoigne watched the octopus for a long time, eyes narrowed in thought.

*

I knew the phone call heralded some form of disaster the moment I heard the plummy voice. "It's Jeremy Hancock. Put Gascoigne on!"

"Yes, sir."

I tapped on my employer's door, waited the required four beats, then went in. "Jeremy Hancock on line one for you, sir."

"Righto." He snatched up his receiver and stabbed at a button with one meaty forefinger. "Jezza, you big poof! Calling to gloat?"

I closed the door and returned to my desk. I was about to hang up when something stayed my hand. Nervous of making any sound, I lowered my ear to the handset lying on my leatherbound ink blotter, holding my breath.

" . . . told you so, didn't I?" That was Hancock.

"So Spain won. Pretty easy fifty-fifty guess on the part of the bloody octopus." My Lord's derision dripped from every word.

"And I'll be making an extra thou from you, old chap! Ha ha!"

"Yes, yes. Well done. Don't gloat, you sound like a peasant."

Hancock laughed again. "It's remarkable! Eight from eight is more than just chance."

"It's unusual," Gascoigne said. "But hardly remarkable."

"Well, I think it is. I plan to make an offer for that octopus."

"An offer?"

"Certainly. I want it for my own. Then we'll see how psychic it is. I'll ask it about more important stuff than bloody football."

Gascoigne laughed heartily. "You're mad, Hancock, you know that? Let me know how you get along."

"I will!"

The line went dead. I hung up and busied myself with booking accommodation for his Lordship in the Loire Valley, the Rhone and the Alsace. I made sure to find the classiest chateaux I could. Perks of the job meant I'd be going along, so I booked myself rooms with huge baths. Gascoigne's door swung open.

"What are you doing?" he asked.

I felt guilty, left-over shame from listening in on his conversation. "Working on the France trip, sir. We leave in two days." He'd only decided upon it a few days before, but that was ever his way.

He nodded, pulling on his heavy moustache. "How long are we there?"

"Seven days. You want to change that?"

"No, no, no. Can't upset the ladies. It's their little treat, after all."

He really believed he was doing a favour for his friends' wives, having me organise this trip. His own wife had died young, several years ago. I knew for a fact that all the ladies loathed the drunken blundering around the French vineyards, constantly embarrassed by their husbands' anachronistic imperial pomposity. But it wasn't my place to say, so I went with, "Of course, sir."

"Keep on with that," Gascoigne said, with a conspiratorial wink. "But I have a little side project for you."

"Yes, sir?" I picked up my pen and notepad, expecting another crazy idea requiring detailed notes.

I wasn't disappointed about the crazy part. "You know about that Paul fellow? Octopus, psychic, lives in Germany?"

I smiled. "Yes, sir. I've seen him in the news."

"I want him."

"You want the octopus, sir?"

"Yes, I bloody do. Make it happen. Bear in mind that Hancock is trying to get it as well and he mustn't succeed, nor must he know I'm after it. Get me that octopus, Rebecca, whatever the cost. Money is no object, all right? There's a bonus in it for you."

I let my notepad sink onto my lap. "Certainly, sir. I'll get onto it."

*

The negotiations heated up very quickly. Paul's owners were happy to 'retire' him for the right price, but there were apparently several interested parties. I didn't get much chance to enjoy the French wine trip; every bit of spare time in between organising private cellar door visits was spent on the phone to Germany, talking to agents, hiring private detectives to track the other buyers and talk them into backing out. On an ethical level I'm not proud of some of the things I do, but I am damned proud of the fact that every time I'm tasked with a job, I do it well. By the time we returned from France, the bidding for the Psychic Octopus had degenerated into an obscene war of wealth between my employer and Jeremy Hancock. I'd become nervous, as both had more money than sense.

"How much is 'no object'?" I asked Lord Gascoigne.

"What do you mean?"

"For this octopus, sir. The owners are prepared to sell and I've chased off all the other competition except one, and he's not giving in. Do you really mean money is no object?"

"Who's this other bastard trying to buy my octopus?" Gascoigne asked stupidly. He already considered the thing his, probably had since he'd first asked me to get it.

"Your friend Hancock," I replied.

He nodded once, his face very serious, and disappeared into his office. The light on my phone told me he was using his private line, but he wasn't dialling Hancock's number. It was one I didn't recognise, which made it quite unusual.

About twenty minutes later I got a phone call from the German owners. "You are successful in your bid," they said, happiness evident in their tone. They *should* have been happy; their annual income had increased by a ridiculous amount. I had no idea who he'd called or what the call entailed, but Hancock dropped the subject like a hot rock. I thought it best not to consider what someone like my employer might do when he felt cornered in a deal.

*

The octopus arrived with his tank and associated paraphernalia on a Thursday afternoon. Gascoigne made a nuisance of himself as the thing was set up in the drawing room. I made sure to pay attention to all the care instructions he plainly ignored. If the octopus died after all this, there would be hell to pay. And I'd be writing the cheque. I made a mental note to organise my promised bonus forthwith.

Once the delivery had been finalised the proud new owner stood in front of the tank, staring as poor Paul tried to hide himself under rocks, colours shifting to match the stone. Gascoigne crouched, hands on his knees, for a closer look. His huge belly pressed against his thighs as his bloodshot nose pressed onto the glass. He made me jump when he stood suddenly. He still stared at the cephalopod, squeezed up against the stones with nowhere to hide. "I wonder if this thing is really legit," he said, almost to himself.

"Legit, sir?"

"Truly psychic!" he said gruffly.

The hairs on the back of my neck shimmied. "So, what are you planning to do now? What will you ask Paul to predict?"

Gascoigne spun on his heel, heading for the door. "Organise a soirée, Rebecca. Get everyone here on Saturday night for a dinner party. Tell them it'll be a special event and make sure Hancock attends."

*

The gathering came about with the usual pomp and ceremony. 'Everyone' — the dozen couples that made the highest echelon of society in Gascoigne's opinion — had all responded in the positive. The guests arrived and I welcomed them, guiding them into one of the many reception rooms where they tucked into canapés and alcohol with abandon.

My employer appeared late as always and made a big show of welcoming everybody. He particularly delighted in Hancock's presence. "You're going to love this party, old chap!"

The guests drifted into the dining room and sat at the long oak table that had purportedly held the feasts of King Henry VIII and other notable royals.

Soup was served in silver terrines and met with hearty congratulations to the chef. The main course followed, rich with fat, wine and value. Once almost everyone had been served, Gascoigne stood, planting his hands on the table where his own plate should have been. "Dear friends," he said, moustache quivering with mirth. "I'm so glad you could all attend tonight. You're probably wondering where my meal is." He paused for effect and a low mutter scuttled around the table. "Monsieur Perdue!" he yelled.

His chef arrived carrying a huge covered silver platter. He put it down before his employer. I shifted from my place near the kitchen doors for a better look.

"I want you all to meet my new pet!"

I listened to Gascoigne, but watched Hancock. I saw his eyes narrow, then widen as he stared at the mirror-like silver bell cover over the plate. He seemed to be mouthing something to himself.

"It cost a small fortune, but I gained possession of Paul the Psychic Octopus and this dinner party is in celebration of that."

"What are you playing at?" Hancock asked, his voice strained.

My employer smiled. "It's said that the Inca ate their enemies' hearts in order to imbue themselves with their strength and courage. I plan to employ a similar methodology." He grinned broadly.

Hancock shook his head. "You can't be serious!"

My Lord removed the silver cover with a flourish. Paul, whole and char-grilled, sat on a bed of lettuce and tomatoes, steaming gently, his skin a patchwork of pale grey and brown scorch marks. "I'll eat this blighter and be psychic myself!" Gascoigne's belly heaved with laughter.

Hancock stood, outrage on his face. "You bloody fool! You know I wanted that octopus and you pull something like this? You think this is a joke?"

Gascoigne sat, picked up a knife and fork. "Not a joke at all, old chap," he said, though his face betrayed his amusement. "A scientific experiment. If there really is something special about this octopus, I want it *in* me." He plunged his cutlery into the carcass of football's biggest star and proceeded to eat.

Faces around the table were a mix of horror, disgust and amusement. Except Hancock. He just fumed.

*

By the time Gascoigne neared the end of his very expensive dinner his face glowed red, grease slicked his chin and his eyes betrayed a deep discomfort. But he forced the meal down until the entire unfortunate cephalopod had been consumed. He grinned at his horrified guests, particularly the furious Hancock, and the party wound down quickly after dinner. It interested me to see that even Lord Gascoigne's set had limits.

His Lordship seemed inordinately pleased with himself, though his hands kept dropping to grasp his huge rotund belly, as if in pain. When the guests had gone he retired to his rooms, dismissing me to my own for the night. I prepared for bed and sat reading, wondering if the image of my employer forcing an entire octopus down his gullet, bit by quivering bit, would ever leave my mind.

I'd dozed off when around midnight the shrill report of the private line woke me. "Yes, sir?" My voice was slurred with sleep.

"Bloody agony!" Gascoigne wheezed. "I need you, Rebecca."

I asked if I should call a doctor, but he'd already hung up. I made my way to his rooms and tapped nervously on the door.

"Yes, yes. Come."

He sat propped up in his massive four-poster bed, which was hung decadently about with silk curtains. His face shone like a prized tomato, bathed in sweat. He clutched the covers over his swollen body. "Bloody pain in the gut, Rebecca. And nightmares!"

"Nightmares?" I asked.

"I've never felt so nauseated. Fetch me something. To settle my stomach and help me sleep."

I nodded, hurrying out, questioning again exactly how all-encompassing my job description was. I returned with milk of magnesia and sleeping tablets that Gascoigne swallowed with agonised winces. He looked truly discomforted, utterly miserable. I waited until he drifted off into a disturbed, twitching kind of slumber, then left. I'm sure I awoke during the night, disturbed by screams.

*

In the morning, Gascoigne looked awful as he sat at the long table with dark purple bags under his bloodshot eyes, his mouth downcast in personal pity. A steaming coffee sat before him, next to an untouched plate of poached eggs.

"Good morning, sir. You don't look well."

"Very bloody observant, Rebecca, give yourself a gold star."

Clearly his humour matched his appearance. "What's on the agenda for today?" I asked.

"I'm never eating octopus again," he said miserably.

Taking a plunge I said, "Perhaps it wasn't so much the octopus itself as the sheer quantity?"

Gascoigne's jowls wobbled as he shook his head. "Not at all. I've eaten far more in a sitting before. I've made a terrible mistake, Rebecca. I feel awful."

I tried not to scoff. "Really, I think it's just a case of excess. Indigestion."

"No. More than that. Last night, Rebecca, they were more than dreams, terrible visions of underwater temples and reaching tentacles. Grasping hands in shadowy depths and creatures, oh my god." He buried his face in his meaty hands.

I didn't know how to respond. "I'm sorry to hear that, sir," I said. "Let's hope it passes quickly."

Gascoigne didn't answer, his glazed eyes looking into nowhere. I excused myself and left to get on with my work. As I shut the dining room door behind me I heard a great heaving sob, like a child unable to wake from a terrible dream.

*

His Lordship did not improve during the course of the day; his appearance and demeanour only worsened. I did my best to avoid him and his gruff self-pity, and those horrible glazed eyes. Repeatedly he would stare into the distance and moan. During the night his shouts and screams rattled through the house again. The following day he seemed further debilitated.

"Let me call the doctor, please," I insisted. He refused, but by the third day, after another night of insomnia and terrors, he finally relented. Doctor Bryant arrived and I explained the history of the illness.

My employer was bedridden by now and Bryant looked quite disturbed at first sight of the Lord. "You should have called me sooner," he said, annoyance evident.

Gascoigne screwed up his face, grey and sweat-soaked as it was. "Bah. Load of nonsense. I'm bloody poisoned, Doc. Poisoned by some creature of the Devil."

"The Devil?" Bryant asked.

"I've made a terrible mistake, Doc. I'm done for."

The doctor looked at Gascoigne's belly suspiciously. "You've certainly gained a lot of weight."

Gascoigne looked down with a wince. "My bloody gut just keeps swelling up." He threw the covers aside, revealing his usually rounded abdomen distended to twice its normal size, the skin stretched taut and shiny. Dark veins striped the corpulent mass, like snakes frozen in jelly.

Bryant shook his head and busied himself with blood pressure tests, temperature taking and a myriad other observations. He drew blood to send to a lab and left, promising to return the next day. "Keep your fluids up and only eat very inert foods, simple carbohydrates, stuff like that," he ordered.

My Lord snorted. "I haven't touched a bite of food or a drop of anything to drink since I ate the bastard thing."

The doctor frowned. "Three days without eating or drinking? Lord Gascoigne, you must at least drink water to avoid dehydration."

"I bloody can't! And I certainly don't feel dehydrated. I feel like I'm drowning!"

I saw the doctor out and assured him I would try to get my employer to eat and drink. I failed in that task.

*

I jerked awake to a high-pitched scream, more agonised than anything I'd heard before. It came from the other end of the house, far from Gascoigne's bedroom. Perturbed, I slipped on a dressing gown and followed the sound. The scream echoed again, muffled by something. My ears led me to the hallway and I screamed myself, jumping as the cellar door sprang open. Gascoigne stumbled out, his nightclothes soaked in sweat, his grey face drawn and exhausted. His eyes seemed more glazed than ever, staring right through me. "Sir, are you all right?"

He ignored me, staggering past as if I wasn't there. His stomach appeared to have deflated, far past its original girth. He seemed emptied somehow, slack like a half-filled wineskin, wobbling on uncertain legs.

"Sir, can I help you? What were you doing in the cellar?"

His face swung to me, his eyes swimming. His mouth fell open like a corpse, his breath foul and tangy. He looked right through me, but spoke in a strained whisper. "Don't go down there, Rebecca. It's nothing."

He staggered away, leaving me staring after him. I looked at the half open cellar door and a wave of dread washed over me. My hand shaking in fear, I grabbed the handle and pulled the door closed, turned the key in the lock, and headed back for bed.

I'd barely made two steps when I heard the front door rattling as it opened. I looked out a nearby window and saw Gascoigne climbing into the front seat of his Land Rover. The vehicle coughed into life and sped out of the driveway with a spray of gravel.

Without thinking I grabbed the keys to my own car from the rack on the wall and hurried after. By the time I'd pulled out of the long winding driveway I could see Gascoigne's tail lights disappearing up the lane. Travelling as fast as I felt I safely could, I followed him through the village and onto the main road into London. He drove through the night, his big silhouette hunched over the wheel. It was the first time I'd ever seen Gascoigne drive himself anywhere. I'd had no idea he even could.

He headed into central London and turned left and right with seeming abandon. He finally screeched to a halt on the banks of the Thames, parking across the footpath of the Embankment. As I pulled up behind him, he stepped from the car and half fell towards the railings by the river. Without pause he clambered over and held the railing in one hand.

I jumped from my car, calling his name. He paid me no attention at all. As I reached the fencing he let go and dropped from sight with a tremendous splash. I screamed his name, hoping anyone might hear, but the street stood ghostly still and quiet. I reached the concrete edge and looked down into the river. I saw his rounded back drifting out into the stream, his face underwater, arms outstretched like a crucifixion. Bracing myself to jump in and try to save him, movement caught my eye. Twisting, undulating grey shapes shivered under the surface all around Gascoigne. With quiet splashes, dozens of long, writhing tentacles broke the surface and grabbed all around his body. He didn't even twitch as the tentacles pulled him down. He disappeared without a sound, a rippling eddy all that marked his passing.

I stared, dumbfounded.

*

I should have stayed. I should have called the police and spent hours explaining that my employer had gone mad after eating a ridiculously expensive psychic octopus. But I didn't. I decided that events had finally exceeded my position description. A line had been reached.

I made the drive back to Gascoigne's estate in the smudged grey light of dawn. By the time I reached home, wondering where my life went from here, all I wanted was sleep. I'd worry about everything else after I'd slept off the dizziness and the headache.

When I got inside, trudging single-mindedly towards the stairs, I heard a muffled banging. My body was wracked with a terrible trembling, my mind spinning, trying to hold itself together. Mechanically I followed the sound, back through the hallway to the cellar door. My stomach turned to water, my knees weak as I stared at the thick oak planks, listening to the thudding from the other side. Someone, or something, wanted out. My eyes fell to the key I'd turned earlier.

In a haze of exhaustion and terror my hand dropped to the cool metal. Compelled beyond my ability to ignore, I turned it and stepped away. The banging stopped. A heavy silence hung over the house in the wan early light. After several seconds listening to my heart beating in my throat, I watched the doorhandle slowly turn. The door swung open, revealing nothing but the shadows of the cellar stairs. A scuff of movement rooted me to the spot and a figure emerged into the hallway. Gascoigne, fat and healthy, smiling broadly, walked into the light.

My employer stood there, proud and good humoured, the over-indulged Lord in every hearty respect. Except his eyes. Looking into them — seeing the elongated horizontal pupils twitching in beds of soft brown — made my knees buckle and darkness swept in from the edges of my vision.

*

I woke in my own bed. I felt hollowed out by terror as everything from the night before flashed through my mind in vivid, movie-like detail. The phone beside me sang out, making me jump. I reached for it with one shaking hand, my heart threatening to burst through my chest.

"Rebecca!" Not-Gascoigne barked. "Good, you're up. I have lots of plans. Get to my office as soon as you're dressed. And tell that doctor blighter not to worry, I'm perfectly well."

I tried twice before words would emerge from my dry mouth. "Yes, sir. Be right there."

AFTERWORD

This story is a combined homage to two different myths. It's a blending of the classic kraken legend and the ever-popular Cthulhu mythos. I always like to think that the idea of the kraken in Greek mythology came from ancient sightings and run-ins with the Great Old Ones. Of course, given that Lovecraft created his mythos in the first part of the 20th century, we know this isn't true, but why let truth get in the way of a good myth?

Anyway, it always occurred to me that the idea of the kraken rising was something not to be taken too literally. The great monster literally rising up from the depths of the ocean seems a little crass. He's more likely to rise gently and surreptitiously in a human body and start his takeover from there. And I for one welcome our new cephalopodic overlords.

THE FOAM BORN

ERIN UNDERWOOD

Marshall Goodwin stood at the stern of the Sea Dog, feeling the familiar vibration of the lobster boat's engine and the gentle sway of the ocean beneath his feet. Coming from a long line of fishermen who had carved their lives from the sea, he felt betrayed by the ocean he had once loved. Looking at the horizon where the sky disappeared under the endless blue water, he cursed the sea for taking his family away, for leaving him alone. Out there, past the Gulf of Maine toward Georges Bank, that was where he had buried his wife and son. That's where he'd spread their ashes in the deep cold waters of the Atlantic Ocean.

It was eight months since Eleni's car had skidded off a bridge in Maine and into the icy water. The cops hadn't found her car until after the nor'easter had passed. When the crews had finally pulled the vehicle from the water, they'd found Eleni and Reese drowned, holding onto each other. It was an image that haunted Marshall; an image conjured every time he looked out at the stretch of ocean where their ashes mixed with seawater and foam.

JJ, the ship's captain, cut the engine, bringing the lobster boat to a crawl before stopping it next to a set of green and red buoys. Marshall supervised as Charlie, the new deck hand, leaned over the side to hook and haul up the closest lobster pot. Adjusting his thick blue gloves and his baseball cap against the sun's glare, Marshall stood ready to guide the cage aboard.

"Damn, I'm good," Charlie said, cranking the winch. The yellow cage burst from the sea in a spray of water that doused the lower half of their overalls. Inside the cage's parlour were five medium-sized lobsters.

"Easy now," Marshall said, securing the trap to the sorting table. He watched Charlie measure and store the catch, throwing back one that was too small.

"You girls need some goddamned nail polish back there? Get that pot back in the water," JJ said from the helm. On the better side of fifty, Captain James "JJ" Johnson was a long time Marblehead lobsterman. He was a good man and a great captain, not to mention one of Marshall's oldest friends.

Charlie dropped the pot into the water, and Marshall hooked the line to the second buoy and pulled the next pot. Several feet from the surface, sunlight hit the cage's webbing, revealing a pale object attached to the outside. It looked like a body.

"Charlie. Hand me that net," Marshall said. He pointed to the one with the extra wide mouth.

Marshall took the net from Charlie. Gently, he slid it into the water, angling it beneath the pot. Meanwhile, Charlie slowly turned the winch, careful not to dislodge whatever was caught on the cage.

"It's a kid!"

In one smooth motion, Marshall scooped the body into his net before dumping its contents onto the boat. A naked boy, no older than five years old, lay sprawled on the Sea Dog's deck. A single lobster skittered from the child's hands. A clanging sound made Marshall jump, eyes flicking away from the child for a second or two. Charlie had dropped the empty trap next to the boy, its door swinging open. Charlie's face was ashen beneath his yellow baseball cap. Marshall stood slack-jawed, staring at the child even as his heart beat against his chest in an unholy rhythm.

"Jesus, what's he doing out here?" JJ asked. The man's sun-brown wrinkled face was drawn, his eyes haunted.

Unable to take his eyes off the lad, Marshall bent down to turn the boy's face up. The child screamed and scrambled away, crashing into a stack of empty lobster pots. Marshall's hand hung frozen in the air, his eyes locked on the boy.

"Jesus, he's alive!"

JJ's words energised Charlie, sending him backward, slipping on the wet deck where he nearly tipped himself over the railing.

Trembling, the boy wrapped his arms around his legs and pulled his knees to his chest in a foetal position. His skin was sea-foam white. From beneath a mass of black curly hair, he looked up at Marshall. Marshall felt the world tilt a little to the left, threatening to send him to his knees until JJ grabbed his arm with a steady grip.

"Marsh, is that your boy?" JJ asked in a hushed voice. The old captain removed his hat and crossed himself. He took another, closer look. "Blessed Mary, save us all." He edged away from the child.

"Impossible. It can't be." Marshall stared at the child. He was a spitting image of his son, Reese, right down to the Texas shaped birthmark on his left shoulder.

JJ was shaking his head. "Charlie, get that thing off my boat." Charlie glanced at Marshall, but didn't move until JJ bellowed, "Now! Before we all end up in the deep."

Terrified, the lad looked up at Marshall. Pleading.

"The hell you will," Marshall said, slamming the net down. "We've known each other for a long time. So, I'm going to forget I heard you order Charlie to toss my boy overboard."

"That *thing* isn't Reese," JJ said, squaring off against Marshall.

"Well, what is he? I can't explain it, but this is my boy," Marshall said. His knees threatened to go weak beneath him. "I've never asked you for anything, but I'm asking for this."

The older man turned sheet white beneath his wrinkled skin as he looked at the child. The sky above grew overcast. The water turned rough and choppy.

"Marshall, Reese is dead. This isn't him, but if it were . . . " JJ reached out, gently touching Marshall's shoulder " . . . you have to let him go."

"I can't. Not again," Marshall's voice cracked. Salty tears leaked from his eyes. "You owe me, JJ. How many times have I saved your arse?"

The Captain cursed under his breath.

"Just keep him away from me," JJ said, turning his back on Marshall.

The ride back to Marblehead was strained and quiet. Charlie rode up front with JJ, both of them refusing to look at Marshall or the boy. By the time they reached the wharf, a storm was blowing in. Marshall wrapped Reese in an old wool blanket that smelled of stale air and fish.

Marshall tried to say thank you, but JJ cut him off, hand slashing the air between them. "Just get him out of here. I'm taking the Sea Dog out with Charlie tomorrow," JJ said. He didn't need to be any clearer that Marshall wasn't included. JJ glanced up with an apology in his eyes before turning back to his work, tying off the line.

"Can I ask a favour?" Marshall said.

JJ shrugged, not looking up.

"Give me a day to figure out what to tell people before you say anything about Reese?" Marshall felt small and vulnerable standing on the dock, waiting for an answer. He hugged Reese to his chest.

"I suppose we can give you that much," JJ said, after a painfully long silence.

Charlie nodded his agreement. "Marsh, be careful."

"Thank you," Marshall said.

JJ turned away. Marshall headed toward his pickup truck, leaving the sound of crashing waves and howling wind behind. Nothing mattered except for the small child in his arms. Marshall knew he should question this miracle, but his relief and joy were intoxicating. His son was back.

A few minutes later, Marshall pulled into his driveway and carried Reese inside. The boy wandered around the house, going from object to object and registering odd looks of recognition.

"You know these things, son?" Marshall asked, setting a hand on Reese's shoulder.

Reese let out a windy sigh as he walked through the house still clutching the blanket around him. He touched the grape juice stain on the couch, ran his fingers over the wooden coffee table, and traced the faint crayon designs scribbled on the wall. Reese gurgled a laugh and ran down the hallway, dropping the blanket and throwing open his bedroom door.

Naked as the day he was born, Reese pulled everything from the toy chest. Once it was empty he turned to the dresser, pulling out pants, shirts, underwear, and socks that had been left untouched. Standing in the middle of the room, Reese surveyed his things with a thoughtful, satisfied smile that stretched into a happy grin.

Marshall watched the boy with a mixture of wonder and amusement. Whatever miracle brought him back, there was no doubt this was his son.

"Come on, Reese. Let's get you dressed."

*

When dinner was ready they sat at the table like a family, except for Eleni's vacant chair. Marshall set a chicken strip with a small pile of fries on Reese's plate and poured him a glass of water. The boy watched Marshall eat before trying his own food, which he spat out half-chewed. Reese grabbed at his glass, but drinking wasn't a skill he had maintained. Water slopped onto the table, soaking his food.

After dinner, Reese climbed into bed — a normal act that breathed life back into the house. Exhausted, Marshall dozed in the rocking chair next to Reese's bed. The wind wailed angry and alone, tearing through branches until it finally blew itself out.

In the morning, Marshall woke and stretched, yawning. He jumped at the sound of breaking glass. Reese was gone and Marshall was on his feet — running.

A shattered jar of dill pickles lay on the floor. Green pickle spears, vinegar, and shards of glass spread out around Reese's feet.

"Dammit, Reese!" Marshall yelled, failing to hide the fear and anger from his voice.

Tears brewed in Reese's eyes and spilled down his cheeks. A soft cry escaped his lips. In his left hand he held an open package of raw cod fillets that were half eaten. Telltale bits of fish dotted his lips and fingers.

"I'm sorry. You have to be careful, son." Marshall took a deep breath, forcing himself to calm down. Reese stepped toward Marshall, his foot landing on a jagged piece of glass. He screamed.

Marshall scooped the boy into his arms and carried him to the couch where he examined the cut. It was wide, but not deep, which was good news. However, where there should have been blood, only a thick mixture of salt water and sand dribbled from the gash. Marshall jerked his hands away from the boy's foot. The resemblance to his son was uncanny. Perfect in almost every detail, except the most important one. He didn't bleed. Marshall stared in horror. Whatever he had hoped Reese was, this boy wasn't human.

"What have I done?" he asked in a low voice.

"Dah. Hurt," cried the boy through trembling lips. Fear and pain glistened like rain in the boy's eyes, but it was the desperate need for love and comfort that tore at Marshall.

"Reese?"

"Hurt."

"It is really you? I'm so sorry. You shouldn't have died. She shouldn't have been driving . . . " Marshall's voice broke, releasing the grief and anger he'd held onto for so long. He pulled his son into his arms and cried.

"Dahdee," Reese said, returning the hug.

"No one will take you away from me again."

Marshall retrieved his first-aid kit and bandaged Reese's cut. He then put *Sesame Street* on the TV for Reese and cleaned the mess in the kitchen.

No sooner did he finish wiping the floor than the doorbell rang. He ignored it. The bell rang again followed by loud pounding. Marshall yanked open the door, expecting JJ or Charlie.

Instead he found Jenny. His neighbour's daughter stood fidgeting on the porch, nervously twisting her ponytail around her finger and glancing over her shoulder at Marshall's pickup truck.

"Jenny? What's wrong?"

"You're home! Oh, God, you are here!" she cried. "Why aren't you on the Sea Dog?"

"Why aren't you in Boston?" he shot back, looking at her new Boston University sweatshirt. He'd always wanted to attend college, but never had. Life, the sea, and a child had got in the way. Instead, he'd opened a college fund in Reese's name; he'd wanted to ensure that his son had more opportunities than just fishing the sea.

"I'm house-sitting for my parents while they're in Spain. They left you a note," Jenny said, glancing at the pile of unopened mail on the table by the door. She looked back at him, her eyes going wide. "You haven't heard."

Jenny pushed past him, rushing through the door and into the living room where she grabbed the remote and changed the channel to the local news.

"Hey, Reese," Jenny said automatically. Then she froze. "Reese?"

She stumbled backwards on clumsy feet until she crashed into a bookshelf. Jenny looked from Reese to Marshall and then back to the boy. She screamed. Marshall leaped towards her and then pressed his hand over her mouth, holding it there until she stopped.

"It's okay," he whispered over and over again.

"He's dead. He's supposed to be dead," she whispered never taking her eyes away from Reese.

"There was a mix up. That's why I'm home today. We're trying to figure out how to tell everyone without upsetting Reese or causing a stir." Marshall was surprise by how easily the lies came.

"Dead kids don't come back."

"He's not dead, never was. He got lost in the system due to a mix up."

"A mix up? How do you lose a kid? Who got cremated? What about Eleni? You identified the bodies."

"She's dead, and I was wrong. We don't know who the child was in the car with her."

"That's horrible. What are you going to do?" she said. The news bulletin alert sounded, drawing their attention back to the television, which was showing a picture of the Sea Dog. "I thought you were on board until I saw your truck in the driveway."

A no-nonsense brunette sat at the news desk as photos of the JJ and his lobster boat were displayed on the screen behind her.

"The Coast Guard has been dispatched, but no trace of the Sea Dog or her crew has been found since receiving the Mayday. It's thought that that the lobster boat suffered mechanical problems during a freak storm this morning."

"Charlie and I, we've been seeing each other. It was just a few times but . . . " Jenny said. Her eyes filled with tears.

"JJ is a pro. I'm sure they're fine," said Marshall, his voice hushed.

"Yeah," she said, without sounding convinced.

They watched as a Coast Guard vessel battled against the mercury-coloured sea looking for the lost lobster boat. Marshall ran his fingers through his hair and clamped his jaw shut to keep from screaming. The Sea Dog, it couldn't be gone. His best friend was on that boat. And Charlie, he was just a kid.

"JJ, I'm so sorry," Marshall whispered. He dropped to his knees and covered his face with calloused hands.

A gentle hand touched his shoulder. He looked up expecting to see Jenny, but found Reese watching him with sad eyes.

"Mah," he said, pointing to the television. The sound of his voice was a soft, windy sigh.

Marshall reached up and held Reese's cold hand.

Reese wrapped his arms around Marshall. The boy's skin was cool like the ocean and smelled of salt. A moment later, Jenny knelt down, wrapping her arms around them both. The three of them stayed there on the wide pine floors until Marshall's knees began to ache. The phone rang, giving him a reason to disentangle himself from their arms.

"Hello?" Marshall said, answering the phone. "Seamus, I'm watching it now. Uh, sure. Of course, I can share the watch. I'll see you then."

Marshall hung up and looked at Jenny.

"I hate to ask, but I don't have anyone else I trust right now. Do you mind—?"

"If you and Seamus see them, you call me first. Okay? Reese and I will be fine," she said, ruffling the boy's hair.

"Thank you," Marshall said. "He isn't talking yet, and it's probably best if you keep him inside for now. I won't be gone long."

Jenny nodded and changed the channel to cartoons, which brought a smile to Reese's face.

*

Fort Sewell earned its reputation as an important defensive location and lookout point during the Revolutionary War. Now, it was the spot that families and friends came to watch for returning ships. Sometimes they never returned, but someone always stood watch, waiting.

When Marshall arrived at the Fort's grassy area, he found Seamus sitting on one of the wooden benches that ringed the spot. He was old by any standard, wearing time and experience like a comfortable suit of clothes.

"Got the lemon cake?" Seamus asked.

"Of course," Marshall said, smiling. He held up two cups of coffee and a bag containing Seamus's dessert.

"You're a good boy, Marshall. So much like your ma. Too bad you got your da's looks." Seamus raised a hairy eyebrow and returned the smile. With a nod, he directed Marshall to the empty spot on the bench.

"JJ's too stubborn to go down easy," Marshall said, watching the darkening horizon.

"He's a good captain," Seamus agreed.

"I should have been with him. If I were there . . . he and Charlie . . . this is my fault."

"There's no reasoning with the sea. She takes what she wants and gives what she will," said Seamus. He broke off a piece of the lemon cake. "I know you, boy. You've somewhat more on your mind than the Sea Dog."

Marshall nodded.

"I was thinking about tales you used to tell when I was a kid. Those stories about old lore and sea creatures. Are there any about selkies that aren't selkies? More like merfolk, but with human bodies? My imagination's gone a bit wild, I suppose," Marshall said, smiling sheepishly.

"There are a lot of stories. The Formorians. Atargatis. Oannes. The sea is full of myths for a man who knows where to look."

"What about the dead returning from the sea?" Marshall asked, taking a sip of coffee to avoid looking Seamus in the eye.

The old man let out a low whistle. In a soft voice, he said, "Now, I dunno. Maybe you're thinking of the foam born."

"Foam born?"

"Legend says when Aphrodite was born, she rose from the sea foam fully formed. Now that's a sight I'd like to see."

"I was thinking more about regular people who died and came back."

"There are other versions. Dead rising up from the deep, born of sea foam and salt." Seamus stared off into the distance, seeing something beyond the waves. He was quiet so long the Marshall thought the conversation was over, but then in a soft voice Seamus spoke. "When I was a boy, on my first ship, we made our way across the Aegean Sea. We stopped to deliver supplies on a small island near Crete. There was this old man. He would row his boat into the sea every day, carrying food, sometimes clothing, and he would drop it overboard. The islanders said he had a young daughter, a girl with green eyes and light brown curls, who drowned during a storm. They spread her ashes in the water. A few months later, the old man claimed he saw her swimming in the harbour. After that, he searched for her every day. They say she was foam born."

"You believe it?" Marshall said.

"I was just a kid. What did I know?" Seamus pulled his jacket tightly around his shoulders as the wind picked up. "I can't fault the old man for wanting to find her. If it were me, I'd take her as far from the ocean as I could get."

"Go inland," Marshall said.

Seamus nodded, saying, "It's just an old story."

"Of course." They sat in silence watching the horizon.

*

On the way home, Marshall thought of Eleni. He should have done more to stop her from driving home from her parents' house in Maine. The nor'easter had just started and she'd insisted on coming home.

"Stay an extra night," he had told her over the phone. She'd groaned; the tortured daughter who had already spent one too many nights with her parents.

"The storm isn't bad. Besides, all Reese can talk about is coming home to see daddy. He's giving me *the Goodwin eyes*. How can I say no?" she'd said. He'd heard the grin in her voice.

"You can't," Marshall said, laughing. "It's a four-hour drive in good weather. Take it easy. Call me every hour, and pull over if you get tired. Love you."

"I love you, too, Marshall."

She'd called once more. Their last conversation had broken off midsentence as her scream mixed with screeching brakes and the horrible sound of rending metal as her car smashed through the bridge's railing. A part of him had died that night when Eleni and Reese skidded off the road, plunging into the frigid Maine water. Worse, the part of him that was left could never really forgive her for leaving him behind.

*

He and Reese enjoyed a sushi dinner with sake and maguro plus an extra-large glass of salt water followed by some TV time until the boy fell asleep on the couch. Marshall tucked Reese into bed and stood in the doorway watching his son sleep, listening to the rhythm of his breath. It felt good to have his family home. He turned off the light.

The wind outside howled, rattling the windows. Marshall glanced out at the moonlit branches just as a passing shadow blocked the light, forming the silhouette of someone looking in through the window at him. Then as quickly as the form took shape it was gone, scattered by a thousand shifting branches and moonlight.

Marshall pulled the curtain closed just as a branch the width of a baseball bat crashed through the window. Shards of glass whipped through the air cutting his face and arms.

"Damn it!" he yelled, falling back. He pressed his palm to his chin to stop the bleeding.

Outside, the wind screamed with the fury of a nor'easter bent on destruction. Thunder and lightning clashed, shaking the house to its timbers, as storm clouds swept across the sky, swallowing the last traces of moonlight.

Reese wailed with the wind, his voice lost in the storm. Marshall picked up his son and carried him into the living room, whispering, "You're okay. You're okay." He closed the door behind them and grabbed the phone to call the cops. He stared at the number pad trying to figure out how he'd explain Reese to Officer Simms or one of the others who had known Marshall since they were kids. Small towns held no secrets. Marshall set down the phone and grabbed his gun from his desk. Together he and Reese cuddled on the couch where they waited out the storm, his gun standing guard on the coffee table, housing the single bullet he had loaded after the funeral, but never had the courage to use.

*

Last night wasn't fun. Marshall woke with dried blood on his neck and an ugly scab along his chin. The storm had taken its toll. Storms in New England were known for their eeriness, but last night was one of the worst. At times, he swore there was a keening voice howling in the wind.

With plywood, hammer, and nails in hand, Marshall sealed up the broken window. The storm should have ravaged the room, but it hadn't. Strangely, the walls and floor were bone dry, except for the area right around the branch.

Someone sent that branch through Reese's window, and something unnatural inspired that storm — of that Marshall was sure. Was it Eleni? Had that been her outside the window? If it was Eleni, there was no question that she was angry and that she wanted Reese back. Marshall was angry, too. There was no way he would let her take Reese away again. Had she done something to the Sea Dog? Was she the reason JJ and Charlie had never returned? What had she become?

Seamus's words echoed in his mind. *The sea takes what the sea wants.*

The sea had taken his wife and son once. It wouldn't take his son again. Eleni was a different matter. If she had she thrown that branch through the window, she wasn't his Eleni any longer, which would make this easier. They had to leave. Kansas. Nebraska. Anywhere as long as it was far away from the ocean.

*

Marshall pulled into the driveway, his truck full of empty cardboard boxes. He and Reese would spend the rest of the day packing and leave as soon as the truck was full and well before nightfall.

He grabbed the bag of bubble wrap and headed inside through the kitchen door that stood ajar. He considered a few choice words to offer Jenny for leaving the door open with a five year old in the house.

She lay napping on the couch with the TV remote cradled against her chest and the *House of Fashion* blaring on the television. A set of watery footprints led from the open kitchen door, through living room, and then down the hallway toward Reese's room.

Marshall dropped the shopping bag. He didn't stop; he didn't think. He just ran, racing down the hallway, slipping on the wet floorboards. Reese lay snuggled in his bed, napping quietly, curled against his plush teddy bear. Standing at the foot of the bed, next to the branch, was a naked woman with long black hair tangled with seaweed, and sea-foam white skin instead of her natural olive complexion. She looked different, but it was still Eleni. She looked up at Marshall with familiar brown eyes.

"Eleni?" he asked. He stepped into the room, moving slowly until he was next to Reese's bed.

"Mine," she said. The word came out as a windy hiss. Her heart-shaped face contorted as she snarled — her nostrils flared, and her gleaming white teeth were barred; ready to attack.

A gale blew from her mouth, howling in his ears and sending pictures and books crashing to the floor.

Reese woke. He smiled up at Marshall. Then he sniffed the air and giggled with excitement when he saw Eleni.

"Mah!" Reese said, sitting up and reaching his arms toward her.

"I won't lose him again," Marshall said, snatching Reese from the bed. He backed out of the room with Eleni stalking after him, following him down the hallway.

"Mine," she moaned over and over again, her voice creaking like branches in the wind.

In the living room, Marshall yanked opened his desk drawer, spilling some of the contents on the floor. He swore and looked around for the gun, which sat on the coffee table half covered by magazines.

"Why didn't you listen? Why couldn't you stay with your parents one more night? Why couldn't you just listen to me for once? Why did you leave me behind?" Marshall demanded with tears streaming down his face for the first time since the funeral. White-knuckled, he gripped Reese to his chest.

"Mine," Eleni hissed again.

"He's *mine*!" Marshall roared the words at Eleni and raised the gun.

Eleni howled like the wailing wind.

Jenny slept through it all.

Reese screamed.

Eleni charged, her arms stretched forward to pluck Reese from Marshall's arms.

"No!" Marshall pulled the trigger. The gun's solitary bullet fired in a deafening roar and tore through Eleni's shoulder, missing her heart. His bullet. Salt water and sand flowed from her wound, and she stumbled backward, confused.

"Marshall?" She finally seemed to recognise him. Eleni retreated. Saltwater streamed from her eyes and wounded shoulder.

"He's mine now," Marshall said.

"No." She staggered backward and then turned, escaping through the kitchen door.

Marshall looked down at Jenny, wondering how she could have slept through the last five minutes. He put the gun back on the coffee table. "Jenny, wake up. We have to get out of here." When she didn't respond, Marshall bent over and shook her shoulder. Her head turned to the side and water poured from her mouth and nose. "Oh. Shit. *Jenny.* I'm so sorry."

Marshall walked to the kitchen door and slammed it shut.

*

The next twenty minutes were spent packing only the essentials. It took longer than he liked. Reese sat on the floor, near Jenny's body, where Marshall could keep an eye on him as he carried boxes stuffed with clothing and household items out to the truck. He had spent a lifetime gathering his physical possessions, refusing to be the next lobsterman driven out of town. He'd fought tooth and nail keep the house that his father had built, but now he was leaving everything behind. And Jenny. He didn't know what to do about her. She'd been a good kid and didn't deserve this.

All that mattered was Reese. Eleni would not take his boy again. Not now. Not ever.

The house looked ransacked. Books and papers were spread everywhere, garbage overflowed the bin, and valued objects like the antique brass fishing lantern and the name plaque from his father's boat were tossed aside. Reese's colouring books were spread across the floor, crayon oceanscapes scrawled across every page.

The phone rang as Marshall tucked the last box into the truck. Seamus was on the line and sounded a bit shaken.

"Marsh, I'm wondering if you might be looking for something."

"No, I can't say that I am. I'm in a hurry, heading out of town."

"I just thought that if you had lost something, it might be at the Fort."

"Seamus, what have you found?" Marshall asked, panic ringing in his voice. Reese wasn't in the living room any longer.

"I think you know."

"I'll be right there."

Minutes later, Marshall barrelled down Front Street in his rusty green pickup, heading toward Fort Sewell. He passed the parking lot and drove straight up onto the grassy area. Several people walking dogs jumped to the side, narrowly missing the front end of Marshall's bumper. At the top of the walkway he saw Reese looking out at the glittering water.

"Reese. Come here, son. Step away from the edge," said Marshall.

Seamus watched them both from about thirty feet away, not willing to move closer.

Reese turned and waved happily at Marshall.

"Dahdee. Home now," he said, giggling.

Marshall sprinted the rest of the distance, but not before Reese leapt over the side, laughing in delight. He splashed down and resurfaced once before going under again.

Marshall ripped off his jacket and tossed his shoes aside. In the distance, he saw the Sea Dog being towed in by the Coast Guard. A fleeting moment of happiness rocked him at seeing his friends. Moments later he vaulted over the side of the cliff after Reese.

The waves were calm, but the tide pulled him down below the surface. He tried to swim up for another breath, but cool, strong hands held him in place. Reese swam in happy circles, welcoming him. Eleni floated in front of him, holding his arms and keeping him deep beneath the surface. Her eyes were dark and angry.

"I love you," he said with the last of his breath bubbling from his mouth. Her eyes softened. Seeing her, feeling her touching him with Reese swimming happily around them reminded him of everything he'd lost and everything he had again. They were alive.

"I'm sorry," she responded.

"Me too," he mouthed back, growing desperate for air.

She pulled him close, placing her mouth on his, sending water into his lungs. When she pulled away, she smiled sadly. His vision narrowed to a single pinpoint of light as a small body swam by him, waving.

Daddy, Reese cried happily.

Reese, he tried to say, but no sound escaped his lips.

Eleni let go. Marshall felt himself floating up toward the surface, face down. She took Reese's hand and swam toward the deep, toward George's Bank, just before Marshall's world turned black.

AFTERWORD

"The Foam Born" was inspired primarily by the recent death of my mother and our family's tradition of spreading our ashes at sea. The image of ashes mixing with salt, sea, and foam has always held a special meaning for me. One day, while I sat on a bench at Fort Sewall, I watched a turquoise coloured Jonesport lobster boat heading out to check its traps. With the need to spread my mother's ashes still weighing on my mind, I began to wonder what would happen if the ashes could somehow reform, returning the dead to life. I did some research to see what creatures (if any) might come close to this idea, and I found an old Greek myth that told the tale of how the goddess Aphrodite was born, rising from the sea foam after Chronos had cut off Uranus' genitals and thrown them into the ocean. While not a perfect match, the story idea solidified from there and "The Foam Born" came to life inspired by imagination, love, and longing for the lost.

SKIN

VIVIAN CAETHE

Her skin sloughed off in a thousand colours, dried bits and pieces of herself cascading to the floor. Ellen rubbed her hands gently over her still-sore stomach, feeling a scale-like crackle as she was born anew.

Those who had seen beneath the swaths of clothing asked if it hurt. The question implied a sense of continuity, the pain of transformation carried through to a new existence. Transformation was part of her nature, had always been part of her nature.

It had hurt at the time, but with a flavour of pain that promised release. The other customers in the tattoo parlour sometimes came over to watch, wincing and gasping. She looked at them impassively over the tattoo artist's hands. Their fascination was a fear of pain, of misshaping of the original form. They had never changed their skins, become something else. She smiled at them while her bones rattled with the electric buzz of the tattoo machine. To her, the human form was painful, more so than the momentary inconvenience of a day's sitting.

Ellen turned to look in the mirror, rubbing lotion into what remained of her former self, ensuring the healing of her new form. The lines and colours traced up and down her arms, black and purple standing out starkly against her pale skin. Blue like the veins tracing memories of the sea. She was becoming a different creature entirely, the daughter of colours, brought forth through the ripping of the epidermis, the destruction of the outer shell. Peeling back layers to reclaim the skin stolen from her. Or perhaps she was becoming a mockery of what she had once been.

They had finished the last of her new skin two weeks ago; it was almost done healing now. It had taken ten years before she even started to get the work done: ten years of research and false starts, ten years to find the only solution, her only salvation. Her belly had been the last to be tattooed, everything else spiralling toward the core of her being. After fifteen years of tattoo work, she was ready, her body covered with the intricate whorls and symbols, memories dredged from her life before this one. Only her face was free of markings.

Tomorrow she would she go to the beach. There, she would walk down to the sand, under the light of the full moon. She would remove her clothes, baring herself to the night. She had known which beach it would have to be, and on which night. She had waited for Henry to die out of love. Despite herself, he had kept her on the land, had made her happy, had held her when she cried at night. But now she was ready. Now she could return to the sea.

Ellen looked at herself in the mirror, pleased with the effect. It wasn't the same as her lost skin, but it was an improvement on the skin she had been forced to wear for ninety-four years. At least she hadn't aged. She smiled to herself, wondering what Henry would think of her now.

*

All those years ago, she had seen him standing on the beach, tears dripping down his face as he twisted the stem of a poppy in his hands. Curious, she had crept from her hiding place in the dunes, so moved by his sorrow she had left her skin behind. She had taken it off, leaving it on the dunes to bask in the moonlight. She cursed that curiosity, that momentary inattention.

He had taken off his hat, its emblems marking him as a soldier. She had seen soldiers before, the ones in the water, floating dead, the others in boats, staring sadly into the distance. Kneeling at the tide line, he had set the poppy gently in the water, watching the surf carry it away.

She'd known him from the pain he felt; his tears had carried it to her, hidden as she was the depths. It had drawn her to the shores, had drawn her to *him*. His tears had been almost as salty as the sea. She'd wanted to know what would make someone so sad.

Firm hands had grabbed her from behind, one over her mouth to keep her from screaming. Fighting, she'd seen three men, eighteen years old at most; one had held her firmly, laughing quietly at her struggles. They had dragged her away from the man who stood his lonely vigil. Rough hands against her lips, filthy fingers on her flesh. Her skin—the one she'd left carelessly in the moonlight— had dangled from the hands of a chubby man; he danced with it, chortling obscenely. They had dragged her down the beach to their campfire; she hadn't seen it from her own place in the dunes. A driftwood pyre had burned and the two men had twirled around it, while one held her down.

She'd scratched and bit and fought, trying to get her mouth free to scream, to curse them. The one who'd grabbed her had thrown her to the ground and leered at her. The second, a skinny, thin-faced man had held her firmly against the sand while the third, the chubby man, had danced with the skin. Holding it high, he'd laughed at her as he dipped it toward the fire. Tears had trickled from her eyes; they had to know what she was now. No one who didn't know about selkies would torture her like this. They had to know what they were doing. She fought harder, her feet drumming against sand strewn with broken bottles, remnants of their carousing.

The man's fingers had dug into her skin and she'd twisted her mouth free to scream. The sound had seemed muted against the dunes, their voices drowning her out as they'd laughed and jeered at her. The thin-faced man snatched her pelt from the chubby one and held it over the fire, watching her as she tried to break free, tried to rescue her self. As she wrenched away from her captor's grip, the thin man had dropped it into the blaze. She'd screamed, the pain searing through her and they'd grabbed her again, holding her down, pulling her hair, ripping hanks from her skull, as they added fuel to the fire — a bonfire for her to mourn her skin.

Henry had burst into the campsite then, punching the man who had held her. The other two yelped and ran, leaving their companion to save himself. Throwing sand in the soldier's eyes, the man had made his escape. She'd reached toward the fire, burning herself to try to salvage her skin. Henry had held her while she sobbed and fought, realising eventually he wasn't like the others. She'd remembered his tears had tasted like salt. He had given her his coat, a poor substitute for the skin he didn't know she had lost. In the days that had followed, as she'd learned how to adjust to her new skin, her hated skin, he had given her a name, Ellen.

Eventually, she had learned what caused him to mourn. That same sense of loss had plagued her every day since she had lost her skin. It was losing a part of herself, a part of himself. Their pain brought them together.

Years after they were married, she'd told Henry the story; when he aged and she did not. They had shared loss that day, loss of innocence, loss of identity. Enough to bring them closer, if only to fill the jagged holes within. He never spoke of that day on the beach, or the battles in the war that had preceded it. Any mention she made of her own loss was in the context of her love for him. She had told him she would wait to return to the sea until he had died.

The memory had turned sepia with age, the fire charring the edges with pain. Close to a century among humankind had taught her how simple her worries were that day; the virgin fears of her kind when they lay on the beaches. The fears she had known in the sea of her childhood were simple things — fierce, vicious creatures embodying ceaseless hungers.

On land, in the company of men, she had learned the spectrum of greed, anger, lust and more. All of the animal cruelties had been sharpened on the human intellect. Horrific deeds justified through convoluted moral codes and social norms. She had learned how they excused their nature.

She had learned about revenge.

There were days when she would rage, when even Henry's kindness couldn't keep her contained. She would cry and scream and beat her fists against the walls that held her. The land that trapped her without her skin. Those days had kindled the fires that had fuelled her quest to find her freedom.

Henry had died twenty-five years ago. With his death, Ellen was freed to begin her project. Years later, she felt the first buzz of the tattoo machine, the first piercing of her skin, the first drop of blood. The first taste of magic.

Picking up her phone from the breakfast counter, she checked her friends' updates. Brian had changed his relationship status again. She smirked as she finished her makeup. Blind dates were always such a disappointment. Especially when they never showed up.

She saw Joseph Jr had eaten dinner at the bistro around the corner from his work. It was the third time this week. Opening her planner, she made a note on the date. If this continued another day, she would consider it a trend. It would make it more difficult if people expected him immediately after work, rather than in the space of a commute to the suburbs.

The men had been easy to find, easier than she had expected. Years of phone-book research and libraries had made the task seem impossible. But the Internet had put all three men only a click or two away. Luke Stafford. Joseph Macarthur. Matthew Smith.

They were dead now, of course, and their sons aged beyond usefulness. The men had been teenagers when they had stolen her skin; they had aged and died like anyone else. She couldn't truly have expected them to live for over a hundred years. All three of them had had sons, only children raised by the men who had stolen from her, their wives pale and passive like most women of that era.

And those sons had had sons, cut from the same cloth as their grandfathers. She had found Joseph Senior early on, had watched him wipe away tears at his grandson's college graduation. He had been the speaker, an honoured veteran and pillar of the community. She had stood at the back of the crowd, watching him, the fury burning unsated in her breast. He had been the last remaining of the three. The one who had burnt her skin. He alone had survived for her to see her revenge, but by the time she was prepared, even he was dead.

The sins of the fathers would be visited upon the sons, and upon their grandsons. On Brian, on Joseph, on Mark.

Ellen's phone beeped to remind her of the pile of emails she had been ignoring. She pulled them up, seeing the latest was from her boss. One of the girls had called in sick, could she cover? Referencing her planner, she checked. Yes, she could. Tonight was free. Tomorrow was not.

*

It wasn't really a job and Hyssop wasn't really Ellen's boss, but for all intents and purposes their relationship was closer to employment than friendship. She had always found it difficult to make friends among humans; most women were put off by the ineffable otherness she possessed. Even the girls she worked with, who were typically attracted to otherness in a variety of forms, found her to be too much. One of them had even mentioned it, smiling as she suggested that was perhaps why Ellen was so good at their form of employment.

The night had worn on by the time she made her way to The House. The men's club was in one of the seedier parts of the city, close enough to the seaside tourist district to be respectable, but near enough to the docks to lend to itself a certain danger. She arrived at quarter to nine, an hour early for her shift. The bouncer nodded to her and opened the side door to the hallway that led to her room. Striding down the hall, she made it to her dressing room without incident, unusual for a Friday night. There were typically strays waiting around, some of whom were not as well behaved as her customers.

In addition to being well-mannered, her clients were always on time, a trait that pleased her greatly. And although most of them were the shy, retiring type, there was a certain dignity in their submissiveness. A gentility to their bearing, despite the leather and vinyl.

*

Taking a taxi home, she rubbed her aching feet. She had never become accustomed to shoes. Only one more day, a couple more tasks and she would be done. She would be free.

The sea crashed in her dreams. Waves broke on her form and she stood in the water, wanting to become what she once was. The yearning grew stronger with each wave. Yet no matter how much she wanted it, she couldn't change. The sea rejected her, breaking around her and never once touching her soul. The cold waves retreated from her, leaving her skinless, broken in a land of heat and pale sun. She shattered into dust and dry bones.

Ellen woke early the next morning, sweating and drained. A shower returned some level of normalcy and she took her imagination fiercely in hand. She had just been nervous. It would all be fine. It wouldn't be a problem. She would be home soon.

Dressing, she put together her purse, paying careful attention to make sure she had everything she would need: a paper bag, a plastic container, keys, phone. As she left the apartment, she closed the door and rattled the knob making sure it locked behind her. A lifetime of habits, even now when it didn't matter. Her purse hung heavy on her shoulder, the rough texture of the vinyl rubbing against her side where it swung.

Her heels clicked on the pavement, the morning air tasting of the sea only a mile away. A raw reminder of what had been stolen from her. Cars whizzed by in schools, tightly controlled by the predatory movements of police vehicles and the shifting lights and signals. The walk to the station took fifteen minutes, but it was a nice day and she had the time. The crowds thickened as the morning wore on and she found herself easily joining the flow.

*

By midmorning, she arrived at the office complex where Luke Stafford's grandson worked as a security guard. Luke had danced with her skin, laughed as she screamed.

She took the stairs to the top of the fourteen storey building. Pushing open the exit, she was pleased to hear the alarm that shrieked when the door opened. She hadn't been completely sure it would alert. Stepping out onto the roof, she propped the door open with a loose bit of concrete and walked across the gravel to the edge. A short retaining wall separated the roof and the forty-six metres to the ground. Standing there, she could look across the city to the sea that glimmered in the distance. The morning sun turned the water silver, the waves glittering diamonds just beyond her reach.

Footsteps thudded up the stairwell and he came through the door, huffing slightly. She heard Brian cross the gravel, his shoes crunching with each step. "Miss, you can't be up here."

She tore her gaze from the ocean to look at him. He took after his father, chubby and red-faced after exertion. His retreating hair was pulled back into a greasy ponytail. She held her hand out to him and he took it, befuddled.

"Hi Brian," she waggled her phone, showing him her dating profile. He frowned and peered at it.

Hope glimmered in his eyes as he looked up at her. "You never showed up for our date yesterday."

"Sorry, I got held up at work."

"Why are you here?"

"I wanted to make up for last night. Your status said you were at work."

She pulled him into an embrace and took a couple steps. He smiled foolishly as she danced him around the roof. Pausing at the edge, she leaned in to kiss him, releasing his hand to put hers on his chest. He closed his eyes as she ran her other hand through his hair. She shoved him from the roof.

Arms flailing, he almost caught himself before he fell over the edge. Ellen kept her grip on at his hair, tearing off a hank as he fell. She smiled and folded it into the paper bag. One down.

Wiping his sweat from her hands, she hurried down the stairs and into the lobby of the office building. No one saw her exit the stairwell. She turned at the sound of the screams, running out of the building with the rest of the people in the lobby to see what was wrong. Turning the corner, she slowed her pace to a brisk walk and hailed a cab.

*

Joseph Macarthur was the name of the man who had thrown her pelt into the fire. His grandson worked across the city, an accountant in a private firm. He was still checked into work, and had posted that he was looking forward to a quiet night with his second wife. He often worked late.

It was late evening by the time she got to the northern business district where Joseph Jr worked. She had changed into a work outfit, hiding it beneath her coat. The janitorial staff took an hour break for dinner and Joseph Jr always stayed until after they came back. She watched the staff leave. The last man out propped the back door with a brick and went around the corner for a smoke.

Walking to the door, Ellen opened it and kicked the brick out of the way. She eased it closed behind her and blinked to adjust her vision. The interior of the building was dimly lit, except for the office where Joseph Jr still worked. Ellen pulled Henry's service revolver out of her purse as she walked down the hall and unbuttoned her coat. Joseph Jr didn't look up as she entered. "I told you; I'll be out of the way in an hour. Leave me alone until then. Some of us have real work to do."

Ellen eased herself into the room, holding the revolver behind her back as she moved into his peripheral vision.

"I told you—" He blinked as he failed to recognise her. "Who are you?" He shook his head. "We're closed. Business hours are posted on the front door. Damn ingrates should have locked it."

"We have some business that couldn't wait until morning." She smiled at him as she edged closer. She saw his eyes widen at her outfit. She figured people didn't wear corsets and fishnets into his office very often. Or have tattoos that covered ninety per cent of their bodies.

"I'm sorry. I don't think we've met." He eyed her with growing amusement. He thought this was a game.

"I'm sure we have. Didn't Mark introduce us?" She let her smile reach her eyes. Mark was the grandson of Matthew Smith, the three boys had grown up together. Joseph Jr, Brian and Mark.

"Oh, that sneaky bastard. He planned this, didn't he? My wife is going to kill him."

"She will never know." Raising the revolver, she shot him in the throat.

He jolted backwards in his chair. He sprawled on the floor. Blood pulsed from his throat, pooling around him on the carpet. She put the gun in her purse and walked to his side. Paralysed, he looked up at her with pleading eyes. She knew she'd worn a similar expression when his grandfather had helped burn her skin.

As he gurgled around the blood that welled from the wound, she took the plastic container from her purse. She let the blood ebb into the quarter cup, watching the expression in his eyes as she collected her due. Two down.

*

Business at The House was slow when Ellen arrived. She leisurely changed out of the clothes she'd visited Joseph Jr in and examined her wardrobe. A leather corset with spikes, glimmering red fishnets, boots to match the corset. She fixed her makeup in the mirror, darkening the eye shadow, putting on dark red lipstick. Her tattoos writhed in the dim light as she stepped back to examine herself in the mirror.

One more to go.

Matthew Smith's grandson, Mark, showed up fifteen minutes early, as she'd known he would. This side job had given her practice, something to do in the years since Henry's death, ways to prepare for this very night. Hyssop had been sure to sell her positive traits. Mark's tastes and behaviour took after his grandfather's; both had a penchant for taking from unwilling women. She sipped her wine, making him wait.

At ten, she took up her whip, opened the door and beckoned him in. Pointing sternly at the table where she had arranged a gag and chains, she folded her arms and stared at him impassively. Licking his lips, he leered at her and didn't comply fast enough. She flicked the whip, catching him on the thigh. Fury in his eyes warred with desire, and she hoped that this would work.

Inwardly, she sighed with relief as he clicked the cuffs closed on his hands and his neck. She grabbed the chains and yanked him to the St Andrews Cross while he struggled playfully. She thinned her lips. No matter how well he paid, he wasn't a sub. He just wanted to control women who dominated.

She chained him firmly face-first to the X and double checked that his hands and feet were tightly secured. Stepping back, she rotated her wrist, readying the whip. His skin was flawless. Starting the session, she gently flicked the whip across his back, increasing the strikes as he groaned. She stopped suddenly, leaving him to wait for the next strike as she strode to the table. Picking up a knife, she hefted it, getting a good sense of the weight.

She traced the blade across his shoulders. This was not part of the script he expected. He made a strangled gagging sound, the ball in his mouth preventing words forming. She pressed the knife harder, drew blood, so he would know this wasn't a game any longer. His muffled shouts increased as his shoulders twitched with his efforts to escape, but he was firmly chained to the cross. She smiled as she cut gently into the skin at the top of his back. This was what revenge felt like. He began to scream against the gag, the terror in his voice as muted as his pleasure had been.

The cuts weren't as straight as she wanted as he fought against the cross, but she had patience. It took longer than she expected to skin his back, but the task became significantly easier after he passed out. It was important to get the entire skin whole from his back, from shoulders to buttocks, in one piece. The welts from the whip didn't matter. They were superficial.

Finally the rectangle of flesh hung messily from his lower back.

The floor and her hands were covered in blood. Deftly cutting the skin free, she lifted it and eased it onto the table. She folded the tablecloth over it tightly and put it into a large freezer bag. Pulling the cooler out from under the table, she placed the package gently in the ice water. Then Ellen cleaned up, but she left Mark hanging.

All these years, almost a century among men, and now she had a chance to be free. To go home. Dressed once more in her street clothes and carrying the cooler, she nodded to the bouncer as she walked out into the night. It wasn't uncommon for her to run errands while she made her clients wait. They wouldn't find the mess until hours later. By then, she would be gone.

She put the cooler's strap over her shoulder and carried it like a purse as she walked out into the tourist district. None of this had been here ninety-four years ago. Instead it had been dunes and sand, the city a small town in comparison to what it had become. The boardwalk under her feet was laden with almost a century of salt and sea, the boards turned silver by age and moonlight.

In the skies above, the moon glowed brilliant, casting the world in monochrome and platinum, bringing back memories in black and white. The beach was only a half hour walk from the club and she inhaled the sea air, stench of the docks and all. The buildings gave way to nature. Before long, she stood in the place where they had burnt her skin. Kneeling, she sifted the sand through her hands, wondering if there might be a remnant left, a slight particle of ash amongst the grains to keep her tethered to the land. But it didn't matter if there was. She could feel the place in her bones; some scars burnt deeper than the skin.

After making sure no one was watching, she stripped, dropping her clothes carelessly onto the sand. Naked, she opened the cooler, took out the package, and removed the bundled skin. Unrolling the table cloth, she spread it out on the sand, the piece of flesh unrolled on it. She pulled the paper bag and the container from her purse, kneeling next to the tablecloth in the moonlight.

Her hands trembled as she swirled seawater into the plastic container, mixing it with the blood. She painted symbols on the piece of skin, a rough mirror to her tattoos. Her mouth grew dry and the memory of her nightmare haunted her. If she failed at this task, if she didn't perform it perfectly, then all would be lost. She couldn't lose another skin.

She arranged the hair on the symbols, crossing them, intersecting them like the ripples of a wave. She hummed the songs of her childhood as she worked, calming herself, drawing the smell of the sea up into her as she inhaled. The tide crept up as she worked, lapping at the edges of the symbol-covered flesh. She cupped her hands, pouring the sea onto the centre of the skin. As the saltwater flowed over the symbols, they glowed blue, iridescent in the moonlight. She exhaled. It was working.

Picking up the cloth and skin, she walked into the surf until the water came halfway up her chest. She let the tablecloth drift away as she supported the skin on the gentle waves. The blood washed out into the ocean, black tendrils in the light of the full moon.

She had done it perfectly, and the skin floated on the waves as if it belonged there. There were no scars, no disfigurement that would prevent her attaining her goal. Of the three, she had suspected he would be the one who would serve best. He had been too cruel, too selfish, to allow others to harm him; the pain he felt throughout his life had been inflicted on others.

Now was the moment. Even if she failed, the revenge was worth it. She had not been able to go into the sea in her true from for ninety-four years. Now she felt the water move around her, the gentle caress of a lover long denied. Her nightmares fell away and she knew it was time.

In the light of the moon, she swung the skin over her shoulders, water and blood spraying through the air. Clammy otherness clung to her back. She felt it lay there, a dead thing against her skin. For several moments she waited, praying, hoping that it had not all been in vain. Fear made her heartbeat quicken.

As if the flow of blood had triggered it, her tattoos crawled to transform the new skin, inch by inch reclaiming what had been stolen. In a burst of a thousand colours, pain and pleasure washed through her. Triumph bubbled in her veins as she dove through the waves. The water splashed around her, welcoming her. Her pelt shone in the moonlight, the fur coloured and swirled with the marks of her tattoos.

She swam out into the ocean, never looking back.

AFTERWORD

Selkies have always intrigued me, particularly in the way the myth is often told as a story of literal control. Like many fairy tales and myths, women very rarely have choice in their lives; their options are often forced on them by male desires and traditions. It is unusual to see a story in which the selkie chooses to marry a human. Rather, they are often coerced by the theft of their skins, forced to stay human. Only when they steal or otherwise recover their skin can selkies return to their seal forms and the sea. But what happens if the skin is destroyed?

In this story, I wanted to explore what a selkie would have to go through to gain her freedom and what that could mean when responding from a place of revenge and necessity. Tattoos as transformative choices were the starting place for this story; I wanted to expand on their meaning of identity and self-determination. Tattoos will, after all, mark you for life.

THE SKIN OF THE WORLD

STEPHANIE GUNN

There are monsters in this world.

I know, for I have seen them.

They are hidden beneath the skin of the world, if you only know to look for them. Most people cannot — or will not — see past the surface, but I can. I can see the bones and tendons, the things that bind the earth together.

It is a tangle deep beneath the skin, a writhing, undulating mess, raw and bleeding.

Like me.

But you shouldn't listen to me. I'm insane.

I.

This is the first truth, the first thing I was taught:

I was born to parents unknown, in a place unknown. They left me on the steps of a church, three days old, thin and helpless in the dark of midwinter. I wailed through that night, wailed until my nascent voice was gone to a harsh croak. The priest, emerging from his warm rooms to check on the church, thought there was a raven dying on the stoop. He opened the door, and instead of feathers, he found me, cold and blue and barely breathing.

He called it a miracle, the spirit of God bringing a frozen babe back to life.

I don't know what I call it, even now. A death, a birth, a truth.

I was baptised the next day, given a good, Christian name: Maria.

Even though they told me that I was too young to remember, I have a memory of blood-warm water dripping on my forehead, the priest's voice shaping words. I remember his arms, hard as stone, as he handed me over to the people who would be my parents. Their arms were harder.

It should have been a miracle, my new life, my second birth. And for a while, it was.

2.

The first fourteen years of my life were normal.

I attended church every evening. I went to school, where I excelled at nothing and was terrible at nothing. The only thing that set me apart from the other children was my sleep pattern. From the first night in my parents' home, I slept as soon as the sun sank below the horizon. No dreams, no waking, no crying. Just sleep, as though I was a machine that had been switched off.

The day of my fourteenth birthday was the same as every other day. I woke when the sun rose, I went to school, I went to church. There was cake that night, a rare pink confection with a hidden layer of raspberries drenched with syrup. As I bit into the first raspberry, juice bursting in my mouth, I felt an unfamiliar warmth between my legs.

My mother took me aside, explained the miracle that was happening to me.

I stared at the blood, tasting raspberries and sugar on the back of my tongue. I used what she gave me and went back to the table. I opened the present that waited next to my plate—a new, white Bible. I ate no more cake.

That night, I sat with my curtains open, the light of the dying sun filling my room. I had bathed and dressed in my white cotton nightgown and now sat, slowing sipping at the warm milk my mother had made me. It was a nightly ritual: the milk, the Bible open on my lap. On the shelf next to me stood thirteen other identical Bibles. That was another ritual: the new Bible given for each birthday. Every year I would read it through, and on the eve before my birthday, slide it onto the shelf next to the others.

My attention, for once, wasn't on the milk or the familiar words before me, but on the sunset. My room was on the second storey of our house, my window host to an unobstructed view of the sun as it sank over the mountains. I drank my milk, and as I swallowed, I tasted the colours I saw in the sky. The deep purple was a delicate violet, the gold honey, and the red was raspberries, rich and dark. I watched as the sun sank and the colours swelled and then faded, waiting for the beginning of the familiar black wave of sleep.

I waited, and waited, and it never came. For the first time in my memory, I was sitting, my glass empty, awake long after the sun had set and the moon had risen, fat and yellow in the sky.

I shook myself, aware of the chill that was beginning to seep through the window. I set my glass and Bible aside and repeated the rituals that my mother had drilled into me. I checked that the door was locked, the window, too. The space beneath the bed was empty, the wardrobe held only clothes and shoes. I sat down in bed again, the Bible on my lap, and still sleep did not come.

A thin thread of panic drew taut within me. I rose again, and crossed to my dressing table, picking up the mirror that rested there. Did I look different, now I was a woman? My hair was still the same straight, thin blonde, so pale it was almost white, my lashes and brows colourless in the moonlight. Only my eyes were defined, a brown so dark they appeared black. I looked nothing like my parents, nor anyone else who lived in town. As one, they were swarthy and squat, their bodies always looking to me as though they were carved from the earth. I was tall and pale, my limbs long and wiry, my features sharp. I tilted my head to one side, trying to decide if I was pretty or ugly. I just saw me. Just Maria.

"Not Maria. Minerva."

I started, the mirror sliding from my hand and shivering to pieces against the floor. The voice had come from directly behind me, unmistakably male and tinged with an odd accent. But there was no man there. In the wide open window — the previously *locked* window — sat an owl, its talons clawing deeply into the soft wood of the sill. The owls I knew were small and brown, their faces always oddly lumpen. This one was larger and as finely made as china, its feathers pure white, its eyes glistening black.

I stood, making a vague shooing motion with my hands, expecting the owl to take flight as the small brown ones always had when approached. Distantly, I was aware of sounds on the lower floor of the house: my parents, no doubt roused by the breaking mirror. The owl didn't move, just stared at me. Those eyes looked through me, sliding past the fabric of my nightgown to skin and muscle and bone. And I felt, unmistakably, something move deep within me, like a finger gently brushing my heart.

And then.

Oh, and then.

The owl stepped forward from the window sill and, instead of falling or flying, it *changed*. Those soft feathers slid over one another with a sound like a sigh as its body expanded. As it changed, a hazy opalescent light filled the room, along with a fluttering warmth that moved like velvet over my skin.

I stared, as unblinking as the owl had been, watching as the bird became a man.

He was naked, his skin so white that I could see the blue tracery of veins at his throat and wrists. His hair was paler even than mine, hanging long and straight past his hips. I looked away from the pale thatch of hair there, and found myself caught by his eyes. They were as black as the owl's had been, his brows and eyelashes startlingly dark against the pallor of his hair and skin.

That warmth shimmered through the room again, deeper now, hotter, and I felt something like feathers moving against my skin, *through* my skin to twist and curl and fold like wings within the narrow cage of my ribs. A warmth blossomed there, spreading through my limbs. I became aware suddenly of the shape of my breasts pushing against my nightgown, the pulse of my heartbeat at my wrists, my throat, between my legs.

He closed his eyes, his lips shaping words as if in silent prayer, and fell to his knees before me.

With his eyes off me, I found myself able to move, to think, to speak. "How . . . how did you get in here?" I asked. A part of me wondered at my calmness, my lack of fear.

He spoke without looking up, though I heard the curve of a smile in his voice. "I flew."

"Oh."

A sound moved through the room, a rhythmic thudding. It was my mother knocking at the door, her voice sharp with panic. I took a step towards the key, but the owl-man looked up again, his eyes capturing me before I had taken more than one step. The sounds of my mother faded, everything faded but for him.

"Who are you?" I asked. "What are you?"

He tilted his head to one side. "You're bleeding."

I felt a sudden urge to cover myself. "How do you know that?"

"I can smell it." He smiled, something feral in that expression. "How old are you?"

"Fourteen. Today is my birthday."

He closed his eyes, an expression of pain crossing his face. "So long." He shook his head, an action like that of an animal trying to free a burr from its fur. "You've been having the dreams, then?"

"I never dream."

He stood then, circling the room, his long fingers brushing against the dresses in my wardrobe, the row of Bibles lined up like teeth. At the glass that had held my milk, he paused, leaning low to sniff its edge.

His eyes had left me, and I was free to move now, able to hear the sounds outside the room. My mother's voice had been joined by my father's, his shouts rough and angry as they argued about the whereabouts of the key to my room.

The owl-man straightened. "Don't they know that they can't tame a wild animal?"

He stepped forward, a sudden, fluid movement, his fingers closing around my wrist, his thumb on my pulse. The warmth blossoming with me became heat, a drowning urgency to strip away my nightdress and press my bare skin against his. That feeling like feathers moved under my skin, deeper now, and darker, somehow.

"They have been lying to you. Drugging you," he whispered, his lips close to my ear. "You cannot trust them."

Something crashed into the door. The heavy wood shuddered, but did not break.

The owl-man pulled back enough that he could look into my eyes. "Come with me. Learn who you are. What you are."

His fingers tightened around my wrist, and at that moment, as I began to follow him to the window, the door crashed inwards.

In the doorway stood my mother and father, an axe in my father's hand, a heavy crucifix in my mother's. My mother was growling, a deep animal sound that sent shivers of revulsion through me.

"This is not your territory, owl," my father said. "She is not yours."

"She belongs to no one but herself," the owl-man said, taking a step closer to me, his hand tightening on my wrist.

My mother bared her teeth, stepped carefully over the broken pieces of the door. She thrust the crucifix forth, and as I watched, the metal liquefied, twisting and lengthening into the shape of a squat dagger.

"You forgot one thing, owl." She spat the last word as though it were an insult. "I was chosen because of my talent."

She thrust the dagger at him. As the metal touched his flesh, he screamed, the sound high and harsh and unlike anything I had ever heard from a human throat. He flashed me an anguished glance before he changed again, his skin folding in on itself, his hair becoming feathers, hands and feet melding to wings and claws. His fingers around my wrist became talons, slashing deep as he lifted into the air. Then he was gone, leaving only a hint of animal musk in the room.

I turned back to the empty window, loss aching within me. I noticed for the first time the pieces of mirror scattered over the floor. The largest piece reflected me: a pale girl with hair and skin damp with sweat, blood flowing freely from deep lacerations that curved around her wrist in the shape of an owl's talons. Her hand was still outstretched, reaching to nothing.

She looked like an animal, caged.

3.

My parents took me to the hospital that night. I had babbled, at first, trying to tell the doctor everything. He had listened, smiling, and then the smile had faded. Eventually he had slipped a syringe into my arm, and a soft haze had descended, as though I had fallen into a cloud.

My mother murmured to the doctor as he stitched my wrist, her words ebbing and flowing like waves. The thread pulled at my skin over and over, dragging at me as though he wanted to unravel my veins and nerves, pull me inside out.

Her words fell like stones into a well as he pulled and stitched, pulled and stitched: *delusions, hallucinations, self-harm, attempted suicide . . .*

My father stood back from the bed, as though separated from me by my mother's invisible wall of words. He lifted his hand, and I thought I saw the axe still there, coming down slowly. But it was only a pen, held tight as he scrawled his signature on paper after paper.

I blinked, and they were gone, only the doctor standing there with another syringe. The liquid he injected was like ice splintering beneath my skin, a layer of frost sinking down to my heart.

For a long time after that, there was nothing but the cold.

4.

I was stone, buried beneath the earth.

Images and impressions wormed down to me from time to time. Leather snaking around my wrists and ankles, the edges dark with something that might have been blood. Green walls, grey walls, walls of dirty cream. Bars on the window, always. The sound of static bleeding through heavy doors. White shoes, food ground to tasteless mush. Needles giving fire, needles giving ice, needles hungrily sucking blood. Pills of yellow, of blue and white and green.

Occasionally I surfaced completely, gulping at the air as though I had truly been buried. And each time there was the owl, beyond those bars, watching.

I spoke, at first, to the nurses and doctors, each time I surfaced. Telling them of men who became owls, fathers who bore axes. Their dark shapes pressed down on me, something about them scraping at my skin as they handed me new pills, new colours to sink me further into the earth.

I stopped talking.

And slowly, so slowly, I rose. The leather restraints were removed, the pills less, their colours more consistent.

Finally, even the colour of the room stayed the same for more than one round of pills.

The final room had walls the mottled colour of sandstone, worn carpet the colour of damp slate. The bed frame was metal, its edges chipped as though worried by teeth. I didn't think it had been me; my teeth, as far as I could tell, were still intact.

The days were measured out by the pills: two yellow, one white and one green with breakfast, one yellow and one green with lunch, one white and two blue with dinner. I ate them dutifully, and each time I did, the earth closed over me again.

The world was turning to stone as I collapsed onto my bed, pulling the thin blankets up to my chin. The lights flickered and then went dark. I closed my eyes, waiting to sink into the darkness.

"They found a splendid cage this time."

It took an effort to open my eyes, the lids scraping against the dry surface of my corneas. It took even more effort to focus on the room. The door was locked — from the outside, no key here — and the corners of the room were empty. I wanted to check beneath the bed, but the earth was weighing me down, turning my body to stone . . .

"*Fight it, Minerva.*"

That name hooked into me, dragged me out of the earth long enough to focus on the window. The bars were intact, the night outside silvered with moonlight. A leafless branch pressed up to my window, and on that branch was the owl.

I blinked slowly, the bird sliding in and out of focus.

"Fight it, Minerva," the owl repeated. "They're just chemicals. They can't affect you, not if you don't want them to."

Though my vision was blurred, I saw light flow out from the owl, the shadows of the bars slicing across the room. The light fell on me, fell *through* me. My heart leapt like an animal in my chest, and my vision and awareness snapped sharply into place.

As before, the man was naked, but he was much changed. His hair was shorter, falling in thin, ragged hanks around his shoulder. Through the small window I could see the sinews of his throat, a gnarled scar in the deep hollow where his neck met his shoulder. His bones pressed against his skin, knife sharp.

He leaned his forehead against the window, just looking at me, immense sorrow shadowing his face. As though deciding something, he drew in a deep breath and sat up, pressing one hand on the glass. He closed his eyes, and warmth seeped into the room, rolling across the empty air towards me. It moved against my skin, achingly familiar, and I closed my eyes for a moment, releasing a slow, shuddering breath. When I opened them again, I saw that his hand had moved, impossibly, through the windowpane, his fingers now curled around one of the bars. His whole body shook as he pushed against the bar, and then he slumped as he withdrew his hand back through the window, the solid glass reforming as though it had never been touched. He leaned against the window sill, his breath coming fast and shallow.

"Are you really here?" I asked, my words thick in my mouth. "How did you do that?"

"I'm here," he said. "The answer to the second question is somewhat more complicated."

"They said . . . " The taste of chemicals was suddenly thick in my throat. I swallowed down bile, reaching for the water jug which rested on my side table. I took a gulp of the tepid water, which moved like a stone down my throat. "I'm having an episode. I need more meds." I reached out to my blankets, trying twice before I was able to close my fingers on them and pull them aside.

"You're not mad." His voice was sharp, stilling me. "You're something else. You're Animae. You're like me."

That word shot through me like a physical blow. I turned back to him, saw the stars reflected in his eyes.

"There's a war being fought beneath the skin of the world," he continued. "A war fought by people like me. Like us."

I placed my feet on the floor. The linoleum was cold beneath my soft soles, focusing me. His eyes on me made it easier to force back the earth, to focus on walking towards the window. Each step felt like I was walking on razors, but I kept moving. Halfway there, bile surged in my throat, and I made use of a bin in the corner to empty my stomach. When I straightened, I felt shaky, but my mind was clear. I walked the rest of the way to the window and placed my hand on the bar he had touched. It was warm.

He smiled, the expression sparking something in his eyes. Hope? I didn't know. "Greetings, sister Minerva."

"Why do you keep calling me that? My name is Maria."

He shook his head. "Your parents named you Minerva."

"You know my parents?"

"I knew them."

Loss, sharp and unexpected, pierced me. "Oh." He was sitting up straighter now, evoking the image of a king on a throne, for all that he was a naked man perched in a tree. "Who are you?"

"I am Kai. I carry the spirit of the Owl." He spoke the words formally, his hands held palms out.

"You're an owl."

"When I choose, yes, I can fly in the shape of an owl."

"And you can move your hand through solid objects."

"Not everything. For me, just glass. The Animae, as well as carrying the spirits of animals, have their own kinds of magic. Each one is unique. Some can conjure flame, some can read minds, some find that substances respond to their wishes. I have an affinity for glass." His words triggered a memory of a crucifix warping.

"Can I do that, too?" My hand tightened on the iron bar, squeezing.

"You can do something, but it is something that will be yours alone."

I let my hand slide from the bar. "Can I turn into an owl, then?"

"You have the ability, no doubt. Discovering the spirit one carries requires a ritual of kinds. A ritual which we cannot perform here."

I slumped. "So I'm useless. A useless, mad girl locked away."

"Not useless. Just untrained. And absolutely, completely not mad. Though I admit, it was a clever idea of theirs, to hide you away here."

A shadow moved against the stars; he glanced up sharply, every muscle in his body growing tight. "What is it?" I asked, craning to see.

"This is not my territory," he said. "They will have sentries, and if they catch me . . . " He watched a moment longer, than relaxed, turning back to me. "Just a night bird, I think. I'm sorry that it has taken me so long. Each time I found you, they would move you, deeper and deeper into their territory. What they've done to you . . . "

I looked down. Where my body had once been lithe, I was now soft with fat and fluid. The fabric of my pyjamas strained over the swell of my belly, and my feet were already aching from bearing my weight. I shifted from foot to foot, wrapping my arms around my thickened waist.

"Not that, Minerva," Kai said. "You are beautiful, and you will always be beautiful. It's what they've done to you within. When we spoke the first time, your spark was so bright that it was almost blinding. Now I can only just discern it."

"The doctors said I needed it. The treatments. They said that I was mad. That I was dangerous."

"They lied. The doctors, the people who called themselves your parents. Your parents, your real family, they would have nurtured that spark into something glorious, something that could change this war, this world. They would have loved you."

"But they left me." My voice broke on that.

He shook his head. "They trusted someone they should not have. And you were stolen. I would have—"

He broke off, his body alert again, his face somehow sharpening, becoming more feral. His eyes widened, darkened, shifted to owl form. It should have looked strange, even frightening; an owl's eyes in a man's face, but somehow it was comforting. It was *right*.

"The sentries." His body shimmered with light. "Hold fast, Minerva. I will return as soon as I can."

He let the owl take him, and he flew. I watched him, my cheeks pressed against the bars, as he lifted, powerful and glorious, into the night sky.

"Kai," I whispered. His name tasted like light, like honey. It tasted like a home I had never known.

A darker, larger shape moved against the stars, its wings beating slowly but strongly as it intercepted Kai-as-owl. I watched them clash, over and over, dark meeting light. Each time they drew apart they moved higher and higher until they were above the roof of the hospital and out of my sight.

I stayed there for a long time, my body growing cold, but the sky stayed empty. Finally, I returned to my bed and pulled back my blankets. They smelled sour, as though a stranger had been sleeping between those sheets. Still, I lay down and wrapped myself tightly. There was a spark of warmth deep within my cold body, soft like feathers, deep as ancient amber. When I focused on it, I tasted sunshine, honey and air and freedom. I curled myself around the spark, kept it safe, determined not to let the earth take it.

5.

Days passed, then weeks, then months.

I did my best, taking my pills, eating my food, pretending to sleep. At first, I feigned sickness to remove the worst of the chemicals from my body. The nurses frowned, added some pills, took away others. I went within, focusing on that spark of amber, listening to it as it taught me the secret pathways of my body. I learned that I could sweat out the chemicals, bleed them out each month. Nightly, I left my blankets and sheets soaked with bitter sweat, and every month, I bled and bled and bled, but it worked.

I thought I was getting away with it.

I was wrong.

They were watching, and they found me standing by the window, the full moon a spotlight catching me frozen. They started a twenty-four hour watch, a nurse with a syringe always at hand. More pills, of course. Then the insulin therapy, which felt like claws tearing at my body from within, trying to rip me to pieces. They always smiled after that, murmuring that it was for my own good, my own sanity.

After that, isolation.

The isolation room was tiny, the floor not even large enough for me to lie prone, every surface padded and coated with plastic. No furniture, the only break in the walls a window no taller than the span of my hand, the glass, as always, reinforced by bars. A door with no observation window.

A nurse marched me there in restraints, through corridors that twisted and turned like a serpent into parts of the hospital I had never seen before. These rooms were empty, unheated, the cold sinking into my skin until my wrists were rattling against my restraints.

The nurse bid me wait by the door as she placed two buckets in the back of the room. She moved the one filled with water carelessly, slopping a good third of it over the concrete floor of the corridor. She shoved me into the room, hard, so I tumbled to the floor, the plastic crackling beneath me.

"Two nights, Maria. Scream and shout, no one will hear you." Her mouth twisted in the mockery of a smile. "It's for your own good."

"It's barbaric!" I spat. "You wouldn't do this to an animal!"

That smile widened, revealing yellow teeth worn almost down to the gums. "One of the doctors has a new treatment. Experimental surgery, sliding little electrodes into your brain, switches that'll let him turn off these delusions of yours. And more, if we want."

I looked up at her bulk, silhouetted against the corridor's light. And there, hidden in the shadows of her face, I saw something moving. Something serpentine, something bestial.

"You're one of them," I breathed. I struggled to my feet; my legs shook. "You're like me! Why are you doing this?"

She said nothing, just slammed the door. I listened to the sound of each bolt snapping into place, then the hush of her soft-soled shoes as she retreated down the corridor. Just before the sound of her footsteps faded, she began whistling, the tune bright and merry. Finally, that, too, faded, and I was alone.

I lay down in the resultant silence, curling into a tight ball. The spark within was barely glowing now, its colour gone to a pallid yellow. Each 'therapy' dimmed it more and more. I wondered if, after this experimental surgery, anything would be left at all.

I turned over so I faced the window. Through it, I could see a slice of sky. No blue, just scudding grey clouds. I watched them, and I prayed for Kai.

6.

The first night I waited.

No one came.

7.

The second night I slept fitfully, waking at the slightest sound.

8.

The third night I screamed. For the doctors, for the nurse who had failed to return. For the people who adopted me, for the priest. For the God who did not hear me. For my parents. For Kai, for Kai, for Kai, always for Kai.

I drank the last of my water, shoved the other, putrid bucket as far away as I could.

No one came. No one came. No one came.

9.

On the fourth night I made no sound. I lay on my side, my face pressed to the crack beneath the door.

The scant amount of air that flowed in through there smelled sweet and fresh. I didn't smell the stink of the cell any more, thankfully, but I knew that the amount of oxygen ventilating in was small. Every time I stood now, the cell grew hazy around me, and my bones seemed to melt.

They had left me here to starve, to dehydrate, to suffocate.

They had left me here to die.

The tapping sound had been audible for a while before it registered to my conscious self. I turned over slowly, dimly aware of the fact that even though I was lying down, the world swam.

Kai-as-owl was there. He barely fit into the small window, wings crammed against the glass.

I turned back over, pressing my face to the gap beneath the door again.

"Minerva, please, look at me."

When I looked back, it was Kai's human face pressed there, angled back so that some of the light illuminated him. I turned over fully, then, pushed myself up onto my elbows. His cheeks were dark hollows, his face so thin that I could see the shadows of his teeth against his skin. His hair was completely gone from one side of his head, and what remained on the other side was sparse, the ends appearing chewed. Worse, his left eye was gone, the socket a raw, oozing mess.

"What did they do to you?" I asked.

He smiled — tried to smile — the expression pulling at the raw flesh where his eye had been. "We're losing. We're lost." He swallowed, and I could see the cartilage and tendons of his neck working. "I wanted . . . I wanted my last to be with you."

"Your last?" The words caught in my throat, rougher than the torn flesh they passed.

He hung his head. "There is nothing more to fight for, now."

Suddenly, I wanted desperately to be able to comfort him. I forced my body to stand, to cross the cell to the window. Without thinking, I reached to him. That spark struggled for life within me, sputtering like a flame trying to catch on damp wood. I drew everything I had, visualised myself breathing on it, giving my life to it. Let it all burn, this muscle, this bone. It was worth nothing to me now. The spark shimmered, and almost went out, but then leapt once, a single surge of energy. I reached out, and when my hand touched the iron bars, it found them warm, then hot, and then my hand moved through them until I could press my fingers against the glass beyond.

Kai's eye widened. "Maybe there is something." Tears welled and spilled onto his cheek as he pressed his hand on the other side of the glass, mirrored to my own. He closed his eye, shaking with the effort, and the glass was suddenly gone, his fingers lacing with mine as a great gust of cool, wonderful air flowed into the cell.

The touch of his skin on mine was like nothing I had ever before experienced: ice and fire and sunlight and liquid desire. The spark within me exploded, became a bonfire: orange and crimson and scarlet and amber. The fire flowed through me, and then he was changing to an owl, tumbling through the frame of the window, changing back into a man.

And then he was there, naked and cold and shivering and *there*.

For a long time, we simply lay there, his slight weight on me, his breath rasping in my ear. His heart was a rapid flutter against the cage of his chest. Beyond him, I could see the remains of the iron bars: still-molten lumps that oozed slowly down the wall, filling the cell with sullen orange light.

Finally, he lifted his head, and I saw afresh the horror of his eye socket, bone gleaming white through pulped muscle and skin. There were other wounds, too-cool blood seeping into the fabric of my pyjamas in at least a half dozen places.

"Who did this to you?" I asked.

"It's the cats," he said. "They've formed an alliance underneath a new leader, and they're pushing into territory they've never before touched. There are great swathes of land falling to desert, to ash, because of their greed."

He coughed, a liquid sound, and struggled to sit up. Between us we managed to get him propped up against a wall. When we were done, we were both breathing fast, and fresh blood filled the well of his empty eye socket.

He smiled, then, one hand coming up to rest against my cheek for a moment. He was trembling. "Iron, then. Why does that not surprise me?"

I glanced up at the melted bars, now cooling into ugly lumps. The glass Kai had exploded had vanished, though physics said it should have fallen into the cell. "Maybe we can move back through? You can become an owl, and maybe I can—"

He shook his head, cutting me off. "Even if you could shift, there are a dozen cats out there, waiting. Cats at full strength, hungry for my flesh and yours." He smiled again, the expression weaker now. "And even if they were not there, I have not the strength for another shift."

I knelt down before him, taking his hands in mine. My body was still weak from a lack of food and water, but I felt stronger. Strong enough to run away from this place. Strong enough to carry him, if needs be. "There has to be a way."

"I always knew this was a one-way journey, Minerva," he said. "Though I expected to end it outside, not in here with you." His skin against mine was dry as paper, his bones sharp beneath. "We would have been mated, I think, if things had been different. Our children would have been warriors and queens."

I was crying now, tears streaming down my cheeks despite my dehydration. "They still can be."

He closed his eye; I saw the rapid fluttering of his eye beneath the lid, as if he was dreaming. "No, my love."

I shook my head, knowing that it was a useless gesture even as I made it. I could see the light going from him, feel his spark fading. I closed my eyes, leaned over and pressed my lips to his. It was a chaste, untutored kiss, but I could feel the echo of heat in it, the possibility of what could have been.

My own spark flared again, and I saw all at once, everything that lay within me. I saw my own self as a delicate iron vase, that fire cradled within. But the vase was an incomplete vessel, jagged pieces knocked out in too many places. It was a vessel that would never hold anything, not completely. Even as I watched, the fire leaked out, oozing slowly as the iron bars had. And I knew then that I would never shift, never find my animal form, never know any magic beyond that one resonance with iron that had delivered Kai into my arms.

My magic was gone, but I was not. And I would *not* fade.

Kai's lips curved against mine, and I felt his words against my skin, more than I heard them. "You will go on, Minerva. And if I can, I will wait for you. I will find you. You are my life, my love. I give you the only gift I can now, the last of me. Everything I have."

I opened my eyes, and saw that the cell was bathed with his light, the edges of his body silvered. As I watched, the light pulsed in time with his heart, each pulse growing dimmer. And when the light was gone, so too was Kai's body. All that remained was a single white feather in my hands.

I cradled it close, embracing it as I would have embraced him. A smaller light flickered around its edges, a wash of cobalt and amber that licked against my skin. I lifted the feather to my lips, kissing it once, and then I breathed it in. That light flowed in, and as it did, I knew Kai. I knew his family, his life, his loves. I knew he had watched me, that he had waited for me, that he had loved me.

Again, I saw the broken vase that was me, and then cobalt-amber light flowing into it, filling it, forming an inner skin that kept the fire contained and whole.

You will not fade, Kai's voice echoed within me as the feather fell to ash in my hands. *You will not fade, and when the time is come, I will see you again.*

10.

The nurse came soon after, and when she did, I was standing there waiting.

She looked past me towards the window, and I saw something like fear blooming behind her eyes. I smiled, and held out my hand. It was she who hesitated, and when we moved out into the corridor, it was I leading her, my head held high.

They would take me to a small room, and they would slice into my scalp, peel back the bones of my skull. They would slide fingers into my brain, slice metal into flesh. There would be more drugs, more operations, and with every one, they would shatter more pieces from that iron vase. They would shatter me over and over, but they would never, ever break me.

With each step, I felt that light expanding within me, and like images flickering in the corners of my vision, I saw the things that were to come.

One day a man would come here, and he would love the strange, shattered creature that I would become. He would take me away from here, and together we would fly to the ends of the earth.

And one day, when the light shone a warm amber, I would hold my daughter in my arms. And her eyes would be black, and she would hold wings in her heart. And one day, she would fly.

The nurse frowned as she lay me down on the operating table. The metal was cold, but I barely noticed.

"What are you smiling at, missy?" she asked.

I shaped my arms to the place where my daughter would one day rest. "There are monsters in this world."

She grabbed my wrists and strapped them down, cinching the leather tight enough that my fingers went numb. "Well, you won't see them after this." She licked her lips, turning to pick up a syringe from a nearby table.

"Maybe not," I said. "But I will always be one."

She slid the needle into my vein, but she looked away before she depressed the plunger.

II.

I was in a room.

It was a small room. There were metal shutters on the window, rough sheets of what looked like hand-beaten copper. They were closed. The walls were the colour of dirty sand, the floor a colour that I found myself unable to name.

There was a numbness, a *lack* that surrounded me, that was in me. As though I was filled with holes.

The door opened, and there was a woman there. Dark hair, eyes the same colour as the carpet.

"Who are you?" I asked. Even my voice was unfamiliar.

She smiled then, close-lipped. "I'm a nurse, sweetheart. You're in a hospital." She handed me three white pills, a glass of water. "You've just had a treatment. Things may feel strange for a while."

I swallowed the pills, washed them down with water. It tasted like nothing.

"Good girl." She took back the glass. "Get some rest. In the morning, you're being transferred to another facility. There will be different treatments there, patients, even some students."

I nodded, lay back, closing my eyes as she closed the door.

In the darkness behind my eyes I saw images. An owl, a baby, a fire. It was all jumbled up, like a vase broken and then put back together the wrong way. I could place none of it.

The nurse came back later, found me lying beneath the bed. She coaxed me back up onto the mattress, gave me another pill.

It was a blue so dark it was almost black, swallowing the scant light in the room. I swallowed it dry, felt that darkness expand within me.

"What were you doing down there?" she asked. "Looking for monsters?"

"There are monsters in this world," I said, though I had no idea where the words were coming from. The blue-black pill was working, dragging me down.

"What did you say?" Her voice was sharp, worried.

I shook my head, the movement slow and ponderous. "And I am one of them," I whispered.

And I was crying as I sank down into the black, into the holes beneath my skin, and I had no idea why.

AFTERWORD

"The Skin of the World" is part of a series of stories and novels that explore the Animae, my own interpretation of the shapeshifter mythos. Specifically, "The Skin of the World" is a prequel of sorts to the novel that I've been working on for the last few years, currently titled *The White Raven*. I have a deep fascination for how magic could work in the real world—would people feel awe or fascination when confronted by it, or would they be more inclined to believe that anyone who expresses belief in magic is actually insane? This was the starting point for "The Skin of the World"—a girl witnesses a shapeshifter and is then deemed insane and institutionalised. This idea deepened into something more as I wrote and rewrote, with deeper machinations than simple disbelief sending Minerva to the asylum (if asylum it is). I love playing with the idea that magic exists in the real world, if you simply know how to turn your head the right way to look beneath the skin of the world, and that wars are fought just beyond the borders of human knowledge, and this story only deepened that love.

ABOUT THE CONTRIBUTORS

JOANNE ANDERTON lives in Sydney with her husband and too many pets. By day she is a mild-mannered marketing coordinator for an Australian book distributor. By night, weekends and lunchtimes she writes science fiction, fantasy and horror. Her short fiction has most recently appeared in *Light Touch Paper, Stand Clear* and *Epilogue*. Her debut novel, *Debris* was published by Angry Robot Books in 2011, followed by *Suited* in 2012. *Debris* was shortlisted for an Aurealis award and a Ditmar. Joanne won the 2012 Ditmar for Best New Talent. Visit her online at http://joanneanderton.com and on Twitter @joanneanderton

ALAN BAXTER is a Ditmar Award-nominated author of dark speculative fiction. He rides a motorcycle, loves his dog and teaches Kung Fu. Alan is the author of the dark fantasy novels, *RealmShift* and *MageSign*, and over 40 short stories in a variety of publications in Australia, the US, the UK and France, including the *Year's Best Australian Fantasy & Horror*. Alan is also a freelance writer, contributing editor and co-founder at *Thirteen O'Clock*, and co-hosts *Thrillercast*. Read extracts from his novels, a novella and short stories at his website—www.alanbaxteronline.com—or find him on Twitter @AlanBaxter, and feel free to tell him what you think. About anything.

JENNY BLACKFORD's first poem for decades was the only one included in the Ticonderoga *Year's Best Australian Fantasy and Horror 2010*. Her stories (in places including *Cosmos, Aurealis* and Jack Dann's *Dreaming Again*) have received several Honourable Mentions from Ellen Datlow and Gardner Dozois. Alison Goodman described her novella set in ancient Delphi and Athens, *The Priestess and the Slave*, as "A compelling blend of vivid storytelling and meticulous research", and Pamela Sargent called it "elegant". Her current major project is writing the violent, sexy life of Bronze Age princess Medea.

VIVIAN CAETHE was introduced to speculative fiction at an early age by being born in the Land of Enchantment. She grew up hearing stories about her grandfather's work on the Gemini, Apollo, and Mercury programs. She writes on the side while sticking to her day job of telling people what to do and being mildly surprised when they comply. An avid tea connoisseur, she knits and cross-stitches in her spare time.

M.L.D. CURELAS lives in Calgary, Alberta with two humans and three guinea pigs. Raised on a diet of Victorian fiction and Stephen King, it's unsurprising that she now writes and edits fantasy and science fiction. Her most recent short fiction can be found in the anthologies *Damnation and Dames* and *Blood and Water,* and she is the editor of *Ride the Moon,* an anthology of modern moon myths and legends.

THORAIYA DYER's short fiction has appeared recently in *Nature, Redstone SF* and *Apex* magazine. *The Company Articles of Edward Teach*, published by Twelfth Planet Press, won the 2011 Ditmar Award for Best Novella/Novelette. In the same year, "Yowie" (*Sprawl* anthology, TPP) was joint winner of the Best Fantasy Short Story Aurealis Award. In 2012, Thoraiya won the Aurealis Award again (same category) for "Fruit of the Pipal Tree" (*After the Rain* anthology, Fablecroft). TPP will publish *Asymmetry*, a collection of four original stories, as part of the Twelve Planets Series in 2012. Find out more at www.thoraiyadyer.com.

DIRK FLINTHART lives in Tasmania. He teaches ju-jitsu, practises Iai-do, raises his three kids, handles a fifty-acre property, handles the cooking with flair, elan, and a good deal of chilli, co-operates with his long-suffering rural GP wife, is half-way through a Masters degree, and writes stuff like this in his spare time. His wife is trying to convince him to take his flute and join a local orchestra with herself and the kids. Next time around, Mr Flinthart is planning to outsource a number of aspects of his life . . .

STEPHANIE GUNN is a lapsed (mad) scientist who decided that words were better fitted to explaining the strange madness of the worlds in her head. She has been nominated for a Ditmar Award, and has won a Tin Duck Award. She currently resides in Perth with her husband, son and requisite cat. She can be found online at www.stephaniegunn.com.

RICHARD HARLAND has been a full-time author for fourteen years. He lives near Wollongong, south of Sydney, between golden beaches, green escarpment and the biggest steelworks in the southern hemisphere. He has collected six Aurealis Awards, the A. Bertram Chandler Award (Australia) and the Tam-Tam Je Bouquine award (France). His sixteen novels have spanned adult, YA and children's, and fantasy, horror and science fiction. His big international successes have been his two steampunk fantasies, *Worldshaker* and *Liberator.* His next steampunk novel is *Song of the SLums,* coming out in May 2013. Richard's website is at www. richardharland.net. He's also put up free 145-page guide to writing speculative fiction at www.writingtips.com.au.

PETE KEMPSHALL is a writer and editor living in Perth, Western Australia. His stories have been published internationally by the likes of Morrigan Books, Big Finish, Dark Quest Books and Apex Publications, and he has been nominated for the Australian Shadows, Aurealis and Ditmar Awards. He blogs about his various projects at www.tyrannyoftheblankpage.blogspot.com.

PENELOPE LOVE lives in Box Hill, Australia. The background for this story was gathered during a trip to Malaysia early in 2012. The trip included a stay at a jungle resort where each night she got a torch from the pool pavilion and walked uphill along a jungle trail to her room. One night she picked up the torch that didn't work properly. It kept going out during the walk and had to be shaken vigorously to start again. The local wildlife kept all their spookiest noises for these long, long moments, and man, that jungle was dark.

KAREN MARIC is an Aussie expat who lives in the gorgeous, mountainous south-eastern province of Fujian in China with her husband and two young daughters. She has had more than a dozen short stories published in Australia and in the US in publications such as *Andromeda Spaceways Inflight Magazine*, *Aurealis*, *Orb Speculative Fiction Magazine* and the anthology *Year's Best Australian Science Fiction and Fantasy* Vol. 5. Visit www. karenmaric.com to learn more about Karen's writing and her life in China.

CHRISTINE MORGAN works the overnight shift in a psychiatric facility and divides her writing time among many genres. A lifelong reader, she also writes, reviews, beta-reads, occasionally edits and dabbles in self-publishing. She has over a dozen novels in print and more due out soon. Her stories have appeared in several anthologies, been nominated for Origins Awards, and given Honorable Mention in two volumes of the Year's Best Fantasy and Horror. She's a wife, mom, and possible future crazy-cat-lady whose other interests include gaming, history, superheroes, crafts, and cheesy disaster movies.

NICOLE MURPHY is a writer and editor who sometimes gets to read as well. Her fantasy romance trilogy *Dream Of Asarlai* is published by HarperCollins. She mentors and publishes new writers through In Fabula-divino and is heavily involved with the Conflux SF conventions. Find out more at her website nicolermurphy.com.

KAT OTIS lives a peripatetic life with a pair of cats who enjoy riding in the car as long as there's no country music involved. Her fiction has appeared in Orson Scott Card's *Intergalactic Medicine Show*, *Daily Science Fiction* and Marion Zimmer Bradley's *Sword & Sorceress XXVI*. She can be found online at www.katotis.com or on Twitter as @kat_otis.

DAN RABARTS is a speculative fiction writer, sometime narrator of podcasts, occasional sailor of sailing things, and father of two wee miracles in a little house on a hill, under the southern sun. As well as in *Bloodstones*, his short fiction has been published or is forthcoming at the *Wily Writers* podcast and in *Andromeda Spaceways Inflight Magazine*. His narrations can be heard on the *StarShipSofa*, at *Tales to Terrify*, and on the *Wily Writers'* Podcast. He has twice been nominated for a Sir Julius Vogel award. Find him lurking on the web at dan.rabarts.com, or in the dusty corners of the house tapping frantically at a keyboard.

ERIN UNDERWOOD is a writer, editor and publisher. She is also the founder of Underwords, a small press for YA science fiction and a popular fiction book blog. Her fiction, nonfiction, and interviews have appeared online and in print. Erin is the co-editor of *Futuredaze: An Anthology of YA Science Fiction* in addition to co-authoring "The Bag of Holding", a quarterly column published in the Science Fiction Writers of America Bulletin. Visit her online at www.underwordsblog.com.

ACKNOWLEDGEMENTS

All stories appear here for the first time.

AVAILABLE FROM TICONDEROGA PUBLICATIONS

TICONDEROGA PUBLICATIONS LIMITED HARDCOVER EDITIONS

978-0-9586856-9-6   Love in Vain by Lewis Shiner
978-0-9803531-1-2   Belong ed Russell B. Farr
978-0-9803531-9-8   Basic Black by Terry Dowling
978-0-9806288-0-7   Make Believe by Terry Dowling
978-0-9806288-1-4   The Infernal by Kim Wilkins
978-0-9806288-5-2   Dead Sea Fruit by Kaaron Warren
978-0-9806288-7-6   The Girl With No Hands by Angela Slatter
978-0-9807813-0-4   Dead Red Heart ed Russell B. Farr
978-0-9807813-3-5   Heliotrope by Justina Robson
978-0-9807813-6-6   Matilda Told Such Dreadful Lies by Lucy Sussex
978-1-921857-00-3   Bluegrass Symphony by Lisa L. Hannett
978-1-921857-07-2   Bread and Circuses by Felicity Dowker
978-1-921857-16-4   The 400-Million-Year Itch by Steven Utley
978-1-921857-27-0   Midnight and Moonshine by Lisa L. Hannett &
                    Angela Slatter

TICONDEROGA PUBLICATIONS EBOOKS

978-0-9803531-5-0   Ghost Seas by Steven Utley
978-1-921857-93-5   The Girl With No Hands by Angela Slatter
978-1-921857-99-7   Dead Red Heart ed Russell B. Farr
978-1-921857-94-2   More Scary Kisses ed Liz Grzyb
978-0-9807813-5-9   Heliotrope by Justina Robson
978-1-921857-98-0   Year's Best Australian F&H eds Grzyb & Helene
978-1-921857-97-3   Bluegrass Symphony by Lisa L. Hannett

THE YEAR'S BEST AUSTRALIAN FANTASY & HORROR SERIES EDITED BY LIZ GRZYB & TALIE HELENE

978-0-9807813-8-0   Year's Best Australian Fantasy & Horror 2010 (hc)
978-0-9807813-9-7   Year's Best Australian Fantasy & Horror 2010 (tpb)
978-0-921057-13-3   Year's Best Australian Fantasy & Horror 2011 (hc)
978-0-921057-14-0   Year's Best Australian Fantasy & Horror 2011 (tpb)

WWW.TICONDEROGAPUBLICATIONS.COM

THANK YOU

The publisher would sincerely like to thank:

Elizabeth Grzyb, Amanda Pillar, Joanne Anderton, Alan Baxter, Jenny Blackford, Vivian Caethe, MLD Curelas, Thoraiya Dyer, Dirk Flinthart, Stephanie Gunn, Richard Harland, Pete Kempshall, Penelope Love, Karen Maric, Christine Morgan, Nicole Murphy, Kat Otis, Dan Rabarts, Erin Underwood, Cat Sparks, Jonathan Strahan, Peter McNamara, Ellen Datlow, Grant Stone, Jeremy G. Byrne, Sean Williams, Garth Nix, David Cake, Simon Oxwell, Grant Watson, Sue Manning, Steven Utley, Bill Congreve, Jack Dann, Jenny Blackford, Simon Brown, Stephen Dedman, Sara Douglass, Felicity Dowker, Terry Dowling, Jason Fischer, Lisa L. Hannett, Pete Kempshall, Ian McHugh, Angela Rega, Angela Slatter, Lucy Sussex, Alex Adsett, Kaaron Warren, the Mt Lawley Mafia, the Nedlands Yakuza, Shane Jiraiya Cummings, Angela Challis, Talie Helene, Donna Maree Hanson, Kate Williams, Kathryn Linge, Andrew Williams, Al Chan, Alisa and Tehani, Mel & Phil, Jennifer Sudbury, Paul Przytula, Kelly Parker, Hayley Lane, Georgina Walpole, everyone we've missed . . .

. . . and you.

In memory of Eve Johnson (1945–2011)